Summoning a Lost Fey

Also by S. K. Kilburn

Consort to a Dark Fey

SUMMONING A LOST FEY

S. K. Kilburn

Fiction

This novel is entirely a work of fiction. The names, characters, businesses and incidents portrayed in it are the work of the author's imagination or used in a fictitious manner. Any resemblance to actual persons, living or dead, events or localities is entirely coincidental.

ISBN-00: 979-8-9912704-0-3 (Paperback)
ISBN-00: 979-8-9912704-1-0 (Ebook)

Cover art and design by Mihaela Voicu
Edited by Theresa Halvorsen
Published by Wild Pict Creative, Inc.

Website: www.scottkilburnwriter.com

Table of Contents

Dedication

Thank you to my mother and father who encouraged me to dream. To my ScHoFan writing group, thank you Ken, Carol, Darklighter, Robin, Taguhi, and Lee.

Chapter 1

Visitations

Tyler is going to get himself in trouble," said the spirit.

Aiden Moray eyed the winged lizard at the other end of his desk. The spirit was small, no bigger than his hand, covered in blue-black scales except for a splash of red on its neck and belly. It flexed and then folded its bat-like wings, its gleaming black eyes fixed upon him.

Aiden closed his laptop on his programming work and said, "Are you threatening my son?" Aiden had dealt with spirits before, but never had they specifically mentioned Tyler. It gave Aiden a queasy feeling.

The spirit's tail flicked once. "Oh no. No threats, but he is dabbling in things best left alone after all these centuries."

"If you guys would give him a moment's peace maybe he'd relax."

"I promise you it's not me taunting him but he is disturbing some of the old ones who don't have my sense of humor."

"Old ones?"

"You and I don't want to know who they are otherwise I would tell you." The spirit gazed at the adjacent bookcase as if it had found a place to hide something like a squirrel burying a nut. It contained a few programming books, a couple of tech manuals of sensor specifications, a scattering of photos of his parents with his brother and his family at Christmas, a picture of Tyler at three tossing a ball, and his framed Computer Science degree from UCLA.

The lizard hopped to the bookcase, reached under its wing with a foreclaw and dropped a shiny green stone in front of Tyler's picture.

"Things are afoot." The lizard spread its wings and vanished in a burst of light.

Aiden picked up the bauble. It gleamed in his hand, but appeared completely ordinary, something he could find in any rock shop out in the desert. Frequently, the spirits left things behind, so Aiden only set it back on the shelf in case there was a reason the spirit dropped it there. This spirit, like many, enjoyed speaking in riddles, and most of the time it meant nothing. It seemed strange that it mentioned Tyler though, on the other hand spirits had a habit of testing he and Tyler just to see their reaction.

He sat in his home office which doubled as a guest room. To his left was a single bed covered with a blue comforter, an Ansel Adams print, his meager attempt at decorating, hanging above it on the pale blue wall. He had spent all day at work and he wanted to get these specs done, but the spirit had broken his concentration.

He sighed and left the room, passing the bathroom on the left and paused at the head of the stairs, glancing at the closed door of his son's room. He shook his head, he didn't want to disturb Tyler now, and walked down the stairs to the living room.

The bare white walls bothered him, but he had nothing worthwhile to put up on them. He entered the breakfast nook and finally the family room with the TV above the brick mantel of the fireplace. A sliding glass door, often cracked open to let a cool breeze through from the back yard, sat to the left of the fireplace. He'd decorated the room in comfortable warm tones, though the furniture was mismatched from years of random purchases.

Giving up on work entirely, he grabbed the remote off the coffee table and sat on the worn couch. His attention was immediately drawn to the small woman sitting on the raised fireplace hearth.

The spirit stood and stretched to her full two feet of height, tossing her long green hair with brown roots over her shoulders almost reaching the floor, small goat horns protruding from her forehead. She was slim with a narrow chin, upturned blue eyes and a deep brown skin tone that reminded him of freshly turned earth. She wore a grey UCLA tank top and blue jeans with bare feet, her toes kneading the carpet.

She lowered her arms. "How do you feel?"

Aiden shrugged. "That's an odd question. Why do you ask?"

"My peers tell me it's polite to ask of a human's feelings at the start of a conversation."

"You have my attention. What do you want?"

"Items that have remained dormant for centuries are on the move. I am concerned as you should be."

"What are these items? Why should I be worried?"

"The old fey are powerful and dangerous, particularly to humans."

Aiden raised his brows. "Dangerous?" He wanted to ask how these old fey and the items were connected but the fey had their own round about way of talking. Directness was not their forte.

"Many of the old ones would kill and eat humans."

"Sounds like a bad horror movie."

She gave him a sour frown. "I'm not exaggerating." She winked out of view.

Aiden shook his head and sat on the couch pointing the remote at the TV.

A hand-sized, blue humanoid with antlers and a bushy tail ran across the shelves to the right of the TV, knocking a book and a snow globe onto the carpeted floor.

Aiden scowled at the blue spirit and said, "Stop that." This was the third spirit tonight. It was getting ridiculous even for him.

The diminutive blue spirit giggled and tossed a small figurine of a dancing woman onto the floor. Luckily, it was metal and merely bounced on the carpet.

Having had enough, Aiden stood and swatted at the spirit, though he knew his hand would pass right through it. He'd hoped the spirit would get the point, but the little blue creature doubled over in laughter, slapping its knee.

This was why Aiden couldn't have people over, even if most couldn't see the spirits. Anyone watching his reactions to things they couldn't see would question his sanity.

His house wasn't haunted; the spirits followed Aiden from house to house. It might take a few weeks for them to catch up, but they always found him and Tyler. The worst part was he had always failed in his search for people who saw or heard them like he and Tyler did.

"DAD!" Tyler stampeded down the stairs and to the den where Aiden was standing. "That blue antler spirit shut down my laptop! I lost half my homework!" The fourteen-year-old's brown hair flopped over one eye.

Aiden turned from the bookshelf. "Yeah, he was here, knocking things off the shelf."

Tyler rushed over. "Where? I'll… I'll…!"

"He's gone."

"Really? I'm tired of them screwing up my laptop. Last week, the red one stole my pen too."

Aiden set the remote onto the coffee table. "You know the drill. At the end of the year, they get more active."

"Can't we do something about it? Use a stronger protection spell or something?"

Aiden took a deep breath to calm himself. He had gone over this with Tyler at least a hundred times. "If we do anything more, they get excited and disturb us more. It's best to ignore them."

Tyler stomped his foot. "Somebody has to know how to get rid of them!"

Aiden walked past Tyler and the kitchen table into the kitchen itself. "Let's have some popcorn." He had to defuse his son's mood, so he tossed a packet of popcorn into the microwave perched above the stove. The kitchen was a typical suburban style with dark wood cabinets, white tile floor, beige countertops, and recessed lighting. It was a comfortable normality that allowed Aiden to feel that everything was ordinary and free of the fey.

Tyler grimaced at his dad and then sat at the wooden kitchen table. The boy worried his finger in a dent on the surface. Aiden kept telling himself that he needed to fix that along with the other dings and scratches, but he couldn't ever find the time.

Aiden leaned against the refrigerator. "I've told you a million times, no one else sees or hears the spirits like we do. I've looked. There are a lot of people who claim to see fairies, ghosts, or spirits, but they only think they do, or it's a game they play."

"So what?"

"If you tell people all you'll get is people thinking you're crazy."

"Is that why Mom left?"

Aiden shouted, "Tyler!"

Tyler glared at Aiden for a long moment. He sighed and tossed his head. "Tomorrow, I need to go to Kevin's house after school to study."

"You know tomorrow is Friday, right?"

Tyler paused. "Yeah, well, we wanted to get started on a school project."

It seemed odd for Tyler to study on a Friday, but Aiden didn't want to discourage him from schoolwork. "Sounds good. Just be home in time for dinner."

The microwave dinged, signaling that the popcorn was ready. Aiden poured the popcorn into a couple of bowls. Tyler retrieved a soft drink from the refrigerator and sat down as Aiden set a bowl in front of him.

Aiden said, "No drink for me?"

Tyler sighed heavily and shuffled to the refrigerator and back with another soft drink. Setting it down on the table, he said, "It's not fair. The spirits get to do anything they want and we can't do a thing about it."

Aiden sat down beside Tyler. "Life is not fair. The more we react to them the worse they get."

"But do we have to just take it? Every year it's the same. We can't do anything and the spirits get to play around more and more." Tyler stuffed some popcorn in his mouth.

Aiden sipped his drink. "Not all of them are irritating. A lot come here to watch and learn. Then there are the ones that help us, too. Remember the time last year when the long-tailed one helped to find your game controller you'd lost?"

"Still, I hate waiting for them to do… whatever they're going to do. We should be able to defend ourselves, something other than our protection spell." His chair scraped on the tiles. Tyler picked up his snack and stormed upstairs to his room.

Aiden sighed. After a while, he followed Tyler upstairs with his own popcorn and drink, passing his son's closed door and entering his office. Sitting at the desk, he opened his laptop. He had to finish the code that he was writing to optimize pipeline flow rates before work tomorrow. Despite the spirits, their warnings, and their noise, he still had bills to pay.

Chapter 2

The Old House

Tyler Moray was fed up with the constant irritation of the spirits scampering about him and his father. For once, he wanted to be the one to annoy them and losing his homework last night was just one more reason to take a stand.

He stared out the window of the school bus, watching the suburban houses pass by like posts on a fence, a fence that hemmed him in with its regularity and overbearing security to be quiet and to stay within the status quo. The houses were so similar, positively stifling, walling him in with repetitive rules and warnings. His father was the worst. Always worrying about what other people would say or do as if they'd be burnt at the stake or something. He'd had it. Thankfully, it was Friday and he was on his way home. He didn't need to pretend with his dad like he did with the other kids to be normal all weekend.

"Did you get everything?" Tyler said to Kevin Adams as the school bus leaned into a turn.

Kevin turned from the window to face him. "I'm cool. Dude, you owe me after I told Matt and Eric about your ghosts, so you better have your shit together or they are going to have your ass." He was a sophomore, a year older than Tyler and on the school baseball team, a real athlete, in charge and confident.

Today Kevin wore the prep school-like clothes he always did, a green pullover and brown pants, looking like he was going to a job interview. Most of the time, his clothes suited him, but not today. Eric Tallman and

Matt Solis, the older boys they were going to meet would be pissed Kevin hadn't worn black for the ritual.

And that could screw up Tyler's one chance to hang out with people who weren't *afraid* of the spirits.

Stifling his worries, Tyler said, "I told them where to find those stones they wanted from that spirit, which is why we were invited back. Do you really think it will work?"

Kevin shrugged. "Doubt it. But Dude, it's a thing to do a week before Halloween. Or are you scared? Are those ghosts of yours buzzing around?" He said this last part in a sing-song way, making fun of Tyler.

Tyler winced, wishing he'd never told Kevin about the spirits he'd encountered, but they were the reason he was able to get the location of the stones in the first place. "What I meant was, do you think they know what they're doing?"

"Sure. Whatever, dude. It's something different to do on a Friday. I'll meet you at your house as soon as I get my stuff and we'll go over to the park together." Kevin slung his backpack over his shoulder.

"Don't forget to change your clothes," Tyler called after him.

"Yeah, yeah."

Tyler watched him go. He was nervous about the ritual, but pleased Kevin wasn't too afraid to hang out with Tyler, though his friend gave him shit every once in a while. Since finding out about the spirits, Kevin had told his friends Matt and Eric, about Tyler's spirit and ghost stories. And then they'd invited him to hang out with them.

At their first meeting, Matt wasn't very interested but Tyler remembered a frustrated spirit coming to him days before complaining how a guy with a wavy bladed dagger wasn't listening to him.

When Tyler asked Matt if he was the guy with the blade, he got all defensive, raising his fist. "How did you know?"

Tyler's stomach dropped. Was Matt going to hit him? "The spirit said you were looking for some stones and he was yelling at you. He even knocked a book off the shelf but you ignored him, so he came to me."

Eric glared at him. "How did you…?"

Matt cut Eric off with a wave of his hand. "What did he tell you?" He was laser focused on Tyler.

“That he was jumping up and down pointing at the big book in front of you. He tried to tell you that the stone is on the cover of the book. The upper right corner.”

There was a long pause as various emotions played across Matt’s face. Tyler thought he’d blown it but then Matt and Eric grinned at each other. Matt said, “You know, kid. You’re pretty cool. Wanna help us?”

Getting the stones, whatever they were for, would allow him to hang out with upper classmen like Matt and Eric. Finally, he was getting somewhere about how to control the spirits.

Jennifer Brooks sat down beside Tyler, shocking him out of his reverie. She bounced once or twice as she usually did setting her books on her lap. “So, what was that all about? You guys have been so secretive all week.” She wriggled her eyebrows at him. With thick brown hair hanging to her shoulders, she looked strait-laced and stuffy despite her blue jeans and pale blue sweater. She was nice enough, he supposed, though she might as well be his sister. For the past few years, his dad and her mom had traded child-watching duties every weekend.

Tyler grimaced. “Hi, Jen. It’s nothing.”

She nudged him playfully. “I’m older and wiser than you, so you should tell me before you get in any trouble.”

“One month older doesn’t count.”

“Whatever. Anyway, don’t forget to remind your dad that we’re coming over on Sunday for dinner. We’ll bring everything and warm it up at your house.”

Tyler shrugged. “Oh. Okay.”

“Wow,” she deadpanned. “Don’t get too excited. At least my mom isn’t dragging you off to church first thing Sunday morning. You know how she is,” Jen grumbled.

They had that in common. Tyler laughed to himself that he knew more about spirits than any preacher. “At least I’ll have a chance to sleep in.” Thank God he had hadn’t told Mrs. Brooks about the spirits. She’d insist on dragging him to church every chance she got. He didn’t need that headache, or the lack of sleep.

The bus stopped again, this time in a non-descript section near the edge of the development. Low hills rose behind a couple of rows of houses ahead. Tyler said goodbye to Jen, stepped off, and walked towards the hills until the road made a sharp turn to the right, away from a large tan boulder and continued to the end of his street. His house was on a cul-de-sac and identical to all the other houses in the development. He felt that repetition was okay for little stuff like cookies, but wrong for houses. The uniformity irritated him and his skin crawled whenever he thought of living here; the sameness, the familiarity, and the safety of it all nettled him.

He unlocked the front door and went upstairs to his bedroom. Frodo looked down at him from the *Lord of the Rings* poster above the bed with the Ring of Power held out like a warning. After he unpacked his books from his backpack, he reached into the back of his closet and pulled out the paper bag with the things he had bought over the last two weeks: a box of black candles and some small candleholders, a chunk of clear quartz about four inches long, and a ceramic skull. Opening his favorite graphic novel, *Sandman*, he retrieved the piece of paper containing the words he had memorized for the ceremony. He went over the words again, double checking though he knew them perfectly. Tyler didn't need to bring the note but felt better having it nearby. Then he put everything into the backpack and went downstairs to wait.

He sat at the kitchen table, which was older and more dented than the one at Kevin's house. Kevin's parents had all new or nearly new furniture and electronics, his cell phone was the latest model and he had the newest video games. Then again, Kevin had two parents who got along. Once again, Tyler wondered if he would ever see his mother again and whether he would hit her or hug her first. She never called or texted and hadn't even sent a stupid email. He remembered the weeks after she left and how moody his dad had been. Dad denied it, of course, but as Tyler got older, he pieced together how much her leaving had torn up his father. Tyler hoped her new and fancy law career was good for her. Somebody should be happy about the situation, even if it wasn't them.

The doorbell rang, interrupting Tyler's thoughts. Kevin came in lugging a lumpy gym bag. "Dude, come on. I don't want to be late." Kevin still hadn't changed into darker clothing, not even a black T-shirt.

Tyler scoffed, "I thought you were going to change into something black."

"Eh, it doesn't matter."

"Dude, I don't want Matt mad or anything because you're an idiot."

"They should be happy that I'm doing this shit at all. Are you coming or are you going to argue fashion like a girl?"

Tyler scowled and opened the door. "Let's go."

He and Kevin began walking down Mallory Street, toward the huge tan boulder and their destination: Franklin Park. At the boulder, they turned south and followed the roads circling around the enormous rock to get to the park. The park wasn't very big or very special, just a wide spot where the city had required the developers to put in an open space, in return for stacking houses shoulder-to-shoulder to maximize profit. It had a small parking lot, space for maybe ten cars or so, and some picnic tables spread around the trees. A swing set stood east in front of the large red boulder and a jogging track went around the perimeter. There was a gate at the top of a rise about two hundred yards away to the north, marking the boundary of the park. The sky was Southern California clear and almost unreal – an intense shade of fluorescent blue. Tyler and Kevin sat in silence on a picnic table. The sun beamed through the branches of the tree above them bright and warm. The sunlight seemed incongruous to Tyler; with what they had planned, there should be clouds and maybe a thunderstorm lurking in the sky.

Matt and Eric pulled up in a battered red Nissan and climbed out, each carrying a backpack. Eric wore black jeans and T-shirt. He was sixteen and a junior in Tyler's high school. He looked hard, like he had a mean streak just out of sight. His eyes were brown and set a little too close together, and Tyler noticed that he had started to grow a goatee. It was really just a few hairs on his chin that he had twisted together, but still more than what Tyler could grow.

Matt was a senior and he too, wore all black including a matching duster reaching past his knees. Even his shoes were black. He had a shock of blond hair and pale blue eyes that burned with intensity. He walked with a mean confidence like he would step on anyone stupid enough to get in his way. While Eric had to work at it, Matt carried off the look naturally, without an extraneous thought or action. Tyler was thankful he had memorized and practiced his lines. Eric was unnerving whereas Matt was terrifying. He didn't want to risk making Matt mad.

The pair stopped and regarded the two younger boys. Tyler forced himself to meet their appraising gaze. Matt declared, “Green shirt, Adams? At least Moray wore black.”

Kevin opened his mouth.

Matt waved his excuse away. “No time. We’re burning daylight.” He shouldered his pack and followed the path between two small hills northwards out of the park.

Eric sneered at Kevin, “If we didn’t need four people for the ritual, you’d be history.”

As soon as they turned their backs, Kevin flipped them off.

At the top of a hill, the manicured grass gave way to brown tufts of weeds. A metal gate with a ‘No Trespassing’ sign stood between the hills, blocking the trail. They climbed over it. It was really lame. A mountain biker could easily go around it. Apparently, the gate and short stretch of fence were there to keep out cars and trucks because the fences on either side just went up a short distance. A faded dirt track wound down the other side of the rise and then straightened. At the bottom, it went past a big rock about the size of a panel truck leading to an old, unimpressive single-story house several hundred yards away.

Kevin said, “All the way out there?”

Eric scoffed. “Quit whining. That’s where we did the last one.”

Tyler wondered if they had been successful the last time and what the experience had been like. Would he be able to talk to the entity they were going to conjure? Could he ask anything? He bit back his questions because he didn’t want Eric and Matt thinking he was a complete idiot. He was lucky to get to spend any time with Matt and Eric. It gave him hope that he could learn more from these two, especially today when they were summoning a spirit to divinate the future, at least that’s what Matt had told him.

As they approached, Tyler saw the house was in a bad way - all the windows were broken out, the whitish paint was almost completely gone and the gray wood bones of the house showed through. The roof sagged so much that it looked ready to collapse at any moment, but the fact that so many of the shingles were missing probably saved it from caving in. A sprawling oak stood off to the right, about fifty yards — the trunk too large to wrap his arms around, its branches gnarled, ready to grab at anything that got too close. The ground was sandy and covered with patches of green grass interspersed between brown weeds from the previous summer. Scrubby bushes and trees grew in a dry streambed winding beyond the trees.

The porch groaned in protest as Matt led the way onto it and inside the house. Tyler, as the freshman, entered last. The house smelled old and musty, but underneath he felt a sense of vague power, dry and prickly, just like the time he'd encountered a powerful ghost with his father. Dad had made him wait behind in another room while he talked to it and had never told him a word about it. Tyler never forgot the experience — so scary and yet so tantalizing. This time, his dad wouldn't be here to shoo him away.

Leaves and dust covered the wooden floor, except for the one room that Matt entered; someone had swept away all the debris. There was a window on the north side, the glass broken out except for a few dirty shards. On each of the three remaining walls someone had drawn a different angular symbol and strange geometry surrounded by a double circle. The same someone had painted the symbols with red paint, not spray-painted like graffiti, but carefully done with a brush. Here the residual power felt the strongest but was still a mere tickle on Tyler's senses. The energy was nebulous and diffuse. This must have been the room where Matt and Eric tried to perform the last ceremony.

Matt and Eric set down their packs at the edge of the room and began pulling spell materials out. Tyler sensed it when Matt removed a large book. Bound in brown leather, the tome looked horribly ancient, emanating power, making Tyler's stomach clench. It didn't feel right. But something about it excited him.

Kevin stared. "What's the book?"

Matt smirked. "It's the *Spiritorium de Infinitus Maleficus Profundum.* It's an ancient grimoire in Latin. My great, great, grandfather got it when he came back from Europe after World War I. It's been sitting in my grandmother's attic until I figured out what it was. Now, be quiet while we mark the circle."

Without a word Matt and Eric marked the cardinal points in the room and began chalking a large circle on the floor. Tyler and Kevin watched in silence from the edge of the room as the other boys drew a five-pointed star within the circle. Then, in a red liquid too thin to be ordinary paint, they marked various symbols — circles around angular and geometric designs — inside the circle between the lines of the pentagram. Some of the symbols looked benign, while others appeared angry. Then Matt unfolded a piece of paper and studying it, copied a strange symbol unlike the others. Instead of harsh angles and lines, this one consisted of graceful swirling curves. Tyler stepped closer, entranced by its beauty.

Matt stopped and pointed at the edge of the outer circle. Tyler halted and walked around the outside until he was as close as possible without stepping within. The symbol was incredible, elegant, and powerful in equal measure. It held whirling water and a branch with leaves around a skull, evoking fecundity, and withering death in equal measure.

When Eric and Matt finished, they carefully stepped outside the circle to avoid smudging any lines. It was apparent that they had done this several times before.

Matt removed his cell phone from his pocket. "Everybody take out your phone and turn them off. Then put it by the south wall. Phones and other electronics can screw up spells."

Tyler followed the instructions, thinking they were strange since the spirits that he had dealt with delighted in shutting down various electronics at his house, especially his laptop.

Matt ordered, "Moray, Adams come here and hold out your hands, palms down." He put his finger in the jar of red liquid and dabbed it on the backs of their hands and on their foreheads. The red paint smelled metallic like blood. As he did, he intoned, "May you be protected from the infernal ones. Amen." He turned to Eric and did the same to him, and, in turn, Eric performed the same protection on Matt.

Matt set the jar aside. "Now take your places like we practiced. Don't throw anything and don't ever touch the circle or I will personally kick your ass."

Tyler and Kevin nodded. Tyler sat cross-legged at the western side of the circle facing the interior with all the designs between the lines of the star. He quickly set his candles on either side of his position with the ceramic skull and the clear quartz chunk in front of him. Kevin did the same opposite him facing a metal cup full of water.

Eric walked around the circle, lighting the candles. Then he sat at the south side of the circle, his back to the south wall several feet from where their phones were. Eric sat in front of a small brazier with flames dancing within. He tossed in a yellowish lump and smoke began to rise, emitting a strange, sweet odor. It wasn't pot. It was sweeter and more mysterious.

Eric glanced at him. "It's frankincense."

Matt sat at the north point of the circle. He also had a censor with incense and a shiny wavy-bladed dagger lay beside his knee. The weapon looked wicked and powerful, a dragon-headed handle with a red stone gripped in its mouth. It seemed to Tyler the perfect tool to control arcane forces, similar to the video games he played and the books he read. The Spiritorium lay open in front of him. Holding down one page was a smooth oblong stone a little larger than a golf ball painted a shiny blue glaze with gold symbols. It must have been one of the stones that the spirit had told Tyler about. The amulet shone with a strange blue iridescence flowing around the surface like chromatic tar. The symbols were a cross between what his dad once identified for him as cuneiform and Sanskrit. They seemed to radiate such aggression that they made Tyler's stomach lurch. As he watched, the symbols began to shimmer softly, twinkling, trying to lure him closer. Then they slowly flowed along the surface, stirring the blue iridescence. Gradually, they gained speed, occasionally bumping into each other. They stopped and began to move in the opposite direction, slowly at first, then gathering speed, bumping, and jostling into each other.

Tyler blinked trying to clear his vision, but the symbols still slid around the surface. His eyes flicked to each of the guys and if they saw anything, they weren't reacting to it at all. He took a few deep breaths, forcing himself to get his breathing under control. He had to remain calm if he was going to be any use while summoning a spirit.

Tyler turned his attention to the chunk of black obsidian sitting on the other open page of the Spiritorium; the other stone the spirit had told Tyler about. The stone glittered in the low light, enticing him to come closer, the air around it fading in and out of focus. A region of blue blackness seeming to expand around the stone, then contract suddenly like some kind of alien respiration. It left black streaks in the air that flowed slowly back into the stone, leaving a pale blue coldness behind. The blue amulet felt as if it held something in check, but the obsidian felt like it was trying to reach out and grab anything that strayed too close. His stomach knotted with a mixture of fear and excitement. The stones in the presence of the book seemed to be highly charged. He could feel a buzzing in the back of his mind forcing his attention to the stones. Tyler hoped that was a good thing.

Kevin breathed, "Dude. Shouldn't we do this at night in a graveyard or something?"

Matt scowled, turning up his lip. "That's movie crap. We're doing the real thing here and we need a specific alignment of the sun and moon, in this case late afternoon." He shook his head, as if to clear it. "Okay, we're going to start. Nobody talk except for your lines, and don't move from your spot, no matter what you see or hear."

Everyone nodded.

Matt raised his wavy-bladed dagger. "Spirits of the Air be with us. Lend us your quickness and intelligence in what we're about to undertake."

Tyler raised his quartz. "Spirits of the Earth be with us. Lend us your power and steadfastness in what we're about to undertake." The stone became heavier as he lowered it. He could feel warm energy coming up from the ground around him. This was real and he was right in the middle of the whole thing! For the first time he was instigating contact with the spirits instead of being at their mercy. It made him feel more powerful, and in control.

Eric raised his hands, wafting a column of incense above his head. "Spirits of Fire be with us. Lend us your energy and heat in what we're about to undertake." Tyler felt an additional crackling of energy.

Kevin followed, holding the cup in front of him. "Spirits of Water be with us now. Lend us your depth and wisdom in what we're about to undertake." Another wave of power washed over Tyler.

Tyler felt more energy in his quadrant than any of the others, but it may have been because he was closest to it. The room felt off balance to him, but since Matt and Eric knew what they were doing, he said nothing. The ritual continued with Matt and Eric saying their lines in what Tyler assumed was Latin, but most of the rite was in English. He and Kevin repeated what Matt said at certain stages.

Matt spread his arms. "Hear us. Come hither before this circle, without..."

The energy built at the center of the circle. The candles began to smoke. Instead of continuing to travel upwards, the incense and the candle smoke began to stream to the center of the circle and started to swirl in a slow-motion whirlwind. Every so often, white light flickered at the center. The increased energy worried Tyler. This seemed very different from the spirits he'd encountered before.

The power continued to grow and coalesce into a malevolent form, focusing on Tyler and ignoring the other boys. It raked across his senses causing his teeth to itch. Tyler couldn't see a thing though because the smoke was so thick.

Tyler thought of running, but he feared any motion would attract the entity's attention. The quartz in front of him radiated a warm glow and yet he felt exceedingly cold. Slowly, to avoid drawing the entity's attention, he reached for the quartz and held it to his chest. A feeling of warmth and safety flowed through him. The being manifesting at the center of the circle turned its attention away from him and swung around directly across from him to the weakest quarter of the circle — Kevin's quarter. Tyler couldn't see through the swirling black smoke and sparkling light in front of him, but Kevin was in trouble. Protecting himself against spirits was second nature to Tyler. His dad had taught him protection exercises at a very young age and made him practice often. Kevin had never had that kind of training.

Tyler reached out, not physically, but with his mind. He directed his energy around the circle, following the counterclockwise swirling direction of the smoke to Kevin, giving him some much-needed shielding. Tyler could feel Kevin's shock, sense him just sitting there, dumbly staring at the smoke and lights in front of him. Luckily, Tyler felt the being turn away from Kevin.

The floorboards listed, as if a great weight bore down in the middle of the circle. Over Matt's and Eric's chanting, Tyler heard the floor creak loudly. Immediately the scent of hot iron and burning pitch filled the air, making him gag. Tyler still couldn't see anything but swirling smoke, but he sensed the creature manifesting was big, and in a foul mood. He hoped Matt and Eric understood what was happening, because it was all he could do was protect him and Kevin. He was completely out of his depth with this entity, whatever it was.

It growled, huge and throaty. Tyler's gut vibrated and the temperature dropped a few more degrees, despite the warmness of the quartz. The floor screeched and shifted in front of him, as if the creature had taken a step. It shouldn't have been able to do that. The magic of the circle should keep the creature contained! Tyler held his breath, clutching the quartz, not daring to move for fear of attracting the being's attention.

Matt screamed, and something struck the wall to his left with a dull thud. Tyler shuddered, realizing that must be the sound of Matt's body hitting the wall. The sounds of glass shards breaking counterpointed the heavy thudding of footsteps that grabbed his attention. He willed himself not to move.

Then all was silent.

The candles stopped smoking. The smoke in the center of the circle evanesced quickly as if it had been only steam. The sparkling lights disappeared, yet the candles remained lit, and the incense floated upwards rather than horizontally into the circle. Tyler looked to Matt's position. Matt was gone. The little bits of glass shards in the window behind his position were gone also. Had the entity gone through it? Kevin and Eric remained at their quarters staring where Matt should've been.

Someone was moving to the left of Tyler. "Fuck!" Matt propped himself up against the west wall, his right hand pressed tightly to the left side of his abdomen.

Tyler hissed, "Are you okay?"

"Shit burns like a mother fucker."

Eric shook his head to clear it and went to Matt, walking across the circle. "Here, let me see."

Matt grimaced when he lifted his hand from the wound. Eric pulled at Matt's shirt. "Ow!" Matt shoved Eric's hand away.

Eric breathed, "Hey, it's just a scratch." He went quiet, his wide eyes darting around the room. Was this the first time they had ever successfully cast a spell?

Matt hissed through clenched teeth. "Get the Spiritorium, the blue and black stones and take them with us along with our phones. You two," he pointed at Tyler and Kevin "Pick up the rest. Hurry up!"

"And put out the incense in the bowls," Eric ordered. "The last thing we need is the fire department here." He quickly gathered the ancient book, rock, and amulet and crammed them into a pack. Slinging it over his shoulder, he helped Matt stand.

Matt snapped, "We must separate, just in case. They can't follow us."

Eric turned to the other two. "The two of us have to go together, but you two will have to split up or the demon will know which way to go to hunt us down. Comprende?"

"I guess, but why would it come after us?" Tyler said.

Eric sighed with impatience. "Because we're the only ones that can send it back. Now move." It felt to Tyler that Eric was putting on a brave face. Tyler was used to strange things happening but this ritual had rattled Eric. Matt was in too much pain to comprehend what had occurred.

Tyler extinguished the candles and picked them up. When Eric and Matt had told him they were summoning a spirit, they didn't say that it would want to hurt them. Obviously, the spell had gone horribly wrong. Tyler's hands trembled; he took care not to bang the metal candleholders too much as he stuffed them into his and Kevin's bags.

As Eric helped Matt from the house, Tyler noticed that Kevin still hadn't moved. Tyler grabbed the water bottle next to Kevin. The charcoal in the incense bowls hissed angrily as Tyler poured water over them. "Kevin? Are you all right?"

Kevin uttered in a barely audible voice, "It really worked. That shit really worked. We summoned a demon."

"Yeah, it did. Can you help me pick this stuff up?" Tyler didn't want to hang out here any longer than he had to. The scent of the demon on his mind disturbed him. Even though it was no longer here, he could sense its residue like a wisp of chlorine vapor that burnt his nose.

Kevin stood, his eyes bulging, and pointed with a shaking finger at the center of the circle. "But that shit was real! Right here! Don't you get it?"

Tyler stopped and glared at Kevin. "I do get it. I was the one who told you that the spirits were real, remember? Now help me pick this shit up."

Kevin paused, the excitement leaving him in a rush. "Yeah… Yeah, sure."

Soon they had their packs on their backs and their phones in their pockets. Tyler wanted to leave as soon as possible. The acrid residue smelled too dangerous. He thought of himself as brave, but not stupid.

At the door, Tyler walked east. It would take him behind the housing development and to the rear of his house. Kevin trailed him, his mouth still agape. Tyler stopped. "You can't follow me. Go that way." He pointed west.

Kevin frowned. “Why?”

“Some demon thing appeared and wants to hunt us down. Duh.”

Kevin could be so dense. Tyler had saved his ass during the summoning, and he probably didn’t even know it. That demon would’ve gone in Kevin’s direction if Tyler hadn’t prevented it. Couldn’t he smell the demon’s stink still lingering in the air, in his mind? No, Kevin had never had to deal with spirits before, much less demons. Tyler couldn’t be bothered with his gee-golly wonder right now. He had lived with weird stuff going on all his life and now he just wanted to get home. Matt and Eric had told him that it wasn’t a big deal summoning a spirit or demon; that they weren’t really evil, that the bad rap came from stupid prejudiced people. Now Tyler wasn’t so sure about that. The demon they called up seemed pretty mean to him. This was going to be a huge problem.

His stomach knotted with worry; Tyler followed the dry streambed to the large oak tree. He paused there. Glancing behind, he saw Kevin heading away from him. The tree looked greener than when he entered the old house. He could have sworn that new growth had appeared around the base and buds appeared at the end of the branches in the last hour. It smelled greener too, like damp earth and fresh acorns. He shook his head. This was getting to be too much for him. He wanted to get to his room and figure out what he should do next.

Matt and Eric called the thing they summoned a demon – and for all Tyler knew, it was. He had never dealt with anything like that. It was big, vicious, and was probably upset at the four of them yanking it out of wherever it was. In his previous experiences, the spirits appeared when and where they wanted to and were never that nasty. This felt entirely different. That thing had been so angry.

He climbed through the gap in the back fence of his house. He felt better, despite the way the repetitiveness of his neighborhood jangled on his nerves. This was his place, his home, his place of safety despite the spirits that came and went. He crossed the green, irrigated lawn to the back door. Fitting the key into the lock, he opened the sliding glass door and ran up the stairs to his room. He carefully wrapped the quartz and the candlesticks in plastic grocery bags and stashed them in the back of his closet. He went into the bathroom and rinsed off the red stuff Matt dabbed on his hands and forehead.

He went back into his bedroom and sat on his bed, breathing hard, his heart thumping against his ribs. The red eyes of Frank Frazetta's "Death Dealer" burned down at him from the opposite wall, almost seeming to accuse him of the horrible wrong that he had done today. The ax dripping blood hinted of the price he might have to pay for his mistake. Tyler looked away. He remembered he had told his father that he was studying with Kevin this afternoon. He went to his desk and opened his American History textbook to the chapter on the Civil War. Even the picture of General Sherman seemed to know the nature of his crime, the severe eyes boring into his own. He sat down and tried to read the chapter.

There was a tapping from downstairs. Carrying the book to the door of his bedroom, he listened. There it was again, so faint he almost missed it.

Tyler descended the stairs. As he walked to the kitchen and the den, he thought he heard a soft tapping sound, like something dropping onto a thick carpet. Glancing into the living room, there wasn't anything there. He stopped a moment and he heard it again.

Thump – thump – thump.

It definitely wasn't from the living room, more like from the breakfast nook. Tyler slowly approached that area. As he set the open book on the kitchen table, a motion caught his eye by the sliding glass door of the den, the same door he'd entered the house through earlier. Had the demon followed him? His breath stuck in his throat. He didn't think a glass door would slow it down. It had felt enormous, so large it made the floor creak in the old house with its weight.

He forced himself to take a breath and walk slowly to the door. He had to know what it was before his father came home. The fear of the thing outside balanced with the fear of his father finding out he'd performed a summoning.

He rounded the couch and just as the thumping sound came again. A large, pale green lump lay against the glass and a snake-like object twitched to one side of it. After a moment the snake-like thing tapped against the glass.

Thump – thump.
He squinted at it, trying to make out more details.
Thump – thump. The snake-like thing was a tail.
Thump – thump.
The pale green lump started to vibrate.

Chapter 3

Visitor

Aiden! This is all screwed up!" Seth Carson leaned over Aiden's desk at work. Seth's distinguishing features were his unibrow, a proclivity for expensive watches, and his tendency to take credit for work he had very little to do with, thereby ingratiating him with higher management. In other words, he was an average, ladder-climbing back stabber.

"What's the matter?" Aiden turned from his computer monitor, running his hand through his salt and pepper hair.

"The temperatures and pressures are all wrong. Didn't you read the specs?"

Aiden took a breath and modulated his voice. "I did read the specs and the rest of the documents that you gave me." He pulled up a page from one of the sources on his computer. "Right here, it states that the parameters need to be in this order." If Seth had read that far he would have known that.

"That's the old specs. You're supposed to use the new one."

"Newer than two days ago? This is what you sent me on Wednesday."

"Yeah, I forwarded it to you yesterday. Read your email." Seth stalked out of Aiden's cubical.

Aiden checked his email but there was nothing from Seth yesterday. Typical for Seth to not send him anything until too late and then blame whoever was nearby. With a tight jaw, Aiden emailed Seth reminding him to send the new specs.

Carol Hodges poked her head over the cubicle wall. "Come on, I'll buy you a coffee." She was a fortyish woman, reading glasses perched on her forehead, dressed plainly in a fuzzy green cardigan. She reminded him of a high school librarian, despite her razor-sharp perceptions of people.

Aiden joined Carol. The so-called breakroom was really an alcove with dingy walls containing the coffee machine, a battered microwave, and a refrigerator. Fortunately, Aiden and Carol were the only ones there.

"You're not the only one to suffer from Seth's disorganization." Carol turned to the coffee maker. "Regular or unleaded?"

"Unleaded. My partying days are over." Aiden dumped the dregs from his mug into the sink so Carol could refill it.

Aiden was tearing a sugar packet open over his java when his spine tingled.

The sensation crept up his body like a stalking cat, or like someone was tracing shards of ice up his spine – chilling, but not painful. Something was happening. The cold, prickly feeling perched on his right shoulder. Aiden blinked. He had dropped the entire packet of sugar, including the paper wrapper, into his coffee.

Carol reached for him and stopped just before touching his arm. "Are you all right? You look pale, like someone told you your mother-in-law was going to stay for six months."

Aiden turned. "I've got to go. I'm ill. Let the others know, will you?" Carol was a friend and all that, but he wasn't going to tell her the real reason. If it got out that he had regular visits from ghosts and spirits, or strange premonitions that preyed on his mind, his next residence would be a mental institution. He would not only lose his job, but more importantly, he would lose Tyler. No, he was feeling ill. If the sensation hadn't rattled him so much, he would have come up with a better excuse rather than just running out.

As a young man, Aiden had searched for others like himself, but all he'd found were pseudo-psychics and wannabe wizards who had less of a clue of what was going on than he did. Many times, he had wished there was a secret society that could whisk him off to some safe house where he didn't have to hide his abilities. He didn't conceal his talents in order not to offend people. He hid them so that he didn't lose what he already had.

All too often, he was reminded of the story of a mob of angry villagers who descended on some accused witch and burned her alive.

His shoulder tingled again. He had this feeling whenever he encountered one of the more powerful spirits or there was a major change in his life. Sometimes that change entailed the death of someone close to him. The problem was he had no idea what it was. In the back of his mind, though, Tyler's odd request to study on a Friday afternoon kept replaying.

***

Aiden drove as fast as he could, weaving in and out of the Southern California traffic, not caring about a speeding ticket. The way people drove these days, he wouldn't stand out, but if Tyler was in danger, seconds mattered. He tried to call the boy's cell phone but the call went to voicemail. The feeling in his shoulder persisted, though it diminished as he approached the house. Either the danger was over or he was too late. The thought of losing Tyler sliced through his heart and settled in the pit of his stomach. If he could just find Tyler, everything would be all right. They'd figure out the rest later.

He pulled the car into the garage with a screech of tires. Leaping from the convertible, he burst through the door that led to the house.

"Tyler? Tyler?" Late afternoon sunlight streamed into the high-ceilinged living room. Nothing seemed out of the ordinary. The same bare off-white walls that he never had gotten around to decorate. The same overstuffed tan sofa and chairs which Sandra had splurged on and then abandoned after the divorce.

"What's the matter?" Tyler came from the den.

Aiden dashed to Tyler. "Thank God." Aiden met him next to the kitchen table. He hugged his son fiercely.

Tyler twisted out of Aiden's arms. "Dad, come on!"

Aiden let him go, looking him up and down. The gangly fourteen-year-old wore the same loose jeans and a black T-shirt as this morning. "You're sure you're all right?"

"Why wouldn't I be?" Tyler stepped to the kitchen table draping his hand over the back of a chair. He moved with an awkward attempt at smoothness that reminded Aiden of himself when he was that age.

Aiden sighed, passing his hand over his face. "I thought something had happened." He felt a bit silly, but still paused, remembering their conversation from last night. "Where's Kevin? I thought you said that you two were going to study this afternoon."

"He just left a few minutes ago."

"Well, never mind, I…"

Thump, thump. The sound of something soft hitting thick glass interrupted Aiden as he turned toward the den. The feeling in his shoulder remained, although it was less intense. *Thump-de-thump*. "What's that?"

"Don't know," Tyler said with a shrug, not meeting Aiden's eyes.

Thump-thump-thump.

"Why is the curtain closed on the door?" Aiden entered the den past the kitchen table, passing the couch and TV. He was sure he had opened the drapes to the den's sliding glass door this morning before breakfast as he did every morning.

"Dad, it's nothing. It was too distracting when we were studying."

"What was distracting?" Aiden pulled open the curtains and leapt away from the glass.

There was something, a form, curled up against the glass door, hunched up, and face down. How did someone get into the back yard? The lump was person shaped, but pale green in color with some sort of deformity on its back and… a tail. The four-foot-long tail behaved much as a cat's, curling and swaying, then tapping on the heavy glass of the door. Yet, it wasn't furred like a cat's tail but green and smooth like the rest of the strange body. A strange semi-transparent membrane covered the person from head to toe.

There was something unsettling about the lump on the creature's back. Aiden couldn't be sure, but he thought he saw something move underneath the membrane. The head was turned away from the window so he couldn't see the face, just the back of the head with dark hair plastered down under the translucent film.

Aiden stared for a moment. "Have you seen this before? Is that why you closed the curtain?"

"No, I've never seen it. We closed the curtains because was too bright outside." Tyler was too nonchalant about the whole thing to be telling the truth. He'd deal with that later.

Aiden put his hand on the door handle.

"Dad, don't! It might be…"

Aiden ignored him and opened the door. A riot of arboreal smells assaulted him — pine, and cedar among others, the conglomeration reminding him of the safe woods behind his boyhood house. A small square of concrete lay in front of the door and the person had curled up on one side with plenty of space left over for Aiden to step out. Looking closely, he saw the person was a woman, a very different woman, but female, nonetheless. Her arms and legs were tucked underneath her, but he could see her slender shoulders and hips. Her slim hands covered her membrane covered face. She trembled and leaned away from him against the window yet remained on the artificial stone of the small patio.

Maybe she was reacting to something behind him. He glanced around, but nothing unusual was in the backyard. He spoke to her. "It's okay. Who are you?"

The creature did not respond. The hands tried to reposition themselves to hide her head as much as possible but failed to cover it completely. As he approached, he saw hair and pointed ears beneath the sheer membrane enveloping her entire body. The membrane itself was inconsistent, transparent in some areas and thicker in others. The covering on her hump was stretched thin, revealing layers of tissue that squirmed as she breathed.

Aiden squatted down, holding his hand out. "Are you hurt? I want to help you." Aiden couldn't fear a creature so obviously terrified. Still, her presence worried him. Why was she at his back door? Who or what was she?

The shivering woman lay as flat as she could on the concrete, keeping her hands over her head. She was a spirit, a powerful one judging by the sensation in his shoulder, but deeply frightened. That a spirit would be scared of anything surprised and unsettled him. He crept forward and touched one of the narrow hands. The membrane felt like thin rubber, tacky on contact. As soon as he touched her, any misgivings he had about her vanished. He thought his sudden calmness was particularly strange, but what surprised him even more was that he actually had physical contact with a spirit. He didn't think that was possible. None of his other encounters had involved touching a spirit directly. The other spirits were ghost-like without physical bodies or had stayed beyond his reach.

She flinched and raised her head to face him. At first, he thought she had no eyes, but then he saw that her eyes were sealed shut beneath the membrane. Her face was triangular with a small nose and her mouth hung half-open in surprise. Her mouth was the only opening in the membrane. She was smaller and definitely frailer than Tyler, almost like a child, yet at the same time, cracking with energy. With the amount of power she exuded, she had to be ancient. Although her eyes were closed, her head followed him as if she could see him. Massaging her delicate fingers gently, he noticed her hand was unusually warm, almost as if she had a fever. Rubbing her hand was the only movement Aiden allowed himself because he didn't want to alarm her any further.

He examined her hand closer and realized she had six narrow fingers. He regarded it as an interesting curiosity, but it didn't distress him, especially considering the tail, long ears and humped back. They stared at each other as her tail wrapped tightly about her body. He smelled trees - cedar or pine, sometimes maple, sometimes a woodsy scent he couldn't identify.

The idea that she might be a threat crossed his mind since she was a powerful spirit with an odd appearance, but he didn't sense any aggression from her, only fear. Although it amazed him that he could hold her hand.

He murmured, "I won't hurt you."

She flinched, her unseeing eyes studying him. At least she could hear.

Aiden helped her up. "Let's go inside." She stood unsteadily, as if injured, and her tail wrapped itself around one of her legs. She was not tall – no more than five feet, frightened, and obviously blind.

Tyler leaned out the door. "I don't know, Dad. Is it safe to bring her in?"

The green woman fell to her hands and knees and began curling up protectively in a fetal position, tucking her arms and legs beneath her, her tail wrapped tightly around her. Aiden immediately knelt and encircled her with a protective arm. "Tyler, she's scared out of her mind." Turning to the woman, he breathed, "Hey, hey, it's going to be all right. This is Tyler. He didn't mean to scare you."

The woman continued to shiver beside him. Aiden pulled gently on her hand, helping her to stand up. Using her other hand, she steadied herself against the glass of the sliding door, her tail tapping gently around the ground Aiden's feet like a blind person's cane. When she lifted her head to face Tyler, she folded in on herself again.

Aiden held her up by one hand, but the rest of her body shrank away from Tyler. He waved his son out of the doorway and led the trembling woman inside, sliding the door closed behind them. When her feet encountered the carpet, she scrunched her toes on the fibers. The vague forest smell seemed to follow her into the house. She bent down and ran her hand across the carpet with her head tilted to one side as if concentrating on the sensations coming from her fingers.

He gently guided her to the sofa that faced the den and the TV. She reached out and touched the sofa, squeezing the cushions and sliding her hand slowly over the fabric. Behind the couch was the breakfast nook with the kitchen table.

Aiden patted the cushion. "Go ahead and sit."

She tilted her head at him.

"It's okay. Here." Aiden took her hand again and sat down beside her.

She sat, but then sprang up, her mouth opened as if to shout, yet she made no sound.

Tyler stammered, "Um, Dad. She has fangs."

The woman curled up on the floor between the couch and the coffee table. She trembled anew. Her tail wrapped about her again.

Aiden glanced at Tyler. "Did you do anything to her?"

"No."

"So why does she hide when she hears your voice?"

"I don't know. I've never seen her before."

Again, with the evasiveness, but he'd deal with that later. Instead, he reached down and helped the woman up and onto the couch. He was no bodybuilder, but she weighed practically nothing. She faced him. He could have sworn she actually saw him although her eyes were closed. "It's all right." Aiden grabbed the light blanket on the back of the couch and covered her.

She responded by wrapping her arms tightly around him, laying her head against his shoulder. Her tail insinuated itself around his ankle.

"So, what are we going to do with her?" Tyler kept his voice low. The woman clung tighter to Aiden.

"Try to help her the best we can. She's different from…"

She coughed. Aiden tucked the blanket around her. She shook her head and coughed again. He patted her humped back. She released him, dropping her face to her knees, and coughed for a longer period. Was she sick? He had never encountered any spirit that was ill. When she raised her head, blood ringed her mouth and ran down her chin to dribble onto the carpet. She began to sway as if drunk, one hand still grasping Aiden's knee.

"Dad, she's bleeding!"

"Hang on."

Aiden tried to hold her so she wouldn't fall off the couch. She squirmed out of his grip and staggered to the end of the couch. Tyler backed away standing in the breakfast nook watching, his face pale. A wave passed upward through her body, forcing her to straighten up and back. She shook off the blanket and stumbled to the kitchen table in the breakfast nook. Tyler jumped away as if she were going to bite him. She seemed to be searching for something, touching each chair back as if it could unlock some information. Her hands fell onto the tabletop, sliding along the wooden surface. Her head tilted, listening to what the wood told her.

Aiden followed her, picking up the blanket. "Hey, it's all right. Why don't we get this around you?" He dropped the blanket over her shoulders.

She coughed again, at first lightly, then longer, and deeper like something was stuck in her lungs. Blood dribbled out of her mouth in long elastic ribbons, leaving small puddles on the chair and running onto the tile floor. The air whistled in her lungs as she drew another breath and fell to the floor with her hands slapping against the brown tiles. She gasped and hacked, while her whole body contorted with her head practically between her knees. Aiden patted her back not sure of what else to do. Tyler backed away, his eyes wide, but didn't run. Aiden worried about Tyler seeing this terrible scene of pain but sending him away didn't seem reasonable. Besides, he would hear everything, which was often worse.

The woman got up onto her hands and knees, her cough stopping, though blood ran from her mouth. Her whole body undulated, starting at her gut, and traveling up her torso, finally stretching her neck and opening her mouth. She spat and sat up, holding her stomach – red saliva running down her chin and chest. A thick brown lump hit the tiles with a wet splat, smelling of decaying leaves. She screamed – a tortured, gut-wrenching cry.

Aiden attempted to quiet her, wrapping an arm around her. Her hands went to her face and explored her contours. The fingers started at her forehead, tracing down her nose to her mouth and spreading the blood. Then her hands flew to either side of her face and she began tearing at the membrane covering it. Aiden backed away but couldn't stop watching.

At the back of her head, the membrane ripped away, revealing black strands of dark wet hair. She pulled the membrane from her face as gobs of milky fluid streaked with red dripped onto the tiles. Her eyes opened for the first time and she turned her face upwards toward Aiden. Those eyes were the most alien he had ever seen, like a domestic cat with vertically slit pupils, colored an intense gold overlaid with a faint green cast. They twitched side to side. In the next instant, they locked onto him and she shrank away from Aiden, bumping into the kitchen chairs. She threw her arms up, blocking him from her. Then she shook her head to free her long hair from beneath the membrane on her back. Crimson fluid sprayed everywhere.

Aiden held out his hands to show that he wasn't a threat. "I know it must be a shock, but I'm the same guy you held onto before."

Her long, pointed ears swiveled around to orient on him, then shivered to shake off the ichor that coated them. They reached almost to the top of her head. She scooted away while leaving a bloody smear on the tiles, keeping one arm up. Catching sight of Tyler, she jerked away from him too. Like a grotesque bib of snakeskin, the membrane from her head hung in front of her. Milky red goo streaked her face.

Aiden took care to sidestep the gore and blood on the floor. Using his softest voice, he spoke, "It's okay. You're safe." She shrank further from him, the whites of her eyes showing.

She screamed again, her golden cat-like eyes growing even wider. Her body writhed and flopped on the floor as she convulsed. Then she was still, lying face down on the floor, breathing heavily. A rip started in the membrane over her large, humped back. Mucus and blood splashed out as a bony appendage stuttered from the tear in the membrane, splattering crimson all around. Aiden backed away as another red-streaked appendage sprang out, splattering more blood and pus around the room. She pushed up, using her arms and raising her torso off the floor.

The woman continued to scream as the extra limbs from her back unfolded and stretched above her. Aiden gaped as the bony appendages with flaps of skin unfurled. The rip extended from the back of her neck to her tail. Her twelve fingers trembled as she gripped the floor, her mouth open and wailing. Aiden gasped.

Large bat-like wings unfolded from the woman's back.

The green wings popped and straightened as the skin stretched betwixt the long delicate bones. Globs of red slime slapped the floor, hitting with a staccato beat accompanied by the smell of fresh blood, pine, and leaves. Aiden tried to tell himself that this couldn't be happening, but it lay before him in all its gruesomeness. He could practically taste the blood coating the walls and floors. Never before had he dealt with a spirit like this.

Her screams terminated in a hoarse cry. The silence stunned Aiden, yet the bat wings continued to unfold and expand. He winced, hearing the joints clicking and popping into place in a nightmare of arthritis. One of the wings touched the wall above the kitchen window, leaving a bloody streak on the drab whiteness. The other wing stretched out over the living room area, spattering puddles of red ichor on the pale beige carpet. She shook as her wings vibrated to their fullest extent. Tyler moved out from under the wing when it unfolded, standing in the kitchen opposite Aiden.

She raised her head, tears running down her face, washing the bloody mess from her cheeks to reveal streaks of pale green skin. The membrane from her head still dangled from her neck, her fingers still gripping the slick tiles. Her open mouth showed both upper and lower fangs, resembling a dog or cat. The lank, wet hair hung about her face, the long, pointed ears poking through the mass like small horns.

She turned her head towards Aiden and her head jerked back, eyes widening. With her hands, she tried to retreat from him, but managed only to slip on the slime coating the floor. Her elbows slid out from under her. Then her eyes closed and she sank to the floor with a moan. The raised wings also descended as one draped awkwardly over the kitchen table and the other sprawled into the living room, resting on top of an overstuffed chair, leaving a crimson smear.

After a few seconds, Aiden realized that he was holding his breath. He released it slowly, looking down at the blood and slime covering him. He looked up and saw that Tyler was also spattered with thick red liquid. Tyler blinked, his mouth opening and closing without words.

Aiden rushed to him, jumping over the outstretched wing lying on the floor. He held Tyler, and for the first time since he was ten, Tyler didn't push Aiden away. Aiden hoped that this grotesque transformation wouldn't scar Tyler. Tyler sobbed silently as Aiden looked down at the winged creature. She wasn't dead. Her chest rose and fell with each breath she took.

He had never seen such a being before. The spirits he encountered before hinted that there were others more powerful and rare than they. This one had flesh. He had touched it and it had bled… a lot. He glanced at his home, swathed ceiling to floor in blood and purulence — four rooms smelling of wet forest rot.

As Tyler's crying lessened, Aiden patted his shoulder. "It's okay. It's over. She's not like our usual spirits."

Tyler raised his head from Aiden's chest. "Wha… What do we do now?" He wiped his tears, smearing crimson over his cheeks.

"You had better take those clothes off and run upstairs and shower."

Tyler stepped back. Looking at himself, he grimaced. "Yeah." He glanced at the prone form beside them. "What about her?"

"I'll clean her up as best I can and put her in the guest room."

"What is she?"

"I'm not sure, but she's had a very bad day."

"Isn't she dangerous?"

"She is frightened and she's fortunate to find us. Anyone else would have shot her without a second thought. I think she deserves a chance to explain herself."

Tyler nodded.

Aiden walked into the kitchen and pulled out a box of plastic garbage bags. "Get out of those clothes and put them in one of these."

After Tyler ran upstairs, Aiden went to the nearby bathroom and washed the blood from his hands and face. Normally the sight of blood disgusted him, but there was so much that his senses were overloaded. He just had to get through this. His fingers trembled, and he clenched his hands into fists, yet they continued to shake. Suddenly his knees buckled and he found himself curled up against the cabinet as sobs wracked his body. He sat on the floor of the bathroom for a few minutes, wiping tears from his eyes. He hadn't had an episode like this since Sandra left him. Fleetingly, he wondered if all women in his life were meant to affect him this way.

Afterwards, he pulled himself upright and washed his face again. Returning to the breakfast nook, he sighed, scanning the chaos before him. The woman hadn't moved, remaining face down on the tiles. Retrieving a bucket and some rags, he started to clean her wings. They were so large that he merely tried to remove the worst parts of the bloody goo. She'd have to bathe later. She was still warm to the touch and smelt of trees — pine, cedar, maple, among others — her scent subtly shifting over time. As he reached the base of her wings, he found finger length black fur running from under her hair at the back of her neck, down her spine covering the space between her wings, and tapering off to a point as it approached her tail. Her wings connected just below her shoulders. They were of soft skin that attached down her back in parallel, stopping at the top of her hips.

He found an old blanket and spread it out by the stairs. He carefully folded her wings and slid his arms underneath her. He lifted and almost lost his balance. She couldn't weigh more than a large sack of oranges. Impossible! Once he recovered, he carried her to the blanket and gently rolled her onto it, face up.

She was beautiful — fine features, narrow nose with a small mouth. She looked to be in her early thirties with a slim body, narrow hips, and small breasts. Perhaps the membrane had obscured that feature. He continued to wash off the worst of the scarlet blobs but ignored her breasts and hips; it wasn't fair to her to take advantage of her state. He refilled the bucket several times with clean water. There was so much blood. How had she not bled to death?

He wrapped her loosely in the blanket and carried her upstairs. Tyler stood watching him, his hair still damp from his shower. Aiden reached the top stair. "Can you open the door to the guest room?"

"Uh, yeah." Tyler stopped staring at the woman in the blanket and pushed the door open.

"Thanks." Aiden lay her on the bed at the far end of the room underneath a photo by Ansel Adams called "Moonrise, Hernandez." It was a startling picture with the moon looming over the houses like a portent of doom, yet it possessed beauty and serenity too. He folded her wings, trying to make her as comfortable on the bed as possible. The tail was very flexible and ended only with a minor taper at its end, similar to a monkey's tail. It could curl in on itself several times without any effort at all. He stretched her out and covered her with the blanket.

Tyler murmured, “What's that tree smell?”

Aiden brushed a lock of wet hair from her face. “It's her, though it changes.” He stood suddenly. He thought he should leave her be. “You hungry?”

Tyler shook his head. “Not really.”

“Me neither. I need to shower this gunk off me.”

“We're just going to leave her here?”

“Yes, at least till morning.” Aiden closed the door to the room. He sighed as a wave of exhaustion washed over him.

Chapter 4

Siamura

Aiden awoke with a start, bright sunlight creeping past the drapes. He'd slept later than he'd intended. It was a Saturday and there was always a lot to do on Saturdays. He threw the covers aside and the previous day's memories rolled over him, especially his terror for Tyler and the green woman sprouting wings. He quickly dressed in a T-shirt and jeans and opened the door to his bedroom. Soft, indirect sunlight illuminated the stairs and the mezzanine that overlooked the living room below.

He stepped from his bedroom, hoping that last night was some sort of hallucination brought on by a bad dinner or something. Looking down over the banister, he saw the bloody chair in the living room. That meant the breakfast nook and kitchen were also thick with gore from last night's metamorphosis. He stood in front of his closed office door. He must have been insane to allow the green creature to stay in his house. She was quietly powerful; his senses hummed just being near her yet was also deeply troubled and lost.

She wouldn't have stood a chance with anyone else or on her own, and she was so frightened yesterday. He couldn't turn her out. She had a dismal hope of survival without his help. The spirits of his past may have been mischievous, but they were never malicious. They never harmed him.

He debated whether to knock. Eventually, he took a breath and tapped lightly on the wood. Hearing nothing except the distant birdsong from outside, he opened the door slowly. The scent of trees pervaded the room, with the freshness of a forest after a brief rain. The curtains were open, allowing the direct morning light to stream in over the desk. The picture "Moonrise Hernandez" seemed to mirror the eerie green beauty on the bed beneath it. She was crouched on the bed with the blanket he had wrapped her in last night piled around her. She blinked and her large cat-like eyes followed his movements. Her mouth opened slightly regarding him, yet she made no movement to cover her breasts. In fact, she made no movement at all, except for a single twitch of the tip of her tail. The membrane from last night was gone, although red stains and dried gunk still clung to her in places, marring the pale green of her skin, and her hair was matted and stiff with crusted blood.

In embarrassment, Aiden lowered his eyes. "Oh, sorry. I thought you were still asleep." He felt his cheeks redden at her state of undress. Hell, he would be uncomfortable around any nude woman, green or not. He backpedaled toward the hall.

She shot backward, bumping into the corner behind her, still remaining on the bed. Her eyes were wide and locked on Aiden. The blanket lay forsaken in a heap in front of her.

She seemed frightened. He couldn't leave her like that without trying to help her, so he approached the bed. In his most soothing voice, he tried talking to her. "Look, I'm not going to hurt you. What's your name?"

The green woman tried to shrink further into the corner, her legs drawn up to her chest and her tail wrapped around them. Her wings had a joint at her hip level that allowed them to fold underneath her as she sat.

Aiden stopped and with one hand, waved her to him. "It's okay. You're safe here." When she didn't move, he crept to the bed and sat on the edge of it.

She wrapped her arms tightly about her legs, only her uncanny eyes peered above her knees.

As Aiden's shoulder continued to buzz, he reached out and touched her hand. A warmth spread from the contact. His heart rate decreased and found a sense of calm within him that quieted any misgivings he had about her.

Those golden eyes of hers blinked. She raised her head so her chin was above her knees. Her eyes studied him, the eyebrows raising slightly and then relaxing. She opened her mouth, then swallowed as if gathering her courage. Her voice was low pitched and smooth, like aural silk. She asked, "Scisce Latine?"

He hadn't any idea what she said. "I'm Aiden." He pointed to himself with his other hand.

Her ears stood at attention, listening to him, tongue peeking from her lips for a moment. Again, she spoke, but in a guttural sing-song style, sounding like an exotic medieval song. Her voice retained its lustrous tone.

"I don't understand you. What's your name?" He gave her hand a gentle squeeze as he shifted closer to her.

Her hand turned to grasp his firmly. She spoke again. This time the words weren't as guttural, but still wonderfully melodic, tumbling from her lips like pearls.

Aiden smiled. "That's all right. I'm sure we'll manage somehow."

She uncurled and knelt close to him. "I mene to thee non harme." Her free hand went to the back of his head. She dropped his hand and wrapped her arm around him, drawing him close. What was happening?

Her lips pressed onto his, her pine and cedar scent overpowered his senses. Her head turned slightly and she kissed him in earnest. Startled, he tried to pull away, but she held him fast somehow heavier than he remembered from last night. One of her hands was at the back of his head while her other arm was wrapped tightly around his torso. He tried getting his feet under him to escape, but her legs encircled his waist holding him fast.

Her mouth opened and her tongue invaded his mouth. She tasted of wood and blackberry, surprising and pleasant, yet her fangs grazed his lips as if warning him not to bite her. Her agile tongue twisted around his. A brilliant flash of green assaulted his senses. Then her tongue retreated and she fell away. He was free of her, but all he could see, hear, and feel was green. Blinded, he breathed deep until it passed.

She curled into a fetal position beside him, barely making a sound. He jerked away, almost falling off the bed. Stunned, he wouldn't have believed that a tongue could be sprained. Nonetheless, that was the sensation he felt. He considered himself lucky though after losing all his senses in a green flash. He wanted to flee, but she moaned in pain. She clutched her head as her fingers ran over her matted hair and clumps of dried blood. He scooted to the foot of the bed, away from her.

"Please… wait. Ah, hurt." She folded up and writhed on the sheets, her tail flopping back and forth beside her, her eyes squeezed shut and her wings twitching erratically.

Aiden wanted to yell at her, but it didn't seem fair, given the obvious pain she was in and the fact that his numb tongue prevented him from speaking. He stared at her. A wave of vertigo gripped him and he slid back so he could lean heavily against the wall. The room circled about his head like a drunken dancer. The woman continued to contort beside him, crying softly. Aiden thought he should run from her, but the idea of escape seemed as remote as Antarctica and a calm sense of morbid curiosity settled upon him. Not to mention he was too dizzy to stand anyway.

After a couple of minutes, she stopped her thrashing and moaning. Initially she faced away from him, still and unmoving. Slowly, she collected herself into a sitting position, her back pressed against the wall away from him, her legs drawn up underneath her. The wing joint at her hip level allowed her wings to splay out at right angles on the bed to allow her to sit, as her tail wrapped protectively about her legs. She again made no attempt to cover her nudity, but merely watched him.

He stared, mesmerized by two sinuous tattoo-like bands of dark green that curled around each breast, then swirled down her abdomen in parallel, disappearing in her groin. These bands did nothing to obscure her nudity. Instead, they highlighted her svelte form. He looked up to her golden cat-like eyes. She in turn regarded him with a tilt of her head, ears raised at attention. She held his gaze to the point of making Aiden flinch.

Aiden's dizziness had dissipated a bit. "What did you do?"

Her ears flipped down. "Sorry. Mean not I to a fright thee. Please…" She closed her eyes and trembled. Her voice was timorous, yet still rich and melodic. The ears stayed down as if to make herself as small as possible, her wings folded tightly behind her, a foot above her head. She opened her eyes after a moment.

"You shouldn't go around kissing people like that — wait, you spoke English. How did that happen?"

She winced. "Use I magt. Touch mine tongue to thyne to learn. Hurt head." Her tail tightened about her. Her hand on her head came away with a smear of crusty brown blood.

"You're kidding."

"Speak I truth." Her eyes blazed at him and her back straightened like she was offended at his remark.

Aiden still didn't believe her, but there were other, more important things to ask. "What's your name?"

She began licking her bloodied hand, cleaning it like a cat, the previous affront seemingly forgotten. "Siamura. Call mine self Siamura this time." She pronounced her name with a long I and rolling the R. Her accent sounded like a jumble of European languages, archaic and mysterious.

"I'm Aiden. Here, you don't need to do that," He waved to the hand she licked. "There's a bathroom next door. Then I'll find something for you to wear." He stood, bracing himself on the wall. He couldn't decide whether to be mad at her or to pity her. One moment she had him in a death clinch, and the next she was on the bed, writhing in pain.

"Wear? Cold I not."

"Well, you've got to wear something. You can't run around nude." He held out his hand to help her up, out of habit rather than conscious thought. His thoughts were skittering around, refusing to lock onto anything for too long, which was probably a good thing. If he thought about anything, he would probably run. Siamura ignored his proffered hand and stood, holding her head. The top of her head only came up to his mouth – her body couldn't be more than five feet in height. Yet her folded wings towered over her, reaching his height.

He stepped through the door.

Following him, her wings sounded like curtains as she shook them. She blinked and looked about her, gawking over the railing down into the living room, her ears up and her mouth open in wonder. Aiden stood by the door to the bathroom and waved her over. She stared about her, then at him, her tail hovering in mid-air as if afraid to touch anything.

He pointed at the bathroom. "You can wash in there." He reached around the doorway and flicked on the light.

Siamura jumped, bouncing off the railing behind her.

"Be careful."

Siamura fell to her knees, trembling. "Forgive me. Not know I." She bowed deeply.

"What's the matter?"

"Use thou magt." She remained on her knees, her face to the carpet.

"Magt? What do you mean?"

"Light without fire." She pointed at the bathroom.

He smiled. "No, that's electricity. I just flipped the switch."

She stared at him blankly, those large cat eyes of hers holding him in their gaze. She firmly held her vibrating hands in front of her.

"Come here. I'll show you."

She didn't move, except for a single twitch of the tail.

He reached for her hand. Tentatively, she allowed him to lead her toward the bathroom. "Here is the switch." He placed her hand around the doorway and onto the switch. "Now push down on it to turn the light off."

She stared at him with wide eyes, her ears plastered to her skull.

"Go on. It's perfectly safe."

Siamura did so and extinguished the light. She flinched, and opening one eye, she watched him. He smiled. She returned a cautious smile.

"See? Perfectly safe. Now push up to turn it on."

She did and the light came on. Siamura grinned and flicked the switch a couple of times. "This ele… elect…"

"Electricity."

"Not magt?"

"No." He pointed to the shower. "You can wash there." Opening a cupboard, he pulled out a towel.

Siamura stepped inside and gaped at the mirror that hung above the sink and covered the wall opposite the tub. Hesitantly, she reached out with her hand to touch the glass. "Such wealth," she murmured.

Aiden blinked. "Wealth? Everyone has mirrors. Well, maybe not that large, but it's no big deal. Over here is the shower. This is what you need."

She turned around and looked up and down at the shower-tub combination, running her hand in the bottom of the basin. "Where water?"

"Uh Siamura, don't you know anything of electricity and plumbing?"

She straightened, her hands balling into fists. "Know I plumbing. Plumbing bring water. Water where?" Her ears stood up, vibrating as she glared at him.

Aiden reached in and turned the chrome handles. "Turn these knobs." Water splashed into the tub. "And turn this center knob to shower. Then slide the glass door closed to keep the water from coming out. Got it?" He opened the door again and turned off the water.

"This not electricity?"

"No, these knobs are for water."

Siamura turned the knobs on and off, and then looked at the tub. "It small. I need pond, lake."

"It's small? It's big enough."

She shook her wings and frowned. "Have not thou these."

"Hmm, good point. Here, let's try my bathroom. It's a little bigger." He picked up the towel and walked out.

"Have thou another bathing room?" She stared after him.

"Yeah, I do. Come with me." He led her through his bedroom and into the master bath. The shower stall was larger and square. The tub stood to one side under the window, facing onto the back yard. It was wider than the tub in the other bathroom.

Siamura stared at the bathroom around her, the double sinks with brass taps, the walk-in closet, the dual banks of towel racks, and finally the large mirror over the sinks. "This thyne?"

Aiden nodded.

"Be thou the lord of this manor house." She knelt on one knee in front of him, her head bowed.

"Please, that's enough. You're embarrassing me. Here's your towel and I'll find something for you to wear." He had to leave before she totally rattled him, as the curving stripes on her torso were becoming more than merely distracting.

She stopped at the shower door. "Aiden, can thou help bathe?" Her long ears flicked up as her tail waved at him.

He cleared his throat. "Help you? With what?" His brain was racing with confusion and possibilities.

"Can not I reach mine back. Wings."

"Oh." He relaxed. "Uh, there's a bath brush hanging in there, along with soap and shampoo for you to use." He retreated from the bathroom, closing the door.

He hunted in his dresser drawers for something she could wear. She looked bizarre, green wings, tail, long ears and fangs, stripes tracing her body like some exotic dancer in a psychedelic dream. Her behavior was stranger still, though maybe it made sense if she was from another world. She thought nothing of running around naked and had no idea what electricity or real plumbing was, not to mention she thought of basics like mirrors as signs of wealth. Yet he felt responsible for her. He needed to help her learn and do whatever it was she was here to do. She certainly didn't come here on her own, or something had happened to her in the transition if she had. He hated to think of her outside, dealing with the other modern machines, buildings, and transportation by herself.

Aiden found a pair of shorts and a T-shirt and placed them on the bathroom counter. She was playing in the water like a child, wings stretched above the shower stall, dripping water on the floor outside. Turning this way and that to clean her wings, she didn't seem to mind the fact that the water at her feet was red. Aiden tore himself away. She made him uncomfortable, but he couldn't abandon her. She was lost and frightened, yet she projected the impression of profound age and below that of repressed rage.

It concerned him that she might be a figment of his imagination, a trick of his isolation. He would have to be careful to get Siamura back to wherever she belonged as quickly as possible.

He descended the stairs into the hell left over from the previous night. Dried blood and chunks of gore covered the breakfast nook and spilled over into the living room, the kitchen, and the den. The deep red blood of last night had darkened to brown, making the room look like a grisly murder scene. The only things missing were carved-up body parts and a grim detective searching for clues.

He did the sensible thing and bypassed the horror. He went to the far side of the dark wood kitchen free of the bloody mess to fix himself a cup of coffee. The sun streaming through the window above the sink brightened the gore-spattered rooms. He peered out the window, which looked beyond the front door upon his patch of happy and safe suburbia. He thought of waking Tyler, but he didn't want to deal with a cranky teenager just yet. Besides, Aiden's feelings about Siamura and her odd behavior confused him. Siamura was badly frightened and in shock. She desperately needed his help, regardless of her appearance. Besides, he had experience with strange happenings, and she was just one more spirit.

No, she was not just another spirit. Siamura wasn't like the others he had encountered. The other spirits were self-confident, sure of themselves and always testing or playing, as consequences seemed only temporary for them. Siamura was different. She had a history and power. He could feel it, an undercurrent beneath her small, timid demeanor, which made him all the more curious as to why she was so unlike the previous spirits he had come across.

Aiden set his coffee mug down with a sigh. The horror show of crusted goo wasn't going to clean itself. He opened the cupboard under the sink and retrieved a bucket and some rags. He set about scrubbing down the kitchen first. A clean food preparation area was more important than a place to sit.

He had started to clean the second counter when a motion drew his eyes away from his work. Siamura had come down the stairs wearing the shorts and T-shirt he had left her, but not the way that most people would wear them. The white shirt barely covered her breasts as it hung up on the base of her wings just below her shoulders, leaving her midriff bare. The khaki shorts were on backward. Aiden couldn't figure why until he saw her tail swing behind her. Obviously, her tail snaked out of the fly of the shorts, very resourceful for a… whatever she was. Siamura wasn't watching him, her eyes flicked from place to place within the interior of the house, her mouth hanging open. She advanced slowly towards the bloodied breakfast nook. When her eyes finally alighted on Aiden in the kitchen, she stopped.

Siamura dropped to her knees and pressed her face to the blood speckled carpet. "Forgive me, mine lord. Offended I thee."

Aiden dropped his rag into the bucket with a muffled splash. "What are you doing?"

She remained prostrate on the floor in front of the breakfast nook, wings down, her tail tucked underneath. "Please, mine lord, mean I none offense. In thyne service am I. Prepared am I of thyne judgment."

"No one is being judged. Call me Aiden, not my lord and sit up."

"Yea, mine… Aiden. May I be of service to thee?" She sat up. The lower part of her wings splayed out behind her on the floor. Her ears were down and her brows went up, as she held her hands tightly in her lap.

"Well, if you want to help, you can help me clean up this mess. There's another bucket under the kitchen sink." He pointed with his thumb at the sink behind him.

Siamura didn't move, except her eyes, which closed. Green wispy fog flowed from where her body touched the carpet, as if some deadly chemical reaction had begun. Thick and dense, it spread from her, obscuring the floor beneath it. Old movies of World War I poison gas attacks sprang to Aiden's mind and his stomach tensed. The greenish fog thickened and tendrils covered the tiles of the breakfast nook and began to creep up the table and chair legs. Aiden stared at the fog that seemed heavier than air and yet slithered up the furniture legs. He noticed that it came closer to him like noxious swamp gas that would dissolve human flesh on contact. He yelled as it headed toward him and ran back into the kitchen.

The gas stopped instantly and evaporated. He glanced over at Siamura who had retreated into the living room, cowering behind the coffee table, a wing shielding her trembling form. He took a breath and crept towards Siamura. She shivered, eyes wide, ears laid back, her tail twisted around her leg, and an arm raised to protect her head.

"What the hell was that?" Aiden demanded.

Siamura squeezed her eyes tight, shaking her head, saying nothing.

His anger evaporated, seeing that he had frightened her. He knelt beside her. She flinched, trembling anew. She hadn't known any better. "I'm sorry but… but you scared the crap out of me. I'm not going to hurt you. I just want to know what that was."

One golden eye, its vertical pupil contracting, peeked over her arm. "It me, magt of mine."

"I don't understand."

"Ask thee for help for clean. Help I."

Aiden glanced about him. Everywhere the green fog had touched, the awful mess of dried gunk was gone. "Oh, I see. It just surprised me." He stepped behind her. "I'll stand out of the way, though." It may have worked, but he didn't want to touch it. Who knew what it did to living flesh?

Siamura unfolded from her position behind the coffee table, her tail tapping cautiously around her. "Want I to clean?"

Aiden nodded slowly. "Yeah."

She gave a slight bow with her head and crawled to her original place where she had sat earlier. She folded her legs underneath her and spread her hands flat on the carpet. She looked as peaceful as an alien monk in meditation. The green fog once again emanated from her hands and legs, anyplace where she contacted the floor. It spread quickly over the clean carpet and tiles, slowing when it touched blood. It spread up the table and chairs, across the tabletop, and climbed the walls. It covered the sofa in the den and the chairs in the living room near Aiden.

Aiden backed away from the vapor, but it only went as far as the splattered chaos. It did, however, dive into the cleaning bucket he had left on the kitchen floor. Within two minutes the thick green mist had enveloped the entire room, flouting gravity, and air density to crawl up the floors, walls, and even ceiling surfaces without ever filling the space itself. Then as he watched, it began to thin and break apart. Soon it completely dispersed and all the blood vanished, even the smears where Siamura's wing brushed the wall above the window.

Siamura turned. Opening her golden eyes, she looked at Aiden.

Aiden exhaled. "Wow. What was that again? Ma…?"

"Magt. It is me and I it. I am the house, the floor, the table, and I… push things to where they should be."

"Is that like magic?"

"Perhaps. Words of thyne are full of shades of meaning." She brought her legs under her and stood, clasping her hands in front of her.

Aiden walked into the kitchen. Even the water in his cleaning bucket was clear. "Magic? We don't believe in that sort of thing. This is the twenty-first century, after all." Aiden reached into the cabinet for drinking glasses.

Siamura stopped and almost doubled over as if he had punched her in the stomach.

"What's the matter?" he asked.

She dropped to the kitchen floor, sobbing. "Nay, nay, nay. Oh, Macha, nay."

He knelt beside her. "Are you okay?"

She sniffed. "Dost thou count years on the church calendar?"

Aiden stood and reached for some napkins on the counter, and then knelt beside her again. "Church calendar?"

"Yea, the Church calendar, Anno Domini… ah… Is thou sure?"

"Oh A.D. Yeah, I'm sure it's the twenty-first century."

Her wings and ears sagged. She shook her head. "Nay, nay, nay…" She covered her face with her hands and sobbed anew.

When he held the napkins out, she didn't notice, so he placed them in her hands. She wiped her eyes and curled into him, her face in his chest. Aiden at first held his arms away from her; it didn't seem appropriate to touch her. But as her sobs continued, dampening his shirt, he gingerly encircled his arms about her, taking care not to disturb her wings. She leaned heavily onto him, which with her slight weight wasn't much. He didn't know quite what to do. She had confused him with her basic questions, terrified him with her power and then was scared out of her mind by him. She was fragile and possessed an eerie beauty yet was so alien-looking and acted half-human, half-beast.

Her wracking sobs shook her entire body.

Her wings were soft and warm on his bare forearms. They were strange, flexible yet resilient, though not entirely distasteful. Her scent of pine and cedar filled his nose, reminding him of happier times, when as a boy he'd explored the woods behind his parents' house and his world was full of possibilities and promise. He'd had no concerns of people singling him out as weird and ostracizing him. He hadn't had the knowledge and fears he had as an adult. He absently stroked the black hair that hung down her back between her wings. It was thick and soft, so black as to almost be deep blue. As his hand traveled down her human-like hair, he found finger-length fur covering her back underneath it. Also black in color, it continued beyond where her hair stopped and ended at the base of her tail. It was softer than her hair, yet thick like a cat's. However, her green tail was bare of any fur.

Siamura's crying began to slow as Aiden continued to caress her head and back. It seemed to calm her.

Tyler's voice said something, and Aiden jumped away from Siamura. When had his son come into the room?

"I'm going over to Kevin's," Tyler mumbled again. His son stared from the living room; his brows raised.

With a jolt, Aiden glanced at his son. "What about breakfast?" He felt his face flush. His question hung in the air, a non sequitur that failed to hide the obvious situation of him holding the green creature.

"I'm not hungry." Tyler stalked out of the room, the front door opening and closing with a bang. Aiden couldn't guess how long he'd been watching them, but it had been long enough.

Siamura sat at Aiden's feet, wiping her tears. "I sorry."

"It's not your fault. He's a teenager."

She nodded.

"Why does the date upset you?" Aiden helped her up and led her to the table.

She sat delicately, arranging her tail and wings around the chair back. Her care in seating herself reminded Aiden of a woman wearing a long dress. "The last time was I here was… seven hundred years ago." Her eyes welled up again.

Aiden stopped mid-reach for a pair of drinking glasses. "You're kidding. There's no way that you are over seven hundred years old. You don't look that old for one thing, never mind the physical impossibility of it."

"Kid not I, though I not seven hundred years old."

Aiden relaxed.

She continued, "I… over four, six, thousands? Forgot I how many thousands of years."

Aiden frowned, giving a small shake of his head. "Well, I've never heard of anyone living beyond a hundred twenty years old. Unless you're telling me you're a tortoise."

"Agreed, can not human live much beyond a hundred years, but I not human." She shook her wings for emphasis.

"No, you're not human, but what are you? You look like some sort of…" Aiden couldn't bring himself to say the word. He didn't want to insult her. Emotionally, she was at a low and he didn't want to make her feel worse.

Siamura dipped her head, a strand of dark hair falling in front of her face. "Wants thou the word of *demon*. That is what thou calls me if Christianity is still practiced."

Aiden went to the fridge and without thinking, pulled out the orange juice. He concentrated on pouring it before answering, "That sounds overly dramatic. What do you call yourself or creatures like yourself?"

"Is not drama. Banished I from Earth, home of mine, birthplace of mine, seven hundred years ago because called was I a demon. Kind of mine, very long-lived."

He set the orange juice down in front of her and sat across the table corner from her, his back to the window. "So, what are your kind called?"

"Call I a *mearoch*." The ending consonants had the same hard sound as the Scottish word loch. "A mearoch in thyne tongue could be forest spirit."

"That would explain why you smell like trees." He sipped his orange juice.

Siamura turned her glass of orange juice in front of her eyes, examining it intently. She hesitantly took a sip, her lips pursing as if expecting a bad taste. Then her eyes widened. "It sweet! Sweet orange and amazing the glass. So well made."

"It's just plain orange juice in a plain glass. Nothing special. Why don't you know about plumbing, electricity, oranges, and glass?"

"Not I stupid. In early fourteenth century bitter were oranges, glass expensive, mirrors more so, plumbing had not levers when it existed at all and none electricity." She glared at him, her ears standing at attention.

Aiden swore her eyes glowed slightly. "No, I didn't say that you were stupid. Where have you been for the past seven hundred years?"

She blinked. "After mine forest destroyed, exiled I to Irgale."

Aiden thought for a moment. "So, you haven't had any contact with Earth for seven centuries. What's Irgale? Why were you exiled? Who did it and why are you back now?"

"Destroyed by Christian priests mine forest. Exiled me to their underworld called Irgale." Her tail flipped behind her as she shuddered. "The priests in their perversity made it so I could be summoned back here. Someone called me. Is why I here. Are thou not the one who summoned me?"

Aiden shook his head. "No, I didn't." He wondered if he had made some horrible mistake to admit that. She was a demon, no, a mearoch, after all. She would be free to shred him with impunity.

She bowed her head. "I glad thou did not summon me. Mine good feelings for thou shall not be tainted by the act of summoning."

He sipped his orange juice again. This entire conversation had an element of surreality. "Summoning is a bad thing, I take it."

"For me it… dreadful. Disorientation and much pain. Appearing at a time and place not of mine choosing. Then I… am… to be ordered about like a pet… monkey." She spat the last word with obvious distaste.

"I see your point." Aiden thought for a moment. For some reason, the idea of someone summoning her made him see red. His reaction surprised him. Best to change the subject. "Do you want to go back? Back to Irgale?"

"Yea, at some point when mine summoners release me. But it is pleasant to be back in Earth."

"Is Irgale pleasant?"

"Yea. Many call it the Sunset Lands or the Land of Fairy. I sure the priests thought it their place of punishment they call Hell."

"So, you don't want to go back."

"I not sure where I should go." Siamura stared off into an upper corner of the room as if her memories crowded around her. She then fingered the T-shirt that her wings prevented from covering her torso completely. As it was, it barely covered her breasts. "Lor… Aiden? Must I wear these garments?"

"You can't go around nude. Besides, you'll catch a cold."

"I am not cold and why may I not be nude? Less to tangle mine wings."

"It's just not done. It… It makes people uncomfortable if you don't wear any clothes." He couldn't think of a better way to put it.

She smirked. "Ach, it still forbidden. But this fabric… this fabric much too fine for one such as I, since… I shall… need to alter it to fit me."

"That's just an old T-shirt and shorts. I'll get a pair of scissors and we can cut them to fit better."

"I would rather use mine magt." She paused, looking at him from beneath her brows. "That is, if thou would allow me."

Aiden stopped. "Ummm, yeah, okay. I guess." He wasn't so sure how safe it was, but he had survived her house-cleaning spell so it couldn't be that bad.

Siamura closed her eyes and the material of the white T-shirt shifted, flowing like viscous milk, and darkening to black, to become a halter-top that covered her breasts. Her tail whipped behind her as the brown shorts sloughed into a pair of black ones that hung low on her hips and ended at mid-thigh, shorter than the original.

Aiden stared as she opened her eyes. She cringed when she saw his expression. Her top concealed her breasts, but both dark green stripes still emerged from underneath her top and undulated down her slim torso on either side of her abdomen to dip under her shorts. They seemed more like arrows pointing to her private areas rather than merely decoration.

"Did I do wrong?" Her ears lay back like a spooked house cat.

Aiden drained his glass and rose. "No, not at all." He rinsed the glass in the sink.

"Then why are thou angry?" She turned in the chair to face him, one green-skinned arm across the back.

"I'm not angry. I'm… Can't you… well, wear something that's not so revealing?" He felt like an old prude complaining about her showing too much skin.

Siamura stood by the chair, her body in profile to him. Shaking her wings, she said, "These make it difficult to wear much more than this." She narrowed her eyes at him. Indeed, the roots of her wings started at her shoulders and ended just above her hips. Her svelte form reminded him how he missed being in the close company of women.

"What about a robe or something?"

"Trip would I on it or it would get in the way of mine wings when I fly."

Aiden sighed. Opening the refrigerator, he rummaged around and found some eggs and sausage. "How about some breakfast?"

"It cold in there." Siamura sprang to his side instantly and put her hand into the refrigerator. "What manner of magt is this?"

"It's a machine to keep food cold. It's not magt. What is magt? You didn't explain it very well last time I asked." He held up a carton of eggs and a package of sausage, raising an eyebrow.

She cocked her head to one side examining the packages. After a moment she said, "Yea, I… would like to eat. Magt is power. It is an energy that drives things, gives them impetus to move, and the quality to exist. One must become and feel the object or desire and gently move it in the direction one wants." She went to the sink with her empty glass and mimicked Aiden's motions to rinse it. "The people in mine day called it magic, but that is not correct."

"Sounds like magic to me." Aiden stepped around her to the stove and brought out a couple of pans. "How do you like your eggs?"

"I like them cooked, but how will thee cook them? Thee lacks fire." She giggled. "Magt is energy. Thee is strong in it."

“This is a stove. The electricity will heat the eggs. How about sunny side up?” He set the pans on the burners.

“Sunny side…?” Siamura collapsed on the floor in a sitting position, her eyes closed and her wings askew.

Aiden turned off the stove and knelt beside her. “Siamura?”

She ignored him, merely nodding her head with her ears up as if listening to someone else. Her hands lay limp in her lap, wings folded casually behind her, her tail curled around her knees. Instinctively, Aiden took her hand and held it. She seemed to be in some sort of trance, head nodding, turning subtly left and right. He waited for a minute or more, worrying if she was all right.

Then she exhaled and her eyes opened. Relief spread over Aiden. He hadn’t realized that he held his breath too. He couldn’t explain it, but he worried for her. She clung to his hand.

Aiden breathed, “What happened?”

Siamura’s eyes focused on him, the vertical pupils contracting to slits. “It was mine summoners. They called me.” She gripped his hand tightly. “I swear I did not tell them where I am or about thee. They have bad thoughts. I trust not them.”

“Who are these people that summoned you? Do they have names?” Again, Aiden felt his heartbeat begin to race. It had been a hell of a morning.

“I know not their names and it forbidden for me to speak of them.”

“Forbidden?”

“The spell of summoning prevents me.”

“Wait, I didn’t see anybody. How did you talk to them?”

“We talked using mine magt.”

“So, your power allows you to communicate long distance, learn English quickly, and clean up the kitchen? Oh, and sprout wings too. How can I even believe in all of this?”

“It is nothing to thee. Thou has skilled workers of glass, sweet orange, clothes of fine thread, a power thou calls electricity and plumbing with knobs. Surely, mine powers are well within thyne capabilities and thou has wealth beyond mine custom. With all these developments, why would I be summoned? What other things are thou withholding from me?” She glared at him.

"We've built machines to do all of these things based on scientific principles. With you it's a snap of the fingers and it's done." He tried to fight his frustration with her; it was hard to explain the basics to someone who didn't have any comparison.

"I snap not my fingers." Her hands balled into fists. "To me thyne electricity is magic. I think thou is envious of mine abilities. Where thou art grow thyne sweet oranges and the rest of thyne food? I do not see any fields or animal pens out of any of the windows of thyne manse." She flung a hand indicating the window.

"The food is grown someplace else and trucked in. We don't need farms in our backyards anymore."

"What is… trucked?" She huffed.

"A truck is like a wagon to haul materials except without horses."

"A wagon without horses? How does it move?"

"It has an engine. Here I'll show you something similar. It's in the garage." He extended his hand to help her stand.

She followed him to the garage. Once through the living room door, she tightened her grip on his hand. He tried to loosen his hold and let her go, but she kept his hand in her grasp.

Aiden led her in and pointed out the convertible. The top was down. He had forgotten to put it up yesterday in his haste to return home to Tyler. "This is a car. It has an engine to make it move like a truck." When the door closed behind them, her head snapped around to it. He patted her hand to calm her down.

She wrinkled her nose. "It smell bad."

Aiden walked her around to the side of the convertible. She stared at the glossy blue paint, turning her head as if to see if it was a threat. The shine of the body paint seemed to heighten her curiosity yet she kept her distance, her tail held still. Aiden stepped forward, opening the driver's side door. She leapt back, dropping his hand, and arching her wings.

"Hey, it's okay. It's not going to bite you. Here, get in. I'll start it up."

Her eyes bulged and she took another step back.

Aiden walked around and opened the passenger side door. "Go on, get in."

Slowly she moved around the car, never turning her back on it, her hands out to defend herself. He waved her in. Warily she sat in the seat, every contact with it making her wince and shrink. She looked miserable. Aiden started to close the door, but her hand shot out and blocked it from closing.

"I trust not this metal thing," she murmured.

Aiden went back around, sat on the driver's side, and closed his door, causing Siamura to jump. He pulled out his keys, stuck them in the ignition and turned. The engine came to life.

The next instant, Siamura was gone, the door wide open to the living room. Aiden couldn't believe how quickly she moved. He hadn't seen her cross the distance at all. The door squeaked as it slowly began to close. He turned off the engine and went back into the house.

He found Siamura cowering behind the coffee table in front of the living room sofa, eyes wide, peering over one wing that shielded her from the door. Her ears were down and she shivered violently.

Aiden closed the door and went to her. "I'm sorry. It can be loud when it starts up." He sat down and put his arm around her.

She sat up stiffly, her wings snapping behind her, throwing off Aiden's arm. "I not afraid." Yet her arms were still wrapped around her trembling form.

Aiden said, "You'll feel better once you have some breakfast."

Haltingly, she followed him into the kitchen and watched him with interest as he cooked the eggs and sausage. Her ears flicked forward at the sizzling sausage, and her nose twitched, smelling the food. She absently wiped her mouth with the back of her hand.

When Aiden put bread in the toaster, she crept closer, watching her reflection in the metal skin of the device. Waving her hand over it, she at first withdrew, but then returned, rubbing her fingers over the heat. When the toast popped up, Siamura yelped and leapt backwards, almost hitting the ceiling as she did so. Her wings opened slightly, catching the air of the room. She touched down in a crouch, her fingers curled like claws, ready to rip the innards out of the little metal monster. In the same instant, she bared her fangs and growled at the offending appliance.

Aiden swore he saw a large cat ready to attack his toaster. "Siamura, it's okay. It's supposed to do that."

She ducked her head, covering her mouth and hunching down slightly.

He continued, "Come on, you should wash up before eating."

He led her to the powder room and taught her how to wash her hands. When they sat down at the table, she again arranged her wings and tail before sitting. Then she promptly grabbed a sausage in her fist and stuffed it in her mouth.

"No, no." Aiden raised his knife and fork. "Use these."

She looked at him with her wide cat-like eyes, her cheeks bulging with sausage. She blinked and swallowed noisily but took his guidance well as he taught her how to use a knife and fork. However, he tried not to stare as she carefully threaded the fork between her fangs. Despite all the effort, she was remarkably patient and quickly learned how to eat with utensils. She ate ravenously after her lessons. After all, using utensils didn't slow her down that much. Aiden showed her how to cook more eggs and sausage, and she wolfed those down too.

Afterwards, he showed her a few printed newsmagazines that he had laying around. Entranced, she began reading. Her spell to speak and understand English apparently included reading it too. Aiden canceled his golf game because he was afraid to leave this strange creature alone, although he felt like he had forgotten another appointment. He would have to worry about that later as every noise made her jumpy and she looked to Aiden to discern whether it was a threat. She asked questions about what she had read. He tried to turn on the TV, but she leapt onto the couch cushions and hissed at it, much as she did with the toaster. The TV spooked her, though she wouldn't admit it. It seemed that most modern objects upset her well-being, especially electronic ones. Although she looked the part of a terrifying demon or mearoch, her actions resembled those of a scared kitten. He had doubts that she could function in this world, but she persisted in learning about everything as quickly as she could.

Chapter 5

Easy Money

Tyler slammed the door behind him, jogged down the driveway, and onto the street. His dad and that green creature hugging had been weird, not to mention the way he had been petting her like a cat. At least the creature at his house didn't seem dangerous; she didn't feel the same way the demon did at the summoning. That demon was horrible and wanted to rip everyone to shreds. The green spirit with his dad was small and frightened and didn't seem like she was about to kill everyone.

It occurred to him he didn't really know what had happened yesterday at the summoning. Before yesterday, he had no idea what a summoning was or that it was possible. The green woman and whatever they had summoned might not feel like the same, but the two had to be related in some way. And yet, the summoning hadn't been that bad. Matt only got a scratch, and the green woman didn't seem to be a danger, so maybe his dad wouldn't have to find out about his involvement.

He wanted to find out if the green woman and the demon were related, but Tyler knew Dad wouldn't let him near her. It was too risky, he'd say. Tyler couldn't be sure whether it was the green woman who attacked Matt or not, because he never got a clear look at whatever was summoned. It worried Tyler that nobody knew where the attacker went or whether it would come back to try and hurt the rest of them. They could be in a lot of trouble.

The sun warmed his back as he slowed to a walk. Everything seemed more normal out here than in his house. The Kesters' blue-and-white-striped mailbox stood out two doors down, the scandal of the neighborhood association. Whether a whimsical landmark or an eyesore, it was just stupid. The idea of a blue-and-white-striped mailbox was stupid, and that someone would get upset about it was stupid too.

Some houses had their association-approved Halloween decorations out: orange plastic pumpkins, cartoon ghosts, and black cats. He and his dad would carve a pumpkin closer to Halloween and that would be it for their decorations. Halloween was for kids, but Tyler still liked to dress up in costume and go to a party. He liked the candy, liked the revelry, yet there was something more, as if he knew on some level the spirits were out too, just not visible to most people. But the way things were going, he'd be lucky to get out at all. And he hadn't even decided on a costume.

If their neighbors knew what happened at his house almost every day, they would freak out. Things moving around by themselves and phantoms hanging out weren't normal by most people's standards. Green, bat-winged women weren't normal, even for him.

As Tyler approached the road to Franklin Park, kids played on the swing set and a couple of families spread out their lunches on the picnic tables. It was a typical Saturday in the park.

He walked the fifteen minutes to Kevin's house, his thoughts circling. He didn't want to think of yesterday's botched summoning or the creature that hatched in his house anymore. The image of his dad holding, hugging, and petting the creature rose in his mind. He shuddered. No, he couldn't think about it anymore. He was going over to Kevin's house to play video games and nothing more.

Kevin's house was similar to his — mailbox out front and a single tree in the small front yard. A few dark leaves scratched along the pavement, pushed by the wind. This was a normal household with two parents, nice furniture, and no spirits. Sometimes he yearned to be normal without spirits interrupting his life. He rang the doorbell.

Kevin opened the door with a swagger and an attitude. "Cool, dude. You're lucky I'm still here. Had to fight off my parents from dragging me along to the mall." He wore a bright blue shirt and khaki pants.

Tyler stepped inside. "You got anything to eat?"

"Yeah, sure, in the kitchen."

The house was decorated more grandly than Tyler's beige and boring house. The living room had new, off-white leather furniture with a large glass and metal coffee table in the middle. The only color was an abstract painting in shades of dark blue on the wall above the couch, providing a sense of dim coolness to the room. Tyler wasn't really sure if he liked it or not, but it was better than the barren sameness of his own house.

The kitchen was a sleek composition of blond wood cabinets with granite countertops. A dark red wooden table with a glass inlay top and matching chairs stood nearby. A modern glass chandelier, the crystals sharply pointed toward the table, hung over it like a set of knives. Tyler grabbed cereal and a bowl, sat down at the table, and began to eat.

Kevin joined him, munching on a pop tart. "Dude, that was pretty cool yesterday. I didn't think anything would happen, then all that smoke and shit. Then BAM that thing appeared. That was awesome."

Tyler nodded. "Yeah, and you were scared shitless. You were lucky it didn't go for you." *And I was the one who made sure of that, you idiot.*

"Who wouldn't be scared? Oh, I forgot. You deal with ghosts all the time."

"It wasn't a ghost."

"Then what was it?"

"Matt and Eric called it a demon." Tyler crunched loudly on his cereal.

"You're the expert with all those stories you've told me. Come on, what was it?"

"Don't know, but it wasn't like anything I've seen before. It was the most powerful thing I've ever seen."

"Where do you think it went?" Kevin leaned forward in his chair.

"Probably to hide and rest, but who knows?"

"Was Matt right about it wanting to hunt us down?"

The cereal turned bitter in Tyler's mouth. "Hey, I've got no idea what it wants."

"Come on, you have to have some clue."

"Can you just let me finish eating?"

With a huff, Kevin grabbed an apple from the bowl on the table and bit in. He was worse than a little kid. At least Tyler could keep Kevin at bay with having to eat. After he had finished, Tyler put his dish in the sink.

Kevin tossed his half-eaten apple in the trash without a second thought. "What do we do if that thing finds us?"

Tyler threw up his hands. "I don't know. Run? Matt and Eric seemed to know how to handle everything and look what happened to Matt."

Kevin paused.

Shit, Kevin had everything so easy — nice house, the latest games, even school was easy for him. Tyler always had to study hard to do well.

Tyler dropped his hands. "Where's the new video game you were talking about?"

Kevin brightened. "In my room. It's really cool. There are new character classes and everything."

A big flat screen monitor hooked up to his computer dominated Kevin's bedroom. On the opposite wall hung a skateboard poster and another poster of a Dodgers' pitcher. The game was up and Kevin showed Tyler the basic mechanics of play. Then Kevin brought out his laptop so both could play at the same time.

This was what Tyler needed, to forget everything for a while. After a bit, they tried the player versus player mode, with Tyler losing more than he won. Tyler didn't care. It seemed to bend Kevin out of shape more when he did win, which made it all the sweeter. After another win by Kevin, his cell phone rang. Tyler listened to Kevin's side of the conversation, but all he could get was that Kevin was excited about something. *What, had his parents gotten him a new car already?* He tried not to roll his eyes.

Kevin tapped the phone, hanging up. "That was Eric and you'll never believe it."

"So, tell me."

"We're doing another summoning tonight!" Kevin playfully hit Tyler in the shoulder. "Wicked cool, huh?"

"Another summoning? Are you guys insane? We don't even know where the last spirit went." Tyler rubbed his shoulder.

"Dude, it's cool. Matt and him did a divination spell and got all the shit on the demon to bind it this time."

"Isn't that what they had last time? And he jumped through an open window."

"No, dude, chill. Eric told me that you might be scared to try again, but he promised me that they got all the spells right this time. That's why they did the divination thing. And this is the coolest part…" Kevin paused meaningfully. "He wants to teach you how they did it because this time there wasn't any problem."

Tyler hesitated. This was what he had always wanted — to contact the spirits when he wanted to, not at their convenience. It was an easy decision to make. "Okay, so when and where? And do we need to bring anything?"

Kevin grinned. "Dude, I knew you'd be in. Eric will pick us up near the park and take us to his place at five o'clock. I need to bring the bronze bowl from last time and you need to bring the rock you had last night."

"Shit, I left the quartz at my house and my dad's still there. Hey, what about Eric's parents?"

"He said his parents are going out tonight so they're not a problem. I'll come with you to get the rock."

Tyler stopped. No way did he want Kevin at his house with the green demon woman there. "Nah, I'll get it. You wait here." He didn't want to tell Kevin about the green woman. The other boy's smug excitement, acting as if he knew what to do about yesterday's summoning made Tyler's stomach turn. What bull. He had been scared shitless and had just sat there gawking at the lights and smoke. Tyler set the laptop aside. "I'll go now so we won't have to worry about it," he added before Kevin could insist on going with him.

Tyler walked as fast as he could back to his house. As he passed by the park, the families had cleaned up their lunches, but the kids were still playing on the swing set.

Tyler had to sneak in and out without his dad knowing, or his dad would ask questions he didn't want to answer. Opening the front door as quietly as he could, he headed straight for the staircase. He didn't see his dad, but he didn't stop to look around either. He dashed up the stairs and into his room. Breathing heavily, he opened his closet door, looking for the crystal when he heard a noise from downstairs.

His father's voice shot up from the ground floor piercing him like a spear. "Tyler? Where are you?"

His breath caught in his throat. Jumping out the window was a possibility, but he didn't have the quartz. Thinking quick, he decided to delay his dad and buy some time. "In here." He tried sounding noncommittal, as he clawed through his closet, but he was sure Dad could tell something was up. That damn quartz had to be in here.

"Can you come down for a minute?"

"Yeah, hang on." Tyler winced. That sounded too obvious.

There it was — still wrapped in the plastic grocery bag. But he couldn't just carry it downstairs and out of the house. It would raise too many questions. Tyler glanced about the room, his eyes finally landing on his backpack. He snatched it up and jammed the quartz in it. He pulled a couple of black T-shirts out of his dresser drawer and threw them on top of the quartz. Grabbing his American History textbook, he stuffed it on top of everything for good measure. He hoped that would deter any questions. Tyler stopped when it occurred to him that Dad might want him to meet their green guest. On the other hand, his father was probably going to tell him to stay away from her. She looked like a demon out of the video games he played. Dangerous, but really cool. Slinging his backpack over his shoulder and remembering that Kevin was waiting for him, Tyler galloped down the stairs to the living room.

"Tyler?" Dad poked his head from the den. "Can you come here?"

Tyler leaned his bag by the front door as he walked to the den. "Yeah?" It almost sounded like he was in trouble, so he cautiously stepped past the couch into the room. At first, he didn't see her, standing behind his dad but she had to still be here though he smelled her scent, the sweet, soothing smell of trees. Then he spotted her, peering around his dad's shoulder. Her weird cat-like eyes were wide open regarding Tyler with wonder, fear, or something else. Her folded wings were taller than his dad's head. She looked wicked cool, but also scary with her long ears, black hair, black clothes, and the dark green tattoos down her torso.

"Tyler, I want you to meet Siamura." Aiden stepped aside.

As Tyler held out his hand, Siamura knelt on one knee and bowed her head, flattening her long ears. She murmured, "I honored to meet thee, Tyler Aiden-son." She had a sexy foreign accent that sounded like she was from Europe somewhere.

Tyler flushed. She was weird, but really cool. He hoped she wasn't going to attack him. He stared at the top of her head, her dark hair, and her wings. He dropped his hand.

Dad broke his trance. "Siamura, it's customary to shake hands rather than kneeling, and our name is Moray, not Aiden-son."

Siamura turned her head upward to look at Dad, her eyes wide. Dad offered his hand to help her up. She took it and faced Tyler. "I honored to meet thee, Tyler Moray." She rolled her Rs with that wicked accent of hers, making his name sound really exotic. She inclined her head to Tyler, with her hand extended palm up, as if in supplication.

She looked so sad that Tyler felt sorry for her. He reached out and gently clasped her warm hand. As he held her hand, any misgivings he had about her dissolved. Somehow, he knew she was frightened and wouldn't hurt him or his father. There was no way she could be the same demon that attacked Matt at the summoning. She gave a small sigh, the tension between them ebbing away.

Tyler blurted, "You're not a demon, are you?" He winced, suddenly wanting a giant hole to open and swallow him. He couldn't believe how stupid that sounded. What an idiot he was!

His dad said, "No, she isn't. She's a…"

"Mearoch." Siamura interrupted, bowing her head slightly. It was strange, but Tyler's fear was gone. He only felt sorry for her.

Dad continued, "All the more reason you shouldn't say anything of Siamura's presence until we figure out what's going on."

Tyler shook his head. "I haven't told anybody."

"Not even Kevin?"

"Nope." A wave of relief washed over Tyler because he didn't have to lie about that.

"Siamura is our guest until she can find her way back home. You're going to have to help me teach her about life here. She's very new to our world."

Siamura's ears flicked between him and Dad as they spoke. She reminded Tyler of a dog or a cat watching people in a room, picking up clues about what was going to happen next.

Tyler spoke to her. "So where are you from?"

Siamura glanced at Dad before speaking. "I from a place called Irgale. It is in the fairy realm and not of this earth. Though I come from here too." Every time she spoke, Tyler got lost in her voice; he could listen to her all day long.

Then Tyler remembered the bag against the door. He didn't want to go, but not only was Kevin waiting, but Eric and Matt were too, and there was no way he was going to piss them off. "I've got to get back to studying. I definitely want to talk to you some more."

"Yea, I would like that." Siamura lowered her eyes.

His father said, "Remember, though, not a word."

"Okay, Dad." Tyler picked up the backpack and left the house. The pack felt heavier, and his feet dragged as he trudged to Kevin's house. It seemed to take forever. The sanitized pumpkin and ghost decorations seemed to mock him as he passed. Finally, he knocked on Kevin's door.

"What took you so long?" Kevin asked.

Tyler paused, wondering how much to tell Kevin. He was so tempted to tell him, tell anybody that there was a green demon — no, a mearoch — living at his house. Yet, he couldn't betray her. His dad was always telling him what to do, but on this, deep down, he knew his dad was right. He couldn't bear the thought of someone like Kevin, or worse, Matt, ridiculing Siamura.

"You okay?" Kevin asked.

"Yeah, my dad told me to take out the garbage."

Kevin gave him a strange look.

"Hey, we don't have a housekeeper like you do."

Kevin gave a long-suffering sigh. "Come on. I need to finish kicking your ass."

Time passed quickly. Kevin did indeed beat Tyler at first, but after a while, Tyler began to win a few. After Kevin won a spectacular victory, he set the console down and flicked off the screen. "Come on. Let's do this shit for real now."

For once, Tyler wasn't mad about stopping. Kevin gathered up his bowls and candles. Tyler reached into his bag and tossed a black T-shirt at Kevin. "If we're going to have any chance, you are going to have to look the part." Tyler pulled out the other one and slipped it on.

Kevin glared at him but changed into the Immolation T-shirt. "Dude, It's too small."

Tyler hefted his bag. "It'll keep Matt and Eric happy, so deal." Kevin grumbled under his breath, but Tyler ignored him. He wasn't going to have

Kevin screw things up this time. This time everything was going to go right.

They left the house and walked to the park. Tyler felt like he could name every blade of grass after all the forays between his house and Kevin's. The fading light gave everything a surreal quality. The long shadows distorted the trees and neighborhood houses, twisting everything around. A dog howled in the distance. Tyler was sure there were creatures lurking in the shadows ready to tear his and Kevin's souls out and eat them.

A familiar battered Nissan pulled up beside them and stopped. Eric called out, "Get in."

Tyler and Kevin crawled into the back seat. Tyler tossed an empty soda can to the floor before sitting. The car reeked of stale cigarette smoke, in marked contrast to Siamura's scent of forest and trees. Tyler slammed the door shut.

"You have the quartz, Moray?" Matt, in the front seat, turned just his head to look sideways at him.

Tyler jumped a little but composed himself quickly. "Uh, yeah. Right here." He positioned his backpack on the floor between his knees.

Matt grinned. He seemed to enjoy rattling Tyler. To Kevin, he said, "Nice shirt — better than yesterday, that's for sure. You got the bowl?"

Kevin nodded. "Yeah, I'm cool."

Matt thrust a piece of paper at Kevin. "Here are the words, same as before." He reached in front of him and returned with another paper. "Moray, just minor changes for you..." He gave him a conspiratorial smile. "...But you knew that."

"Let's rock and roll!" Eric gunned the engine and they took off down the road. He cranked Metallica on the stereo, drowning out any further conversation.

Matt's statement shocked Tyler. What did Matt know about him? He studied the paper looking for clues. Besides, he didn't want to embarrass himself by being unprepared. But the words were identical to the last ritual except for a few lines near the end.

Ten minutes later, they pulled up to a shabby house. It was older, the dry lawn bare in spots, a big weed flowering on the far side of the yard. The exterior stucco had a big crack by the front window with dark stains running down the walls. Tyler wasn't so sure, but he thought he saw a retreating shadow on the side of the house.

Eric screeched to a stop in front of the house. "Mi casa, es su casa." He laughed and slammed the car door shut. "Come on." He wrestled with the key in the front door and let them in. Additional stale smoke odor wafted over them. Tyler worried that Dad was going to smell it on him and Tyler would have to come up with some explanation. The worn curtains in the front room were pulled closed against the sun. Despite the lights Eric switched on, the interior remained dingy with a yellowish cast. A torn couch and easy chair sat behind a scarred coffee table. Stains marred the carpet of indistinguishable pale color. The only thing missing were roaches. However, the flat screen TV was brand new and pristine, its remote gleaming on the thrashed coffee table.

Eric ignored everything in the front room and walked straight to the kitchen. As they followed, Matt kept a cryptic smile on his face. Eric opened the refrigerator and pulled out a plastic container of dark fluid. "My parents are out so we're cool for a few hours."

Kevin pointed at the container. "What's that?"

Eric smiled. "Blood. Always need a sacrifice. We didn't want to offend little Tyler here and kill it in front of him."

Matt must have seen Tyler's shock because he said, "Don't worry. It's not human." Matt smoothed his shirt over his stomach. He seemed to hold onto the left side of his abdomen like it pained him.

This was getting worse. Tyler tried to put on the most confident voice he could. "So why are we doing another summoning?" The other three boys stopped and stared at him as if he had invited the Pope to join them. "I mean, how can you be so sure it's not going to end up like last time?"

Eric sneered, "Don't be stupid. It's still out there. It's looking for us. We have to control it."

"Eric and me did a divination earlier," Matt said in a soothing voice as if he were explaining something to a dim-witted child. "We found out the proper name and spells to use to control the demon. It's not going to get away this time. Eric's right. We have to try again before it finds us or we're all in trouble. Happy?" His hand gripped his stomach again.

Tyler fidgeted with his pack. "Well, okay." It did make sense. The demon was still out there and they had to do something before it came back. He followed the other boys upstairs.

The stairway and subsequent hallway were much like the rest of the house, dingy and ruined with old stains and deep marks on the walls. Eric pointed to an open doorway as they walked past. "That's my room, but we're going to use the spare room."

Tyler glanced in the door. On the wall was a poster of a guitar player flashing the devil horns with one hand. A goat's head in a flaming pentagram was in the picture above him. All manner of papers and clothes lay strewn about the floor. Along with a couple of soda cans on the floor. A book was open on the unmade bed. Out of the corner of his eye, he saw Kevin curl his lip.

Eric led them into the next room and turned on the overhead light. "My dad never got the carpet down in here. Lucky us." The carpet lay rolled up on the opposite side from the door, exposing the composition plywood beneath. An exercise bike and a sewing machine were against the far wall on either side of the single window in the room. Somebody had recently taped an old bed sheet over the window. On the wall to the left of the door was a closet, its sliding doors closed. Eric and Matt had inscribed a pentagram in chalk on the plywood floor. Like the previous one in the abandoned house, this one contained many complicated angular symbols within its lines. It also had Tyler's favorite one with the swirls and the skull, beauty and death together. This time the swirling symbol was in the middle and larger than the rest.

Eric poured the blood into a ceramic bowl and carefully placed it at the center of the circle. The Spiritorium was open at the north side of the circle opposite the window and beside the door. Crap, that put west, Tyler's place, against the far wall with the rolled-up carpet and no escape route, should things go wrong again.

Everyone again turned off their phones and put them by the door. Candles were already in place around the circle. Tyler went to his position and withdrew the quartz from his bag, setting it in front of him. The black glowing stone wasn't anywhere in the room, but the blue amulet sat on one open page of the Spiritorium, its golden symbols staying rooted to the surface this time, but the stone itself was shimmering and shifting position like it wasn't quite in this reality. Tyler didn't like the feeling it gave him, similar to a high-pitched buzzing sound like a large mosquito.

Eric lit the candles around the circle and turned off the overhead light. Everything fell into a dim reddish hue, their shadows projecting onto the walls, making grotesque shapes and exaggerating their every move. Eric sat, his back to the window, and lit the incense in front of him.

Matt pulled a corner of the bed sheet aside and peered out the window. The sunlight was dying. "It's time. Moray, Adams, just like last time. Then follow our lead." He seemed to hold his left hand on his stomach a lot since they entered the house.

Matt stepped around the circle, closed the door, and took his position at north. Standing, he picked up the wavy bladed dagger and intoned, "Spirits of Air, be with us now. Lend us your speed and foresight to our endeavors." As he sat, Tyler saw him flinch and hold his stomach again. It was the same place that he was scratched yesterday.

Tyler lifted the quartz. It felt heavier and cooler than a few moments ago. "Spirits of Earth, be with us now. Give us your strength and stability to guide us."

Eric said his supplication to the spirits of fire. Then Kevin gave his to water, though he didn't sound very confident. Eric and Matt launched into the ritual itself. They began with some complicated lines in Latin and another language that Tyler couldn't place. For several minutes, they went back and forth between each other. Matt would start with a line and Eric answered with a different litany. The smoke from the incense curled up towards the ceiling and the darkened electric light.

Matt and Eric paused. Then in unison, they said, "Demosura, be with us now. You will not use deception or lies against us, but will appear in your true form, harmless to us." Through the frankincense haze, Tyler smelled trees. As Eric and Matt continued with more strange words, the scent of trees grew stronger. The glow from the blue amulet illuminated Matt's face, giving him a sickly, cold visage, as if the amulet was feeding off him. Eric and Matt together said, "Demosura, be with us now. Heed our call and do not delay. Bow to our will and obey us."

In the center, the air wavered and shifted. Small swirls in the incense smoke spun into the center. Then something appeared. Starting at the feet, the body slowly materialized upwards, until finally the head was visible.

The demon was green with bat wings and a tail, wearing black shorts and a black halter-like top.

She dropped to one knee, facing Matt. "I come." Even her accent was identical to one Tyler had heard earlier. Tyler gawked at Siamura as he realized that she lied to him and his dad.

She was the demon!

Matt smiled, one of the nastiest that Tyler had ever witnessed. "Welcome, Demosura. You may enjoy the sacrifice of blood we have provided."

She reached down and picked up the bowl delicately. She sniffed at the blood and wrinkled her nose slightly. She drank the entire contents in one gulp, and then shuddered, like she hadn't liked the taste.

Matt snickered. "It's not human, I know, but you can't have any of mine." He touched his dagger to the amulet. The amulet flashed brighter than all the candles, casting everything in a cold, bluc light.

Siamura/Demosura yelped, dropping the bowl. She collapsed onto the floor folding into herself. Her mouth was open, only a hoarse scream escaped before she fell silent. Her fangs shone in the hideous blue glow, blood-drenched saliva dripping from them. Mouth still open, she writhed and twitched as if her bones were going to break. Her wings began to twist in on themselves.

"Stop it!" Tyler couldn't stand it. Demon or not, this was cruel.

"She attacked me. She deserves worse." Matt held the blade and amulet together several seconds longer, staring at Tyler. He pulled the objects apart and the room plunged into darkness, save for the dim redness of the candlelight. Oddly enough, with all her thrashing about on the symbols of the circle, not one line appeared smudged or erased.

Demosura lay on her side, panting, her wings and extremities twitching erratically. Slowly, she brought her hands and feet beneath her. Her spasms hampered her efforts, but as her twitching lessened, she brought her limbs under control. On both knees, she bowed towards Matt. "What thyne wish, Master?" She kept her face towards the floor, away from him.

Matt pumped his fist with the dagger. "Yes, I fucking own you now!" Yet he flinched, as if his side hurt.

Eric shouted, "Right on!"

Kevin smiled and nodded. Only Tyler seemed horrified at Matt's actions. Demosura remained kneeling, face down.

Matt continued, "I want you to break Stan Rutherford's legs, he's the captain of the football team, and fuck up his friends, in the most painful way possible."

Demosura sat up and opened her eyes, the ends of her wings splaying out behind her. "I can do that, Master, but thee will need to point him and his friends out to me." She kept her voice even and respectful.

"Bitch! Do as I command! I gave you his name. You can bind him."

"That is not enough. Thee must point him out for me to carry out thyne wish. I must be sure."

"Damn you!"

"I am already damned."

Matt flung the dagger. It struck her on one side of her abdomen through one of the dark green tattoos and remained embedded for a second. Then it slid out from her and clattered to the floor, covered in blood. She gasped, her eyes wide. Blood started to flow from her wound and down her hip. She bent in on herself as she clasped her hand over it. Her eyes began to glow.

"Give me back my knife."

Breathing deeply, she kept one hand over her injury. After a few heartbeats, she picked up the blade with the other, wiped it on her bare leg, and set it down in front of Matt. She grimaced as she sat, remaining inside the circle. The blade gleamed in the candlelight.

"Move back."

She scooted back to the center of the circle, watching him.

As Matt reached for the weapon, her tail snapped out and snatched up the dagger before he could touch it. She moved impossibly fast. As Matt screamed, she flipped the dagger above her head. The blade sunk into the ceiling halfway to the hilt, the sound of splintering wood echoing through the room. Plaster dust floated down on top of her, incongruous as a summer snow. Her black hair dusted with white gypsum, she said in a calm tone, "Master, that is the second time thee has harmed me with that accursed blade. I may not survive a third time."

"Fuck you! Give me my dagger!"

"Alas, it resides beyond the boundary of the circle. I am powerless to retrieve it for thee."

"What? You lie!" Matt's face had reddened even in the light of the candles.

Her head tilted by a fraction. "I would dare not deceive thee. Only if thee releases me from the circle can I bring it to thee." Trembling, she bowed her head. She removed her hand from her wound, but the gash had vanished.

Matt frowned and felt his abdomen again. He shuddered.

With her head still bowed, Demosura licked the blood off her hand. Remaining seated, she turned to Kevin. "And thee? What does thee wish?" As she faced away from Tyler, the tip of her tail twitched like a cat's, yet small tremors rattled down her wings.

Kevin jumped. "Uh, me? I want a sports car. A Ferrari."

"May remind mine second Master that it is too large to fit within the circle, is this not true?"

Demosura shifted again and turned to Eric. "What is thyne wish?"

Eric grinned. "I want five million dollars."

Her ears stood up. "What are dollars? What do they look like?"

Eric fished in his pocket, pulled out a bill, and tossed it into the circle. "That's a twenty. I want you to make a whole bunch of those."

Demosura smoothed the bill and examined it. "Does thee have leaves or something similar?"

Eric glanced around the room. "What about that carpet?" He pointed at the roll against the wall.

Demosura nodded, her ears flattening again. "That would be perfect. Thou will need to put it into the circle."

"Just don't grab me."

"I will not."

Eric dragged one side of the rolled carpet within the circle, forcing Tyler to jump out of the way. Eric dropped the roll and snapped back his arms. Tyler knew if she wanted to grab him, she had plenty of time, but she sat placidly in the middle of the circle, her ears down until Eric retreated.

"May I approach?"

"Yeah, go ahead."

Deliberately, she moved closer and set the twenty-dollar bill beside the carpet. She sat, laying her left hand on the bill and her right on the roll. Tyler thought he saw her hand on the roll tremble slightly. She began to mutter something and the hair on Tyler's arms stood up. Her eyes didn't close, but they started to glow with an eerie green light. Then her hands glowed green and the green glow crept from her to envelop the bill and the roll of carpet within the circle. Dim green light bathed the room. Occasionally, it brightened, competing with the candlelight.

Then Demosura stopped muttering, and the green radiance vanished, leaving the candlelight as the only source of illumination. A disheveled pile of twenty-dollar bills had replaced the carpet. There was a sheared off edge next to Tyler and the rest of the carpet behind and to the side of him.

Eric shouted, "Awesome!" He reached in, mere inches from Demosura's hand, and grabbed a handful of bills. As he inspected them, he said, "Perfect! I'm rich!"

Kevin's eyes widened at the sight of the instant wealth. "Cool! Screw the car. Make me some of that and I'll buy my own."

Eric leapt up. "Then come on and help me drag more in." Kevin and Eric yanked on the remaining roll dragging another section within the circle.

Demosura glanced at Tyler. Ducking her head and looking away, she wrapped her tail protectively around her knees and hips. Tyler didn't know what to do except stare, as she pulled her wing around to shelter herself from him.

A flurry of bills scattered as the two boys dropped one end of the roll in the circle. Demosura laid her hands on the roll and muttered her incantation. After the green light dimmed, two huge piles of bills had replaced the roll within the circle. Again, a sheared edge was at the border of the circle with the remaining carpet extending by Tyler.

Eric and Kevin reached in, again heedless of their proximity to her and grabbed handfuls of bills, yelling, "We're rich!" They laughed and high fived each other as they snatched more bills from the circle. Tyler watched one drift down, narrowly missing a candle. It was amazing they hadn't set any of them on fire.

Demosura bodily turned to Tyler, ignoring Eric's and Kevin's celebrations. "Mine fourth and most powerful Master, please have mercy on me, thyne subject. Thou wrath is most terrible." Still kneeling, she bowed, her nose practically touching the floor, and trembled anew. "How might I please thee?"

Kevin and Eric interrupted their partying to watch in silence. Tyler shivered and fidgeted with the quartz. "Uh nothing… Thank you." The idea of asking her for anything not only made him feel guilty, but it also terrified him. The stories of horrible things happening when you asked for gifts from demons and other spirits shot through his mind. And he wasn't sure whether to feel sorry for her pitiful situation or angry at her for deceiving him and his dad about her being a demon in the first place.

She turned towards Matt and made a shallow bow. "Mine first Master, what is thyne wish?"

Matt still had his hand pressed against his side. Sweat beaded on his forehead and his lips were pulled down in a grimace. The scratch must be getting worse.

"Perhaps thou would allow me to heal thee."

Matt barked, "I'm fine. No thanks to you, bitch."

"I assure thee, I did not harm thee."

"Shut the fuck up!" Matt brandished the blue amulet in his right hand. It glowed balefully, bathing Matt's face in its cold light.

Demosura groveled, her head pressed firmly on the floor. "Please Master, mercy! Have mercy. I do not intend to offend thee."

"You should have thought about that before you tossed my dagger away, you whore."

"I am sorry, Master."

Matt staggered to his feet. "You're worthless to me! You can't even take care of that asshole, Stan." He raised his arms over his head. "Begone, demon, back to the depths of Hell where you belong. I command you to leave us." Wincing, he wrapped his arms around his stomach.

Demosura stood and bowed low, but she didn't immediately disappear. Her ears flicked up and her eyes widened. Then the air wavered and warped as she went out of focus. She vanished, leaving them in silence.

"Woo-hoo!" Kevin shouted and high fived Eric. "Dude! We made a killing!" The two of them started to stuff bills into their pockets. Twenty-dollar bills covered the floor so thickly Tyler couldn't even see the circle.

Tyler put out the candles next to him. It annoyed him that Eric and Kevin got all that money for nothing.

Matt collapsed to a sitting position, his hands remaining on his stomach. The amulet dropped and rolled up against the book. A drop of sweat fell from his face onto the floor. His shirt was soaked through. Even in the dim light of the candles his skin had become pale. He groaned.

Tyler stepped to Matt. “Are you all right?”

Matt’s hand came away from his stomach covered in blood. “Fuck.”

Tyler turned to the others. “Guys, I think Matt had better go to the hospital.”

Kevin and Eric didn’t pay them any attention, still giddily counting and shoving money into bulging pockets.

Tyler went to the door and turned on the overhead light, forcing everyone to shield their eyes. “Eric! Take Matt to the hospital.”

Eric stopped. Tyler half expected Eric to hit him. Instead, Eric’s eyes flicked to Matt. “What the fuck happened?”

Matt grimaced, holding out his reddened hand. “The bitch did this. Hurts like fuck.”

Eric stopped. “Shit. Help me clean up and don’t take any of my money.”

Kevin and Eric along with Tyler carried the candles and holders to Eric’s closet, which was more of a mess than Tyler’s closet. The reek of old laundry turned Tyler’s stomach. Tyler retrieved his quartz and his backpack. Kevin boosted Tyler up to retrieve Matt’s dagger from the ceiling. He should have made Matt get his own stupid knife except he was still on the floor holding his guts. Eric took it and the Spiritorium and put them into Matt’s bag along with the amulet. The four of them filled several grocery bags full of the money and stuffed those into Eric’s closet too. Then they rolled the carpet over the sub floor. The carpet no longer covered the entire floor so they positioned it so it would at least cover the chalk circle they had drawn.

Finally, with everything put away and hidden, they piled into Eric’s car. Eric blasted the music so loudly that nobody said anything. Tyler could see that Matt kept flinching whenever Eric hit the brakes or rounded a corner. Tyler ground his teeth the whole way until Eric dropped him and Kevin near Kevin’s house.

They had to walk a long way back to Kevin's house. Kevin's backpack bulged with all the cash he had stuffed into it, although most of it stayed at Eric's house.

Kevin shook his head. "Eric better not screw me out of the rest of my money."

Tyler adjusted his pack on his back. "Didn't any of that bother you?"

"The only thing that will bother me is if Eric keeps my share of the cash. Oh, I forgot. You didn't ask for any. That was stupid. She asked you what you wanted. You could've had anything. You could've been rich."

"Never mind." Tyler turned and walked to his house. Siamura had lied to him about being a demon. On the other hand, she had talked Matt out of breaking Stan Rutherford's legs, even when Matt insisted on it. She'd also had thrown the knife above her head where no one could reach it, instead of at Matt. That's what he would have done.

It was strange. She knew Tyler's name, and according to Matt and Eric, that meant she could command him, yet she didn't. Maybe she couldn't command him because he didn't ask for anything. If that was the case, he narrowly avoided being demon bait. It didn't make sense, but it didn't matter because Matt sent her back to Hell anyway. That was the last time he'd see her. He felt relieved, yet oddly sorry that she was gone. Relieved he wouldn't have to explain why she was here to his dad or worried Siamura would order him around like a stupid robot. However, he was a little sorry he wouldn't have the chance to talk to her. But it was safer this way.

Chapter 6

Snack

Aiden hung up the phone. Janine, Kevin's mother, didn't know where Kevin was either, although she had said that Tyler was there earlier. It was past dark on a Saturday evening and both their sons were missing. People had warned him how difficult teenagers were, but he'd thought he had a year or two before this kind of thing happened. Tyler had always let him know where he was, with whom, and when he'd be back. To top it off, Siamura had left over two hours ago, saying that she had been summoned and had to appear or there would be dire consequences for her. Not knowing where either of them were, was just… He pounded the counter, rattling the plates in the overhead cabinet. Tyler and Siamura had run off and neither one had told him the full story.

He went into the kitchen and fixed a cup of coffee — anything to distract him. Afterwards, he sat down in front of the TV and flipped through the channels. One-hundred-fifty channels later, and he still couldn't find anything to keep his interest and keep the worry at bay.

Some time later, the front door opened. Aiden rushed to it. "Tyler?"

His son came through the door, carrying his backpack half off his shoulder.

Aiden continued, "Where have you been?"

"I was over at Kevin's house, studying."

Aiden paused. This was one of those stupid parenting tests. "Oh, I see. Aren't you supposed to call me if you're going to be late?" He didn't want to bust him for lying, at least not yet.

"Well, yeah. I forgot."

"Look, all you need to do is pick up your phone and tell me you're running late. You're old enough to do that."

Tyler stood there glancing from one spot on the floor to another. Aiden could tell something was bothering his son, something bad, but now wasn't the time to press him. Whatever had happened was still too fresh.

"Hey, you had me worried. Set your pack down and I'll scrounge up something to eat. How does that sound?"

"Yeah, okay."

They walked into the kitchen and Aiden pulled a few things out of the refrigerator — pot roast and mac and cheese. He popped them into the microwave while Tyler got the plates and utensils out. Tyler looked relieved Aiden hadn't grilled him as soon as he came home. However, Aiden hoped he would be more forthcoming after some food.

They sat down and began to eat in silence. Aiden stopped for a moment and looked at his fork. "You know I had to teach Siamura how to use this?"

Tyler paused, a forkful of pot roast halfway to his mouth.

"She left here a while ago, something about someone summoning her. She didn't sound too happy about it. I haven't seen her since."

Tyler shrugged and popped the food into his mouth.

"What did you think of her?"

"She's pretty cool, I guess."

"Yeah, she's interesting, to say the least. She seems all alone, though."

"Yeah." Tyler chewed his food.

After a few more bites, Aiden said, "I talked to Kevin's mother earlier and she told me that both you and Kevin weren't there."

Tyler stopped eating and stared down at his plate.

"Did you realize that some guy was attacked in the park down the street last night? He's in critical condition at the hospital. I was worried. So where did the two of you go?"

Tyler pushed his remaining mac and cheese into a pile on his plate. "We went to Eric's house."

"Do I know this, Eric?"

"He's a guy from school, Eric Tallman. We were studying."

"See? Not so bad. And you're not in trouble for going to someone else's house. I just need some information, that's all."

Tyler shrugged but didn't say anything.

They finished the meal in silence. Tyler went up to his room, saying he had to finish his homework. *One of those teenager moods.* Aiden caught himself quickly tapping on the table. He knew Siamura was still out there. Maybe she wouldn't be coming back. He had to keep busy, cleaning up the kitchen and straightening things up in the den. Grabbing a beer, he sat in front of the tube again and channel surfed.

About an hour later, a thump outside in the backyard shook him out of his TV-induced trance. Could it be a prowler or a wild animal? Aiden turned off the set and put his feet down, listening. Something bumped at the back door, followed by scraping sounds of someone trying the door. No one but he and Tyler had the key to that door, and Tyler was upstairs. Aiden leapt up and pulled the curtain aside.

The sliding door opened and Siamura stumbled in. Dirt and mud covered her and her wings, and sticks and leaves clung to her hair. The smell of trees and earth followed her. In her hand was a deer's rear leg, covered in fur and ending in a hoof. With her other hand she leaned on the wall, leaving a muddy smear. She swayed as if she were intoxicated.

Lurching, she rotated her head to face him. "Sorry, mine lord." She ducked her head. The leg slipped from her grasp and landed on the floor with a loud thump.

Involuntarily, he put his hand to his mouth. "Are you hurt?"

Unsteadily, she looked at herself. "I made a mess." Her eyes glowed, then the radiance spread and covered her whole body in green light. When it dimmed, she was spotless and uninjured. "There, all clean." She shook her wings like a bird after a bath.

Aiden pointed to the mud-smeared wall. She swung around, overshot and came back. Green light covered the stain for a moment, and it disappeared. He pointed to the glass door and she cleaned that too with her magic. The door closed by itself, along with the curtain. He pointed to the animal leg on the floor. "What's that?"

Her head lolled. "A snack for thee?"

"Where were you? I thought you were summoned. You didn't kill them, did you?" He backed up towards the couch.

She shook her head. "Nay, nay, nay, I do not hunt humans. After the summoners dismissed me, I went a-hunting." Her wings shot out, nearly hitting several things like the ceiling light and the TV, although she miraculously missed them all. "I went flying!" Her wingspan was too large to spread fully so the tips grazed the opposite walls and the ceiling.

Aiden could imagine how buildings might make her claustrophobic because he felt very small under those wings, so he backed up until he felt his calves touch the couch. He marveled at her enthusiasm. It was the first time that she hadn't seemed frightened of everything. He didn't want to dampen her mood so he didn't interrupt her.

Ears alert and eyes bright, she continued, "I flew over houses. Then no more houses. I was free!" She stretched her arms above her head and leapt onto the coffee table in front of him, her wings still partially spread. "Then over hills and trees. Trees! Glorious, fantastic trees. I landed in the top of one and waited." Her wings snapped closed, and she squatted down with her arms between her knees. Aiden sat on the couch as his empty beer bottle on the coffee table wobbled like a drunken man and fell onto the carpet without a sound.

Her eyes grew wide. "I could smell him. The stag, he came closer. I crept down the tree in silence till I reached the lowest branch." She mimicked her climbing motions on the coffee table. "There he was, just below me. I leapt onto his back!" She flipped backwards, landing on all fours on the floor between the coffee table and the TV, tossing her head violently. "Mine teeth tore into his neck and we went down!" She rolled on her back, breathing heavily. Her chest rose and fell rapidly. Aiden realized he'd forgotten to breathe, that he'd been watching her display with his mouth slack.

Siamura rolled quickly onto all fours, facing him. "It was a blood frenzy feast!" She shook her head again as if she were tearing into the carcass right on his carpet. "I was feeding. Then I heard them — small wolves. Coming closer. Wanting to steal mine kill, mine food. They yipped and whined, so I turned and growled." Her growl rent the air. Aiden's legs shot straight out, his eyes bulging, heart racing. Her glowing eyes and sharp fangs had replaced all thought. He couldn't move, and only stared at her.

She laughed. "That is what they did. They turned tail and fled, like the little puppies they were, leaving streams of piss in their wake." She continued giggling. In one leap, she landed beside him on the couch, although the couch didn't move or wobble with her slight weight jumping onto it.

Aiden couldn't move. Siamura pressed herself against him, her breath tantalizingly close. His fear vanished in the instant she touched him, and a vision filled his mind. He was sitting on a log with her beside him. He could make out a campfire with meat spitted on sticks, roasting. Large trees stood at the edge of the firelight, their limbs forming a canopy above them. A couple of stars winked through the leaves. The smoke curling up brought the aroma of spicy, freshly cooked meat to his nose. He felt relaxed and safe.

Siamura kissed him lightly on the cheek. The kiss had so much promise and energy that he turned to her. Her eyes were positively smoldering, a very different kind of predator. A soft, thrumming sound emanated from her throat, oddly soothing and invigorating. It awakened feelings that had remained dormant since his wife had left. She kissed him on the lips, smiling and flashing her fangs as she pulled away.

Fangs? Aiden blinked. The campfire and trees disappeared. His den returned, with him sitting on the couch with a strange, green-winged creature in his arms. Her bizarre cat-like eyes regarded him. He shook his head. "Wait, what's going on?"

The thrumming sound stopped. Her ears flattened and her eyes widened. "Oh. So sorry mine Lord. I did not mean…" She extracted herself from him, her eyes looking at the wall, the coffee table, anywhere but at him. Her arms wrapped around herself making her appear smaller.

As she pulled farther away, Aiden grabbed her hand to stop her retreat. "No, no. It's okay Siamura. I'm not angry, just surprised." *And confused.* First, he was delighted at her energy and happiness, then scared shitless, and then finally he was kissing her. He felt like he was on a wild roller coaster ride of emotions trying to catch his breath.

She seemed to fold into herself, her head almost tucked under an arm, but she left her hand in his as if powerless to withdraw it. "Please, I mean to thee none harm. I… I…" She began to tremble.

He felt terrible. He hadn't meant to frighten her. "Come here." He scooted towards her. "You're safe." She placed her other hand against his chest to push him away, but he captured that hand in his free one and eased her head to his chest. She stopped fighting him and she fell into his arms. Aiden stroked her head and down the soft fur of her back.

Her breath hitched. “I wanted to run away, but thyne is the only kindness to me. There… There are so many humans everywhere.” She sobbed against him.

“Shhh, tell me in the morning.” He held her like that for several minutes before carrying her up to her bed. He laid her down, and she turned her back on him, facing the wall, still sobbing. Pulling the blanket up over her, he patted her shoulder, then retired to his bedroom.

Chapter 7

History Lesson

The next morning, Aiden found the door to the spare room left open after he was sure he closed it the night before. Cautiously peering within, he saw the Sunday morning sun beaming through the window, but there wasn't a trace of the green mearoch inside. He wiped his face. He hadn't slept well at all. Visions of winged, fanged demons had filled his dreams. Tying his robe, he looked over the railing. She wasn't in the living room either. He hoped she was still in the house. If she were outside, there was no telling the trouble she could cause or the danger she could be in from whatever attacked the man in the park. Though judging from her hunting story last night, she could probably hold her own.

He hurried down the steps, a fanciful worry that a media circus would greet him on his front step filling his mind. Instead, he saw the green woman curled up at the foot of his sofa in the den. She rolled quickly to kneel facing him.

"I… I am sorry," she stammered. "Did I wake thee?"

"Uh no. I was worried… I mean… Did you sleep down here?" Aiden pulled his robe tighter.

She nodded. "I did not feel comfortable upstairs. I was afraid thee would be angry with me." She knelt in the middle of the room on both knees, hands clasped together. "I am very sorry about last night. I had not fed in such a long time and when I did, I became light in the head. It shall not happen again. I promise. Please let me stay." Her ears folded down like a frightened kitten. "I have no other place to go."

Aiden blinked. He hadn't expected such a display. "Okay, get up. Don't worry. You can stay. You surprised me with the animal leg, the hunting story and… the kiss."

She ducked her head. "I lost mine-self."

"What happened? I swear I was in a forest clearing last night."

"Mine magt was too much and uncontrolled. I had not fed here in a long time."

"So, your magt just overflowed and made me see things?"

She nodded, not meeting his gaze.

"So why did you have to hunt in the first place? We have plenty of food here."

"I must feed, not just eat."

"But you killed an animal. That's barbaric."

She turned her head up to him, her eyes hard. Her ears stood straight up and she bared her clenched teeth and fangs. "It is not barbaric. It is life. Thee eats meat too." Her wings unfurled partway making her look larger.

Her anger startled him. Stepping back, he said, "But I don't kill anything."

"Thou benefited from the death, nonetheless. It matters not that someone else did thyne bidding." She seemed to realize the effect her demeanor had on him and ducked her head to face the floor. Her voice softened. "I require not only the sustenance, but I am needing the connection to this world. I need the meat of animals that live here." Her ears flipped down and her wings folded tightly behind her back, almost like a turtle retreating back into its shell.

Aiden blinked. He hadn't seen Siamura display any sort of aggression except last night. "What was that growling last night? You scared the crap out of me. I couldn't even move."

She faced him, her brow raised. "I did not mean to…" Her ears flattened. "Please forgive me. I… I…"

"It's okay. Just tell me what happened."

She blinked back tears. "Mine magt… Mine growl paralyzes people with fear when they hear it. I did not mean to do that. Again, because I had not fed here in so long, the magt sought ways of flying from me. Was thee afeared long?"

"No, when you jumped on the couch and… kissed me, I was no longer afraid."

"Ach," she turned away, though he thought he caught her blushing. Her cheeks became less green and more red. "Yea, that would be so. The fear is removed by mine touch and…" She ducked her head again.

Aiden stepped around to face her. "And what else?"

"Mine desire to remove the spell afearing thee."

Spell? What was she hiding? "But there's something you're not telling me."

"The magt… the magt makes me incautious and too… responsive."

"Oh… I see." He cleared his throat. The room seemed to feel too close.

She touched his arm. "Aiden? Mine wings are cramped from flying last night. I need to be out in the sun to stretch them."

He took her hand and led her to the living room. The ceiling here was open to the second floor and a shaft of morning sun fell across the carpet. "There should be enough space here."

She hesitated.

"Go on."

Tentatively, she extended her left wing and then her right. She closed her eyes and a long sigh escaped from her as she extended her wings fully. They were huge, at least twenty-five feet tip to tip, and they vibrated as she stretched the muscles. She twisted them back and forth, flexed them up and down. Even the narrow fingers that traversed the skin of her wings contracted and relaxed. Siamura reached over her shoulder, pulling one wing forward to try to rub her back. She stopped and caught him staring.

"Sorry." He turned away.

"Could I ask thee to help me? I do not want to embarrass, but could thee rub mine back?"

"Okay. Sounds reasonable." Aiden ducked under her left wing.

Siamura lay down, keeping her wings spread open, one wingtip at the foot of the stairs, the other on top of his off-white chair on the opposite end of the room. She rested her head on her folded hands. He knelt down behind her, next to the tail flipping back and forth. Fur covered her back between her wings, thicker at her shoulders and thinning to a stripe near the base of her tail just above her shorts. He wasn't sure if she was more human or more beast or whether the thought troubled him.

He bent over and brushed her long hair aside. Running his fingers through her soft fur, he began to massage her shoulders. Her musculature was very unusual, but having wings, her muscles would have to be in different places. He had been massaging her for a few minutes when he heard a low thrumming sound from her. He'd heard the same sound last night.

Aiden sat up, his hands falling away from her back. "What's that?"

Siamura coughed and the thrumming stopped. "It is me. I uh… purr, for want of a better word. I am sorry."

"So, you were… responsive again?" He stood.

She closed her wings and sat up, her arms and tail wrapped around her knees. "I purr for different reasons. I am not an evil beast that needs to be put down. Your massage felt good." Her eyes were reduced to mere slits as she pursed her lips.

Aiden stood and walked into the kitchen. "So should I get you a saucer of milk or do you want coffee?" He turned on the radio as he did most mornings.

She followed him to the kitchen. "Thou jests with me. I would rather have the sweet orange if it pleases thee." Her tail snapped quickly like a whip.

"Go ahead and stretch out. I'll bring it out to you." Aiden smiled. Her tail seemed to show her moods, and right now, she was annoyed. He liked that better than her usual frightened self. She stepped back into the living room as Aiden cleaned out the coffee urn and the news came on.

"…of an unusual number of dogs and cats reported missing. Please be careful and bring in your pets at night. And now for the weather…"

Aiden switched the radio off, frowning. He started the coffee maker and poured a couple of glasses of orange juice. He walked back into the living room and gave a glass to Siamura. She had spread her wings out on the floor again.

Pulling a chair from the kitchen table, he sat down facing her. "So, you're sure you didn't hurt a dog last night in your thrill to feed?"

"Did I not show thee the deer leg last night? Do dogs now have hooves and antlers? I will show thee again." She folded her wings with a rustle and walked to the back door, her tail caressing the couch and wall as she passed. Opening it, she looked both ways and stepped out. She returned a moment later with the leg.

Holding it up she said, "This is the rear leg of a deer. The worst thing I have done is poach."

"Okay, okay, it's a deer's leg. So why all the missing pet reports this morning?"

"I know not, this is the first that I have heard of it. When I was flying last night, I felt a ripple of magt. I fear that I may not be the only being using magt in thyne town." She lowered the leg.

"That's it? Maybe something else is out there? No more details?"

She shook her head. "I tried to follow it, but it disappeared. I am sorry."

"Could there be a connection between what you saw and the missing animals? What about those summoners of yours? Could they be using black cats in their ceremonies somehow?"

Her tail crooked upright, almost over her head, the ears stood at attention. "I did not see anything. I tried to follow, but I saw none-thing. I do not know of this connection of which thee speaks. As for mine summoners, they are craven." She stared at him. "I swear to thee, the next time I am out I will try to find this ripple of magt."

Aiden frowned. She seemed to be trying her best to help and was certainly better equipped than he was to find the mysterious source of magt. It still bothered him. He snorted as he motioned at the deer leg. "Why did you bring that home?"

Her tail dropped. "It was a gift for thee and thyne son." Aiden couldn't help but gawk, for as slight as she was, she hefted the leg as if it weighed nothing at all. She walked into the kitchen and set it on the counter. The leg thudded on the countertop as it landed, making the cabinet shake.

He stood. "That's all right. We've got plenty of food." The leg didn't look very sanitary. The hip joint that originally attached to the rest of the deer had dirt and leaves on it, and the sight made his stomach woozy. He was used to seeing his meat in little plastic-wrapped containers in a supermarket's refrigerator.

Siamura pulled a large knife from the block and proceeded to skin the leg. Placing the knee joint in her abdomen, and the torn part away from her, she grabbed two handfuls of loose skin and jerked towards her. The skin peeled away from the flesh like a band-aid from a wound. The tearing sound made Aiden's skin crawl. He could never be a farmer.

Siamura, using the knife, cut the meat into sections after first removing the torn and dirty upper chunks. "That can go into thyne cooling box, er… refrigerator, and thou can have it for later." Blood covered her hands. She picked up the dirty sections, rinsed them under the faucet, and ate them raw.

"Don't you cook it?" Aiden winced.

Her fangs shredded another piece. "And ruin the flavor? I ate the rest of him before his body cooled."

Aiden pulled out the plastic wrap and wrapped each piece of meat. "You don't look like you ate an entire deer last night."

As she chewed on another chunk, her eyes almost closed with a dreamy, faraway look. "It was delicious. I function different from thee. When I eat, I absorb energy directly. I am not sure where the body goes, but I still derive sustenance from it."

"You can eat all you want and never get fat? That hardly sounds fair." He patted the paunch he had been trying to lose for years.

"A mearoch is mostly magt or magic. Therefore, anything I eat is converted into magt. That is why I do not get heavy. Besides, if I became too heavy, I could not fly."

"But if you're all magt, then you shouldn't be here at all."

"True, but someone summoned me. The last time I was here, Robert the Bruce had defeated the English and Scotland was independent again. After his death, his son, David II, was crowned king."

"This isn't Scotland. You're in the United States, on the western coast of the continent of North America. You probably have never heard of the New World to the west of Europe."

"I have heard of land west of Europe. The Danes had settlements in Greenland and there was land beyond that. Just yesterday, I saw the maps in the newsmagazine that thou had given me. May I ask thee a question?"

"Sure."

"If I offend thee, please forgive me. What happened to the mother of Tyler?" Her tail explored the cabinets and countertop, brushing against the doors and knobs, as if testing the environment around her.

"Oh, Sandra and I divorced when Tyler was four." Aiden poured two cups of coffee. "I'm sorry, all I have is decaf." He handed her a cup.

Siamura made a face when she smelled the coffee. "May I have more of the sweet orange? I liked that very much." She carried the cup and glass to the kitchen table, her tail trailing along the cabinets.

Aiden poured another glass of juice and handed it to her.

"I thank thee." She sat at the kitchen table, arranging her wings and tail around the chair back as if she were wearing a long flowing gown.

He sat to one side of her and facing the den, looking at the back of the sofa where she had kissed him last night.

Siamura drained her juice and smacked her lips. "The Church allows divorce?"

"Yes, but there are many different churches, and it's the government that actually oversees who gets married and divorced."

She smirked. "The Church is much weaker than in mine day."

"You sound happy about that."

"After what they did to me, it does give me a certain amount of pleasure. Does thyne wife, Sandra, contact thee or Tyler?"

"My ex-wife Sandra. No, she doesn't."

"Why did thee divorce?"

Aiden didn't want to go into it, but she'd honestly asked, and he didn't want her to feel awkward. Besides, he was over Sandra. "She left when Tyler was four. She served me the divorce papers after she settled in New York."

Siamura frowned as her tail tapped silently along the border of the tile floor and the carpet. "Thou hast told me how she left, but not why."

Aiden opened his mouth to speak, but he stopped. Should he tell her about the other spirits? Then it dawned on him that she was the only person he could talk to without any fear of being ostracized. He sat across from her at the table. Her tail flicked behind her, waiting for him to continue.

He smiled. "I have always been able to communicate with spirits, not only you. When Sandra and I were together, the spirits would move things around, and Sandra became angry about it. She could never see or hear them like I can, or at least she never admitted to it. I'm sure she thought it was me who was hiding things. But then the spirits returned two diamond earrings of better quality than the ones that they originally took. She even had them appraised. She panicked. It was one thing to have the original object turn up, but better quality ones? She had to realize that it wasn't all in my head. She'd had none of the experiences that I had. I grew up with spirits and now you're here. But before you arrived, I had never touched a spirit."

"I am a mearoch, which is a version of what thee calls a spirit. I have substance — mayhap not physical but magt."

Aiden frowned. "But I can feel you nearby, a sensation in my shoulder, like a spirit."

Siamura smiled. "That is magt thee is sensing. As I said before, thee is strong in it. Otherwise, thou would not be able to sense me or the other 'spirits' as thou calls them."

"I suppose so." *Did he really have this magt in common with Siamura?*

Siamura raised her eyebrows, seeming to be on the verge of another question about his relationship with his ex-wife. Instead, she asked, "May I help prepare some breakfast?"

"Sure." He stood up. "What did you do before you were exiled to Irgale?"

"As a mearoch I watched over the forest, mine forest. I am… was the forest." She paused, as if confused. "I also helped people with herbs and spells. Not many people came to me, but when they did, I tried to help. If they were coming to see me it meant they were very desperate."

"You helped them with herbs and spells?"

"It was the thirteenth century. There were few medicines, at least none that thee would call as such. Yea, I would heal them and tell them to bathe. The new religion made them so afraid of their own bodies. It made me ill." She stood, shaking her great wings. Aiden could imagine the fear she would engender when a medieval farmer encountered her. She was unnerving him just sitting at his kitchen table. But she fascinated him as well. He had to know more about her.

"Why were you exiled?"

"The priests of the new religion, Christianity, came to mine forest and cast me out. Then…" Her eyes welled up with tears.

"Hey, hey, it's all right, but don't you want revenge?"

She quickly wiped her eyes. Clenching her teeth, she said, "Aiden, they are dead now. Their children, grandchildren, and many-great-grandchildren are all gone. What would I prove taking revenge now, and on whom would I take it? That would prove that I am some beast, a monster. Before the priests came, I helped people, healed them, and told them to stop cutting down mine trees. I tried to be fair. There were too many of them and only one of me."

They spent the next few hours talking about the changes of the past centuries. Aiden picked up his Sunday newspaper and Siamura read it too. He'd been planning on getting rid of getting the Sunday paper delivery for years, but today was glad he hadn't as she peppered him with questions. He also had to describe the concept of advertisements in the media.

Aiden heard a familiar galloping down the stairs. Tyler entered the living room, stopping suddenly. "She's still here?" Tyler gawked at the mearoch. Siamura shrank into herself, avoiding eye contact with Tyler.

Aiden looked between the two. "Where else would she go?"

Tyler shrugged, wiping his cheek. "Uh, I don't know. She wasn't here last night."

"She came back after you did. Do you…"

"I gotta go. I'll be at Kevin's, okay?" His son dashed out of view.

"Tyler, just be home before dark." Aiden yelled after him.

"Okay!" The front door closed and Siamura's shoulders relaxed.

Aiden said, "What's the matter?"

"Not a thing."

"Every time you're around Tyler, it's like you're scared like he's going to hit you or something. Why?"

She shook her head. "I cannot say."

"Why not?"

"I cannot discuss it."

"Did he say or do something to you?"

Siamura stood, her tail snapping behind her. "Stop, Aiden. I am bound to say none-thing."

Aiden sighed in anger, balling his hands into fists. It didn't make sense. She cringed every time she saw Tyler, yet Tyler carried on as if nothing were wrong. This had to end. He had to figure out what was going on.

[illegible] all gone. What was [illegible]

[illegible]

[illegible] they were glad he had [illegible]

[illegible] he had been [illegible] getting out of [illegible] was glad he had [illegible] with [illegible]

He also [illegible] the concept [illegible]

Aiden heard a familiar galloping down the stairs. [illegible] the living room, stopping suddenly. "She's still here?" [illegible] at the [illegible] shrank into her [illegible] avoiding eye contact with [illegible]

[illegible] between the two [illegible]

[illegible] "I don't know." [illegible]

[illegible] back after you [illegible] you.

[illegible] "I'll be [illegible]" [illegible]

[illegible]

[illegible] "What's [illegible]"

[illegible]

[illegible]

[illegible] Well?

[illegible] shook her head. "I cannot say."

"Why?"

"I cannot discuss it."

"Did he say or do something to you?"

Saminara shook her head, [illegible] "Stop, Aiden. I am bound to say none [illegible]"

Aiden sighed [illegible] his hands into fists. [illegible] make sense. [illegible] was wrong. This had to end. He had to figure out what was going on.

Chapter 8

Voices

Tyler couldn't believe that Siamura or Demosura or whatever her name was hadn't gone back to hell as Matt had ordered her to do. Or rather, she had left, but then showed up again at his house. He didn't know if he was relieved or scared out of his wits. Once dismissed, demons should return to Hell, or that's what everybody said in all the books and movies. Yet he was oddly pleased she had come back.

He didn't know what to think about her.

He continued walking to the park. When he had called Kevin, Kevin said that they needed to talk, but that he was grounded for not telling his parents where he'd been and couldn't leave his house. Since Kevin sounded freaked out, Tyler felt he should go along and try to calm him down. Kevin had agreed but told Tyler to meet in the backyard, away from his parents. It sounded strange, as if he was hiding something, but Tyler dismissed it. Kevin occasionally was weird about what his parents thought about him.

The sky was clear, the sun shining, and a warm breeze typical of Southern California rustled the leaves on the trees. It certainly wasn't the dark and stormy weather that always foretold terrible events in the movies. But a rainstorm would be appropriate now. He was living with a real live demon in his house, and his dad had invited her to stay. She made a point of not crossing Tyler, though he had no idea why. Maybe he could beat her up or say her name three times and send her back. However, which name to use, Siamura, Demosura, or some other name? He hadn't a clue.

On the other hand, she was so cool. Dangerous as hell, but cool. She was powerful and she looked absolutely awesome, not to mention sexy in her own way. But she was staying at HIS house. That was too close for comfort. He was going to have to do something and soon.

When he arrived at Franklin Park, he envied the kids playing on the playground and the families with their picnics. They were lucky. They didn't have a demon in their midst ready to devour their souls without a moment's notice.

Tyler was about to continue on, when he noticed a few people standing at the rise near the gate that led to the abandoned house, looking and pointing in the direction of the old house they'd summoned Demosura in.

He walked past the picnic tables and up to the gate. Peering down, he saw a forest of small trees or bushes had grown up behind and up to the house. They weren't taller than a foot or two but were bright green and went as far as the base of the hills in the distance. They contrasted against the bleached color of the vegetation on the comparatively parched hills. None of those plants had been there when they'd performed the summoning two days ago. He couldn't believe that the ritual caused all that. He shivered, pulling his jacket around himself and walked on.

When he reached Kevin's house, he bypassed the front door and went directly to the side gate leading to the backyard. Kevin was sitting in a chair by the pool. He clutched his hands together, staring at the concrete at his feet.

Tyler strode up to the chair across from Kevin. "So why are you grounded? You sounded freaked out on the phone."

"My parents are stressing. They won't leave me alone." Kevin wrung his hands as if to wash away some stain.

He never does that. Cautiously, Tyler asked, "What happened?"

"Nothing."

"What did you tell them?"

"I didn't tell them nothing. It was Reverend Woodward."

"Reverend Woodward? What did he say to your parents?" This was sounding worse by the minute.

Kevin glanced up at Tyler. "Look, I can't take it. Matt's gotten really sick. That scratch got horribly infected. The doctor gave him some powerful drugs, but he's not getting any better. Then there are all the postings about missing dogs and cats. And last night some animal killed my dog and left his guts all over the backyard." He pointed to a corner behind him. The area looked wet as if someone had recently hosed it down.

"My dad went out with a baseball bat to kill it but didn't find nothing. I'm telling you; it was her, dude, that demon we summoned. We, all of us, are to blame. Ever since that first time, I keep seeing things out of the corner of my eye and I hear stuff — voices, whispers. It's getting too weird. And she killed my dog! I want all this to stop, so I talked to the reverend after the service."

"What did you tell him?" Tyler clenched his fist.

"I told him everything, the first summoning and how the demon escaped, then the second time actually seeing and talking to her." Kevin turned to face Tyler. "Do you know what that means? Hell is real. It's not just one of those movies to scare you. It's fucking real, dude. Now I hear other demons, and sometimes they're in the same room and I see them. It's freaking me out. I had to tell somebody."

"I told you that I see and hear things all the time. What's the problem?"

Kevin ducked his head. "But I never thought that…"

Tyler snapped, "Oh, so you thought I was crazy and making up shit."

The sliding glass door behind Kevin banged open. Kevin's dad stormed out. He wore tan slacks and a pale blue polo shirt, as if he was going to the golf course. His dark hair was perfectly combed with grey on the sides. He reminded Tyler of one of those TV show doctors who always had the right answer to any problem.

Another man followed close behind, Reverend Woodward, mid-thirties and brown hair sprayed so that not a strand was out of place. With his pressed blue button-down shirt and dark slacks, he looked like a cell phone salesman.

Kevin's dad pointed his finger at Tyler. "I knew you were no good from the moment we met. What's this I hear of demons and such nonsense? Why did —"

The reverend patted the other man's arm. "Paul, Paul, let me handle this."

Kevin glanced between his dad and Tyler, his brows raised, hands clasped tightly together.

Tyler gulped. His secret was out, really out. His chest tensed, he could barely breathe.

Kevin's dad, Paul, glared at the reverend, pausing a moment as if to consider whether to yell at him instead. He threw up his hands. "He's all yours, Reverend."

The reverend put on one of those false smiles meant to settle everyone down. He took a breath. "So… Tyler. It is Tyler, right? I don't see you very much at my services. But you always come with Wendy Brooks and her daughter, though."

Tyler wasn't so sure about what the reverend was getting at. The secret was out though, nothing else mattered. "Yeah," his voice rasped.

The reverend's smile disappeared. "I would have thought you were a bright young man with a good head on your shoulders. At least that's the impression I got at church."

Tyler couldn't say anything, he couldn't breathe, he couldn't move, petrified of the next words from the man's lips. All he saw was the reverend's brown leather shoe tips surrounded by the solid concrete of the patio.

"Do you know anything about a ceremony that you boys did on Friday night? Your friend, Kevin, told us all about it and he doesn't seem too happy about the results."

Tyler was trying to wrap his mind around the fact that other people, adults, knew his secret. *I trusted Kevin! How could he tell anyone when I told him not to!*

The reverend continued, "Well, it doesn't matter. You boys shouldn't dabble with that kind of stuff. It will poison your mind and make you unstable. Those kinds of activities are only used by the mentally weak. You need something to guide you on the proper path." He paused. "Am I getting through to you?"

Tyler didn't know what else to do, so he nodded.

The reverend smiled. "Why don't the both of you come to Bible study on Wednesday evening? I think it will be a good alternative to candles and black cats, don't you?"

Tyler felt numb. Was that it? "Okay."

Kevin's dad growled, "I don't want to see you around my house or my son. You're a bad influence on Kevin."

Tyler's cheeks burned, he stood and turned away. From there it was easy to decide to leave.

Reverend Woodward chirped from behind him, "I'll see you Wednesday."

Tyler didn't stop. He kept his head down and rushed through the gate. Once he got to the street he slowed. He hadn't gotten into that much trouble, but his chest hurt and his eyes stung. He scrubbed an errant tear from his cheek. His best friend had betrayed him. No, he was wrong. He had thought Kevin was his best friend, someone to be trusted. He could handle the joking around about his voices and visions, but now it was out in the open that he was a freak, and soon everyone would hear about it. He just wanted to go home. His dad knew about the spirits, and if Siamura was a demon or mearoch or whatever, it didn't matter. She seemed more scared of him than a danger. At least at home, he wasn't a freak.

Chapter 9

Dinner

Aiden and Siamura read the paper, with Aiden at the kitchen table with the sports section and Siamura studying the world news section, lying on the floor on her stomach with her wings draped over the living room. She'd found a small sliver of sunlight and had spread out in front of the window like a house cat soaking up the sun. The window faced the fenced backyard and behind the fence was a hill with two oak trees, so there wasn't any real chance of people seeing her. Every once in a while, her tail thumped against the wall beneath the window. Aiden smiled to himself, recalling that when he was a boy, he had a dog, whose tail thumped on the floor when he was happy. He could get used to the sound, he decided. He realized that having her here vindicated the experiences he had had since his childhood. She gave them credence and validity. He wasn't normal, but he wasn't insane either.

Siamura sat bolt upright, her wings snapping shut. "Someone is coming!" She disappeared up the stairs before Aiden could recover from the shock.

"Siamura?" She'd pulled her disappearing act several times yesterday whenever she heard a strange noise or sometimes nothing at all, so he thought this was another false alarm. "There's no one…"

The doorbell rang. In that instant, he realized that Wendy Brooks and her daughter, Jen, were at the door. It was Sunday afternoon. They always came over on Sundays. He couldn't believe he had forgotten. He glanced around, suddenly self-conscious of any clues of Siamura's presence. Not seeing any, he opened the door. “Hi, Wendy. Hi, Jen.” If Siamura stayed hidden, he wouldn’t have to worry about her discovery.

“You look surprised.” Wendy brushed a lock of ash blond hair from her face. She was stocky, yet not overweight, wearing a brown coat and pale green shirt with blue pants. “You feeling all right?”

Jen nodded. “More like Tyler didn’t remind him. I knew he wouldn’t.” Jen bounced in, her brown hair swaying behind her. She wore jeans and a blue shirt under a tan jacket. Aiden had always hoped her perky, outgoing attitude would rub off onto Tyler to counter his more quiet, introspective demeanor.

They both carried grocery sacks with Tupperware containers of food, like a great Care Package of food relief since Aiden rarely had the time or inclination to prepare food. He was always grateful when Wendy came by, not only for the food, but also for the opportunity to talk to an adult outside of work. It had saved his sanity more than once. Their relationship never became romantic, although there were times, he thought it could work, but in the end, they were just too different.

“Here,” Aiden took a bag from Wendy and Jen. “Let me help with that.” He ushered them into the kitchen.

“Is Tyler upstairs?” Wendy took a baking dish out of the cupboard.

Aiden pulled the containers out of the bags. “No. He went out. He should be back soon.”

“Did he leave the paper and orange juice in the living room?” Jen pointed over her shoulder with her thumb.

“What? Oh, that.” Aiden hesitated. “Yeah, he was in a hurry to meet Kevin.”

Jen rolled her eyes. “Those two are always talking about one thing or another.”

Wendy took off her coat and put it in the closet along with Jen’s. “They have been a bit secretive lately, haven’t they?”

Aiden picked up Siamura’s orange juice and paper. “Yeah, they probably need their space for a while.” It still bothered him that Tyler hadn’t told him he’d gone over to Eric’s last night.

Wendy asked, “Have you heard about the attacks? The one was here in the park next door.”

“Yeah, I heard about it, but they still don’t have any leads, do they?”

"The police won't even say whether a person or an animal did it."

Jen looked through the paper as Aiden set it on the table. "Yeah, and there's a bunch of plants growing up like mad behind that park too."

Wendy turned. "You were over there? After what happened? Young lady, I'm going to ground you."

"Mom, Christa and me rode our bikes up here yesterday like we do every week and there's a whole bunch of bushes growing around that old house behind the park. They're not as tall as me, but there weren't that many bushes last week. Pretty weird."

Wendy shook her head and sighed. She started spooning a casserole into a baking dish. "So how are you doing, Aiden? You seem a little tired."

"Oh, I'm fine. It's been a crazy week at work. I had to wrap up a project on Friday."

Wendy gave him a stern nod of her head. "You really should've been at church today. Reverend Woodward's sermon was about how we all should slow down a little for family." Wendy put the casserole into the oven and set the timer.

Jen pawed through the paper. Settling on the lifestyle section, she flounced down on the sofa in the den and began reading.

Aiden was thankful he'd only obliquely hinted about his experiences with spirits to Wendy. She was always trying to get him to go to church, as if the reverend could exorcise the stories about the spirits. If only it were that easy. He hadn't anything against the reverend personally, but he felt the spirits were more than the typical Christian worldview could handle, especially with what he now knew had happened to Siamura. He didn't want to cause any undue attention to himself and jeopardize his job. It was the biggest reason he'd avoided any romantic involvement with Wendy. He didn't want a repeat of his experiences with Sandra. The other was Wendy seemed to have an opinion about practically everything and insisted upon sharing it with everyone.

"How's work with you?" he asked, mainly to deflect any more questions about Tyler or the spirits.

"Oh, it's going all right. Last Friday Joseph had to rock the boat and ask for special priority for computer resources, as if his project were more important than everyone else's. I swear some people think the world turns around them. I'm starting to think I should go back to Consolidated Petroleum…"

Aiden laughed and uncorked a bottle of chardonnay.

***

The wine was more than half gone when the front door opened. Tyler walked in. "Hey, Dad where's…" He turned the corner into the kitchen. "Siamura?" He stopped in front of Aiden suddenly seeing Wendy sitting at the table with him.

"Who's Siamura?" Wendy asked.

Tyler started, "Uh, she's a…"

"…friend who's staying for a little while." Aiden finished. Tyler seemed more flustered than usual.

"She?" Jen peered over the back of the sofa at them.

"That's an unusual name. Where is she from?" Wendy held her glass in mid-air, forgotten for the moment.

"She's from… ah…" Aiden hesitated.

"…Scotland." A woman's voice cut through the silence with her characteristic archaic accent. Everyone turned to the stairs. A small, waif-thin woman with dark hair and pale skin in a form-fitting green dress walked down the stairs. The dress was sleeveless and flattered her figure to the point of distraction. Aiden swallowed. She had the same peculiar walk to counterbalance her wings, though without seeing them, her hip movement made her saunter like a sultry runway model. The voice was Siamura's and her facial structure was the same, yet she had a milk white complexion rather than pale green and short ears rather than long ones. Her eyes were deep green with round pupils instead of golden and cat-like.

She faced Wendy. "Hello, I am called Siamura." She extended her hand.

Wendy shook her hand. "Pleased to meet you. I'm Wendy and this…"

Jen practically jumped off the sofa and gushed, "I'm Jen. Are you in fashion, movies, or something?" Her brown eyes lit up, taking in Siamura's form.

Siamura glanced at Aiden. "Nay, none-thing like that."

Jen dug in the cloth bag she'd brought. "I've got to get a picture. You don't mind, do you?"

As Tyler stepped closer to the table, he brushed against Siamura's hand. Or was it her hand? Aiden thought it was just behind her, where her wing would be. For a moment, her wings and tail flickered into view. Her skin tinged with green, and the ears lengthened. Fortunately, Jen was concentrating on her bag and Wendy was reaching out to Jen to settle her down that they probably didn't notice the momentary flicker of Siamura's disguise.

"I cannot…" Siamura stepped away from Tyler and raced up the stairs.

Wendy looked around. "Where'd she go?"

Jen dashed upstairs, her phone in her hand. "Who is she? I still want to get a picture. I want to figure out how to do my eye make-up like hers."

Tyler raced after her. Aiden and Wendy followed. This was quickly unraveling and would get out of hand if he didn't take control of the situation. Aiden ordered, "Jen, don't open the door. I need to explain."

Jen tried the door anyway. "It's locked."

Aiden interposed himself between the door and the other three people. "Put the phone in your pocket and don't even think about touching it."

"Why?"

"Because Siamura doesn't like it. If you want to meet her, you have to leave it in your pocket."

Wendy asked, "She's camera shy?"

"She's had some bad experiences. Just take everything slowly — no loud noises and no quick movements."

Jen frowned. "You make sound like we're going into a lion's cage. She's just a girl."

Wendy tut-tutted her. "Jen, be polite. The poor girl is frightened."

"Thank you," Aiden said. If Siamura was going to stay, she needed to meet other people, and he had to be sure he wasn't in the grips of some wild hallucination. He put his hand on the door. "Siamura, I promise everything will be fine. Open the door, please."

From behind the door Siamura said, "It is not wise for me to be seen."

Aiden said, "Siamura, you have nothing to worry about. Please open the door."

Wendy winked. "Are you sure she isn't a teenager?"

Aiden shushed her.

After several seconds, he heard the lock on the door click and the door open. Siamura stood, this time dressed in jeans and a blue shirt remarkably similar to what Jen wore.

Jen squealed, “Oh my god. We’re wearing the same thing.” She looked down at herself to confirm. “How did you change so fast?”

Aiden said to Siamura, ignoring Jen, “Would you like to join us downstairs?”

Siamura nodded and latched onto Aiden’s arm as if she would drown if she let go of him.

Wendy took Jen’s hand. “Come on, honey, we’d better check on dinner. You too, Tyler, come along.”

Aiden and Siamura followed Wendy and the children down the stairs.

When they returned to the kitchen Wendy and Jen busied themselves setting the food on the table while Tyler set out the plates and utensils. Aiden stood to the side with Siamura patting her hand which was wrapped around his forearm in a death grip.

Jen looked up from setting the casserole dish on the table, sniffing once. “Is that your perfume, Siamura? It’s really interesting. Very woodsy and natural.”

Siamura’s fingers tightened. “Ach, yea, mine perfume.”

Wendy stood at the table. “Well, let’s eat.”

They sat. Aiden led Siamura to the seat to his right with her back to the den. Jen sat beside her and Tyler across. Aiden sat at the head of the table by the window and Wendy at the opposite end.

Wendy insisted on saying grace. Aiden stopped himself from saying anything, even though she was ignorant of a spirit at the table, a spirit who was real and alive as they were and not a dream or a snatched glimpse. Siamura gripped the table during the short prayer.

Jen passed Siamura the casserole. “So where did you get that perfume? I’d really want to try it.”

“It be… It is mine own creation.”

Aiden noticed that Siamura’s disguise didn’t waver when Jen’s fingers touched Siamura’s.

Jen continued, “Am I going crazy, or does it change? Is it based on your moods?”

Siamura ducked her head slightly, suppressing a smile. "Yea… yea, it does."

Wendy took a sip of wine. "How do you know Aiden, Siamura?" She glanced at Aiden. "You never mentioned her before."

Aiden helped himself to the casserole. "Siamura is a distant relative of ours who's decided to come visit."

Siamura smiled. "I have none other family and I recently found Aiden… and Tyler."

Wendy said, "Your accent doesn't sound Scottish."

Siamura shook her head. "Ach, nay. I come from an isolated island nearby. We have different speech there."

Aiden picked up his wine. "I'm happy she found us. Wendy, you were talking about your new position at that software firm."

Wendy didn't need to be told twice and prattled on about her job, instead of continuing her interrogation of Siamura. Dishes were passed and Jen seemed to make a point of touching Siamura's hand each time. They began to eat, but Siamura watched their guests intently. It dawned on Aiden that she was studying them, mimicking their behavior in subtle ways. He almost breathed a sigh of relief that things were going so well.

That is until Jen yelped, "Oh my god! Let me see your hand!"

Siamura reflexively balled her hands into fists, holding them to her chin.

Wendy scowled. "Jen, how rude! What are you on to now?"

Jen's excitement was only mildly abated. She reached for Siamura's hand. "No, no, I'm sorry, but I just want to see your hand."

Siamura glanced at Aiden, then back at Jen as if the girl would bite her. Slowly, she extended the fingers of her right hand, keeping it close to her face.

"It's okay. I just…" Jen gently took Siamura's hand in hers and pulled it towards her. Jen counted, and then counted again.

Siamura smiled, "Yea, I have six fingers."

"That is so crazy. How did you get them?"

Wendy set her fork down. "Jen, that really is rude. I'm sorry Siamura, she forgets her manners."

Siamura blinked. "I was… born with them. It is common where I come from."

Wendy raised her eyebrows at Jen, letting her know to drop the subject. "Why don't you tell us about the school project that you're working on Jen?"

The girl blushed. "Oh… yeah, my teacher, Ms. Dawson, said that I should do my class project on Eleanor Roosevelt…"

The rest of the meal passed by uneventfully, although Jen would sneak glances at Siamura whenever she could. Wendy noticed and with an eyeroll at Aiden, soon took Jen home. As soon as the door closed behind them, Siamura dropped her disguise with a sigh.

Aiden asked, "How are you able to do that? Hide your wings and such."

Siamura shook her wings out. "Mine magt. I can influence the minds of people to make them see what they want to see."

"Couldn't you go out in public with your disguise?"

"I can only influence a limited number of people at a time."

"So, no crowds then."

"I must be mindful of mine wings and tail too. If someone were to touch them then the illusion would fail."

Aiden nodded. That must have been what happened when Tyler stepped closer to her during her introduction to Wendy and Jen. They reentered the kitchen and began clearing the table when Siamura stopped.

Siamura's ears stood straight up. "I must leave. Someone is in dire need."

Aiden paused. "Who is it?"

Siamura shook her head and walked out the back door into the darkness.

He turned to Tyler. "Do you know what she's talking about?"

"No idea."

"Come on. You know something is going on."

"Dad, I swear I don't know anything."

Aiden let the plate he was holding drop to the counter with a clatter. "Okay, just talk to me. What's going on between you two?"

"There's nothing going on. I have homework to do." Tyler ran upstairs.

"Tyler! Get back here!" Aiden tossed the silverware into the sink with a deafening crash. He took a few steps after his teenaged son and then stopped. He punched the air in front of him. He would never get Tyler to talk like this. Aiden didn't want to be like his father, always throwing a fit whenever things got difficult, but having a teenager in the house certainly tested his patience. Although, Aiden knew he couldn't wait too long for Tyler to finally talk to him. If by tomorrow, Tyler still hadn't said anything, then he would have to take a different, more forceful approach.

***

Hours later, Aiden was absently flipping between channels on the TV. It bothered him to have Siamura out on her own, especially at night. She said she was okay, but pets were missing and weird plants had sprung up behind the park. He admonished himself that Siamura could probably see and hear better than he could.

Then a soft thump and a rustle interrupted his thoughts and Siamura came through the back door.

She tilted her head and frowned. "Why does thee wait for me?"

"I worry about you. What happened out there?"

Her ears lay flat. "I was in none danger, but I felt not that other ripple of magt." She sat on the couch beside him. "While about mine errand, I noticed a glow in the eastern sky over the mountain. It was strange, like a great forest fire in the distance. I went to discover what it was. Has thee seen this light?"

Aiden thought, then shook his head.

"I flew east, keeping low. When I reached the mountain, I followed it upwards. To mine fortune, there were no buildings so I could remain undetected. There was a ribbon of stone with many traveling carriages… cars, like the one in thyne garage between the light and the city. They moved very fast. The air smelled bad with that car smell.

"I reached the top of the mountain and landed on a boulder. I saw it then, another city of lights sprawled below. The lights were in rows, in white and yellow for the most part. Then I felt them, like an enormous herd. There was a person for each of those lights.

"Aiden, I knew there were many people, but so many… I tried to count them. So many…" She stared into the middle distance and shook her head. "It stretched on and on. I saw another range of mountains and mine hopes brightened until I realized that there was another glow behind them. Does this city have an end? Are there so many human beings now?" She placed her hand on his.

Aiden smiled at her innocence. "What you saw was the Valley part of the city of Los Angeles, and, yes, it goes beyond that other mountain range to the south. Millions of people live there."

She blinked. "Millions of people? Is the entire human population here?"

"No, there are many such cities all over the world. Each with millions of people."

She shivered, her wings rattling.

"Are you all right?"

Her ears lay flat. "What has happened? More has changed in the past few centuries than in the many millennia before. Why Aiden?"

"Human beings figured out a lot of things. Growing food, conquering disease. Now we're more concerned with making money. There are very few wild places left that humans haven't mapped, cataloged, and claimed as their own." He worried he had said too much and that would overwhelm her in her fragile state.

"This is indeed the age of humans then. Is there any place for me? Have I been cataloged and claimed?"

He smiled. "You are your own person. No one can take that away and I won't let them, if it comes to that."

She hugged him. "I thank thee Aiden. Thee is a true friend. I am realizing with each passing day how much fortune it took to have found thee. I only hope I do not endanger thee."

He returned her hug gently. "Endanger me? How?"

She pulled away to arm's length, wearing a melancholy smile. "I also know how cruel humans can be." She walked away. "I feel very tired. Good night."

She didn't look well, as if her small curiosity had unleashed an avalanche that smothered her old concept of the world.

Chapter 10

Helping a Friend

Tyler rolled out of bed and switched off the alarm. Another Monday morning, yuck, but then again, all mornings sucked. But this Monday promised to be worse than any other Monday of his life since Kevin had told the reverend about how they'd summoned Siamura. Everybody was going to know about it by the end of the day and the last thing Tyler needed was people staring at him like he was some kind of freak. If only he could stay in bed or figure some other way to avoid facing the rest of the school, but his dad would never let him get away with skipping class.

He stumbled out of his bedroom and to the bathroom, dreading the coming day when he heard voices from Siamura's room. He crept closer.

His dad was speaking in a louder voice, a sign that he was irritated. "…a man was killed nearby."

Siamura's accented voice was even, free of inflection, as if avoiding anything to annoy his dad. "Nay, I have not killed anyone. Last night I healed someone. I do not kill people, Aiden."

"But they said the body was ripped to shreds."

"I do not kill people," she repeated in that even voice.

Tyler heard her approach the door. He scurried away and saw her emerge just as he ducked into the bathroom, closing the door. Her light footsteps passed by followed by his father's heavier tread. His dad never yelled at anyone, but Tyler could tell from the heavy footfalls his father was angry. Sometimes he wished his dad would yell every once and while.

He sighed. No, he didn't wish for that. He didn't want someone like Kevin's dad storming around.

Tyler dressed and went downstairs to the kitchen. His dad and Siamura sat at the kitchen table talking. Tyler noted by the tone of their voices that the mood had lightened. Dad pushed back in his chair. "We'll talk more later. I'm going to work, and Tyler's going to school." He paused.

Tyler crossed behind Siamura to get to the fridge and Siamura winced.

"What is it between you two?" That earlier note of irritation crept into his dad's voice.

Tyler opened the fridge and poured a glass of juice. "Nothing, Dad." He quickly drank the juice so he wouldn't have to say anything.

Dad turned to Siamura. "And you won't tell me anything, will you?"

The mearoch ducked her head, ears flattening. "I cannot say."

Dad sighed and shook his head. "Since you're going to stay here, I'll show you how to use the computer upstairs and surf the web." He turned. "And Tyler, I want you directly home after school and we're going to have a talk this evening."

Tyler set his glass down on the kitchen counter. Great. Dad was going to want answers for the mess he'd gotten himself into. With a gigantic sigh he picked up his book bag and headed out the door with a sense of foreboding. It didn't matter where he went or what he did because everything was falling apart. At school, everybody would know that he was crazy because of Kevin, and at home, his dad wanted him to explain why the demon was scared of him. He wanted a hole to open under his feet and swallow him whole.

He dragged his feet onto the bus, not daring to look anybody in the eye. His breathing tightened as he passed each row of seats. Soon the other kids would know about the voices he could hear, they would point him out to their friends, and there would be no end to the ridicule. Tyler grabbed a seat in the middle of the bus stealing a glance at the people around him. No one was looking at him like he had open sores running over his body, thank goodness.

The bus stopped and Kevin stepped onto the bus. He looked terrible, with a haggard face and dark circles under his eyes. Instead of picking his feet up, he dragged them along the floor. He stopped by Tyler's seat. "You mind if I sit here?"

Tyler stared, mouth open, but moved aside to avoid a scene. Kevin had to be nuts to sit beside Tyler after what he said yesterday.

Kevin tucked his bag at his feet and leaned close. “Look dude, I’m sorry about yesterday. You’re the only one who will believe me. You gotta help me get rid of the voices. They kept me awake all night.”

“You have to learn to live with them,” Tyler mumbled. Gods, it sounded like something his father would say.

“What?”

“You just live with them, like I do.” Tyler turned his back to his friend, staring out the window. Kevin could just rot in hell for all he cared.

***

Throughout the day, Tyler dreaded the eventual embarrassment of others learning his secret. Every class he went to, he looked at people’s faces to see if they knew his secret, but all everyone seemed to worry about was themselves. At lunch, he entered the cafeteria with trepidation, sure someone would point him out in the crowded lunchroom. Yet nothing out of the ordinary happened. By the end of the day, relief that he’d run the gauntlet unscathed filled his chest. But he had to figure out a way to keep Kevin’s mouth shut too. He couldn’t risk another outburst. The reverend was discreet, but there was no telling if the next person Kevin blabbed to would have the same manners.

After school, they both boarded the bus for the ride home. Again, they sat in the middle of the bus as the other students sat ahead or filed past them. When the bus lurched into motion Kevin leaned towards him. “What do I do about the voices, and… You sometimes see things, don’t you? I thought you told me one time you did.”

“Yeah, sometimes I see them. You do what I do. You ignore them.”

“Ignore them? They get louder at night. Maybe you could teach me how to do it or something.”

“You just ignore them. I can’t teach you that. Though it has been quieter at my house recently.”

“I should go over to your house then. I gotta get some sleep.”

Tyler hesitated. He wasn't sure how much to tell Kevin. While it was true it was quieter at his house, he suspected Siamura had something to do with it. Things were different with her around, almost as if the other spirits feared her.

"Let me come over," Kevin's voice took on a whining tone. "We could see if the voices stop."

"Dude, you're grounded. Your dad will have a shit if he finds out."

"I don't care. You gotta help me. I'm going crazy."

"You expect to come over after you told the reverend? You're crazy."

Jen turned around from the seat in front of them. Her brown hair tied back today. "What are you guys arguing about? You're best friends. If he wants to come over, let him come over."

"Kevin's grounded. His dad will blame me if he finds out that Kevin was at my house."

Jen frowned. "What did you do to get grounded?"

Kevin said, "Because of the summoning that we…"

Tyler slapped his hand over Kevin's mouth. "Shut up!"

"Summoning?" Jen's eyes sparkled. "Okay guys, spill it."

Tyler dropped his hand from Kevin's mouth. "None of your business."

Jen sniffed with an air of superiority. "Well, I don't know about Kevin, but my mom is picking me up from your house tonight, so I can wait till we get there."

Tyler grumbled, "Kevin's dad doesn't even want me around him."

Jen leaned further around the seat. "Wow, so this summoning thing is real serious."

Kevin groused, "Dude, I'm coming over."

"No, you're not."

"Yes, I am."

The bus pulled to a stop and Tyler led the way off the bus with Kevin and Jen following. They walked in silence toward his house as Tyler noticed more people in the neighborhood had put up the approved cartoon Halloween decorations over the weekend. They shouldn't, but it felt like the decorations were laughing at him, mocking his situation at home. A few curious leaves blew around their feet like clueless puppies, leading them forward, eager for the coming disaster.

For a moment Tyler thought about running all the way home, leaving his friends behind, then slamming and locking the door in their face. But he had no hope of beating Kevin. He was an athlete and faster than Tyler, plus Tyler couldn't abandon Jen outside. Her mother would be pissed. Tyler turned around to Kevin. "I don't know what you think you're doing. You can sit out on the grass for all I care, but you're not coming in."

Kevin didn't slow down. "We'll see."

When they reached his house, Tyler opened the door. As soon as Jen was inside, Tyler tried to close the door on Kevin but Kevin blocked the door and forced it open, pushing his way into the house. Tyler stumbled back into someone and Siamura caught him at the base of the stairs. She was in her human disguise she'd worn when Jen and her mother were over. Tyler yelled, "Siamura, kick him out! I don't want him in the house."

Kevin pointed at Tyler. "Fuck that. I'm staying and you're going to help me."

Siamura glanced at Tyler then at Kevin but made no move towards Kevin. Jen stood away from the group, her eyes big and her hands gripping the straps of her book bag tightly.

Tyler shouted, "Well, get rid of him!"

Kevin slammed the front door shut and stepped forward. "I'm staying. You owe me!"

Siamura murmured, "I cannot do anything."

Tyler tossed his hands up. "Why not?"

Jen stepped back towards the door leading to the garage. "Stop it, you guys!"

"Siamura, throw Kevin out now," Tyler ordered, dropping his bag.

Kevin flung his backpack to the left and advanced on Tyler. "No way, dude. I'm staying."

Siamura held her head in her hands. "Stop! Both of ye cannot order me to do contradictory commands."

Kevin stopped and stared at Siamura for the first time. "Why do you sound like Demosura?" He started towards the disguised mearoch.

"Leave!" Tyler tackled Kevin and Jen let out a yelp, but Tyler only managed to push him aside instead of knocking him down.

Kevin shoved Tyler. Tyler hung onto him and they started to push each other back and forth. Kevin swung at him hard, and Tyler's feet slipped out from under him.

The next thing he knew, Siamura was looking down at him. Her skin was green and her cat eyes glowed. She picked Tyler up as if he weighed nothing and set him on his feet. She held a hand out to block Kevin from coming closer.

Jen screamed and ran for the front door.

Siamura's tail flipped. "Hold, I cannot have ye harming each other." She stepped so that Tyler was at arm's length from her.

Jen tugged at the door, yet it wouldn't open. The door was unlocked. Why didn't it open? Jen spun around and flung her back against the stuck door. Her eyes were wide springing between Kevin, Siamura and Tyler. He had no idea what she was thinking.

Kevin swore, "Fuck! That's Demosura. No wonder I'm hearing shit. It's her!" Kevin raced forward and raised his fist to punch the spirit.

The first blow connected, and Jen screamed, "Stop it!"

Tyler's mouth fell open as Siamura began to deflect and dodge Kevin's punches. It was like something out of the Matrix movie, how she moved so calmly, without straining.

Then she reached forward, grabbing both of Kevin's fists and holding them still. It was uncanny how she was shorter and smaller than Kevin, yet easily overmatched him.

Jen held her hands over her open mouth.

Kevin yelled, "Let me go!"

Siamura said, "Nay, Kevin, not until thee promises not to hit me nor anyone else."

Kevin tried to kick her.

Siamura's tail whipped out, snaring his ankle. She dragged him to the living room spreading her wings in the space and hovering over the ground. Releasing her hands, she let Kevin dangle upside-down by his foot in the air. "Halt! I will not harm any of ye. Please, do not hit me, or anyone else. I cannot allow that." She rubbed her arm where Kevin had hit her.

Tyler gaped at the mearoch floating in his living room, her tail holding an upside-down Kevin by his ankle. She didn't flap her wings at all. She shouldn't be able to do that. She only weighed a tiny fraction of Kevin's weight. Jen followed behind Tyler, her balled up fists held just below her chin.

Kevin panted, "Are you blind? She's a demon! She'll kill us all!"

Siamura folded her arms. "I shall not. I swear it."

Jen squeaked, "You're a demon?" Tears welled up in her eyes.

Tyler shook his head. "She's a mearoch, not a demon."

Siamura drifted downward, gently setting Kevin down. The mearoch made a show of folding her wings, rustling them more than she seemed to need to.

Kevin quickly rolled away from her, but at least he didn't attack. "You idiot! We summoned her. She's a demon. Which means Hell exists!"

Tyler slapped his forehead. "You're the idiot. You just told her." He pointed at Jen, who jumped.

Kevin grumbled, "I thought she already knew everything."

Jen shook herself. "Shut up!" She stopped for a moment eyeing Tyler then Kevin. "What do you mean you summoned her? Like with candles, magic spells, and stuff?"

"Yeah, and she appeared." Kevin pointed at Siamura. "Except her name is Demosura."

"Ha! You expect me to believe that?" Jen lowered her voice and her hands. "Siamura, it isn't true, is it?"

Siamura nodded one quick jerk. "He speaks the truth."

Jen recoiled. "So, you are a demon."

"Nay, I am a mearoch, not a demon, not a devil and not from thyne Hell either. Tyler, thee needs to tell thyne father that thou has summoned me."

Jen sighed.

Tyler threw up his hands. "Oh yeah, right, after my dad said not to do a thing with the spirits. He'll kill me. Besides, I thought you told him."

Siamura's ears stood at attention. "I cannot tell any person until thee does. I cannot violate that."

Kevin groaned, "Dude, she knows your name and there isn't a magic circle. We're in deep shit."

The mearoch shook her head. "I know the names of Matt and Eric too. Knowing the name of a being does not give control over that entity. For instance, Kevin, I command thee to stand on one foot."

Kevin glared at her, his fists clenched at his sides, both feet firmly on the floor.

She continued, "Thee is safe. Having a name gets thyne attention. It forces not a being to do what they are told. As for a magic circle, thee needs not protection from me."

"But you attacked Matt," Kevin insisted, "Well… you did scratch him and you ran away."

"I did not. I went to Matt last night and healed him before the poison could kill him. Use thyne telephone device to call him if thee doubts me."

Kevin lunged at her. "You're lying! You're a demon!"

Tyler dove for Kevin. "Stop it!" He pulled at Kevin as Jen joined him.

Kevin shook them off, but thankfully, he didn't continue to go after Siamura. "She'll kill us all and devour our souls," he screamed pointing at her.

Jen shouted, "Why isn't she killing us now if she's this big evil demon you say she is? She easily stopped you from hitting her and broke up your fight with Tyler."

Siamura bowed her head, ruffling her wings with her tail curling around her feet. "I cannot attack any of mine summoners."

Jen put her hand to her mouth. "What about me? I didn't summon you."

Her ears stood up. "I want not to hurt anyone, and thee has given me none reason to."

Kevin spat, "You're still evil and a demon from Hell."

"I am not evil. I am from Earth, not Hell, and I am not a demon. The priests called me that so they could get rid of me."

"But you look like a demon," Kevin persisted.

Siamura raised her brows. "Does thee call dogs demons because they have fangs, long ears and tails? Are birds evil because they have wings?"

Kevin sneered, "So why do you call yourself Siamura when your name is really Demosura? What are you covering up?"

"Demosura was mine name seven centuries ago. I gave mine-self an unsullied name to begin anew. I have had many different names in the past. Sometimes others have named me and sometimes I have named mine-self. If thee wishes, thee may give me a new name that suits thee."

Kevin opened his mouth, and then shut it, clenching his fist. Tyler could tell he was angry, yet Siamura refused to respond in kind.

Siamura's tail swung wide. "Why did thee come, Kevin? I am certain thee did not come to talk to me."

Kevin snapped, "Don't play dumb. The voices, the other demons, won't leave me alone."

Siamura smoothed her hair. “Thee has never had these experiences before the summoning so their presence disturbs thee. Tyler is the only one of the four who has heard the spirits before. Kevin, the reason thee is hearing those spirits or voices is because they felt what thee did at the summoning. Thee has marked thyne-self by performing the ceremony. Thee is now visible to them and they believe that since thee helped bring me here, thee can help them too.” Her smile hinted that she found his situation ironic.

“Well, yeah. You know them. You can tell them to stop.”

She shook her head. “I have none such ability. Thyne friend, Tyler, would be of more help than I. He knows how to live with the gift.”

“Gift? You control them. You’re a demon lord with legions of demons under you.”

Siamura sighed. “Did Matt fill thyne head with these stories? I am not a demon or a lord of anything.”

The sound of the garage door opening made all of them jump, facing the door. Why was Dad home so early? Tyler couldn’t get Kevin out of the house without Aiden seeing him. This kept getting worse and worse.

Siamura’s ears flattened, she raised her hands, palms up. “Tyler, please tell thyne father that thou summoned me. He already knows thee is hiding something from him.” She rubbed her arm where Kevin had hit her earlier.

Dad’s voice came from the garage. “Tyler, are you here?”

Jen stepped to the garage door. “Hi, Aiden. We’re all in here.”

Great, now Tyler didn’t even have time to hide Kevin. Then there was Jen, who would tell anyway. She could be so uncool sometimes. He thought about running out the front door, but that was a pretty stupid idea. Where would he go? Besides, his dad already knew something was wrong. He looked around, hoping for inspiration, only noticing that Siamura kept her eyes on him, while massaging the dark splotch on her arm where Kevin had hit her.

Chapter 11

Confession

Aiden knew he shouldn't have left work early, but he worried about leaving Siamura and Tyler alone together. There was more to their relationship than merely occupying the same house. Tyler was acting as if he were hiding something, especially around her. And Siamura appeared to be especially fearful around Tyler, but she acted strangely all the time. Maybe it was just that. Something must have scarred her terribly in the past. Considering how little he knew of her history, there could be a universe of possibilities.

He was concentrating so much on getting home that he almost missed the news report on the car radio. "A man was murdered this morning on Grant Street near Franklin Park," the announcer said in the customary urgent tone sure to make people turn up the volume. "Police have no clues except that a large, powerful man or animal committed the crimes." That put the killing two or three blocks from Aiden's house. A murder that close to his house was more than highly unusual and downright scary. Aiden coaxed a little more speed from his car.

Aiden entered the house from the garage. Jen called to him from the doorway. She seemed stiff, like she was holding her breath. That puzzled him — not the fact that she was here, but that she seemed fearful. He entered the house, walking past her.

Aiden came to a halt, doing a double take between Siamura and Jen. Then he saw Kevin staring at anyone but him. His eyes finally fell on his son, who kept his eyes on the floor. He looked at Siamura; she wasn't in her disguise but somehow Kevin and Jen seemed okay about that. Every time he saw Siamura, she gave his senses a start because she was so unusual. Though she wore the black top and shorts as before, her wings, tail, long ears, and especially her cat-like eyes drew him in, dominating his attention. Seeing him, she relaxed her wings with her tail hanging in the air, awaiting his reaction. The small motion of a hand clenched to his right caught his eye. Kevin's hands were balled into tight fists at his sides, lips drawn into a thin line, his jaw set. He looked ready to fight, to bulldoze through them all without much thought.

"What's going on here?" Aiden didn't like the scene. He let the door close behind him and the teenagers jumped at the noise.

No one said anything. Siamura ducked her head, watching Aiden from beneath her brows, almost as if that she was bowing to him.

"Siamura? Have they…? Are they…?" Aiden indicated Jen and Kevin.

The mearoch raised her head and met his eyes. "Yea, Aiden. They see me in this form."

Shit, this is bad. Aiden took a breath. "Tyler, please explain."

"Uh, Dad, Kevin came in and…"

"I thought I told you that no one else is to know of Siamura. Do you realize how dangerous it is to her and to us if people know she is here? Why did you bring Kevin here? And Jen?" This was Aiden's worst nightmare come to life. His chest felt tight, almost suffocating.

Jen folded her arms tightly. "Mr. Moray, my mom will be by later to pick me up. I won't tell, I promise."

Aiden took a breath. "Jen… that's fine. Why don't you sit down over there?" He stepped to his son. Aiden tried to keep his voice under control, yet it grew louder, words he hadn't intended to say in this moment spilling out. "Tyler, what is it between you and Siamura? Why is she afraid of you? And why is Kevin here? I thought he was grounded." All the frustration of the past couple of days rolled over him. Tyler's evasiveness, Siamura's caginess… Aiden's sense of control had slipped out of his grasp.

No one spoke until Kevin mumbled, "I've got to go home. My dad…"

Aiden growled, "Don't… move… from that spot." He pointed at Kevin. "Why are you here?"

"I… I followed Tyler here." Kevin glanced at Tyler.

"Is this true, Tyler?"

"Yeah, Dad, but I told him not to."

"Go on." Aiden clenched his fist.

"He hears voices too. The spirits, they're bothering him. So, he thought that I could make them go away. I told him to just ignore them and go home."

"I thought you told me that Kevin doesn't hear them. What changed? And how does he know about this in the first place? Did you tell him?"

"Yeah, I told him, just the little stuff."

"You told him, after I warned you." Aiden fought to keep his voice flat.

Tyler snapped, "He didn't believe me anyway."

"Well, if he's hearing them too, I'm sure he believes you now." Aiden pointed at Siamura. "So, tell me what happened!" He threw up his hands.

Tyler ducked his head. "We summoned Siamura."

Aiden shouted, "You what?! Of all the…" He stopped and stared at the boys. He couldn't even think. His whole life collapsed into this one instant, nothing else mattered. He always guarded against allowing their secret to become public. Their lives and Siamura's life were now in danger. Damage control, damage control… how to clean this up?

The children cringed, eyes wide, but otherwise remained unmoving.

Aiden sighed and flopped into the chair beside Tyler. He took a moment to rub his temples with his palms. "So, the two of you summoned Siamura and now Kevin is hearing the spirits. Is that why he came here? To… to… figure out how to stop it?"

Tyler clasped his hands together, his words flowing from him in a rush. "It was Matt and Eric too. Dad, I was tired of always waiting, never having any control over whether the spirits would come or go. They always do stuff to us. They shut off my computer, deleting my homework. All sorts of stuff! It's unfair. I was sick of it."

Aiden rubbed his temples. "Shit. Two more people? I suppose they're hearing voices too? What next? Did somebody take pictures and post them on the internet too? Tell all the news stations? Are we going to have the army and the FBI coming through our door to drag us off to god knows where?" Aiden sighed and rubbed his head, modulating his tone. "Are you sure, just the four of you and Jen? At least, so far?"

Tyler shuffled his feet. "Kevin told Reverend Woodward."

Siamura's brows and ears shot up. Her tail snapped in front of her.

Aiden stared at his son, then at Kevin. "Oh, you've got to be kidding. Please say you're kidding."

Kevin mumbled, "She's still a demon and she's from Hell." His fists clenched tight and his jaw set, but he didn't meet Aiden's gaze.

Tyler shrugged. "I don't think he really believed that we actually summoned anything. He just said that we should go to Bible study on Wednesday night. Well, and he told Kevin's dad, that's why Kevin is grounded."

Aiden shook his head. Ripples in a pond… spreading.

Jen sunk further into the chair across from him. "Mr. Moray, you don't really believe this summoning business, do you? And the voices and stuff?"

Her question distracted Aiden from the impending disaster. "Siamura's the result of the summoning. Isn't she evidence enough? I've heard the voices ever since I was little and I still do. I try to explain to the spirits that they shouldn't bother people too much because some people tend to get upset when their nice and tidy worldview gets exposed as a simplistic pile of crap." He glared at Kevin.

Jen flinched and blinked. Even Kevin drew back, dropping his fists. Aiden had never talked about his abilities with anyone except Tyler and his ex-wife, Sandra. He hated to be so forward, but his anger wouldn't let him do any less, especially seeing his whole world blowing up in his face. He sighed. "Let's go and get something to drink."

Kevin stumbled over his words. "Uh, Mr. Moray, I need to go home. You… you won't tell my dad that I was over here, will you?"

Aiden raised an eyebrow. "Are you going to stop talking about Siamura and the summoning?"

The boy stammered, "I… Um, yeah." He seemed surprised that Aiden had listened to him.

Aiden nodded. "Then we have a deal. We won't say you were here and you'll say that you were mistaken about Siamura, that she wasn't real. Oh, and Tyler will help you learn how to deal with the other spirits. Good?"

A smile crept across Kevin's features. "Yeah… Thanks, Mr. Moray!" He gathered his backpack and left through the front door.

Aiden followed the kids to the kitchen as Siamura trailed after them all. Aiden poured soda for all of them except Siamura, as the bubbles hurt her nose. She insisted on 'sweet orange.' They sat around the table sipping their drinks while Tyler told them the whole story of the summoning, Matt's scratch, the second summoning, and the money that Siamura made, until they were back to the present. Siamura nodded from time to time during Tyler's story agreeing with Tyler's version. Jen kept looking from Tyler to Aiden and back again, her eyes wide, as if expecting Aiden to stop Tyler from telling such an obvious lie.

When Tyler finished, Aiden said, "Is that all? There's nothing else to tell me?"

Tyler shook his head, his hands wrapped around his soda glass.

Siamura said, "There is one part that Tyler omitted, if I might tell it." She turned to Tyler. "May I speak without restriction with thyne father from this point forward?"

Tyler shrugged his shoulders, his fingers still clenching the glass tightly. "Yeah, go ahead. It doesn't matter now."

Siamura sighed as if a weight had left her. "Last night I healed Matt. He should recover within a few hours, perhaps a day. It was fortuitous as I tasted his wound and found the poison was not mine but another creature." She rubbed a dark splotch on her arm. It looked to Aiden to be a bruise. She didn't have that this morning.

Jen leaned away from her. "Eww, you tasted his blood?"

Aiden found himself grimacing too.

Siamura frowned. "Of course. By tasting, I can… diagnose, I believe that is the word, the type of poison and apply the proper spell to neutralize it. It was, as I told the four boys earlier, a poison of magt, but not from me. It was another being who uses magt that injured him."

Aiden asked, "There's another mearoch running around? One that has been killing people?"

"I doubt it was a mearoch. Tyler, thee said on both occasions thou drew a magic circle on the floor. Can thee remember the layout of the first one? Perhaps thee could draw it?"

Tyler rose to get paper and pen.

Aiden closed his open mouth. "You mean there's another physical spirit on the loose?"

"Yea. We are both of the fey. I am a mearoch. It is something else, but both of us are of the fey."

Tyler returned and began drawing the magic circle on the paper. A large pentagram dominated the image, but the spaces within contained other symbols. Aiden was impressed at the complexity of the illustration and the fact that Tyler recalled a lot of the details.

Finally, Tyler pushed the paper across the table to Siamura. "How's that?"

She picked it up in both hands, staring at it. After a moment, she laid it down in the middle of the table. Her ears flattened. "From what I can recall of the old ceremonies, this is a complicated layout to call forth a spirit. Can you enlarge the smaller symbols? They are too small to read."

Tyler seemed energized by her interest and took back the paper. He began drawing again on other pieces of paper, referring to his first one to guide his hand, his pen deftly tracing every angle and geometric shape. Aiden noticed one symbol was unlike the others as Tyler spent more time illustrating the swirling, organic mass of lines.

When he had finished, he handed the pages to her. There were letters marking where the smaller ones went on the first diagram. "That's all that I can remember."

Siamura smiled a little. "Thee has done much better than most people." Tyler sat up taller. She continued, "As I suspected, I am called to be thyne protector, though I know not whom or what I am to protect thee from."

Jen leaned forward. "That explains why you wouldn't allow the two of them to hurt each other."

Tyler was deep in thought. "So, if the symbols were in a different pattern, we would be running away from you instead of you being our protector?"

Siamura shook her head. "Nay, I do not attack people." She eyed Aiden as if to make her point. "But I may have not shown up at all. I remember little about that first day except having to find shelter. Where did thee get this diagram and its symbols?"

Tyler said, "From Matt. He has an old book called *The Spiritorium de Infinitus Maleficus Profundum*."

Siamura's ears shot up and her wings spread a few feet on either side. She rose halfway out of her chair like she was about to leap across the table at Tyler. "*The Spiritorium of the Boundless Infernal Abyss*? Who wrote it? Was there anything else?"

Tyler shrank back, startled. “I don’t know who wrote it. It’s really old. There is the black rock and the blue amulet though. Just having those things in the same room gives me the creeps.”

Siamura laid her ears back seeming to realize she’d frightened the teenager. Glancing at Aiden and Jen then back at Tyler, she murmured, “Sorry.” She folded her wings with a rustle. “Where did the rock and amulet come from?” She rubbed her arm again.

Tyler twisted a pencil in his fingers. “I, um, found them. Well, Matt and Eric cast a spell from the Spiritorium to find the stone and the amulet.”

Siamura’s ears stood up. “What was the nature of the spell?”

“It was a simpler spell than this one except they couldn’t see or hear the spirit they summoned.”

“How did they possess the stones if they couldn’t hear it?”

“The spirit came to me really mad because they ignored him. The spirit told me everything. So, when I did meet Matt and Eric and told them where the stones were, they wanted me to help at the next summoning.”

Siamura sipped her juice. “I fear for Kevin. He does not have the experience with the fey like thee and thyne son. I told thee earlier that thee is strong in magt. Tyler is too. That is why thee can talk and interact with spirits and it gives thee a modicum of protection against them. But that boy, Kevin… they will torment until he goes mad.”

Aiden shook his head. “We’ll help him. And I still don’t believe that we are strong in this magt stuff.”

Siamura blinked. “It is the truth.” As if her declaration was all that was needed to prove her statement.

Jen said, “What about Kevin? Can’t you do anything? Wait, do I have this magt thing too?” Her hand covered her mouth. “Am I going to go crazy like Kevin?”

“Nay, thee does not have magt.” Siamura smiled and patted her hand. “I doubt thee will have any trouble. Thee helped not with the summoning.”

“Yeah, but I’m talking to you now.”

“True, thee is, but thee is only using thyne normal senses, not any ones derived from magt. Thee should be safe.”

Aiden stood and went into the kitchen. He had forgotten how hungry he was with all the excitement going on. “Jen, I assume you’re staying for dinner.”

As they ate dinner, Jen looked over at Siamura. “I was wondering why you were eating funny yesterday.”

Siamura froze, staring at Jen. “Eating funny?”

Jen smiled. “You almost got it. Here, let me show you.” She gently wrapped Siamura’s fingers around the fork to show her the proper way to hold it. Yesterday, Aiden had been happy to get the mearoch to use the fork at all.

Jen asked, “How do you normally eat?”

“With mine hands and mouth.” Siamura answered as if she were answering an obvious question.

“Isn’t that messy, especially with spaghetti?”

“I have not eaten spaghetti before. Most times, I bring down an animal and eat it before the flesh cools.”

Tyler frowned. “Don’t you cook it first?”

“Don’t you need a knife at least to cut it up?” Jen followed.

Siamura bared her fangs. “I use these to cut and I never found the need to cook. As for the mess, I bathe afterward. Is that sufficient to answer thyne questions?” Aiden had never noticed how impressive her upper and lower fangs were. She had to be careful maneuvering her fork to avoid her canines.

Aiden’s eyes fell upon the symbol Tyler had drawn with the graceful curves and leaves around a death’s head. It was so different from the rest. “Siamura, can you tell us more about this symbol?”

She halted, ears flipping back. He could have sworn she blanched a paler green. She glanced at each of them.

Tyler said, “What’s the matter?”

Siamura set her fork down, staring at her plate. “It is the symbol that the priests assigned to me, so they may control me.”

Aiden was confused. “Assigned to you?” He knew she was upset, but he felt that this was an important key to the puzzle.

She took a breath, wiping her face. “When they defeated me and burned mine forest, they cut one of mine fingers off and bound me using magt to that symbol. Mine severed finger went into the construction of the blue amulet that Tyler saw earlier at the rituals. The same one Matt used against me.”

Aiden waited a moment for her breathing to settle back to a normal rate. He didn't want to keep pushing her, but he needed to know. "So, I could use this diagram to force you to do things?"

"Yea."

"If it's so easy, why doesn't it happen more often?"

She looked at Tyler. "Not many people know of the symbol and more important, it helps if they are strong in magt."

Tyler didn't meet her gaze.

Aiden continued, "That would explain why you followed Tyler home after the first summoning and not one of the other boys."

She nodded.

Jen asked, "You don't have any missing fingers. In fact, you have six on each hand."

"I healed mine-self." Jen gave her a funny look. Siamura held out her bruised arm over the table. "Observe." The overhead light brought the ugly splotch in sharp contrast on her pale green skin. Her arm glowed a brighter green. In a few seconds, the mark vanished. Her arm was smooth and clear. She rotated it, flexed her six fingers and withdrew her arm. Everyone was silent. She continued, "Aiden, both thee and Tyler have the magt. Thee can be assured that both of ye will have more strange occurrences. Ye cannot ignore it anymore."

Jen looked around the table. "I used to be jealous of Tyler's stories about ghosts and stuff. Now I'm not so sure."

Aiden said, "I'm worried about what Kevin's parents will do about you, Siamura, and the summoning."

Jen said, "I can't imagine that his parents actually believe anything happened. They probably think it's too weird and something that they shouldn't be associated with."

Tyler shook his head. "His dad grounded him after Reverend Woodward told him. I don't think his dad really believes we summoned anything, but the idea made him mad. Reverend Woodard told them after Kevin confessed to him yesterday after church. Kevin went to him because of the voices."

Aiden opened his mouth to say something, as the sense of helplessness returned. It would only be a matter of time before more people knew of

Siamura and that Aiden helped her. He had to concentrate on damage control.

Tyler continued, "The reverend told Kevin and me to go to Wednesday's prayer group. I don't think he believed Kevin."

The doorbell rang, making everyone jump. Jen ran to the door. "It's probably my mom." Aiden heard a man's voice along with Wendy's and Jen's. He turned to Siamura, and instead of her winged form, he saw her as human with pale skin and long black hair, wearing a green T-shirt and blue jeans. She had striking, brilliant green eyes, even though her pupils were round and not slits. Her ears were much shorter, almost human, and only subtly pointed.

Wendy came around the corner. "Hi, Aiden. Hi Siamura." She paused. "Aiden, you do know Reverend Woodward? I wouldn't normally bring anyone over, but he said he really needed to talk to you." A clean-cut man in his mid-thirties stepped beside Wendy. He wore pressed tan slacks and a crisp, powder blue button-down shirt with the collar open. Aiden's suspicions rose because he was too friendly looking and well-groomed, almost like a salesman trying too hard to close a deal. "Reverend Woodward, this is Aiden Moray and Siamura."

Siamura backed away from the table and eyed the space around her. It was as if she was searching for an escape route. This couldn't be good considering her previous experiences with men of the cloth.

Wendy continued, missing Siamura's reaction, "And this is Aiden's son, Tyler."

The reverend stepped around the table to Aiden with a quick and easy eagerness that made Aiden wince. "Pleased to meet you, Aiden. You can call me Steve. I wonder if we might discuss this in private. It concerns your son." He smiled, flashing his pearly whites, extending his hand for him to shake.

Aiden stood. "Um, if it's about Tyler…" *What was this guy getting at?* "Wendy, Jen could you excuse us?"

Wendy shook herself, obviously hanging on their every word. "Of course. We'll see you later. Reverend?"

The reverend smiled. "I'll be able to find my way back in my car. Thank you."

Aiden waved. "Good night, Wendy, Jen." He stepped to the kitchen after the women had closed the door behind them. "Have a seat, Reverend. Can I get you something to drink?" He hoped that it would give him time to gather his thoughts together.

Siamura sat with deliberation and watched the reverend with an intensity that unnerved Aiden. Her fingers gripped the tabletop. Aiden was going to suggest she go upstairs, but she apparently had other ideas.

Reverend Woodward sat beside Tyler. "Just a glass of water please."

"What is this about?" Aiden asked as he collected the water, ice and glass setting it before the reverend and sitting back down at the table. "I don't believe I've ever been to your church."

Steve noisily swallowed some water. "Well, I realize that, but your son Tyler has, and more importantly is a friend of one of my church members. Could we perhaps discuss this between the two of us? No offense, Ms. Si… uh."

"Siamura," she said with a thin lipped smile. "If it concerns Tyler then I have an interest too." Her eyes held onto the reverend practically with a death grip.

Aiden said, "It's okay, reverend. She's family. And Tyler should hear it too."

The reverend nodded. "Okay then. I can tell you're a no-nonsense type of guy, so I'll get right down to it. Kevin Adams, Tyler's friend, came to me about a demon summoning. He told me that he and Tyler, along with two other boys, performed this ceremony. Did you know about this?"

"We were just discussing the subject before you arrived. What of it?"

"Well, it's dangerous. It severely disturbed Kevin. He seemed to think that Tyler here knew more about demons and could help him."

"As a no-nonsense guy I can tell you Tyler does have an active imagination. And you're truly worried about demons walking the earth? Should we hoard wooden stakes and crosses against a vampire invasion?"

Siamura fidgeted in her chair.

"Don't be ridiculous. I'm saying that claims of demons and summonings can upset people. Make them susceptible to psychosis and the other such diseases of the mind. I don't think we should encourage such behavior."

Aiden said, "I'll agree with you that we shouldn't encourage anyone to summon demons. Furthermore, I've told Tyler to stop telling any stories that would offend people."

The reverend paused a moment as if trying to decide whether Aiden was playing him for a fool or not. Finally, he nodded. "I'm glad we had this talk. I would strongly suggest that Tyler join us for Bible study on Wednesday evening at the church since he is in need of guidance along the proper path. I recommend you and Ms. Siamura to join him." He reached in his pocket and handed a business card to Aiden. "I invite all of you to our services on Sunday too."

Aiden glanced at the card and nodded politely. Now maybe he would leave them alone. Siamura's knuckles were turning white, she was gripping the table so tightly.

The reverend continued, "We should close with a prayer. Our Father who art in Heaven…"

Siamura shouted, "NAY!" The sound of heavy wood splintering echoed through the room. She was standing, her disguise gone. Huge dark claws, like knives, the size of Aiden's fingers and gleaming with a deadly blackness had grown from her fingers and reduced part of the table in front her to kindling. Her cat-like eyes blazed green, her wings partially spread.

Steve gaped, his eyes riveted on the creature before him. "Oh… my… word…" He put his hand on the table like he was going to faint.

A brilliant flash of green light exploded in front of the Reverend. "Be gone!" Siamura jumped onto the table on all fours, her tail whipping behind her. The lights above exploded leaving only the flickering light coming from the kitchen area several feet away. Dishes from their dinner shattered on the floor.

Steve fell backwards in his chair. He stared at her in disbelieving horror, too stunned to move.

Tyler leapt up and away from the enraged mearoch.

Aiden snatched Siamura's tail in one hand. "Stop!"

Siamura faced him. Her fangs had elongated so her mouth no longer closed. They were razor sharp and larger than kitchen knives. She raised one hand with its cruel talons towards him. The end of her tail stiffened and wrapped around his arm. He felt the incredible strength of it and realized she had transformed, no longer the wisp of a girl he'd carried up to the room on that first evening. He pulled, struggling to release his arm, and found he couldn't shift her one bit. She was solid, all tendon and muscle.

Her eyes glowed eerily as she stared at him.

Aiden took a deep breath and as calmly as possible said, "Stop. Stop right now." He was facing down a predator. He could not show weakness.

Siamura blinked. Her ears flicked back and her wings snapped closed. She glanced at the disaster about her, as if seeing it for the first time. Her tail released him and slipped out of his grasp in an instant, curling about her leg protectively. She hunched down, covering her mouth with a hand. Then her eyebrows shot up noticing her claws. Shaking her head, she dashed off the table in the direction of the stairs.

The sound from upstairs of the office door slamming made everyone jump, shocking Aiden back to reality. Aiden bent over the reverend, examining him for any burns or other damage. A light that bright could have hurt him somehow. "Are you okay?" Aiden patted the man's shirt, worried that the heat may have injured him, but the shirt wasn't even warm to the touch. The odor of ancient trees hung in the air. The reverend trembled slightly as Aiden helped him up.

Steve dusted himself off, also checking to see if he was unharmed. "What? What was…" His hands shook. "Holy… smokes." He stared at the table and the light above.

Aiden blinked. "Yeah, pretty dramatic." He took a breath to calm himself, righting the fallen chair.

"She's a demon… and dangerous. Why do you let her stay here? She could murder you in your sleep."

Aiden murmured, "I think she's frightened by so many new people and our customs. She's not familiar with our ways."

"Mr. Moray, I don't think I'm getting through to you. Look at what she did. She's unpredictable and murderous." The reverend pointed at Aiden. "She's the murderer, who's been killing all these people and animals, isn't she?"

"No, absolutely not. She's been here the whole time, and Tyler and I are fine." He hoped he wasn't stretching the truth. He also worried that Siamura would not stop upstairs, but would burst out a window, flying as far away as she could. He longed to go upstairs and check on her, but the first priority was damage control. "It would be a good idea if you went home and thought about this before jumping to crazy conclusions. Please don't go talking about her to anybody." With a hand, he indicated that Reverend Woodward should leave.

"She's not only a physical risk, but also for your souls as well," the reverend said. Tyler stood at the foot of the stairs to block him from having second thoughts about pursuing Siamura. Reverend Woodward saw him. "Son, you and your father are in grave danger," he pleaded. "You must take matters in your own hands to protect yourselves."

Tyler gripped the banisters on either side of him. He wasn't going to budge.

The reverend stopped walking to the door. "Are you blind? She attacked me!"

"She ran off like a scared rabbit after I told her to stop. I will talk to her, but please leave now and don't tell anybody." Aiden opened the front door.

The reverend stepped out and turned. "I can't let this go. Please reconsider."

Aiden closed the door and threw the deadbolt as an added precaution. He set his back to the door and heaved a sigh. "Shit. That was just shit." Tyler's eyes widened at his father. Aiden made a point not to use foul language around his son. "Sorry. It's not your fault. That went as badly as it could have. I have to check on Siamura. Could you do me a big favor and clean up the kitchen as best you can?"

Tyler nodded, his eyes still wide. "Sure, Dad." He stepped off the stairs.

Aiden paused. "Did you take any of the money that Siamura made? I wanted to see how good a match it was."

Tyler turned. "No, I didn't even touch it. I was busy trying to help Matt."

Aiden smiled. "Good for you and you did well just now too." He patted Tyler on the shoulder and went up the stairs. Now he had to figure out what Siamura did. She shrank and ran from most everything that startled her. One minute everyone was sitting around the table, the next minute all hell had broken loose. Literally. At least she stopped when he told her to and no one had been hurt. If she were a murderer, she would have killed all of them. He couldn't believe that she would hurt him and Tyler.

He knocked on her door. When there was no answer, he opened it softly. Siamura lay curled up on the carpet, crying, wings loosely about her, her tail wrapped around her leg. As Aiden closed the door behind him, he felt an immense sadness in the room and in the atmosphere. He had to push his way through it to reach her. It wasn't physical and he couldn't see it, but it was still there, dragging at his limbs. He knelt beside her. "Siamura?"

Sobs wracked her body. She faced the wall away from him. He gently closed her wings and slid his arms underneath her. When she didn't protest, he lifted her and he marveled that she weighed less than a child in marked contrast to when he grabbed her tail downstairs. He set her on the bed, arranging her wings and tail to make her as comfortable as possible. The horrible claws had disappeared. Brushing her black hair over her ears and out of her face, he let her cry. "It's okay. You're safe."

She crawled to him and laid her head on his chest. "I… I am sorry. I meant not to do that, to lose mine temper."

Aiden stroked her hair and the fur between her wings. "It's over. You had your reasons, I'm sure."

She began to sob violently. He held her, waiting for it to pass. She was light and fragile, and it was hard to imagine her as a terrible creature. But what had happened? Where did the predator with claws come from? Was she like Jekyll and Hyde?

Her breathing returned to normal though every once in a while, she let out a sob. "That prayer… that prayer that the reverend said. It was the one that the priests used when they attacked me hundreds of years ago in mine grove. They brought their own spirits to attack mine grove and me. They called them angels. We battled for a long time. I remember not how long, but I was outnumbered. Mine kind had been hunted down and destroyed or banished. The fey were constantly losing to the new religion."

Aiden lifted a strand of hair and brushed it behind her long ear. His hand continued down from her head to her back, fingers twirling into the soft fur there.

"I had done none-thing wrong, Aiden. I helped people. I cured them of illness, mended their broken bones and hearts. The only thing I asked in return was for mine grove to remain unmolested. The priests could not abide by that. They saw me as a threat. Other members of the fey had left, or soldiers and priests drove them out.

"I stayed and fought. For hours, perhaps days, the battle raged. I drove many of their infernal angel spirits away. I know several priests died. I admit that and I am not happy that I did so. Despite mine efforts, I was defeated. I was bound, mine grove in flames. The head priest, Father Elringson, hacked off one of mine fingers to make his foul magt. I still feel mine severed digit as though it were only minutes ago that he removed it. He tied mine essence to that awful symbol. I screamed at him. He said I was receiving the mercy of his god. Then he left me to the angels.

"Losing mine finger was none-thing compared to what the angels did to me. They took me to their prison and chained me down. They began to dissect me piece by piece. Each night I would heal and each day they would rend mine flesh anew. For years, they tore at me each day and sometimes into the night. They never seemed to tire in their delight of ripping mine body, breaking mine bones, cutting the meat from me and tossing it onto the fire.

"After several years of this, I gave up. I wished for Death to embrace me, to take me away from mine horror. Each day, each month, each year, Death spat on me and laughed. I gave up trying to heal, trying to remember, trying to do anything."

She paused. Aiden remained silent, controlling his own rage as he stroked the fur between her wings to keep her calm.

"One day the angels failed to come. I thought it must be a trick. They had done it before. More days passed without them returning. Perhaps they were bored. Long ago they ripped mine lungs from me. I could not scream loud anymore. I realized after a few more days that the only bits left of mine body were a bone shard in the ashes and a drop of dried blood that they had forgotten about.

"I dragged the shard with the blood far away, as far away from that place that I could manage. I kept running until I could not run anymore. I started to rebuild mine-self, but I had forgotten how the pieces fit together. Oftentimes I would attach tissue and bone only to find later that I had done it wrong. I had to tear it apart and try again. In many ways, it was worse than the angels because I would get far along only to discover I had to start again. It took me years to heal.

"I had to avoid being eaten by predators. Sometimes I failed, but at least the beasts left mine bones. I spent years keeping hidden and quiet. I knew not where the angels were, or if they were looking for me." She wrapped her arms tightly around Aiden's waist.

Aiden kept smoothing her hair during her story. "Am I the first person you met since all of that happened?" It sickened him that anybody could do that to her or to any creature.

She nodded her head and pressed herself closer to him.

Aiden said, "You told me why you reacted to Reverend Woodward the way you did, but where did your claws come from? And how come I could not pull you away from him when I grabbed your tail?"

Siamura stiffened in his arms. "I am of magt. Mine claws come out when I am threatened or I am hunting. Mine magt allows me to alter mine weight or to bind mine-self to the ground or objects."

"And the flash of green light? And the lights blowing out?"

She rubbed her head against his shoulder. "It was mine magt. Please forgive me. I forgot mine-self."

They remained that way for several minutes while Aiden ran his hand over her hair and wings. The aura of sadness in the room parted and drifted away like a passing rainstorm. A feeling of safety and warmth replaced it. A soft thrumming vibration began inside her.

Aiden startled, pausing in his caresses.

She snuggled closer to him, her leg resting over his. "Please go on."

"It's your claws and teeth. How can I trust you?"

"Aiden, look at them." She sat up on his lap spreading her fingers in front of them. She turned them from front to back. "None claws. I swear to thee I will be careful in the future. The reverend surprised me. It shall not happen again." She placed her head on his shoulder again.

He resumed stroking her head and wings. Her purring increased and her tail wrapped around his ankle. Her hands went up his back and she tilted her head to him. Her catlike golden eyes dilated, practically smoldering. She stretched up to him, her mouth parted, and she kissed him. He tasted blackberries.

Aiden pulled away, surprised.

Siamura sat up, and her hand brushed his cheek. "Please, Aiden. I want this. I need to feel something other than horror, pain, and fear." Her purring receded deep within her, a low rumble.

"But, it's not…"

She put her fingers on his lips, stopping him. "Thee told me of the divorce, therefore thee be not married. Thee greeted not Wendy as a paramour and Tyler realizes that thee needs companionship. As for me, I have been celibate for seven centuries."

"I don't know you."

"Nor I thee. What better way to learn more of each other?" She smiled and kissed around his mouth and nose.

She knew his excuses and pulled them away like wrapping paper. He kissed her, tasting her again. She slipped off her top and shorts, her purring regaining its volume. She reveled, free of her clothing. He stood, gathering her in his arms.

She wrapped her arms around his neck and tilted her head in askance.

He smiled. "Trust me."

He rushed next door to his bedroom. Using her tail, she closed the door. Aiden set her feet onto the floor and they kissed again, giggling softly to each other. Her skin lightened and her wings began to fade from his sight as she pulled his shirt from him.

Aiden stepped back. "What's going on?"

Siamura blushed. "Would not thee find me more attractive if…"

Aiden shook his head. "If I can't see your wings, I might step on them…"

She smiled, her green color returning along with her wings and tail. She leapt into his arms and they kissed again.

Chapter 12

Arrested

Tyler worried about Siamura. She had looked terrified when the reverend first arrived, but when the reverend started the prayer, she'd turned into a raging demon with huge terrifying claws. Her power to knock down the reverend was amazing and when Dad grabbed her tail, Tyler was afraid she'd attack him instead. But he had spoken in his calm voice and instead of attacking, she'd cowered and ran upstairs, upset. She didn't fit the mold of a killer demon. But man did she leave a mess in the kitchen and the table had a huge chunk taken out where her claws had ripped into it. Although she had the power to kill, she hadn't used it on anyone. Just the kitchen table.

Tyler wondered why she attacked the reverend. Siamura said she wasn't a demon, yet she had almost ripped him to shreds for saying a prayer. If she wasn't a demon, why would she care whether he said a prayer or not? Something wasn't right. Although he had questions about her behavior, he sensed that she wasn't a real danger to him or anyone else. That's why he didn't want to disturb her and his dad last night. He understood that she needed some privacy and she seemed comfortable with Dad, so he left them alone.

Tyler opened the curtains of his bedroom, the sunlight beaming in. The air felt better this morning. He was more optimistic, and it was only Tuesday.

But something jangled his nerves. His dad hadn't knocked on Tyler's door to wake him. Dad always knocked on his door, and he was never late.

After dressing in a T-shirt and jeans, Tyler left his bedroom to go to the bathroom next door. Along the mezzanine walkway, the sun brightened a patch of floor in front of Siamura's room. That was strange, as her door was kept shut most of the time. He padded to the doorway and peeked in. She wasn't there. He walked into the room and found her clothes on the floor.

Something was wrong. Where was Siamura? Was she wandering around without clothes on? Was Dad all right? He dashed out of the room and rapped on his dad's bedroom door. Dad always knocked first, since Tyler was a little kid, and insisted that Tyler did too. Despite Tyler's worry, the habit was hard to break.

Through the door he heard a woman's giggle, followed by his father's harried voice, "Hang on." His dad murmured something he couldn't make out and Siamura laughed softly. Tyler was trying to reconcile Siamura's clothing in her room with the fact she was in his dad's room when the door opened. Dad was in his bathrobe. The smell of apples mixed with pine and other trees drifted out the door. "What's the matter?" Dad glanced at his watch, "Oh, no! We're late!" At that, Siamura laughed from the bed. Tyler had never heard her laugh before. It was infectious, and seeing that his dad was fine, he found himself smiling. Even Dad cracked a half-smile.

Siamura padded up behind Dad. "Good morning, Tyler." Her voice had a thrumming quality to it. Her eyes shown brightly, her tail swung around his dad's leg, and she wasn't wearing any clothing. This last point made Tyler's breath catch in his throat. She was stunning. He had seen her nude before, but this time there was no membrane and bloodied gunk covering her body. He couldn't tear his eyes away from her, and the vision of her beauty burned into his memory.

His dad must have seen his reaction because he turned around and closed the door to a crack. "Put some clothes on!" he hissed.

The thrumming sound stopped, and she whined, "Do I have to?"

"Yes, you need to."

"But they are in the other room."

Dad paused, his eyes flicking back and forth between Tyler and Siamura. Then he stepped out, closing the door behind him. "Why don't you finish getting ready and I… we… uh, will be downstairs shortly."

Tyler had never seen his dad this way. He seemed flustered, happy, and embarrassed all at once. It confused Tyler, but Dad was smiling and that made it okay.

Dad nudged him. "Go on, we're late."

Tyler nodded and strode into the bathroom. He went through his morning routine in a daze, trying hard not to think of the implications of what he'd just seen. Stepping out of the bathroom, he glanced down the walkway. His dad's door was still closed, so he went downstairs to the kitchen. It was weird without Dad there to get the breakfast things out, but Tyler had gotten himself cereal in the past. That seemed easy enough. As he was eating, Dad and Siamura entered the kitchen. She had dressed in her abbreviated top and shorts, her arm and tail around Dad, and the faint scent of apple and maple swirled in with them. Even when Dad tried to put a little distance between them, she continued to touch him.

Finally, Dad put a hand on her shoulder. "Siamura, Tyler is here too."

She quickly withdrew from him and sat at the table with Tyler. Her eyes never settled long anywhere, constantly flicking across him then away. Her tail would curl around her chair then his, then the table leg, and then repeat the motions. Tyler held his breath. She made an attempt to smile and put her hand on his. Her ears flipped down. "I am sorry, Tyler. I am as confused as thee is, but for different reasons. I have not felt this way in a very long time. I… I am very grateful to thyne father. Please be not angry with me or with him."

Tyler nodded his head. Oh God. They actually had… he had known before, but with Siamura's words it was vocalized and in the open. He sat there, letting the idea sink to the bottom of his toes.

Siamura brushed his brown hair from his eyes. "It will be okay."

His dad put a glass of juice in front of Siamura and sat down, biting into a piece of toast and sipping a cup of coffee. "We'll have to hurry, but we should make it in time."

Siamura drank and smiled at Dad, who took a bite of toast and returned her smile. Seeing his dad happy felt kind of strange to Tyler, but good too. Then Dad waved at him to hurry up and it became a day like any other, running to get his things and catch the bus to school.

***

On the bus Kevin sat next to Tyler. There was an uneasy silence between them. Tyler could tell that Kevin was tired and cranky. Obviously, the spirits weren't leaving him alone and he wasn't sleeping. After a minute, swaying with the bus's motions, Kevin brought up the subject of Siamura.

"Shh!" Tyler put his finger to his mouth for quiet. "Remember what you promised."

"Okay, okay." He paused. "Is she still at your house?"

"Yeah, why?"

"You're, well, all right and all that? I mean she hasn't like tried to, you know…"

"I'm fine." He wasn't about to tell him about Siamura nearly attacking the reverend last night or ending up in his dad's room this morning. "My dad's fine too."

"You heard that there was another murder in our neighborhood last night, didn't you?"

"No."

"You sure she stayed at your house? She didn't leave even for a little while, like when you were sleeping? Maybe she put a spell on you." Kevin leaned closer. "That makes two murders you know."

"I'm positive she didn't leave the whole night." Tyler rolled his eyes at Kevin's stubbornness.

"Yeah, but how?"

"Dude, stop."

Tyler went through his school day thinking about the morning's events. He couldn't believe how happy his dad had been, and that Siamura and Dad had been together last night. She was kind-of sexy, but… not human. And he worried that Siamura's demon half could resurface and hurt him and his dad. A part of him was angry that she had come into their lives and upset things. For years, he and his dad had been alone with the spirits and now a spirit had come into their lives in a big way. He had always hated how the spirits would flit in, cause trouble, and then flit out. But Siamura didn't seem to be leaving anytime soon, judging from his dad's happy smile, and he wasn't sure how he felt about it. That summoning seemed to give him what he wanted, a spirit with more permanence.

"Tyler?" His history teacher, Mr. Bernard, interrupted Tyler's reverie. Mr. Bernard was an old guy with the jowls of a bulldog. "Tyler, what day did General Sherman occupy the city of Savannah?" He wore a sour expression annoyed he'd caught Tyler daydreaming. His bald head gleamed under the fluorescent lights. "And what did he do when he succeeded?"

Tyler hesitated. He had read this section last night, but with the excitement of the reverend's visit and his dad and Siamura, he found it hard to concentrate. "Uh, December 20, 1864, and he sent a telegram to President Lincoln, saying the city was his Christmas gift to him." He thought the idea of a city as a present was awesome.

"Wrong. The date was December 22. Please pay attention from now on. Although you are right about the telegram," Mr. Bernard grudgingly added.

Tyler gulped. There were mutterings around the classroom, commenting on how harsh the teacher was. Several other students sat up straighter, putting aside their doodles and phones. For the rest of the class, Tyler focused on the lecture, pushing his worries to the side.

During the break before the last class of the day, Kevin found him. Eyes wide, he tapped Tyler's arm urgently. "Dude! Did you hear about Eric?"

"No, I…" Tyler glanced down the hall. Students parted the way for a figure dressed entirely in black. It was Matt, looking as healthy as ever, wearing a superior smirk on his face. He carried a book under his arm. Many students eyed him like he was a dangerous madman.

Matt sauntered up to them. "Guess what?"

Tyler and Kevin stared at him, not saying anything.

"I got that bitch demon to cure me." He slapped his stomach for emphasis and grinned. "Never better." He held up the book he was carrying. The cover said 'Latin' on it. "I'm going to use this to translate more of the Spiritorium. Next time, she won't even question us. You guys be ready. I'll tell Eric."

Kevin interrupted, "Dude, that's what I wanted to tell you. Eric got arrested when we went to the Apple store at lunch. That money she made was fake."

Matt's face darkened. "Fuck. I'll get her. I knew she was going to pull something." The bell rang, making them jump. "I'm gonna fuck her up." He trotted down the hall.

The bell rang and Tyler and Kevin hurried to their separate classes before Tyler could say anything. Eric arrested and Matt pissed off at Siamura — what a great way to finish the day. He worried about her. That amulet really hurt her whenever Matt used it against her. After class, he caught the school bus for the ride home, trying to figure out what to do.

Kevin sat down beside him as houses passed by the bus windows. "I am so fucked."

"Why?"

Jen plunked herself across the aisle from them. "Yeah, why? And Tyler, I'm coming over today."

Tyler glanced at her. "Again?"

"Not my fault. My mom has to work late."

Tyler sighed, "All right, whatever."

Kevin said, "What about Eric and the other stuff?"

Tyler shrugged his shoulders. "I don't know."

"They arrested Eric. They'll ask questions and he'll talk eventually if he hasn't already."

Anxiety churned in Tyler's stomach. Then he had a realization. "If he tells the truth, they'll never believe what he says. Have you thought about that?"

Kevin brightened. "Yeah, you're right."

They spent the rest of the bus ride discussing Eric's arrest and Matt's response. Kevin got off at his stop and Jen went home with Tyler. Tyler told Jen how Siamura almost attacked Reverend Woodward last night and how Dad had stopped her.

Jen put her hand over her mouth. "Oh my gosh. Do you think the Reverend will tell the cops and they'll come by and arrest you?"

"I hope not."

"Should we even be going back to your house?"

Tyler realized the cops could already be at his house, waiting to throw him in jail. Nevertheless, he had to know what happened to Siamura first.

"Yes. Where else would I go?"

There were no cop cars in front of his house, and he let out a breath. He opened the front door and walked in after Jen. “Siamura? Are you here?” He heard a movement from above.

Siamura came down the stairs, her faint perfume of trees following her. “Hello, Tyler. Why is Jen here?” Her wings shook, but she didn’t show any other signs of agitation. She surprised him by putting her warm hand on his shoulder. It startled him.

Jen said, “Tyler told me about last night. I’m really sorry. I gotta stay here until my mom comes. I told her not to bring anybody else.”

Siamura removed her hand from Tyler. She stood straighter and looked him in the eye. She seemed different, more direct and with less hesitation in her movements. She murmured, “I hope not. I do not want to meet any more of her friends. I am in her debt, however. She reminded me that I cannot hide forever.”

Jen blinked. “Tyler told me some stuff, but what really happened after we left?”

“He began a prayer. The last time I heard that prayer I was beaten and tortured for years, perhaps decades. I had a dispute with Christian priests centuries ago and the memory is still vivid. I lost mine-self and became angry. I only pushed him away. He should be fine. I was sure not to injure him.”

Jen eyed her seriously. “You showed yourself, like this,” she waved her hand, indicating Siamura’s green tail, wings, and tail. “To the reverend? Tyler wasn’t pulling my leg?”

“I did.”

Jen gaped at her. “Oh my god.”

Tyler asked, “You also showed your claws. Does that mean you could hurt somebody?”

Siamura’s tail flicked side to side. “Yea, I could, but I choose not to.”

“You seemed ready to attack the reverend until my dad grabbed your tail.”

Her ears flipped down. “It was a mistake. The reverend surprised me. It shall not happen again.” She turned and walked to the kitchen. Her tail and wings counterbalanced her steps. “Does ye want something to drink?”

Tyler and Jen followed, setting their bags on the kitchen chairs. The table and the lights above were whole and undamaged. Tyler gaped around the room. "What happened to the table? And the lights?"

Siamura stepped beside him. "I healed them."

"But there were huge chunks taken out and splinters everywhere. It took me forever to clean it up last night."

"I am a mearoch. Bending wood to mine magt is mine nature."

Tyler flicked the switch for the lights above the table. Nothing happened. "Well, the lights still don't work, but they look better."

"Alas, I cannot do much with the new devices."

"I'll get new light bulbs later."

Siamura stood in front of the open refrigerator. "It amazes me how much food and drink thou has in this age. So many variations, so much in plenty. I am in awe every time I open this contraption." Tyler and Jen told her what they wanted and she retrieved a Coke for each of them, pouring a glass of orange juice for herself.

Jen sat at the table. "Why is food so amazing to you?"

Siamura sat beside Tyler. "Have ye seen people go hungry?"

"Well yeah, because they were too fat and wanted to drop the poundage," Jen said.

Siamura shook her head. "I meant not that. I remember people searching in the muddy fields, looking for a few moldy grains to feed themselves. I held starving babies in mine arms, too far gone to save. People unable to move, an eye blink the only indication they still lived. Many were no more than animated skeletons. Ye are very fortunate."

Jen sat up. "People came to you?"

"They did. I tried to help as best as I could and managed to save a few."

Tyler said, "Yeah, she was the spirit of the forest. Lots of people believed in magic back then."

"There was more magt then too." Siamura paused. "Tyler, when thee came in the door today, thee seemed concerned. Did something happen today?"

Tyler sagged in his seat. "Eric got arrested for trying to spend the money you made."

"That is bad news. I assume the sheriff will investigate."

"Yeah." Tyler thought it strange the sheriff would be interested.

Siamura's tail flipped. "Thee should call thyne father, Tyler. The sheriff or his agents could come here to ask questions at any time. He should be here."

"Wait, how do you know that?" Tyler asked.

Siamura smirked. "The technology changes, but the methods do not." She rustled her wings. "I am here to help thee, and I am concerned." She reached and patted his hand. Tyler felt better, but he knew there was more to Siamura than what she said. He couldn't dwell on it because the cops were on their way, and they would want to talk to him.

Tyler picked up his phone and told his dad about the impending visit by law enforcement. His dad responded by saying he was on his way.

Siamura squeezed his hand, taking him from his thoughts. "I am going to wear mine disguise so I shall be with thee when the sheriff talks to thee."

"What if he asks about the summoning?"

"Thee can answer them but tell them not that Demosura and I are the same person."

"Should I tell them everything?"

"I would not volunteer any more information beyond what they ask for…"

Jen said, "Are you telling him to be difficult? Because they can arrest him for that."

Siamura said, "Aiden will be able to answer that better, but any officials will try to use thyne words against thee, even in mine time. Answer their questions with the permission of thyne father, but ramble not." She sipped her juice.

Tyler nodded. Siamura had changed. Her fear had receded, revealing a calculating, almost cold nature. Her ears remained at attention, and her movements were reserved, as if coiled and ready to strike.

Chapter 13

Interrogation

Aiden left his job early again. He left a message with Seth, his boss, and everyone on the project. He hadn't stayed a full day since Siamura arrived. Before last Thursday, Seth was looking for a way to get Aiden transferred to a dead end department and now he would have good reason to fire him. Aiden needed his job not only for the pay, but for the health insurance too. But he couldn't worry about that now. He had to beat the cops back to his house. He exited the freeway, turning on surface streets to make his way home — his tires chirping around the corners as he went.

Aiden pulled into the garage and leapt out of the car. No cop cars in front, which was a relief. Closing the garage door, he opened the interior door to the house. Breathing hard, he panted, "I got here as fast as I could," and smoothed his thinning hair.

His heart sank as he looked at the people in his house. He hadn't beat the cops after all.

Tyler piped up. "That's okay, Dad. Aunt Samantha was here with us."

Aiden blinked — Aunt Samantha? Tyler stood beside an attractive dark-haired woman in simple jeans and a top that accentuated her figure. Her hair wasn't just black. It seemed to leach out the light from the air around it, but it was her eyes that drew Aiden. Her green eyes were hard, staring down the strangers. Ah. Siamura in a different form. Her hands were drawn into fists, knuckles white, and her posture indicated she was prepared to do battle with everyone.

Jen jumped up from her seat on the other side of Siamura and brushed a lock of brown hair behind her ear. Her eyes darting about told Aiden she wasn't comfortable to be in the room with the police.

One of the cops, a woman stood. She was almost a foot taller than Siamura, with shoulder length brown hair and a prominent nose that gave Aiden the impression of a bird of prey, ready to swoop in and make a kill. She wore a tan trench coat that reminded him of a stereotypical 50's era detective. Aiden realized he did the right thing by leaving work immediately to defend his son from the likes of her. Beside her stood a large black man who looked like he could play football for a living. Even though he was over six feet, Aiden could tell he moved with economy, not with a swagger like most muscle-bound men. He wore a plain jacket and no tie, looking very reserved. Two uniformed police officers stood behind them.

The hawkish woman extended her hand. "I'm Detective Kim Tirzynski of the Oak Springs Police Department and this is Special Agent John Kerns of the Secret Service. These men behind me are Officers Biggs and Evans." They showed their IDs and Aiden shook their hands. She continued, "You must be Aiden Moray. We wanted to interview your son, but your friend insisted on waiting for you." The detective sounded like she wanted to jail Siamura for life.

Aiden said, "I'm sorry if there's been a misunderstanding. Anyway, I'm here. I hope there wasn't any trouble." He eyed Siamura and Jen. "Jen, could you wait for us upstairs?"

Jen picked up her backpack, visibly relieved to leave the room. "Yeah, I've got some homework to do." She darted up the stairs.

Aiden turned to the Agent. "Go ahead and have a seat. So, Agent Kerns, since you're with the Secret Service, why are you here? No one has threatened the President around here."

The man smiled easily, as if he had explained this a hundred times before. "A common misconception is that we only guard the President and other heads of state. The Secret Service also handles issues of counterfeiting, which is why I'm here today. I won't sit down until everyone else does." He smiled like he'd told a joke, but it didn't reach his eyes.

Aiden sat beside Tyler on the couch. Siamura sat on the other side of Tyler, while the detective and Agent Kerns took seats across from them. Agent Kerns continued, "I'm curious though. Samantha, where are you from?"

Siamura stiffened. "Scotland."

Detective Tirzynski said, "Your accent doesn't sound Scottish."

"I was raised all over Europe and the Mediterranean."

Agent Kerns shot the detective a glance and asked, "What's your relationship with the Morays? Are you Mr. Moray's sister?"

"Nay, I am his second cousin."

"And you're staying here?"

"Yea."

"I didn't see any suitcase or bag of yours upstairs when we did our search."

"They were lost."

Aiden glanced into the den and saw that the furniture had been rearranged, items from drawers heaped into a pile in the middle of the room. Apparently, they had finished searching the house. He wished he could have been here earlier, but it couldn't be helped.

Agent Kerns was remarkably calm, despite Siamura's antagonism. There was likely more to him than Aiden initially thought. He could be more dangerous than the detective, who seemed to be biting her tongue in the presence of a federal officer. The agent said, "Thank you, Ms. Darach. I'll get down to the matters at hand. The Oak Springs Police Department found counterfeit bills and that's when I was called in. I'm going to ask some questions, and I'd like to record this, if you don't mind." He withdrew a small recorder from his pocket and held it up. Siamura's eyes widened as if it might bite her.

'Ms. Darach'? Then Aiden caught a quick nod from Siamura. "Okay."

Agent Kerns set the recorder on the coffee table in front of them. "Where is Tyler's mother?"

Aiden said, "She's an attorney in New York, but we haven't heard from her in years."

"No child support?"

"No, I got custody of Tyler and I didn't ask for child support. She waived visitation rights."

Agent Kerns paused. “I see. Tyler, you’re a freshman at Washington High School. Is that correct?” The detective leaned forward.

Tyler looked at Aiden. Aiden said, “Go on.”

Tyler’s voice wavered, “Yes, sir.”

Kerns smiled. “Relax, son, I just want to sort out what happened. That’s all. Do you know Eric Tallman?”

Tyler said, “Yeah.”

“How did you meet him?”

“Through Kevin. He told me about Matt and Eric.”

“What are Kevin and Matt’s full names?”

“Oh, ah, Kevin Adams. We’ve been friends a long time, and Matt Solis, he’s a senior.”

Agent Kerns asked him to spell their names, which he did. “Why did Kevin introduce you to Matt and Eric?” Detective Tirzynski folded her arms, glaring at Tyler.

Tyler shifted in his seat and cleared his throat. “They said they needed a fourth.”

“A fourth? What for?”

“Matt and Eric wanted to do a summoning and they needed four people to do it.”

The detective snorted. Agent Kerns raised an eyebrow at her and continued, “I’m curious why Kevin introduced you to Eric and Matt. After all, they are upper classmen.”

Tyler glanced at Aiden. “I told Kevin some stories… ghost stories, and I guess they thought I’d be good enough to help them out.”

“Those must have been some impressive ghost stories.”

Tyler glanced at Aiden again. “I told him they were true.” Siamura clasped her hands together in her lap.

Kerns smiled and Aiden resisted rolling his eyes. The agent was leaning a bit too hard into his ‘good cop’ routine, humoring Tyler to get the maximum amount of information. “I see. You mentioned a ritual, a summoning, you called it. What was this summoning meant to do?”

Tyler fidgeted, wringing his hands. “Summon a demon.”

Detective Tirzynski pursed her lips. Her eyes flicked away then back to Tyler.

Agent Kerns paused, as if trying to consider such an unlikely event as true. "Can you tell us what happened?"

Tyler described the first ritual in the old house. He started with the smoke, continuing with a large creature that he couldn't see because of the smoke, and ending with Matt's injury. When he finished, he said, "You don't believe me, do you?"

Kerns smiled gently and leaned forward to meet Tyler's eyes. "I believe you saw something unusual."

Detective Tirzynski asked, "You're sure it wasn't the other boys playing a trick on you?"

Tyler shrugged. "I don't think so."

Kerns continued, "Did you see Matt's wound?"

"Yeah. It was just a scratch." Tyler indicated on his left torso where it was.

Thc Agcnt nodded. "Was there another ritual later on?"

Tyler described the second ritual in which they summoned Demosura, starting with Matt asking to break the football captain's legs, continuing with Demosura talking him out of it, then Matt throwing the knife at her, and Eric asking for money. The demon agreed to create the money, and then offered to heal Matt. Matt refused help from Demosura, even though she said the scratch was poisoned and he would die without her aid. Finally, Matt dismissed her and Eric gathered up the money.

"And you didn't ask for anything from this Demosura? Not even a little money?"

Tyler shook his head. "No, it didn't feel right. So, I didn't ask for anything."

The detective pressed, "Why not? You could have had lots of money or anything else."

Tyler faltered. Aiden spoke up, "I've always taught Tyler that there's a price for everything. Right, Tyler?"

Tyler nodded. "Besides, it wasn't right to ask Demosura for stuff. Not after Matt stabbed her with the knife."

"What about Kevin or Matt?"

"Matt wanted to hurt people. Demosura said she wouldn't do that."

"And Kevin?"

"Well, he did want a car, but Demosura told him it wouldn't fit in the room."

"He didn't want any of the money?"

Tyler didn't say anything. Siamura tensed her hand on Tyler's shoulder.

Detective Tirzynski said, "If you withhold information, it can be very serious. It would also reflect on you, your father, and your aunt."

Agent Kerns joined her, "She's right. These counterfeit bills threaten the security of the nation. We need to find all of them and who made them." He waited a beat. "So did Kevin take any of the money?"

Tyler grimaced with distaste. "Yeah, he did. But not a lot, not as much as Eric did."

Kerns pressed further. "And you didn't take even one bill from the pile? Eric or Kevin couldn't possibly know how much they had there."

Tyler grimaced but turned his face to Agent Kerns. "No, not even one. Eric and Kevin were too busy celebrating." His voice betrayed a tinge of bitterness.

"We talked to Matt Solis today, and he doesn't have a scratch like you describe – not even a band aid or a scar."

Tyler stared at Agent Kerns, open-mouthed.

Detective Tirzynski frowned and said, "Tyler, did Matt tell you how he lost the scratch?"

Tyler nodded. "You won't believe me either, but Matt said that Demosura healed him. He said that he had power over her — that he controlled her and made her heal him."

Tirzynski said, "You said that Matt dismissed Demosura. Where did she go?"

Tyler shook his head. "I don't know. I didn't see her leave."

Agent Kerns asked, "How did you know this Demosura was a demon?"

Tyler said, "She had bat wings and a tail."

The agent continued, "Could it have been a costume with makeup and prosthetics?"

Tyler ducked his head and wrung his hands. "I… I guess so. Maybe they were messing with me."

Siamura took advantage of the momentary pause. "What will become of Eric?"

Agent Kerns replied, "We will question him at length. After we finish, we'll release him to his parents."

Aiden said, "You don't think the boys made the money, do you?"

Kerns shook his head. "I'm not at liberty to discuss the details of the case. I'm sorry." He turned to the detective. "Do you have anything further?"

"No, nothing further." Tirzynski pulled her card from her pocket, handing it to Aiden. "If you have anything to add, please don't hesitate to call me, especially if you know where we can find this woman who calls herself Demosura."

Tyler asked, "Is Demosura in trouble?"

Agent Kerns said, "We just need to talk to her and figure out what happened. Then we can decide what comes next."

Tirzynski stood. "Thank you for your time." She shook Aiden and Siamura's hands.

When Agent Kerns shook Siamura's hand, he turned his wrist and examined her hand. "That's unusual. You have an extra finger."

Siamura snatched her hand back as if stung. "It runs in mine family." She kept her hands behind her, out of sight.

"Well good evening and let us know if you remember anything else." Kerns said.

As soon as the police left the house, Siamura sighed and her disguise dropped, her wings and tail shimmering into view. "She will be back. I trust her not."

Aiden eyed her. "She sure as hell didn't trust you. I tried to get here as fast as possible. What did you say to her before I got here?"

"I failed thee, Aiden. I allowed her in because they had something called a warrant. They said it gave them permission to search the house. I am sorry."

Tyler went to the kitchen table, stepping over a fallen chair, and handed Aiden a piece of paper. "I had to tell Siamura to let them in. They had this. If I hadn't stopped her, she would have attacked all four of them."

Aiden glanced at the paper. Across the top, it said *Warrant*. He didn't know what a warrant looked like, but this one seemed authentic. "Well, given the circumstances, neither one of you has failed."

Tyler said, "Then, after they came down the stairs, the detective and the agent wanted to question me. Again, Siamura told them she wouldn't allow it. Luckily, you came home when you did because I didn't know what to do next."

Aiden said, "Siamura, were you honestly going to take on four officers? Even with your claws, I appreciate your commitment, but they have guns and are trained in physical combat. They aren't like the reverend last night. There's no way you could be a match for them. And don't go around slashing people with your claws."

Siamura ducked her head. "I am sorry. I intend to uphold mine promise of protection."

Aiden realized that she truly believed that she could defeat the law officers even outnumbered four to one. Siamura was too small and fragile, even with her claws. He shook his head. She acted like a misbehaving teenager with an over-blown sense of invincibility. "That could have left us in a much worse situation than we are now. Siamura, we can't afford to have the police upset with us."

"They will try to do thee harm." Her tail snapped behind her.

"There are rules and laws to prevent that." Aiden held up the warrant. "They went through the proper procedures. They can't arrest us without cause."

Siamura's ears flipped forward. "With thyne permission, I need to hunt. That would be for deer, of course."

"That's okay with me. Just be careful out there." Aiden could feel her anger pushing him away. Tyler took a step back. The back door slid shut, shaking the house as she left.

Tyler looked at Aiden with wide eyes and hands open in askance. Aiden said, "Somehow I feel we don't know everything about her." He couldn't stop worrying about her though.

Jen cautiously came down the stairs. "What was that?"

Aiden said, "That was Siamura going out. She feels that she has not done enough to protect us."

Tyler flopped into a chair.

Jen said, “I was afraid she would try to fight all of them. She’s a little crazy.”

Aiden nodded. “We all must be a little crazy. Why don’t you two go upstairs and study? I’m going to try and clear a path down here.”

Chapter 14

A Gift

What the hell happened to your house?" Wendy had come over to the house to pick up Jen.

Aiden and Wendy were in the kitchen, away from the children. Thankfully, she didn't bring anyone else with her. Aiden didn't need a replay of Reverend Woodward's visit, not after this afternoon. Aiden had managed to get the kitchen area reasonably cleaned up, but the rest of the house was a mess.

Aiden opened the freezer and found a pizza. After this afternoon with the cops, it took his last bit of energy to pop it in the oven. "Don't start, Wendy. I really don't need any more stress today."

"Reverend Woodward told me that Siamura was a demon with bat wings, a tail, and everything. And I was wondering what would have happened for him to say that to me. He warned me that she was dangerous, that she was the Oak Springs Slasher. And your house…"

Aiden opened a beer. He offered her one because it was the polite thing to do. Everything was automatic with him — always having to make nice and cover his abilities. She accepted it out of habit. She, too, was traveling in the same behavioral ruts. He took a sip before replying, "No, Siamura isn't the Slasher. And maybe Reverend Woodward had some bad chicken."

She looked at him expectantly. "So? What happened here?"

"The cops searched the house. Satisfied?"

"That's awful. Why would they do that?" Her tone sounded genuinely sorry for him, but he knew that her sympathy wouldn't last.

He might as well come out with it. "Apparently, Tyler has fallen in with some less than reputable kids. One of those kids was caught with counterfeit money. So, the cops are searching each kid's house to find how it was made. Just don't start in on Siamura. I've already had a bad day."

Wendy sighed. "Well, what do you expect? You give a kid money, even if he knows it's fake, and of course he's going to try and spend it sooner or later." She sat at the table, pushing up the sleeves of her blue sweater. "You're a good guy, Aiden. I like you. Otherwise, I'd let you get in trouble and not say a word. I don't believe for a second that Siamura is a demon, but the reverend was right about one thing. I think she's dangerous to you and Tyler. She doesn't feel right to me. And don't tell me that BS about her being from Scotland. And Tyler's friend using counterfeit money will definitely get you in trouble. You could lose your job, go to jail, and who knows what else. For all we know she had something to do with that too."

He sat at the head of the table, looking to his left, he sighed as he saw magazines scattered about the den. "Siamura's innocent. Things will settle down."

"The police are going to think you personally had something to do with the money or the murders. You need to clear this up right away before it gets worse. Get rid of her."

The back door slid open, interrupting Aiden. Siamura stepped in wearing her human disguise with blue jeans and a green top and carrying a bulging deer skin. "Hello Aiden, Wendy." Closing the door, she set the skin on the table in front of them. The edges of the supple hide were whitish and streaked with red. Wendy recoiled from it, grimacing. Aiden sat up straighter, trying not to show any distaste at the carnage in front of him.

Siamura patted Aiden's shoulder. "I brought thee a gift." Opening the skin, she showed off the hunks of venison, most with bits of skin still attached. "I wanted to give thee something for the trouble I have caused thee. There was not any fresh meat in thyne refrigerator so I thought this would assist in a small way."

Aiden gawked at the bloody lumps of flesh sitting on the skin of a freshly killed deer. "Uh, thank you. I guess we'd better put it away." He didn't want to seem ungrateful for her gift, but he couldn't believe she'd brought it into the house in front of Wendy. He got up to get something to put it in, tuck it away and hope Wendy would forget she'd ever seen it.

Wendy stood. "Siamura, where did you get that? It looks like you just killed something. He's too nice to say that you are, but you are taking advantage of him."

Siamura's eyebrow crooked upward. "I did just kill a deer. What of it? And I am not here to take advantage of anybody. I am trying to help. There is a creature loose, killing people. I searched for it this evening, but alas I have not had any luck."

"What are you, some kind of TV super cop who can track down murderers?"

Siamura frowned with obvious confusion. "I am not a super cop."

Wendy's voice rose. "So how are *you* going to find the killer?" She looked up and down her small frame. "The police are handling it. You're just fooling yourself thinking you can stop him."

Siamura leaned on the table toward her. "I am the only one who can defeat it." Her eyes were fixed on Wendy's.

"But..." Wendy obviously didn't know what to say because she threw her hands up and turned away with a loud huff. She stomped towards the stairs, calling for Jen.

Siamura's head cocked to one side. Aiden's heart leaped to his throat as he saw her stalk around the table, eyes fixed on Wendy's back.

Aiden ran to block her. "Siamura, stop. Let her go." The last thing he wanted was another incident.

Her eyes flashed, but she spun and went into the den. She sat heavily on the couch, arms wrapped protectively about herself.

Wendy and Jen left and Aiden worked to put the meat away, worrying about the cops, the money, and the murders. When he turned around, he spotted wingtips over the couch, which shocked him back to the events of last night. She must have dropped her disguise when she heard the door close behind Jen and Wendy. He couldn't believe he'd slept with her. Why hadn't he said no? He was a father, and he had to act like a father, not like some sex-crazed pervert jumping into bed with some creature. It seemed like bestiality, yet it wasn't. Was she a beast, a woman, both, or neither? It couldn't be wrong when a person consented, yet what really concerned him was that he had enjoyed it.

Aiden knew from the first moment he had touched Siamura outside the back door four days ago she was different from any other spirit. She had taken his life and turned it inside out. He had promised himself he would help her because that was the right thing to do, regardless of her appearance, but after the encounters with Wendy, the reverend, and the cops, he wasn't so sure that was all of it. There was something more. Aiden could have sworn that she was going to attack the cops when they interviewed Tyler.

Unfortunately, that wasn't the only complication. He knew Detective Tirzynski and Agent Kerns weren't going to give up with just an interview of Tyler. They would track down Siamura, and in doing so discover he was not normal, and that supernatural things happened to him regularly. His life would be ruined.

The timer for the pizza buzzed, interrupting his thoughts. Aiden got the plates out for the three of them. Even though Siamura had eaten already, he wasn't going to exclude her.

Usually, he and Tyler ate in front of the TV, but Aiden wasn't in the mood for the added noise. He cut the pizza and set it in the middle of the table along with napkins and plates. It seemed like any other day, except for the messy house and a winged mearoch. He knew his life would never go back to the way it had been. He wasn't sure he liked it now, but there was no going back.

Tyler came down, slapped a couple pieces of pepperoni pizza on a plate, and went into the den to watch TV. He bent over, reaching for the remote, and straightened in front of the TV when he saw Siamura on the couch.

Siamura stood, her tail swaying side to side, barely missing the boy. "I shall move, have none worries."

Tyler set the remote back down. "Nah, I really don't want to watch it anyway."

Siamura walked around the couch to the kitchen table. "There is a police car with men in it watching the house. I do not want to cause any more hardship for ye. I should leave and stay elsewhere tonight."

Aiden sat at the table, taking a piece for himself. "Siamura, you're staying here. I don't like what the cops did, and it's a great pain in the ass, but I'm not turning you out." He couldn't name or rationalize it, but something in him refused to let her go. Maybe he had lost his sanity and was tired of playing it safe, or he had finally decided not to be ashamed of his ability. Perhaps it was a combination of both. Either way, he wasn't going to back down.

"I appreciate thyne kindness, but I should leave for ye safety."

"If I were concerned about safety, I wouldn't have let you stay to begin with."

Tyler put his pizza down. "You can't leave. How are you going to protect me if you're not here? Aren't you my protector?"

Siamura turned to him with her eyebrows raised.

Aiden had to admit he was surprised with Tyler's reaction too. Aiden smiled. "Both of us want you to stay. You're outvoted. Have a piece of pizza and I'll get you a beer."

She blinked at the both of them. "If ye feels that way, then I shall stay for now. Since I am staying, I should teach ye how to perform magt on a larger scale."

Tyler spoke around a mouthful of pizza. "How?"

Siamura said, "We can put the house back in order."

Aiden stood at the refrigerator, his offer to get her a beer forgotten. "You can do that?"

"The house has a residual memory of where everything was. We become the house and put things back where the house remembers them."

Tyler asked, "The house has a memory?"

Siamura smiled. "Fret not. Take mine hand. Come, Aiden. I shall show thee." She moved to the living room and sat on the floor. Tyler joined her. Aiden felt silly doing this, but he sat down on the other side of her.

She said, "Close thyne eyes and breathe slowly. Ye will feel dizzy at first, that is normal."

Aiden did as she instructed and had a strange feeling of vertigo as if his skin were too small. His perception went out, and he sensed the walls, the furniture, as he glided within the house. Flowing over the surfaces, he felt where things were missing and where the objects were that would fit into those vacancies. It was just a matter of shifting those objects back to the holes where they belonged. Siamura was there guiding them. He could feel her energy coursing around and through him, so when he found a drawer out of place, her power shifted it back to the proper location.

Things like clothes that moved around a lot were more difficult, but generally putting them back into the closet was sufficient. Small things like pens, clocks and books floated to their proper positions. The weird feeling of being in multiple places at once confused Aiden. Not only did he feel his body, but simultaneously he was in all the rooms at once. Somehow could see and hear within them too. All of his senses were active within the space of the house.

Siamura's hand tightened on his. She ushered him from the rooms of the house to return to his body, or rather, constricted his senses from the house to reside only where his body was. From room to room, she chased his perceptions until he sat on the floor of his living room.

Siamura's voice came to him from his ears, instead of within his head. "Open thyne eyes and take a breath."

He blinked. It was like going into the daylight after sitting in a darkened movie theater.

Tyler patted himself as if making sure he was still there. "Whoa, that was intense. Do you do that all the time?"

Siamura smoothed her hair. "Often enough, but not to move anything — only to observe." Her tail twitched behind her.

Aiden asked, "Is that how you were able to follow Tyler with your eyes closed when you first arrived?"

She nodded. "Yea, it is."

Tyler tried to stand but stumbled. Siamura caught him and eased him down to a seated position again. "Be slow. It will take thee a minute to recover."

Aiden didn't feel exhausted, but a sense of tiredness pervaded him. "How much time passed?"

"Only a few minutes — not long. Ye pizza is still warm."

"Good, 'cause I'm starving now." Tyler leapt up and snatched a piece of pizza from his plate, tearing into it. Aiden followed. He had to admit he was hungry too.

Siamura sat at the table and had a piece. "It is normal to be hungry afterwards. Thou has expended more energy than thee is accustomed." She took a long drink of her beer.

They devoured the pizza in silence. Aiden was surprised how hungry he was. He was just about to get up and look for something else to eat when the doorbell rang.

Siamura stood and walked to the wall by the kitchen. Placing her hand on it, she dipped her head for a moment. Aiden was going to ask what she was doing when the doorbell rang again. She instantly assumed her human disguise as Aiden went to the door. Through the peephole he saw Reverend Woodward and another man with him. Shaking his head, he walked from the door.

From the other side of the door the reverend said, "I know you're home, Aiden."

Siamura blocked Aiden from walking further away. "Allow him in. We must stop the stories here."

Aiden stage whispered, "Are you crazy? You almost killed him last night!"

She pointed at the door. "None the less. I need to resolve this."

Aiden stepped to the door. "Okay, but he's going to say another prayer…"

She smiled. "Oh, I hope he does." She positioned herself behind Aiden.

Aiden opened the door. "Yes? What do you want, reverend?" Two men stood on his porch.

Reverend Woodward pointed at Siamura. "There she is! She's hiding herself like last time!"

An older gentleman, shorter and rounder than the reverend with white hair around his bald head save for a tuft at the very front, patted the reverend's arm. He looked like an energetic professor who couldn't wait to tell you the secret of laser fusion. He pushed up his black framed glasses and said, "You must excuse the reverend. I'm Mr. Greg Richards. You must be Aiden Moray. I would very much like to come inside and speak with you." He stuck out his hand.

Aiden stared at the proffered hand, unsure what to do.

When Aiden didn't take his hand, Richards stepped past Aiden and into the house. "My, you're a pretty one. I'm Mr. Greg Richards." He shook Siamura's hand.

Siamura flinched. "I… I am Siamura."

Richards turned. "Well, come on reverend."

Reverend Woodward shook himself and stepped in.

Aiden glanced at Siamura, who nodded. He shrugged and closed the door. "If everyone promises to be civil then I suppose we can talk. Can I get anyone something to drink?" He led the way into the living room.

Richards took a seat in an armchair. "Just water for me, thank you."

Reverend Woodward sat in the other armchair.

Siamura followed Aiden into the kitchen. Aiden whispered, "Are you sure about this?"

She responded in kind. "Have none worry." She carried an orange juice and a water to the living room.

Aiden entered and set the one water on the coffee table in front of Mr. Richards. Siamura smiled as she set the water in front of the reverend. Aiden and Siamura sat on the couch together. Tyler followed and sat on the other side of Siamura.

Aiden said, "This is my son, Tyler."

Tyler nodded, glancing at the reverend.

Reverend Woodward watched Siamura, his hands on the armrests as if ready to catapult him at the mearoch. The tension in the air was palatable.

Mr. Richards grinned, shaking his head. "I've been hearing some quite amazing tales lately. Yep, a giant of a man slaughtering the good people of Oak Springs for the past couple of nights. People's pets done away with in the most gruesome ways. And a green skinned demon walking amongst us."

Aiden set his water on the table. "So, Mr. Richards, what's your connection with Reverend Woodward? Why are you here?"

Richards nodded. "The good reverend here called me about a story of a demon. I have studied the subject in depth." He raised his hand to stop Aiden from interrupting. "I wanted to see this for myself to see if this has any merit. The reverend said that you, Siamura, were a demon and moreover had attacked him. Only through Mr. Moray's intervention was the attack stopped. Is this true?"

Siamura sat up, her hands raised. "I assure thee that I am not a demon. Do I look like a demon?"

Aiden watched her closely. If things got out of hand, he might have to jump into action again.

Reverend Woodward began in a loud voice. "Our Father who art in heaven…" He stared directly at Siamura as he recited the entire prayer, his fingers gripping the armrest tightly.

Siamura stared right back at him as Mr. Richards eyed the two with raised eyebrows. She said, "I am not as familiar with the modern English version as the Latin. Pater noster, qui es in caelis…" She went on for several lines. Aiden could only assume it was correct. "Scisce Latine, Mr. Richards? Et tu, Reverend Woodward?"

The reverend frowned, saying nothing.

Richards nodded. "Ego loquemur Latine. That was impressive. I seldom hear it in Latin."

Siamura placed her hands on her knees. "Can a demon recite that prayer, Mr. Richards?"

"Ah… Well, no. According to the texts, no demon or agent of the Devil can recite that prayer. And I imagine only the Catholic clergy can say it in Latin."

The mearoch in her disguise smiled. "I will have to concede that I am not a member of the Catholic clergy, none-thing more than a student of language."

Richards laughed. "You being a member of the fairer sex I would have to agree with you."

Aiden said, "I hope that clears up any questions of demons. It is getting late."

Richards stood. "Clear as a church bell."

The reverend leapt up. "But I saw…!"

Everyone stared at him, Siamura with a raised eyebrow. Reverend Woodward shut his mouth and exhaled audibly through his nose.

Mr. Richards stood. "Come on, reverend. We've all had a long day."

The reverend nodded, grimacing.

Richards walked to the front door. "I shook her hand and she recited the Lord's Prayer in Latin. She may be a lot of things, but a demon is not one of them."

Woodward frowned at Siamura. "There's something not right about her. I'm going to get to the bottom of this."

Aiden opened the door for the pair. "Good night."

Mr. Richards nodded. "Yep, good night. Sorry to bother you."

Aiden closed the door after them and gave a sigh. "I think that went okay."

Tyler said, "I don't think Reverend Woodward was convinced."

Siamura remained in the living room, her disguise dropped, stretching her wings, and shaking her head. "I feel so unclean after saying that prayer." She shivered and drank all the orange juice.

Aiden's stomach growled. He went into the kitchen and fixed some sandwiches. He was still hungry after the spell they'd used to reorder the house. Tyler started in on his at the table. Aiden opened another couple of beers for himself and Siamura as they joined Tyler at the table.

Aiden bit into his sandwich. "So, what was the difference tonight? Last night you were about to tear into him and tonight you're praying in Latin."

She smirked. "I shielded the house from the effects of that prayer before they stepped in. I made the house a dead space for it, so none-thing would happen when he or I said it."

Tyler said, "What could have happened?"

"That prayer can alert those angels that tormented me centuries ago. I made it so the house deadened the prayer preventing it from going beyond the walls."

Siamura's tail flipped and hovered behind her as she finished her beer. She glanced at Aiden occasionally. He looked at her and she smirked and looked away, shaking her wings slightly, playing a game of being coy.

Tyler noticed her game. "What's the matter?"

Siamura said, "After I hunt, I get…"

Aiden interrupted her. "Siamura and I need a little time alone." She had a maddening tendency to be too direct, regardless of whom she was talking to.

Tyler picked up his plate and took it to the sink. "Yeah, I get it." Aiden detected a slight grin.

Siamura went to Tyler and kissed his forehead. She murmured, "I care for thee very much. Thyne father and I need to be intimate."

Tyler stared at her for a moment, eyebrows raised. "Oh, I get it. I'm not a kid anymore." He glanced at Aiden.

Aiden coughed, "I think that's enough." This was embarrassing.

Siamura gave Tyler a wink and a smile.

Tyler nodded. "Besides, I've got homework to do." He dashed upstairs.

As his footsteps receded, she turned to Aiden. "Was I too forthright? I like not to deceive him. He should know."

"You said you cared for him. Don't make promises that you can't keep."

"It is not a promise. I do care for him. I do not want him feeling worthless and unneeded." She wrapped her arms around him and kissed him. "I care for thee too."

Aiden didn't know what to say. He stared at her feeling like their relationship had rocketed ahead by months. Normally, he would be suspicious, but Siamura spoke with an innocence he didn't doubt.

"Did I say something wrong?" Siamura's wings sagged. "I have ruined thyne mood. I have ruined thyne house. The police suspect thee has some connection to me, they think I am the counterfeiter, and probably the murderer too. …and I have ruined thyne relationship with thyne son."

"No, you haven't ruined anything. I chose to have you stay here. It was my decision too. You say what you see. That's all." He took her hand in his.

She kissed him. "Can we go upstairs?" He swung her into his arms and carried her up the stairs while she kissed him. This time she weighed light as a feather.

Afterwards, as Aiden was drifting off to sleep, content and satiated, he heard Siamura open the door and creep out.

***

The next morning Aiden awoke to purring and the sensation of someone washing his chest. He thought it was a dream until he opened his eyes. He lay face up on the bed and Siamura lay across his body. Two smiling cat-like eyes greeted him. "May we stay in bed for the rest of the day?" She traced her tongue along his chin.

Her rough tongue tickled, feeling like a large domestic cat's. He grinned. "You're insatiable. If I didn't know you better, I'd call you a nymphomaniac." He drew her face towards his and kissed her.

She broke off the kiss. "What does thee expect after centuries of celibacy?" She licked his lips. Sitting up, she threw her leg over him and straddled him.

Afterwards his hand traced along the fur between her wings. Her head rested on his chest as she purred. The vibrations ran through his body. "What are we going to do? This can't last, not with the cops snooping around."

Siamura raised her head. "I left during the night to try to find the other fey. But I was unable to locate it. The longer it is free, the more dangerous it becomes for all of us." She went back to grooming him with her coarse tongue. It was oddly erotic. "I owe thee so much, both of ye. Everything seems unreal to me. Thee has shown me the first kindness in centuries. I keep expecting to awaken from mine dream. I am afeared to sleep then to awaken and none of this be real."

His finger caressed her long ear. "I have the same feeling, and if this is but a dream, then we should promise to each other not to wake up."

The clock radio snapped on and Aiden glanced at it, checking the time. An announcer came on hawking used luxury cars, no payments until next year. Siamura's head turned and she hissed at it, flashing her fangs. Aiden's heart kicked into overdrive, shocking him awake. It was like having a huge, angry cat lying on him.

He gently rolled her off him. "Sorry, tigress, but I need to get up and get to work."

She rubbed against him, protesting, but the newscaster's voice broke through his haze of lust. "In breaking news, police have discovered two more bodies in Oak Springs. Preliminary reports indicate that these deaths are the work of the Oak Springs Slasher. If verified, this would make these recent deaths the third and fourth victims of the Slasher. We go…"

Aiden clicked it off. Today had been starting off so well too.

Chapter 15

Betrayal

Tyler dressed, and before he went downstairs, glanced at his dad's bedroom door. Dad was running late again. Tyler smirked. He felt better about Siamura than that woman his dad had been seeing last year. If Siamura were to stay permanently with him and his dad… Wow, that would be really bizarre, but cool too.

The Wednesday morning sun streamed through the windows of the front doorway. Little specks of dust floated through the rays, glinting like small diamonds. He went into the kitchen and poured a bowl of cereal. His dad was always on him to hurry in the morning, but since Siamura, he'd been the one delayed. Not that he liked his dad being late, but he did like seeing his dad smile more and walk a little taller.

Dad came down in a rush. "We're running kind of late. Are you almost ready?"

Tyler looked up and saw Siamura's wings and tail flipping from behind the open door of the refrigerator. He smiled. "Don't worry. I'm going to catch the bus."

Dad said, "Oh right. Great. Thanks. I want you to come straight home after school, okay? There are too many things going on out there."

"Okay, Dad." Tyler carried his dishes to the sink.

The doorbell rang. That was strange. Nobody visited in the morning; all their neighbors were doing the same morning rush of getting out the door. His dad blinked at the door, not moving toward it. Siamura shifted into her human disguise wearing jeans and a green shirt and walked to the door. Tyler quickly followed her.

Aiden rushed in front of her. After looking through the peephole, he opened the door. "Hello?"

A woman, mid-thirties or so, with blond shoulder length hair stood on the porch. She had blue eyes that seemed to drill into them. "Hi, I'm your neighbor, Tami Samuels, from down the street, and I wanted to make sure everybody knew about the Oak Springs Slasher." She thrust a piece of paper at Dad. "We're all in danger. He's hit all around our neighborhood. It's only a matter of time before he comes to our street. In fact, they found two more bodies this morning."

Dad held up the leaflet. "So, what are you handing out?"

"That flyer has the police phone number and the most recent description. Report any suspicious people or cars to the police immediately. And, if you have a gun keep it loaded and with you at all times. That's my number and address at the bottom. I'm starting a neighborhood watch program and I'm expecting everyone at our first meeting tonight at my house. It's the second house from the big rock." Her words came out in a flood. Aiden closed his mouth, having tried to interrupt several times.

"I'll see you there at seven tonight. Bye!" Without allowing them to ask any questions, she turned, heading across the street. By the time Dad closed the door she was already ringing the doorbell of the Benson's.

Dad shrugged. "I was trying to tell her that the cops are already in that car in front of the Benson's she just ran past."

Siamura dropped her disguise and smirked. "She is frightened, which makes her miss observations. I am relieved that thee failed to tell her. That would have led to more questions."

Dad nodded as they walked back into the kitchen.

Siamura laid her hand on Tyler's shoulder. "She did bring up a significant point. Two more people were killed last night. If thee encounters anything threatening, call mine name, and I shall be there as fast as I can."

Tyler stopped. "Really? How will you hear me?"

"I will sense thyne danger. I am linked to thee, and as thyne protector, it is mine duty that no harm befalls thee."

"Cool." Tyler imagined Siamura swooping out of the sky, her wings wide and dark. He had to fight back a snicker. It would scare the shit out of anybody.

Siamura cocked her head at him, her brow furrowed as if she were confused at his reaction.

Tyler added, "I mean… yeah, that's good, uh, thank you."

Dad turned. "Just be careful. There are strange trees growing near here too."

Siamura's ears folded down, and her wings sagged. "That would be mine forest. I know not why, but it has started around the old house where thee and thyne friends first summoned me."

Tyler said, "Isn't that good? To have your forest back, I mean."

Siamura dipped her head sheepishly. "Yea, I feel better, but I worry. I know how humans react to the unusual as with Tami Samuels."

"Well, I think it's great. It means you'll be staying, doesn't it?"

She nodded. "I imagine it does, but thee has a bus to catch."

"Oh yeah." Tyler picked up his backpack and headed out the door. Siamura was staying. She made his dad happy and was pretty cool to be around. He felt like punching the air as soon as he opened the door until he saw the dark blue sedan with the two cops inside parked across the street. The men glanced at him and then away. Tyler pointedly avoided eye contact and hurried to the bus stop. It was weird to be watched, like they expected to catch him breaking the law right in front of them. He spotted that Samuels woman halfway down the street, still handing out her leaflets.

School seemed quieter than normal, as if everyone feared a monster that would pursue anybody making too much noise. Occasionally he heard people murmuring about the Oak Springs Slasher.

As soon as Tyler entered Mr. Bernard's room, the teacher straightened and blinked at him. Today Mr. Bernard made a point of not calling on Tyler, even when he was the only student with his hand up. It was maddening. Tyler had read the whole section on General Sherman's march through South Carolina and the controversy about Columbia and he could easily answer the questions.

After class, on his way to lunch, he ran into Kevin. He looked anxious. "Dude, I've been looking all over for you."

"I was in Mr. Bernard's history class like always at this time. What's up?"

"Matt and Eric are doing another summoning tonight and they want us to be there. They…"

Matt swaggered towards them, wearing his black duster. Eric was with him, clad in blue jeans and a black heavy metal T-shirt. The crowd in the hall parted to let them pass. Some stared, and others grimaced as if an unpleasant smell followed them.

Matt ordered Kevin and Tyler, "Let's go to the courtyard." He walked in that direction, not bothering to see if they would follow. The courtyard was a square of short grass and dust in between the school buildings with a stunted tree growing in the middle of it. It was forlorn and out of the way. Not many people used it, which probably was why Matt and Eric favored it.

Matt stopped by the tree and turned around to face them. "Okay, we're doing another summoning tonight at Eric's house. His parents won't be home, so we won't be interrupted." He laughed. "So, you guys got a visit from the cops?" He didn't even wait for them to answer. "They've got nothing. They can't believe that it actually happened. What did you tell them, Adams?"

Kevin squirmed about being put on the spot. "They searched my house. I told them the truth and they ran off."

Matt laughed again. "What about you, Moray?"

Tyler said, "I told the truth, but I don't think they believed me. They searched my house too."

Eric seemed oddly nervous, his eyes flicking from window to window as if expecting someone to spy on him. Kevin too, seemed like he wanted to be anywhere but near Matt and Eric.

Matt slapped his fist into his other hand. "I told them that nothing happened. Like I said, they have nothing. They're trying to get us to admit that we made the money, which is a crock of shit. Anyway, I did some more translations and improved the layout of the circle, so that bitch, Demosura, can't resist us. I'm gonna fuck her up good. She's one hot piece of ass, isn't she? I'd like a piece of that." His laughter was mirthless and cruel.

Eric joined him, but his laugh seemed strained. Tyler could feel his face getting warmer, but he had to play along like he didn't know about Siamura. He snorted and struggled to make it sound convincing. Kevin's eyes widened at Tyler, but he too laughed along with Matt.

Matt said, "What time do your parental units leave your house, Tallman?"

Eric replied, "Ah, five thirty or six o'clock. I'll put a flashlight in the window above the garage when they've left. Probably around a quarter past or so." He fidgeted, like he was not telling them something.

Matt grinned. "Cool. Meet at Eric's house at six thirty sharp. We'll need time to set up. And don't forget to bring your candles and stuff." He eyed the two younger boys. "What's the matter? We'll be able to do anything now."

Kevin ducked his head. "I'm grounded. I can't go."

Matt made a fist by his side. "You're not going to wimp out now."

Kevin said a little louder, his voice stressed, "I'm not even supposed to be talking to any of you." He turned to leave the courtyard.

Matt took two steps and tripped him, making Kevin fall into the dead grass. He put his knee in Kevin's back and said, "Listen, choir boy, you will be there tonight."

"But my dad will kill me!" Kevin whined.

"Tell him you need to meet some people for a school project." Matt stood. "Jesus! Are you always this pathetic? I should beat your ass right now until you grow a pair. I'm coming by your house tonight at six fifteen to pick your sorry ass up and don't make me knock on your door. You won't like it."

Tyler backed a few feet away from Matt. Matt straightened and somehow managed to grab Tyler by the upper arm. He whipped Tyler around like a rag doll, making Tyler's teeth rattle. "Don't you chicken out on me either, you little shit. If you don't show up tonight, I will pound you into the floor tomorrow morning and mop the floor with whatever's left. Comprende?"

All Tyler could do was nod. Crap, he was in deep shit now.

Matt squeezed Tyler's arm harder. "Do I need to pick you up too?"

Tyler shook his head quickly. “No, I’ll tell my dad that I’ve got a project too and he’ll drop me off near Eric’s house.” He held his breath hoping Matt wouldn’t kill him.

Matt smirked. “You learn fast, Moray. Don’t piss me off. I expect you to be at Eric’s house when I get there.” He dropped Tyler’s arm and sauntered away. Eric fell into step beside him.

Tyler and Kevin followed a beat later, Kevin brushing dead grass and dirt from his clothes.

Kevin said, “I thought you were going to go berserk when Matt said he wanted to do Demosura.”

Tyler didn’t reply. The thought of Matt doing anything to Siamura made his face go hot all over again. He forced himself to uncurl his fists. She didn’t deserve to be talked about like that. It had only been a few days ago when she’d hatched in his breakfast nook. Yeah, she’d scared the crap out of them when she’d almost attacked the reverend, but she didn’t deserve what Matt had planned. If Matt and Eric ganged up on her, she’d be in trouble.

Kevin continued, “Is she still at your house?”

Tyler eyed him. Even though he was the freshman and Kevin the sophomore, he felt older and surer than Kevin. Tyler opened the door. “She left. I don’t know where she is.” He hoped that Kevin believed him.

The rest of the school day passed uneventfully. It bothered Tyler that Kevin had told the cops about Siamura, but he wasn’t blameless either. He’d told them that Kevin took some of the counterfeit money. He hated himself for that, but he hated Kevin more for telling the reverend in the first place. And he hated Matt most of all for being an asshole. Tyler always thought of himself as being stronger, but it was bullshit. He couldn’t trust anyone, yet no one could trust him either. Everyone was lying and double-crossing each other. And tonight, he would betray Siamura. The back of his throat burned at the thought.

He climbed on the bus for home. Jen wasn’t there, and Kevin didn’t sit next to him, but he did sit nearby. Tyler preferred it that way. He was still trying to sort out how he felt about all that was going on.

When he got to his house, a dark blue car was still there, but different cops were sitting in it. Tyler tried to ignore them as he entered the house and closed the door behind him. Silence pervaded the house, as Siamura came down the steps on soundless feet. “Thee seems troubled.” Tyler glanced at her, but he knew what he had to do and turned away. She came closer, tilting her head with a frown.

Suddenly, she wrapped her arms around him. He breathed deep. Her forest scent had a hint of apple.

“I suspect it concerns me. It will be fine.” She held him, not speaking, patting his back gently for a long moment. Tyler dropped his bag and put his arms around her until his hands bumped into her wings. She felt warm and safe. He thought it was funny he wasn’t afraid or disgusted by her appearance anymore.

He took a breath and released it. Siamura loosened her grasp on him, and he stepped away. He didn’t know how to tell her, but if he was going to betray her, he wanted her to know. “Matt and Eric want to do another summoning tonight. They want me to help them. Kevin too. I don’t want to, Siamura.” He couldn’t bring himself to repeat what else Matt said about her.

“It is not the fault of thee. I was expecting Matt to try to entrap me again. Thee will need to help him too, or he and Eric will become suspicious, perhaps dangerous.”

“Matt did say he would beat the crap out of me if I didn’t show up tonight. But they want to hurt you.”

“Hmm, thee should go along with the ritual until I appear. During the summoning, wipe off part of the circle so that I will be released. It can be a small break, the width of thyne thumb will do.”

“Matt will kill me if he sees me do that. Why do you have to show up?”

“It is mine curse. I must appear or I will become sick. The sickness will not leave me until I comply. If thee breaks the circle, then I shall be able to leave it and deal with Matt and Eric.”

“They’ll gang up on you. What about the blue amulet? Matt is going to use it.”

“I shall distract him while thee takes the amulet. But there is one thing. Do not allow him to touch the knife to it.”

“But Matt is bigger than I am. He threw Kevin to the ground today. Can’t you just take the amulet away from him?”

Siamura shook her head. “I cannot touch it, nor influence it. But I swear I will distract him.”

“Matt’s a senior! There’s no way I can fight him.”

“Do not fight him, take the amulet from him. I will help as best as I can, but thee is the only one that can touch the amulet.” Her fingers brushed his arm. “I am pleading for thyne help Tyler. I cannot do it. The magt prevents me.”

Tyler blinked. It was up to him to give Siamura a chance to break free. He knew she couldn’t count on Kevin or Eric, so that only left him. “Okay, I’ll try.”

She smiled. “That is all any of us can do. Does thyne father know of the ritual?”

“Not yet, I’ll call him.”

Tyler picked up his bag and started up the stairs. He phoned his dad and let him know that another summoning was taking place tonight. His dad told him to wait until he got home and they’d talk tonight — and to get his homework done. He seemed remarkably calm, but then his dad knew about spirits. If it had been Kevin’s dad Tyler could imagine his head exploding.

But he found it hard to concentrate on his schoolwork when the summoning was so near. The candles and quartz were in his bag, ready to go. He had wrapped the stone in a T-shirt to protect it and to give him something to wipe away a bit of the circle for Siamura. After a while, he heard the garage door open. His dad was home. He hoped Dad wouldn’t be angry.

“Tyler?” It was Dad downstairs.

“Yeah?” Tyler opened his bedroom door.

“Let’s eat and I’ll drop you at Eric’s house.”

That was a surprise. His dad didn’t mention that on the phone earlier. “You’re taking me there?” Relief flooded him.

“Yes, I am. I don’t want you walking over there with a murderer on the loose. I’ll park away from the house. Come on. Siamura has fixed us dinner.”

Tyler grabbed his back and headed downstairs. Siamura made spaghetti with a salad. It tasted odd. The meat was different, with a strong tangy flavor. He wasn’t sure if it was safe to eat, but he found that he didn’t want to hurt her feelings. “Uh, what is it?” He tried hard not to sound negative.

Siamura smiled. "It is the venison that I brought last night. It has a stronger flavor than the beef that thee is accustomed to. I cooked it, and it is safe for thee to eat. I can make something else if thee likes it not."

Tyler shook his head. "No, I like it. I'm just not used to it." He took another bite. Knowing to expect the stronger taste, he found that he could not only eat it, but enjoy it. He didn't want to disappoint Siamura.

She had a few bites. It was fascinating to watch her dodge her fangs with the fork. "Aiden, I shall need the rest of the meat after the ritual. I may need to expend a great amount of magt, and I will need to replenish mine-self."

Dad thought for a moment. "I'll put it in the large ice chest and stow it in the trunk of the car." They finished their meal, and Aiden filled the plastic chest with slabs of deer meat while Tyler watched in awe.

"You can eat all of that?" Tyler asked.

Siamura averted her eyes. "Thee has not seen me feed. I can consume an entire carcass."

Dad closed the lid. "Okay, we'd better go or we'll be late. Come on, Siamura."

"I cannot travel in the metal thing," she said, referring to the car.

"Well, how are you…" Aiden hefted the ice chest and walked to the garage.

Siamura shook her wings. "Worry not about me. I have these."

With a shake of his head, Aiden let her go. Tyler rode in the car with his father. The top was up against the night. The streetlights went by like on any other drive. In fact, everything seemed normal, except his dad was driving him to a summoning ritual.

Dad said, "Be careful, okay?"

Tyler sighed and fell into the habit of being annoyed by Dad's concern but caught himself. He tried to sound nonchalant, replying, "I will. Don't worry." He directed Dad to Eric's house.

Dad parked around a corner a block away and turned off the engine. "Make sure the door is unlocked so I can get in."

"You're coming in?"

"Of course. I'll wait fifteen minutes or so, then I'll follow you in. Just have the door unlocked. I'll be downstairs."

"Siamura wants me to take the blue amulet from Matt. She said she can't touch it."

"Then when I hear people struggling, I'll come in and help you. Matt's a senior? Isn't that what you told me?"

Normally Tyler would have been upset about his dad insisting on coming inside, but it made him feel better, knowing that Dad would be close by, considering what he and Siamura had planned. Tyler wasn't entirely sure he could grab the amulet without Matt beating the crap out of him, even with Siamura's help.

Tyler hopped out, slung his bag over his shoulder, and walked the rest of the way to Eric's house. The Halloween decorations on some of the neighbor's houses were a pale mockery of what was about to happen.

The lit flashlight in the upper window signified that the plan was still on. There were three blue sedans parked near the house, but not in front of it reminding Tyler of the car parked outside his house the cops sat in. It was too dark to see if there was anybody inside the cars, but he had the distinct feeling of people watching him. He pretended not to notice and rang the doorbell.

Eric pulled open the door. "What took you so long? Everybody's here. Let's go." Tyler stepped to the side to make sure the door wasn't locked. Eric waved him forward. "Go ahead upstairs, same place as last time."

Tyler saw him lock the door. Then as he turned away, he heard the deadbolt slide back again. Tyler turned around to double-check what he had heard. "Could I get a glass of water?"

Eric sighed loudly. "Yeah, in the kitchen." He turned off the light and walked towards Tyler.

Tyler tried to look around him without being obvious, but he couldn't see the lock. He stepped to one side, then the other. His heart dropped — the deadbolt was undone. Eric had purposely left the door unlocked. He turned around before Eric ran into him and went into the kitchen. Eric grabbed a glass out of the cabinet and filled it with tap water. "Here. Now let's go." Eric was twitchy, his hands never resting long anywhere, not like his usual calm self.

"Thanks." Tyler took a sip. Eric was up to something, and Dad would run right into whoever else was coming. He couldn't think of a way to warn his dad without letting Eric know and had to follow Eric upstairs.

When they got to the spare room, Matt was busy inscribing a circle with white chalk on the cheap plywood floor. Matt nodded in Tyler's direction and went back to copying the symbol drawn on the paper he held in his hand. Eric picked up another paper and piece of chalk and wrote another symbol in the large pentagram on the floor.

Kevin set his candles out. "Dude." He seemed twitchy too, glancing around the room like something was going to grab him. Only Matt was full of arrogant confidence, sketching on the floor in broad strokes.

Tyler said 'hi' to Kevin and walked around the perimeter of the circle. Siamura's symbol, the skull and graceful branches, lay in the center of the pentagram. He took a seat with his back to the wall against the remains of the rolled-up carpet facing the closed door. His spot felt as claustrophobic as last time, the carpet brushing against his lower back. He pulled out his candles and quartz and set them up placing the quartz on the folded T-shirt close to the chalk line. He watched as Matt and Eric continued drawing on the wood floor.

There were new symbols in the layout that made Tyler's chest clench with dread. He didn't know what they were, but with Siamura's symbol in the center, they had to be about her. And with Matt's plans for her, they couldn't be good.

Matt finally stood, dressed all in black, emanating a malevolence that dripped onto the floor and infected the room. Tyler shivered.

Matt murmured, "I have you now, bitch demon." He turned to the others and pounded a fist into a hand. "Come on, let's do this fucking thing. We got demon ass to kick." He pulled his phone from his pocket. "I want to see everyone's phone and I want to see you turn it off." The three of them followed his instructions and returned them to their pockets.

Eric went around the circle, lighting the candles. When he had finished, he turned off the overhead light. The candles radiated a deep red glow, as if Hell itself had decided to creep into the room. Matt opened the Spiritorium to a marked page. He reached into his pocket and pulled out the dark blue amulet, the gold lettering glinting in the candlelight. He set it in the middle of the book. Tyler's fingers itched, filled with a sudden urge to snatch it up and run out of the room. But Matt would kill him if he tried.

Matt launched into his invocation of the Spirit of Air just like the last ritual. Tyler invoked the Spirits of Earth. He lowered the quartz and Eric began with the prayer of Fire. Tyler glanced at the others. Their attention was on Eric. Tyler decided that now was the time to make his move. He made a quick rub over the circle's perimeter with the edge of the shirt as he set the quartz down on the T-shirt. He held his breath, his hands shaking, afraid Matt had noticed his betrayal.

Eric finished, and Kevin spoke his supplication to the Spirits of Water. No one glanced at Tyler as he withdrew his hands from the quartz. He only hoped that it was enough for Siamura to escape the circle. Matt continued with the ceremony. Even though the words were in Latin, Tyler could tell that they were different from the last summoning. Eric started the next section, in English the same as before. They went back and forth for a while. The energy in the room rose but darker than last time, like a sickness rotting from the inside out. It stroked the hair on his arms, leaving an invisible taint. He wanted to crawl into the closet and hide under the boxes there. He steeled himself and repeated Matt's last lines along with Kevin and Eric. Matt clutched the blue amulet tightly rubbing the top of it with his thumb.

Tyler hoped his father could make it inside, but it was bothering him that Eric had left the door unlocked. Eric had to have a plan and he feared Dad would run into whoever Eric was waiting for. This situation was twisting out of control, everybody was double-crossing everyone else. The room reeked with the relentless darkness, coiling in on itself as if ready to strike.

The candles began to smoke. This didn't happen the last time they summoned Siamura. The vapors converged into the center of the circle and swirled like a small tornado. Siamura's green form took shape in the center. First, her feet were solid, then her knees, and her thighs in the black shorts. A wave of visibility flowed up her body until finally her head and wings were revealed.

She made a small bow. "I have come, Master."

The amulet in Matt's hand glowed balefully, giving him a corpse-like pallor. He held the amulet in one hand and his dragon dagger in the other, drawing the two closer together. "Grovel, damn you."

"Yea, Master. There is no need…" She quickly dropped to her knees, but her tail whipped out and snatched Matt's hand holding the knife.

Without thinking, Tyler sprang at Matt, grabbing for his hand holding the amulet. If he could get it away from Matt, they would have a chance. Matt's hand with the dagger was still held fast by Siamura's tail. Matt's mouth gaped and raised his other hand with the amulet to ward Tyler off, placing it directly in front of Tyler. Tyler grabbed it and tried prying Matt's fingers off the amulet. However, Matt was too strong for him, and Tyler began to twist around.

"Let go!" Matt yelled.

Something struck Tyler on the side of his head, but he wasn't going to release Matt's hand. He curled around the hand and the amulet within. He felt himself flung against the wall or floor. He had slipped, losing his sense of up or down, but Matt's hand smacked the surface first, and the amulet went flying. Tyler released Matt and fell forward, landing on top of the amulet. He scrabbled and stuffed it into his jacket pocket.

"Stop!" Siamura's voice cut through the confusion. Tyler rolled face up near the door. Siamura stood over a prone Matt against the wall to Tyler's right. She held Matt back from pursuing Tyler with one hand. She was definitely out of the circle. Eric stood still behind her, watching her tail which still held the knife. It waved in front of him like a cobra ready to strike. Kevin hadn't moved. He remained seated on the floor, gawking at the scene.

Matt spat at Tyler, "You stupid asshole. She's going to kill us."

Siamura picked Matt up by his upper arm and hefted him off the ground like he weighed nothing. Her voice was close to a growl. "I kill not people." Though, it sounded as if she would make a special case for Matt. She turned and her tail drove the dagger hilt deep into the wall where Matt was. The thump rattled Tyler's jaw. Plaster dust puffed out around the weapon. She held Matt over the circle. "Does thee know what this symbol is?" She pointed with a long finger downward. Matt shrank from her, cowed by her speed, strength, and glowing green eyes.

Tyler watched her, afraid she'd grow giant claws and fangs again. And his dad wasn't here to grab her tail. *Where is Dad?* Had he done the right thing by breaking the circle? Her eyes looked positively demonic. She saw him and her eyes not only dimmed but motioned for him to move away from the door. He stumbled back to his place by the quartz.

Matt squirmed in Siamura's grasp. He had both hands on her one, yet he couldn't free himself. "Ow! That hurts, bitch!"

She dropped him casually as if discarding an empty soda can. "Thee knows not what that symbol does, does thee?"

Matt landed on the rolled-up carpet, his head thumping against the wall. "It's to control you, and it would've worked if this asshole hadn't hit me." He lunged at Tyler.

Tyler cringed, but Siamura's tail snapped around Matt's outstretched arm. She was incredibly fast. Matt yelped in pain. Siamura snarled, "If thee touches him, I will break thee. Am I making mine-self clear?" The sound of her furious voice chilled Tyler down to the bottom of his heart.

Matt tried using his other hand to pull her tail from his arm. A wail grew louder in his throat. Desperately, he struggled against her, but without success. Tyler's hands shook as he scooted away from him. He almost felt sorry for Matt.

"I repeat. Does thee understand me?" Her voice was solid and unyielding as an old oak.

Tears ran down Matt's cheeks. He rasped, "Yes, yes, let me go."

"Good. We have progress." Her tail released him.

Matt fell over and curled into a ball around his hand, gasping for breath.

Eric's voice wavered, "So, do you kill us or…?"

Siamura raised an eyebrow at Eric. "I am thyne protector, fool. I am to protect ye from that." She pointed to the nasty symbol that she had indicated to Matt earlier. The symbol was all angles and geometric shapes, and it made Tyler's skin crawl whenever he looked at it.

Eric said, "But you're a demon. You're going to eat our souls and send us to Hell."

"Wrong!" Siamura shook her head. "I do not know what these souls are or what to do with them. I am sick of this game. None of ye know what ye are doing."

They all stared at her, Matt's soft moans of pain breaking the silence.

She continued, "That symbol is not to control anything, as Matt well knows. It is a glyph of another being of magt who will try to kill ye. I have been hunting it for days to none avail." She knelt in front of Matt, and her voice softened. "What was thee attempting to accomplish with these ceremonies, Matt? I want to know."

Matt hugged his arm, whimpering, but didn't answer.

Eric pointed at her. "You were supposed to punish those jocks and other assholes who were on our case." He retreated against the wall by the window, putting the maximum distance between himself and the mearoch. "Instead, you made counterfeit money and got me into trouble. Some protector you are." Kevin crawled towards the window too but stayed seated as if standing would call her attention to him.

Siamura stood and spun to face the door in one fluid motion. Tyler wondered why, but moments later the door flew open. The ceiling light flicked on. Two men in blue windbreakers spread out from the door. One was white, the other black. The third person was a woman in a tan trench coat, with straight, dark hair cut to her shoulders. All three pointed their guns at Siamura.

The black man yelled, "FREEZE! Don't move!"

Tyler cringed. It was one thing to see guns on TV, but when three of them were pointed in his direction, he didn't feel very brave. At the doorway, two more guns pointed at Siamura, their wielders hidden behind the edges at each side of the door. Tyler sank lower, his hands inching up, not taking his eyes from the scene playing out in front of him.

Chapter 16

Protector

Tyler squinted against the bright overhead light. He recognized the black man on the right as Special Agent Kerns and the woman in the center with the hawk-like nose as Detective Tirzynski. He didn't know the third guy on the left, but he was bigger than Agent Kerns and wore a blue windbreaker, probably another federal officer. All of the three were taller than the mearoch, and they each had a gun pointed at her.

Everything seemed to stop for a moment as each person sized up the situation. There was a flicker of shock on the law officers' faces as they saw Siamura with her green skin and dark wings, but it passed quickly. Siamura stood in front of the boys with her hands raised casually. Tyler wondered if Siamura knew what guns could do. She wasn't reacting with any indication she knew those weapons could kill her. Tyler, despite his fear, started to crawl to her. He wasn't going to let her ignorance become her death sentence.

In the next instant, green flashes erupted on the officers' hands. All three yelped as their guns flew across the room and crashed through the window at the far end. The door behind them slammed shut as the men on the other side shouted in surprise.

With a loud crack the plywood floor in front of the door bulged upwards and a tendril of wood shot up from it. It covered the seam between the door and the wall, sprouting more tendrils sideways to anchor itself to the door and wall. The wood continued to grow, the brass knob disappearing under the wood gone wild. The tendrils spread fingers from the edge reaching for the center of the door. Meanwhile more tendrils, like roots, stretched along the wall further anchoring itself. All this happened within the space of a heartbeat sealing the door shut. Tyler stopped trying to get closer to Siamura.

The second agent charged Siamura, looming over her. Agent Kerns, seeing his partner had advanced, took a step forward to assist him. Detective Tirzynski reached for something at her belt. It looked like the mearoch would be squashed like a moth.

The agent grabbed one of Siamura's arms and with a kick, tried to sweep her feet from under her, except her feet weren't there for him to kick. Overbalanced, he landed on the floor on one knee while Siamura shot upwards to the ceiling so fast Tyler almost missed it. She rested, her back against the ceiling having slipped her arm out of the agent's grasp. She hung there, defying gravity, her wings motionless and partially open. Agent Kerns reached for her.

Siamura's leg snapped out, the blow forcing Agent Kerns into the detective and knocking the handcuffs out of her hand with a clatter. Landing behind the other agent, Siamura snatched his foot with her tail, tripping him. Siamura knelt over the prone man, and roots broke through the floor with furious cracking sounds, like blind worms spewing splinters. They wrapped around the agent's outstretched wrists and held him to the floor. The man screamed and Tyler cringed.

"Hold!" Siamura stood in front of Agent Kerns, just getting to his feet to attack again. She blocked him with one hand. Incredibly, he hesitated and the detective did so too. Tyler shivered in place. Everything was happening so fast.

"Stop ye advances," Siamura continued. "Ye are in danger." As she spoke, the man on the floor quieted and tried to turn his head in her direction.

Detective Tirzynski asked, "Are you Demosura?"

Siamura smirked. "They know me by that name." She nodded in the boys' direction. "Though mine name this time is Siamura."

Agent Kerns moved, but far too slowly. Siamura spun, knocked his feet out from under him and had him on the ground, face down. Tyler blinked in disbelief as she held both the Agent's hands behind his back. "Do I bind thyne hands too, Agent Kerns? Or does thee swear to leave me be?"

The detective stepped forward to help, but Siamura's tail whipped in front of her like a snake ready to strike. Siamura shook her head. "Halt, Detective Tirzynski. Stay back. Agent Kerns, does thee swear?" She gave his hands a jerk.

Agent Kerns breathed, "Yes! I swear."

Siamura lifted Agent Kerns as if he weighed nothing and tossed him beside the detective. Detective Tirzynski bent to help him up, but he refused. Instead, he gathered himself to attack the mearoch again.

Siamura snatched him up by the collar. She held him off the floor. "Stop! Thee swore, or are thyne words worthless?" Tyler gaped as both Siamura and the agent rose off the floor.

Agent Kerns gasped and gurgled, both his hands on Siamura's slender one, unwilling to give in.

The detective yelled, "Stop! You're killing him." She drew a fist as if to punch Siamura.

Without turning her head from the man, Siamura's tail whipped around Tirzynski's hand. Siamura rumbled, "Yield to me, Agent Kerns, or thee will pass out."

Agent Kerns sputtered, "Yes, yes."

Siamura dropped the man as if punishing a misbehaving child. He landed in a heap, his legs failing to support him. "Wise choice." She returned to the floor, fixing her cat-like eyes on Tirzynski. "Detective, does thee swear not to harm me and mine charges? Or must we have a trial by combat also?" Detective Tirzynski brought her other hand to try to pry Siamura's tail from her wrist. Siamura slammed her tail towards the floor, forcing the detective to her knees.

Detective Tirzynski looked up at Siamura. "I won't fight you." Siamura released her. The detective held her wrist to her chest, blinking rapidly.

Matt swung his black overcoat around himself and grinned. "Ha! We beat the cops. That'll teach you for interfering." He stepped forward and drew his foot back to kick the prone agent in the gut.

Siamura's tail flicked out and deflected Matt's boot. "What is thee doing? The man is down. There will be none unnecessary violence."

Matt stumbled but regained his balance. "Bitch! I'm your master!"

Siamura backed him to the wall. “That may be, but first I am thyne protector and that includes saving thee from thyne own stupidity. Why did thee call me this time?”

Matt stared at her, but Eric spoke up. “The voices, they won’t shut up. They keep getting louder.”

Siamura faced him in graceful motion, reminding Tyler of a jungle cat — a lion or a tiger. “That is because thee summoned me. The other spirits know that ye brought me through and want thee to help them too.”

Matt screamed, “But you can make them stop. You’re a demon lord.”

Siamura shook her head, laying her ears back. “I do not lord over anything and I cannot make them do anything they do not want to. They view the four of ye as magicians and ye needs to learn to live accordingly. I am sorry.” She halted. “Detective, please tell thyne compatriots at the door to leave the building.”

Tyler could still hear the men pounding on the door. It had started out as a lightweight interior door, yet now the wood of the door had fused with the wood of the surrounding doorway. The two sections had grown together as if they were never individual pieces of wood. No wonder the men outside couldn’t knock it down. They would have to take out the entire wall. It was like the door became stronger the more they tried to break it down.

The detective was about to bang on the wood, but hesitated. Apparently, the thought of touching the mutant lumber repulsed her. Instead, she yelled, “Hey! Stop! This door is not going to budge. You’re making it worse.”

The pounding stopped. A man’s voice came from the other side. “Are you all right, detective?”

The detective called back, “Yes. Just stand by.” She turned to Siamura. “You can’t hold us hostage forever.” She glanced at the door again.

“Kill them, Demosura.” Matt ordered.

Siamura’s ears stood up. “I will not kill anybody. Furthermore, I am not holding anyone hostage. I am thyne protector, and protector of the rest of ye that summoned me. By extension, I must protect thee, Detective Tirzynski, Agent Kerns, and this unfortunate gentleman at mine feet.” She stepped to the circle on the floor and pointed at one of the symbols. “Matt, thee not only summoned me this time, but also this creature. This is the creature that thee wanted to destroy everything, and whom I suspect is the cause of thyne serial murders, detective."

Agent Kerns gathered himself and stood up, brushing off his slacks. "This is really far-fetched, don't you think?" he said to the room.

The detective said, "Drop the costume and give yourself up. And turn off whatever projection you're using to create the… roots and stuff."

Siamura only stared at them, her tail flicking from side to side. The room became suddenly cooler. The light above flickered and then went out entirely. By candlelight Tyler saw small roots emerge from the floor and walls in a wave towards the door. Screams from the other side of the door grabbed their attention. The cries quickly retreated from the door. Detective Tirzynski snatched at her radio. "What's going on out there?" Static was the only response.

Siamura's eyes glowed an eerie green. "I am clearing the house. I cannot prevent the creature from answering the summons, but I will not have people getting killed because they were in its way."

Tirzynski shouted, "You can't expect me to believe that!" She stepped toward Siamura.

Siamura flexed her wings and lowered her voice to a throaty rumble. Detective Tirzynski stopped her advances. "I care not what thee believes. Whether thee likes it or not, I am responsible for ye lives, and ye will follow mine instruction. This creature is coming and it will kill ye. I am charged to protect ye. When it comes through that door, I am going to hold it, and I want all of ye to run from the room and away from this place."

"This is all an elaborate hoax," Agent Kerns said, "I don't believe for a minute that you're a demon and that there's another one coming."

Siamura raised her eyebrow at them, her ears stood up. "Sometimes I think it would be easier to let all of ye die. I leave blameless and the creature kills all the people who are causing me problems. What say thee to that?"

The humans in the room stared at her. Tyler thought it was impressive Siamura still hadn't shown her claws. Apparently, she really meant the promise she made to Dad.

Her tail flicked once. "None more argument. If ye leaves too slow, I will toss ye from the window. This creature is not human. Human beings are its food."

Tyler cried out as the house shook as if a wall had come down. Siamura jumped to the detective and yanked her away from the door. “Stay behind me!” Tyler didn’t wait to be told and retreated from the door. Siamura’s tail pushed Agent Kerns behind her too. The roots holding the prone agent released his hands. He lunged at the winged woman and the detective grabbed his arm.

He stopped, but it wasn’t Tirzynski holding him back. It was what Siamura was doing.

Siamura turned, but her face wasn’t green and human-like anymore. She had black fur and a cat’s muzzle, large upper and lower fangs, sharp teeth filling her mouth, with saliva dripping onto the floor. Claws the length of a finger grew from Siamura’s digits that had become cat’s paws. The claws were black, and edged both front and back like knives, glistening as if oiled. Her feet similarly grew enormous claws. Her legs and arms became furred and jointed like a cat too. Siamura had transformed into a black tiger with green bat wings sprouting from its back — *Wait, not a tiger,* Tyler thought. *More like a panther, but tiger sized.*

Everybody stared, barely breathing. Siamura tossed her cat head and made a feline grunt, apparently satisfied no one was attacking her. She dragged her front claws over the center of the circle, turning the floor into wood chips. Tyler blinked. This was the creature that had been staying at his house for five days. Now she was a winged black panther, sharpening its claws on the floor like some huge house cat. Pausing, Siamura nodded at Tyler and said, “*Worry not, Tyler. None harm shall befall thee. I swear it.*” Tyler tried to smile, but her voice had emanated from the huge panther without its mouth moving — a mouth with such long teeth that it wouldn’t close completely.

Siamura rose on her hind legs, facing the door, her wings half-spread to fill the suddenly cramped room. Tyler couldn’t figure out what she was waiting for until the house shuddered again. The door blew inward, spraying wood everywhere, but the wings shielded the people from much of flying splintered wood, though Agent Kerns grabbed for his shin, blood leaking from between his fingers.

Siamura snapped her wings closed. A huge man, seven feet tall, whose shoulders were wider than the ruins of the doorway, stood blocking the shattered opening. Two tusks the length of Tyler’s hand grew from his lower jaw. His skin was the color of red ochre, an angry heated crimson. His fingers ended in cruel yellow claws. Siamura's black panther was terrifying, but the red beast almost made Tyler lose his mind as his stomach flipped over. The eyes were an unearthly violet that fixed on Tyler as his black tongue ran over his lips. The smell of hot smelted iron permeated the room, competing with the woodsy forest scent. The red thing sniffed the air and snorted, a long stretch of drool running from beside a tusk. Tyler had never felt anything so malevolent in his life before. This thing was an actual demon.

Siamura roared, one paw swiping the air in front of her in warning. Tyler shivered; she was outclassed. The red thing looked as if it could swat Siamura aside like a misbehaving kitten. He roared and the house trembled. Tyler and the others covered their ears, but it was no good — the sound echoed through his very chest. Siamura wasn't wrong about this creature. Tyler wanted nothing more than to escape but the demon blocked the way out.

The red demon turned his massive shoulders to fit through the doorway. Siamura reared up and stepped to block him from the people behind her. The demon swung a clawed hand at Siamura. She latched onto the demon with her claws and swung him into the closet beside her, smashing him through the closet door and into the wall beyond. Plaster dust billowed. The house vibrated, and timbers broke. The red demon destroyed the closet and wall beams as he careened into the wall beside Siamura. The remaining glass in the window shattered, falling from the frame like an afterthought.

Tyler yelled, "Run! Go!" just as Siamura jumped on the red demon, attacking him with a flurry of slashes. The other boys raced through the doorway and down the stairs, their footsteps pounding. Tyler waited by the door as Siamura pushed the brute into the ruins of the closet, making the house shake again.

The second agent dashed out of the room. Agent Kerns limped to the door as the demon shoved Siamura across the room into the wall opposite the closet. The beams snapped beneath the blow and Tyler lost sight of Siamura in the explosion of plaster dust. The house lurched and Tyler held on to the ruins of the doorway. He swallowed. She was gone. There was no way she'd survive that.

Detective Tirzynski rushed the door and grabbed Tyler by the arm. "Come on!" Tyler didn't want to abandon Siamura, but the detective dragged him out of the room.

"Siamura!" Tyler yelled but another lurch from the house told him the building didn't have much longer.

Agent Kerns hung on to the banister as he swung himself to the stairs, limping badly. Tyler heard another crash from the room and Siamura's growl. Tyler and the detective bumped into the wall as the house shook. He was able to shake his arm free from her, as she recoiled from the root-like wooden growths on the wall. They looked similar to what had grown along the floor and walls in the room. Tyler ran his fingers along them knowing instinctively these were the product of Siamura's magt.

"Move! Don't touch those!" Detective Tirzynski yelled.

The lights remained on throughout the house, yet blinked like some perverse disco, making it hard to see. They ran across the mezzanine, taking care not to trip over the new wooden growths.

On the landing halfway down the steps, the house shook again, but this time he kept going. He didn't want Detective Tirzynski to grab him again. As Tyler reached the front door, he passed a cop holding out a gun to Detective Tirzynski. "Detective, what's going on?"

Tirzynski took the gun, saying, "Thanks, Banes." She checked the chamber. "Hell, if I know, but I'm going back in."

"Are the kids out?" another officer asked, patting his arm.

Banes pulled his pistol from its holster. "Yeah, he's the last."

"Okay, let's go." The house shuddered again.

Tyler stepped into the chaos outside – people running to the house, a crowd of people by the street. Dad ran up to him. "Tyler! Are you all right? I saw the cops go running in and couldn't follow. What's going on in there?"

Tyler hung onto his father. "Dad, Siamura is fighting a big red spirit. They're tearing the house down."

"Are you hurt?"

"No, I'm fine."

Two gunshots rang out. The house shook again with a monstrous crash.

Chapter 17

Trance

Aiden stared as the house quivered from the last blow. Then a pair of gunshots obliterated the silence. Siamura was in trouble, he knew that much. "Tyler, stay here," he ordered his son. The cops weren't going to stop him from entering the house this time.

The gunshots didn't seem real. Aiden thought they were too muted, as if minimizing the danger. There was a cop by the doorway, but he was staring inside as Aiden pushed his way through the front door.

The interior was thick with dust that tasted like plaster. Aiden's eyes took a moment to focus on the interior, the lights strobing on and off. He heard a cop muttering, "Oh, shit. Oh, shit," while pressing on an injured person's sternum. Another cop was giving mouth-to-mouth to the same injured person only a few feet from the front door. Aiden stepped closer. It was Eric, the kid with attitude he stopped when he ran from the house.

In front of him Detective Tirzynski turned from the living room, her gun pointed downwards. Plaster dust continued to rain down from a large hole in the ceiling behind her. Aiden whipped his head to the right where a gaping hole in the wall had opened to the outside beside the fireplace. Two other cops, their guns drawn, were investigating the damage as more debris fell from the opening. A pile of stone lay in front of the fireplace. A large hole in the stone façade above showed broken beams. In front of the pile of stone was a flattened sofa. With all the damage, it was no surprise the house shook so much. But where was Siamura?

Despite the dust, Aiden smelled Siamura's scent of trees, but a different smell — a scent of smelted iron with sulfur — also pervaded the room. After a quick whiff, Aiden took short shallow breaths, the smell stinging his senses, making them tingle. His shoulder twitched, and he assumed that this was the taint of Siamura's opponent. Aiden made his way to the living room, stepping on broken wood and chunks of wallboard strewn across the floor. He was relieved he didn't see Siamura's broken body in the wreckage. Detective Tirzynski approached the cops who were assisting Eric. As she holstered her gun, she held her hand on her chest as if she were having difficulty breathing. Another cop followed Tirzynski.

Aiden drew to a stop beside the two officers with Eric. He had talked to him right before Eric had run into the house. Aiden stared. A large bloom of wetness saturated the front of Eric's black T-shirt. Blood covered the hands of the cop pressing rhythmically on Eric's chest. The other cop blew air into Eric's lungs via mouth-to-mouth.

The cop pressing on Eric's chest glanced up to the detective and said, "I don't understand it. He ran right in front of me."

Tirzynski opened her mouth to reply when the cops by the hole in the fireplace shouted as they flexed their now empty hands. Hadn't they just held guns just moments ago?

Siamura walked through the hole in the wall. She looked like she normally did, with green wings, tail, and long ears, but blood ran from terrible gashes across her torso and limbs, red saliva dripped from the corner of her mouth, and blood oozed from her torn wings. She wore a determined, almost cold expression. Her eyes glowed faintly, giving her a demonic air that made Aiden hesitate. He was concerned about her injuries, yet her power and the blood frightened him.

As Siamura walked between the two cops by the opening, the bigger cop, Evans, lunged for her. He was a powerfully built man, like a body builder, easily a foot taller and a hundred pounds heavier than the diminutive mearoch.

Detective Tirzynski shouted, "Evans! Stop!"

Aiden thought it strange that the detective would be protecting Siamura. After all, she considered Siamura a suspect. Then Siamura turned to Evans, grabbed his outstretched arm and trapped it under hers. She touched his forehead and with a small green flash, Evans fell limp in Siamura's arms.

The cop on the other side of Siamura moved toward Evans, but Siamura turned, bared her fangs and hissed at him, a deep frightening sound that grew to a low growl. She spread her wings to shadow the man, making her appear bigger and more threatening.

Tirzynski yelled, “Banes! Leave her alone!”

Aiden now understood the detective’s actions. She was trying to keep the cops out of harm’s way, out of Siamura’s way. Banes backed away from the mearoch, his hands half-raised in surrender. Siamura snapped her wings closed and swept Evans into her arms, carrying him to a chair. Aiden had always suspected Siamura’s strength but seeing her carry a man more than twice her size was eerie. Her speed was exceptional too. It was as if the cops had stood still while she’d incapacitated one and scared off the other.

While Siamura was setting Evans in the chair, Tirzynski reached for her pistol. “Siamura, what did you do to him?” she asked. Aiden could tell she was trying to keep her voice from sounding accusatory and realized the detective was afraid of the mearoch and unsure how to handle what had happened.

Siamura didn’t look up. “He still breathes, though he will have a headache when he awakens.”

Aiden stepped over a pile of wreckage, finally making a decision. “Siamura, what’s going on? Are you all right?” Blood oozed from her many wounds and he remembered how fragile she was when he first took her in.

Tirzynski shouted, “Mr. Moray! Get back!” The detective reached for Aiden, but he jumped towards Siamura, out of the detective’s reach.

Aiden realized he had just chosen sides, Siamura’s side, against all the police in the room. He took a deep breath. He couldn’t allow Siamura to stand alone and outnumbered. He had to at least try to prevent the cops from killing her regardless of the cost to him.

An officer at the front door yelped as his gun sailed across the room and out the hole in the wall by the fireplace. Aiden stared. “You’re doing that, aren’t you?”

Siamura pulled Aiden behind her. “Yea, I am. Stay back.”

Tyler entered the house and stood beside the prone form of Eric. He watched them, eyes wide, taking in the scene of destruction and of the mearoch.

The detective blocked Siamura's path to Eric. "Where's the red thing that attacked us?"

Siamura's ears flattened. "He vanished, as his kind can. I am going to heal Eric. He is one of mine charges, and therefore mine responsibility. Hinder me not."

Tirzynski stood in place. "The ambulance is on its way."

Siamura again arched her wings, this time over the detective. "Move aside." Her voice deepened as she spoke to the men attending Eric. "Ye two — away. Tyler, stay with me."

The detective hesitated but finally stepped out of their way, saying, "You shouldn't threaten people."

Tyler stood behind the mearoch, glancing around. When Tyler's eyes alighted on Aiden, he nodded indicating to his son that it was okay.

Siamura snapped her wings shut and hissed, baring her fangs. The detective retreated further. Siamura knelt beside the cop pressing on Eric's sternum. The bottom of her wings splayed out behind her. Siamura put her right hand on Eric's forehead and her left gently on the cop's shoulder. "Thee may stop now. I shall tend him."

The man was visibly torn between trusting the alien creature or staying despite her orders. "But he'll die if I stop."

She patted his shoulder. "I have him. Worry not." She turned to Agent Kerns, who had appeared at the doorway. "I want the other two boys here right away."

Tirzynski hesitated. "It's too dangerous."

Siamura growled. "They are mine responsibility. There is more of a threat of thee shooting them than from me." The two cops fled from Eric's side. Agent Kerns waved to bring the boys into the house.

Siamura kept her hand on Eric's forehead. With the other, she touched his wound. She brought her reddened hand to her mouth and tasted it, flicking her tongue several times. Someone in the room making a gagging sound. Her own injuries continued to drip down her arms and torso. Tirzynski wrinkled her nose at Siamura's vampiric display. It shocked

Aiden, and he recalled Siamura had said she did the same thing when healing Matt.

Tyler stepped between Siamura and the detective. Aiden could tell he was putting on a brave face, but his hands clenching and opening sporadically betrayed his stress. Aiden stepped beside him also blocking the detective.

An officer led the boys into the house. Siamura turned to them and said, "Matt and Kevin, stay close to me." She turned to Tirzynski. "No one should disturb us. If anyone does, the consequences are apt to be fatal. Do we have an understanding, detective?"

Tirzynski nodded. "Okay, but you're staying put afterwards." Aiden thought it was all bluster on the detective's part after seeing Siamura knock out Evans with little effort.

Siamura continued, "Aiden, put thyne hand over mine on Eric's forehead. Tyler, Kevin and Matt, make sure none interferes." Matt folded his arms like a self-righteous bouncer at a high-class nightclub, putting himself between Siamura and Agent Kerns. Kevin nervously glanced at everybody, not quite sure of his role.

Aiden blinked, then knelt on the other side of Eric from Siamura. He put his hand over Siamura's bloodied one on Eric's forehead. "What do I do?"

Siamura's tail curled around her body. "Close thyne eyes, take a breath, and follow mine lead. Thee shall do fine."

Aiden felt Siamura's hand, warm and sticky with blood, reminding him of Siamura's transformation at his house on that first day. Her hand shook a little, as if she were afraid of the people around her. He realized everyone was staring at them and he understood Siamura's trepidation. By healing Eric, her attention would be diverted and she wouldn't be able to defend herself against so many people. Aiden was sure that Detective Tirzynski considered Siamura a dangerous criminal. He wondered why Siamura trusted the detective enough to put herself at risk. The other cops kept measuring the distance to the door with their eyes, silently debating whether they could make it before Siamura pounced on them or the detective ordered them to stay.

Aiden glanced at Siamura. Blood still dripped from several slashes on her stomach, arms and legs. He couldn't abandon her, not now. He worried about her — she looked so fragile, but she told him to close his eyes. He did, and felt her warmth spread up his arm and into his body. All the noise and distractions vanished. He was in a different place with a haze obscuring his vision. It was quiet, so quiet that his heartbeat dominated his hearing.

Then he heard Siamura calling, "I am here."

At first, everything was black. His vision gradually resolved and as he walked in this foreign land towards her voice, the ground became firmer and more distinct, with occasional sickly yellow tufts of grass. He passed by a tree. It was a straggly thing with small dark green leaves. He saw Siamura standing by another tortured tree. Soft indistinct light surrounded them and illuminated the mud-colored sky.

Aiden asked, "Where are we?"

Siamura looked the same, except without all the wounds. "We are inside the mind of Eric. Thee needs to convince him that I should heal him. Once we do that, thee should go back while I help him."

"What? How are we inside Eric?"

She smiled. "Magt makes the strangest things possible. This is how I heal people, but they have to allow me to do so. I will not knit flesh and bone back together without their consent. Thee has the same potential too, if thee studies and practices."

Aiden paused trying to wrap his mind around that. He could actually do things with his ability? Good things, not just parlor tricks?

Siamura nodded. "Come. We need to hurry."

Aiden marveled at the scenery around him as they walked between some stunted trees that looked like they never had a decent amount of rain. The bark and trunks had hack marks from an ax and the limbs were mostly broken. Only a few had any leaves on them. The sickly grass had disappeared and the ground was hard and rocky. Smoke or fog obscured everything beyond the middle distance. The air felt dry and smelled of dust and the desert after the sun went down — blasted and dead. Aiden followed Siamura closely. He didn't want to get lost in this barren place.

Aiden asked, "The gunshot did all this?"

She said, "I doubt that. This seems to be a troubled young man."

Siamura passed by a boulder. It was vaguely tan with most of the color drained from it, rendering it cold and lifeless. She stopped. “Eric, I have come to heal thee.”

Eric crouched behind the almost colorless rock. When he saw Siamura, he jumped up, his face twisted and he threw up his hand to ward her off. “Get away from me!” He looked awful, pale with hollow eyes and bruises covering his emaciated arms.

Aiden stepped around Siamura towards Eric. This area was even drier and less hospitable. The few tree leaves were small, and most of the limbs were dry, brittle fingers reaching out into empty space. Aiden said, “Eric, she’s trying to save your life. She came back to help you.”

Eric spat, “Liar! She’s brainwashed you!”

“She hasn’t. You’ve been shot. You need help.”

“She’s going to kill me.”

Siamura’s tail flipped. “Thee shall die if I do none-thing. I want to prevent that.”

Eric paused, trying to avoid looking at them, but his eyes always came back to her. He seemed to hate himself for showing weakness.

She pointed to the horizon. “It is coming.” The haze parted and a dark cloud rapidly advanced towards them. Aiden realized it wasn’t a cloud. It was a blackness so total that Aiden felt he would lose himself in it. It had no reference except the trees and rocks disappearing in its path. He wanted to run from it, but instinctively he knew no matter how fast he ran, it would catch him and never let him go.

Eric turned and groaned with hopeless exhaustion. “It… It keeps…”

Siamura stepped forward, extending her hand. “I know. I will make it go away.”

Eric stared at her, not running, yet not taking her hand.

Aiden said, “She fought off the red demon. She’s not going to hurt you.”

Siamura said, “Come. We have not much time.”

Eric crumpled onto the ground. “I don’t know.”

Siamura knelt and took up his hands. “It will be okay. I shall take care of thee.” She turned to Aiden. “Open thyne eyes now, and many thanks.”

For a moment, Aiden thought it was an odd request as his eyes were already open. Then he realized he needed to open his physical eyes. He blinked, his eyes stinging from the brightness in the room. He released

Siamura's hand as everyone turned their attention to him. Siamura's other hand remained over Eric's chest wound.

In a voice barely above a whisper, he said, "He's going to be okay." Despite the light in the room, a green glow bathed Siamura's hands and Eric's torso. The detective and the two cops were still there, along with Matt and Kevin. Tyler still blocked Tirzynski from Siamura. At the door, Agent Kerns stood watching with two more police officers. Another policeman stood at the gaping hole in the wall across the room.

Aiden breathed. Nobody could doubt his or Tyler's friendship with the mearoch. Though, everyone should know that Siamura was working to save Eric's life. He only hoped that revealing his secret was worth it.

For a few minutes, Siamura didn't move and the green light didn't change. Everyone waited, likewise not moving. It surprised Aiden how no one made a sound or tried to interrupt Siamura. After a while, a couple of paramedics arrived at the door as Eric began to breathe on his own again.

The green light around Eric and Siamura dissipated and Siamura released a large sigh. She opened her eyes and brushed Eric's hair from his forehead. She bent down and kissed his brow, leaving a bloody lip print. She murmured, "Awake, Eric."

Eric's eyes fluttered open. "What happened?"

Siamura straightened. "Thee should be fine, though thee shall need to rest for several days." She lifted his hand and placed two lumps into his palm. "These are for thee." She closed his fingers over the objects. Aiden realized that those must be the bullets that almost killed him.

Siamura turned to Detective Tirzynski. "Thee may take him now." Siamura stood and backed away from Eric. She held her wings and limbs close to her body as if presenting the smallest possible target for an attack. She seemed so small and frightened. He couldn't figure out why she should feel that way since she had just saved Eric's life. Surely, everybody knew she wasn't a threat.

Chapter 18

The Hospital

Aiden watched as Siamura backed away from Eric. After two steps, she hesitated, and then seemed to stumble as she moved. She leaned heavily against the chair she had set the officer in earlier. The man remained slumped in it, unmoving, just as Siamura had left him. Siamura suddenly appeared so weak. The powerful creature was gone, replaced by one that needed his protection. He didn't care if she had destroyed a house. He saw beyond her the hole in the stone facade high above the fireplace where the beams also were broken and the huge hole beside the fireplace still sprinkling dust. It was hard to believe a slight creature like Siamura had a part in all this destruction. Despite all the damage and the presence of so many people, Aiden still smelled the smelted iron of the other fey creature.

Meanwhile, the cops were shouting, questioning Eric's miraculous recovery from the two gunshots to his chest. Eric opened his hand to reveal the two reddened slugs that almost ended his life while the paramedics set up to take his vital signs.

Matt folded his arms, puffing out his chest. "I commanded Demosura to save Eric. It was all my…"

No one paid Matt any attention. Kevin watched it all, a confused frown on his face, likely wondering how a demon sworn to end human life would save lives by fighting another demon and then healing someone. Detective Tirzynski didn't speak, but had a faint scowl on her face, as if her suspicions of the people and the situation were battling with her conscience.

Aiden stood and went over to Tyler, quietly speaking into his ear. “Are you all right?”

Tyler murmured, “I’m fine, Dad.”

“Good. Watch Kevin and Matt. Siamura doesn’t look well.”

Tyler nodded.

Aiden wrapped an arm around Siamura, letting her lean against him. “Tyler told me you fought off another creature. What happened?”

Her eyes were unfocused, and blood ran from the corner of her mouth. “That is true. His name is Talot, a destroyer spirit. Is everyone else uninjured?”

“Everyone’s fine.” Aiden felt her tail and wings go limp in relief. “What about you? You don’t look very well.”

Her head lolled onto his shoulder. “I need to rest. Do not have them take me.”

He kissed the top of her head and she smiled wanly. He scooped her legs up in his other arm and was thankful again how light she was. He was about to step towards the door when Detective Tirzynski blocked his way. The attention of every cop in the room was suddenly on him and the mearoch, no longer focused on Eric.

The detective had her hand under her coat, no doubt holding her gun. “Stop right there, Mr. Moray.”

“She needs to rest.”

“I’m taking her into custody. She’s a suspect in our case.”

“She’ll be at my house. You can find her there.”

The detective stepped closer. “Didn’t you hear me? I’m taking her into custody.”

Siamura’s hand snatched the lapel of the detective’s coat and drew her in. Siamura raised her head to look into her eyes. “Detective, if thee does not see fit to let me go, please grant me the mercy of a quick death.”

Tirzynski’s face drained of color as she frantically pulled Siamura’s hand off her like it was diseased. “That’s… That’s not my decision. God, we don’t…”

Siamura turned to Aiden. “Do not leave me. It is not thyne fault, but do not abandon me.” She wrapped her arms around his neck and then was silent. Her arms slid from his shoulders and her head rolled back.

Aiden shook her gently. “Siamura? Siamura?” When he realized that she was unconscious, he held her closer. “I’m taking her home. She’s my responsibility.” He surprised himself with those words. Never in his life would he defy a police officer, but he couldn’t betray Siamura. They would torture her trying to figure her out, like the priests had done centuries ago. He couldn’t allow that. He would rather be thrown in jail than have any harm come to Siamura.

“How can you trust her?” the detective hissed. “She’s destroyed a house single-handedly, is the prime suspect in a counterfeiting case, and is most likely a murderer.”

“She saved my son and everyone else from certain death and you call her a murderer? You’re more of a killer than she is.” Aiden’s voice rose, strong and full of decisiveness. “There is no way I’m going to release her to you.” People in the room gawked at him, and for the first time in his life, Aiden didn’t care.

“I can’t let you leave here with her.” The detective’s hand slipped underneath her coat again. “I won’t tell you again to stop.”

Agent John Kerns stepped beside the detective with a noticeable limp. He was taller and broader than Aiden, looming over them. “Mr. Moray, why don’t you let the paramedics take care of her?”

There was no hope that Aiden could maneuver around the two law officers. Even if Aiden wasn’t carrying Siamura, he couldn’t get around them. He was a pudgy computer geek, not some battle-hardened veteran who could bench press two hundred pounds.

Agent Kerns extended his arms. “Here, let me take her.” A couple of paramedics had taken away Eric on a stretcher. Another two paramedics waited behind the agent, eyeing Siamura curiously. The other cops in the room were starting to move toward him, their hands on their weapons. Aiden was outnumbered.

Aiden relented. “Okay, but I’m staying with her.” He nodded at the paramedics.

Agent Kerns stepped aside and Aiden set Siamura on a stretcher. The dark haired paramedic with a diamond stud in his ear immediately checked her eyes with a penlight. Prying open one eyelid, he shined the light in her eye, then away. He did that three times. He turned and looked at the agent and the detective. "What the hell is she? These aren't contacts. Her pupils react to the light."

"She's our suspect," Detective Tirzynski declared.

The other paramedic stepped beside Aiden. "Please, sir. You need to move away so we can evaluate her." The two men took her vital signs and shook their heads. Examining her wings and tail, they gave up and proceeded to wheel her out. "We'll have to take her to the hospital. We don't dare do anything here."

Detective Tirzynski stopped them and drew the sheet over Siamura to cover her completely, like she was a corpse they were removing. "The less people see of her, the better for now. We'll figure out what she is later." She turned to Aiden. "I expect to meet you at the hospital."

Aiden followed the stretcher out the door, Tyler right beside him. Outside was a confusion of emergency lights, caution tape, and people. Police were cordoning off the house, neighbors were gawking and talking with each other, and a news crew was making a report. It seemed like a hundred people were gathered. A fire truck was the base for firefighters running back and forth from the house. One ambulance pulled away from the curb, while at another, paramedics loaded up the covered body of Siamura. Aiden was about to climb in after Siamura, but he remembered the ice chest in the car. Siamura made a point of having the food to replenish herself. Aiden pulled Tyler with him and made their way back to his car.

Aiden and Tyler walked by the emergency crews without incident. One of the neighborhood men called out to him, "What's going on?"

Aiden shrugged his shoulders. "I'm not sure. Some kind of fight is all I could get."

"Anybody hurt?"

"Not sure. Sorry, I gotta go."

The man mumbled something about a lot of noise but seemed satisfied as his wife nodded. Aiden didn't really care what they thought. His concern was to get to the hospital with Siamura's food and prevent them from dissecting her. He wished he had been less cautious and parked closer.

When they climbed in the car, Tyler pulled a wad of cloth from his jacket pocket and unwrapped it. Inside was a ceramic lump, an amulet about half the size of his palm. Under the glow of the streetlight, Aiden saw it was blue with golden symbols incised around it. Aiden winced. His shoulder suddenly twitched.

Tyler said, "Siamura told me to keep it. Matt used it to hurt her."

"Then you should hide it under the seat until she decides what to do with it." Aiden started the car and drove to the hospital. On the way, Tyler told him more details about the summoning, Siamura's face off with Agent Kerns, and her transformation into a panther. He also described how Siamura held the red demon at bay while everyone escaped from the room.

The news both gladdened and disturbed Aiden. She'd fought with the police and the agents, yet she had rescued all of them from the demon she called Talot. She'd pursued the creature but returned to save Eric from certain death. He wondered how many more surprises she had hidden from him. And what about the demon Talot? Was he still out there?

Tyler interrupted his reverie. "What happened with you and Siamura with Eric? All three of you were glowing green."

Aiden blinked. The memory of the trance flashed in his mind. "Really?" *Yeah, no doubt that I'm associated with Siamura now.* "Siamura showed me that her magt — our ability can be used to help people. She said that we could learn to do the same thing."

Tyler turned to him. "No way. Like we don't have to hide anymore?"

Aiden shrugged. "We will have to be discreet, but yes, it seems we could harness it." Aiden proceeded to tell of his experience inside Eric's mind with Siamura.

"Wicked," Tyler exclaimed, his eyes alight.

Aiden parked the car and they rushed into the emergency room. A couple of news crews crowded around the entrance. It was unreal how fast the media descended on a story. Aiden wondered why one of the news reporters looked familiar. Tyler nudged him. "Hey Dad, that's Kathy Rodriguez from Channel Four. I guess even the big stations are covering this."

Aiden nodded. "Must be a slow news day." They walked past them to the door.

A policewoman stopped them. “I’m sorry, sir. No one except family members are allowed in.”

Aiden pulled up short. “Uh, my friend is in there.”

“What’s your name sir?”

“Aiden Moray and this is my son, Tyler.”

The cop blinked with a small note of surprise. “Go on in, Mr. Moray.”

“Oh. Thank you.” Somehow, he’d expected more resistance, but he and Tyler walked in with no one else saying anything or stopping him. The waiting room was empty, save for a man and woman with their heads down, sitting off to one side, murmuring to each other. Aiden went to the desk to check in, but the woman receptionist told him to wait.

Aiden shook himself, his hand closed into a fist on top of the desk. “I’m Siamura’s guardian. I must be allowed to see her.”

The woman said, “I understand, sir, but no one is allowed back there yet. Those people waiting are the parents of one of our patients and they’re not coming back here either. I’m sorry.”

“Who made that rule?”

“The authorities. Their priority is safety.”

Aiden fumed, but there was nothing he could do, so he walked back to the chairs, sitting with a huff. He wanted to believe he didn’t need to worry, but he had visions of Siamura strapped down to a metal table like a frog ready for dissection. Tyler tapped Aiden on the arm and tilted his head towards the couple sitting down. “That’s Eric’s parents.”

They glanced up momentarily, hearing Eric’s name. The man looked like a construction worker — thickly built, no-nonsense. The woman was haggard, though who wouldn’t be? She’d been called to the hospital for her son in the middle of the night. Eric’s mom had sweet eyes in a face that had seen disappointment. Aiden didn’t know if anyone had told them what had happened. It disgusted him that no one would let them see their son. They held each other’s hands with their heads together. It wouldn’t be fair to let them suffer needlessly. He stepped towards them, smoothing back his hair. “Hi. You’re Eric’s parents, right?”

The man looked up, brows arched, eyes red and raw. “Yes, we are.” He paused.

“I’m Aiden Moray, and this is my son, Tyler. We were with your son before he was brought in here.”

The man said, "I'm Russ Tallman, and this is my wife, Beth. They – "

Beth blurted out, "They didn't tell us anything, except that Eric was here. First, they tell us that he's in trouble and we must cooperate, leave him alone in the house, for some sort of a sting-operation, and now this. We shouldn't have trusted them." She shot a glare at her husband.

Russ was about to speak, but Aiden interrupted him. "Eric is going to be fine."

The couple looked at him, initially with wide eyes, but then their eyes slowly narrowed and their backs straightened.

Aiden continued, "We were there. He was conscious and weak, but he's going to be okay. I just wanted to let you know." He turned and crossed to the opposite side of the room with Tyler. Siamura had affected him more than he had realized. A week ago, he wouldn't have spoken to the parents. He would have assumed the authorities had taken care of it. He wouldn't have stood up against the detective earlier either and he wouldn't have revealed himself as someone associated with a demon or mearoch, yet the cops knew. Hell, probably the whole town of Oak Springs knew by now. If the TV news was outside the hospital door, he could count on everyone knowing. Siamura had made him realize that he wasn't on the edge of sanity.

Aiden and Tyler waited several minutes. Aiden picked up a magazine and flipped through the pictures. After a few minutes, he couldn't stand it anymore. He slapped down the magazine and stood up, only to see Detective Tirzynski and Agent Kerns coming towards him. Agent Kerns still walked with a noticeable limp, but both stared directly at him. Aiden's stomach bunched.

"Mr. Moray?" Detective Tirzynski said, "Can you please join us for a chat?"

"Sure." Aiden turned. "Tyler, wait for me here." Tyler sighed, flopping his hands on his lap. Aiden quickly met up with the law officers.

Agent Kerns pointed to a door. "I think that room is free."

A dark-haired man in a lab coat rushed up to the trio and paused. The doctor frowned, glancing between the three of them. He looked at Aiden as if debating whether to speak or not.

Aiden had had enough of this behavior. "What about Siamura?"

The doctor pulled up short. "Siamura?"

"Yes, the green-skinned, winged-and-tailed woman you have back there somewhere. Her name is Siamura."

The doctor glanced at Agent Kerns who nodded. "We're going to move her upstairs into a room right away. I dare not do anything except observe her at this point until the tests come back."

Thank God for small favors. At least they weren't going to cut her open in the next ten minutes. Aiden stated, "I insist on staying with her."

Detective Tirzynski indicated the room. "Come with us, Mr. Moray, and then we'll decide what to do."

Aiden followed her into the small examination room. Agent Kerns closed the door and sat on the examination table. The detective motioned for Aiden to sit on a chair. She leaned against the closed door, folding her arms. "Look, Mr. Moray, you need to start talking to us or I'm going to arrest you for obstruction of justice, and I'm sure Agent Kerns will charge you at the federal level."

Aiden sat slowly giving himself time to think. "I'll be more than happy to tell you all I know, but I need to stay with Siamura at all times."

The detective was about to speak when Agent Kerns held up his hand. "Why is that?"

"She's frightened and I'm the only one she is going to trust. It's in your best interest too. After tonight's events at the house, I would think you would want to keep her as calm as possible."

Tirzynski frowned. "You're in no position to dictate terms here."

Aiden wanted to tell her to shut up. Instead, he took a deep breath. "Nevertheless, if you don't want her going berserk, I should be with her."

Agent Kerns said, "I'm sure that won't be a problem. Why don't you tell us why you call her Siamura instead of Demosura?"

Aiden paused. "Siamura is the name she wanted to be called this time. Demosura is one of her old names that she no longer uses."

"What is she?"

"She calls herself a mearoch, which translates as a forest spirit. As near as I can tell, she is the protector of a forest. She also helps people, like we saw earlier with Eric. In return, people are to leave her forest alone. Or at least that's what they used to do."

Agent Kerns stretched his leg, wincing like it hurt. "Why did she call for you at the house? Then before she passed out, she wanted you to stay with her."

"She trusts me. I've explained what various modern things are to her, like electricity and plumbing. Our world scares her. If she wakes up in a strange place with people she doesn't know, she will panic, and I don't want her to hurt anyone."

"How can you be so sure that she will panic in unfamiliar surroundings?"

Aiden said, "She's expecting to wake up at my place and I'd say the odds are not in your favor of keeping her here. You saw what she did to the house. Are you willing to take that chance?"

Chapter 19

Impasse

After this declaration, Agent Kerns and Detective Tirzynski left to discuss his request to stay with Siamura. Aiden waited alone in the examination room. If they wouldn't allow him to stay, he'd remain as close as possible to Siamura — even sleep in the hallway if he had to. At least the floor here would be clean enough.

The detective entered the small room, wearing a sour expression as if she had to swallow her own bile. Tirzynski cleared her throat. "We've decided to let you stay with… Siamura." She stumbled over the word.

Agent Kerns was right behind her. "But We will have more police officers outside the room, just in case there's any problem."

Aiden stood. "That's fine. I just need to bring in the ice chest from the car. It has food for Siamura."

The detective stated flatly, "The hospital has food. Surely that's good enough for her."

"I know, but she insisted that I bring the food that she hunted."

Tirzynski frowned then sighed. "Okay, bring it in, but we'll need to search it."

Aiden rushed to the waiting room and told Tyler what had happened. As Aiden left the emergency room, he noticed the knot of news crews and reporters waiting outside had grown larger. This was becoming a zoo. The Channel Four reporter, Kathy Rodriguez, whom Tyler pointed out earlier, called out to him, "Mr. Moray, Mr. Moray!"

Aiden stopped. "How do you know my name?"

She was attractive, almost his height with an air of in-your-face seriousness, and perfectly styled shoulder-length blond hair. "You gave your name to the officer at the door. What is your role in this investigation?"

"Nothing, really." He wasn't going to go into detail about Siamura with a reporter. He turned back in the direction of the car, nearly bumping into Tyler who had followed him outside.

"It's something because I've been hearing your name mentioned at the Tallman house. What is your connection with the Oak Springs Slasher case?"

"I don't have time right now." Aiden hurried to the car, trying to get away from her.

She kept pace with him. "Didn't you see something unusual inside the house?" Tyler kept himself as a barrier between the reporter and Aiden.

"Nothing." He unlocked the trunk.

"Nothing? Part of a wall was missing!"

Aiden pulled out the ice chest. "You seem to know more than me."

Tyler slammed the trunk closed and locked the car.

Ms. Rodriguez pointed at the chest. "What's that for?"

Aiden walked directly into her, forcing her to jump out of the way.

Tyler said, "None of your business." He kept himself between the two adults.

The reporter insisted, "The people have a right to know."

Aiden approached the knot of reporters in front of the door to the hospital, still not saying anything.

"No, they don't," Tyler said.

Fortunately, the woman cop at the door gave the gimlet-eye to the posse of reporters and Rodriguez backed off. He and Tyler quickly slipped back inside the building.

Aiden murmured to the cop, "Thank you."

She smirked. "Don't thank me yet. They want to search that cooler of yours before you go any farther."

Sure enough, two officers were in the waiting room. The tall one said, "Mr. Moray, can you open the chest, please?"

Aiden said, "It's just deer meat."

The Tallmans were still in the waiting room, and they squinted at him as he walked past them. The cops took him behind the desk and opened the ice chest. They grimaced at the chunks of the bloody red meat layered in the container. The shorter one said, “We’re going to have to call in a doc to make sure this is what you say it is.”

The taller cop patted Aiden down, finding nothing — not that he would try to sneak something past law enforcement. Aiden wondered how much of a weirdo they thought he was. They also searched his son and failed to find anything.

Finally, the doctor came in and opened the chest. He snorted, “I don’t know exactly what animal it’s from, but it’s certainly not human.” He closed the lid. “Is that all?”

The tall cop nodded curtly. “Yes sir, thank you.” He turned to Aiden. “You can take it up.”

Aiden sighed with relief. “Thank you.” He and Tyler walked down the hall. He turned to his son. “And thank you out there.”

Tyler said, “Well, we have to stick together.”

A male nurse stepped out. “Mr. Moray, I’m supposed to take you to the room.”

“I think we can find it.”

“I’m ordered to take you and your son up to the room.”

Aiden simply sighed and followed the man to the third floor.

When they arrived, the tall officer who had searched the ice chest knocked on the door. Agent Kerns opened it and the officer said, “We searched Mr. Moray and the ice chest. The doc said it’s probably deer meat. Everything else is all clear.”

Agent Kerns nodded. “Thank you, Officer Barnes. Come inside, Mr. Moray.” When Tyler tried to come in, the Agent held out his hand to block him. “I’m sorry, son, you should go home. You can’t come in here.”

Aiden turned. “You said I could stay with Siamura.”

“Yes, we did. It’s very dangerous, and we’re making a special allowance for you, but not your son,” Kerns said with a nod. “I’m not going to be responsible for his safety.”

Aiden replied, “But I can’t leave him alone at home. That’s crazy, especially with a killer on the loose.” There was a momentary pause as Aiden realized he couldn’t abandon Siamura with the detective and the agent, yet he couldn't desert Tyler either. There was a very real danger of the law officers killing Siamura if he wasn't there to smooth out their differences, plus Siamura needed the food, and Aiden couldn't trust the detective to give it to her if he wasn't in the room.

Kerns said, "None-the-less your son is not staying in this room."

Tyler spoke up, "Dad, I'm not a kid anymore. I'm staying, but I'll wait just outside the door."

Aiden felt pulled in two directions. At least with half a dozen cops outside the room, Tyler should be safe with them.

Tyler stepped out of the room. "Siamura needs the food. Don't worry about me. I'll sleep on the couch out here."

Aiden nodded. "Okay. I'll come back to check on you later." Tyler smiled back. Aiden walked into the room. It was nice enough, with pale blue walls and two beds with privacy curtains currently tucked back. Everything was clean, sterile, and cold, despite a generic picture of a vase of flowers on the wall opposite the beds. There were a couple of chairs, one by the window and one by the door. In the bed near the window lay Siamura, covered by a thin blanket. She was hooked up to a heart and lung monitor and on an IV. The other bed, nearest the door, was vacant. The door to the room closed automatically behind him.

Aiden hurried over to her, sliding the ice chest by the chair beside her bed. His arms ached from carrying the damn heavy thing. He smoothed her hair — she was still unconscious, but she looked better than when the paramedics took her away. But her scent of trees wasn't as strong as usual. Glancing up at the monitors, he saw that her heart rate was low — so low that the warning light was on continuously. He pointed to it. "Isn't anyone going to do anything?"

Agent Kerns stepped towards Aiden. "She's been that way since the paramedics brought her in. Doctor Patel said that with her alien physiology that he is only giving her fluids until he figures out what won't kill her."

Aiden stopped and felt her forehead, which felt warm, but her body temperature was higher than his, so that was normal. He sensed her energy was steady, not declining. She should be in the clear, if she had enough time to rest and got some food. At least the hospital staff had cleaned her up – she wasn't covered in blood anymore and that was a relief. He frowned though, spotting her wrists and ankles tied to the steel railings of the bed by leather restraints, and a handcuff bound her left wrist to the railing closest to him.

Aiden pointed to the metal shackle around Siamura's wrist. "Why the handcuffs? Aren't the restraints enough?"

Detective Tirzynski said, "They're to make sure she doesn't escape."

"She's not going to like it."

"At this point, it doesn't matter what she likes. I saw her destroy a house in a matter of seconds and I'm doing everything I can to reduce the danger. If it bothers you, you can leave."

Aiden stopped. It would do no good to protest and have the detective boot him out. He looked down at Siamura again. She lay on her back. She never slept on her back because it cut off the circulation to her wings. He pulled the sheet down to turn her on her side, grateful that a hospital gown covered her. She may not be modest, but he was. He began lifting her and tugging on her wings.

"What are you doing?" Tirzynski asked, stepping closer like she was going to stop Aiden.

"I'm moving her wings to get the blood to circulate. I don't suppose we could rearrange her so that she's on her side, could we?"

"Too risky."

Aiden pulled the blanket further down. "Could you at least help me?"

The detective shook her head, her eyes horrified like he'd asked her to plunge her hands into a tank full of hungry piranhas. Agent Kerns stepped over to help. Aiden could see him taking a deep breath before touching her. The agent blinked and lifted her. He would have thrown her off the bed, except she was strapped down. "What the…? She weighs practically nothing!"

Aiden yanked her wings free. "My guess is twenty to thirty pounds, but it makes sense if she's going to be able to fly."

"But she picked me up with no problem and I'm two hundred."

"Amazing, isn't it?" Aiden pulled the blanket back over her. "The bed wasn't designed for her." He pointed at the handcuff. "I know you're being cautious, but metal like this is going to scare and upset her. She's had a very bad experience. The straps should be enough."

"Look, if you want to stay, don't bring it up again."

Aiden blinked. He could feel his face coloring with anger.

Agent Kerns asked, “What was this bad experience?”

Aiden said, “Some other creatures captured and tortured her for years. They strapped her down and took her apart over and over.”

Detective Tirzynski snorted, “That’s hard to believe. She’s not missing any limbs. In fact, she has extra ones.”

Aiden said, “I know. Somehow, she’s able to regenerate.”

Kerns sat on the empty bed. “Why aren’t you afraid of her? Personally, she gives me the creeps even when she’s unconscious.”

Aiden sighed. He knew he’d have to tell this story at some point. “I grew up with strange things happening to me and I’ve met others like her. Well, not the same, but with abilities that aren’t explainable. I have a sense when things are going to turn out okay.”

Kerns said, “You said she healed herself. How?”

“You both saw her take two bullets out of Eric and save his life. It’s got to be something like that. All I know is that she was very bad off and it took years for her to recover.” Aiden sat in the chair closest to Siamura. He didn’t want to deal with any further questions. “It’s been a very stressful night. I think we should try to get some sleep.”

Detective Tirzynski said, “Agent Kerns, you should stay on the other bed for your leg. Mr. Moray, aren’t you worried about Tyler being alone out there?”

Aiden shifted, trying to get comfortable. “I would prefer if he were in here with me, but you won’t allow it. I know he won’t go home, so staying outside with your officers will have to do.” He sunk into the chair and closed his eyes, hoping the officers would get the hint. He wasn’t expecting to actually fall asleep.

***

Aiden awoke to rustling and thrashing from the bed in front of him. The lights in the hospital room were dimmed, but not off. He briefly wondered where he was and then the previous day’s events came flooding back. He sat up and Siamura turned to him, except it didn’t look like her. It was some half-beast, half-human creature. Two cat eyes glowed at him set in a green-skinned face dusted with black fur. Her mouth and nose extended from her face to form a muzzle with sharp fangs that were longer than her normal pointed teeth. Her right hand swung from behind her, but it had long black talons extending from the fingers. The claws were flat, double-edged things that glinted black and shiny in the dim light, looking more like blades rather than something from an animal. Over her incongruous frame hung the torn hospital gown that looked as if she had eaten someone rather than having worn it while she was unconscious. Her long ears folded back, her eyes closed to mere slits and she hissed at him, as her wings stretched above her, bumping into the wall.

The sound chilled Aiden. In the most soothing voice he could muster, he said, “Siamura. It’s me, Aiden. It’s okay.”

She stopped hissing and closed her mouth, though her longer fangs protruded, overlapping her lips. A strand of drool dripped from her mouth. Aiden saw that she had cut through the leather restraints. He glanced down at her left hand and caught the sinister gleam of metal from the handcuff. Her handcuffed hand was still in human form. Either the metal stopped her transformation or the shackle’s small size prevented that part of her from changing. Siamura followed his eyes and yanked hard on it, making it clatter against the steel railing of the bed. She screamed and swung her clawed hand at it, slashing her wrist to the bone. Baring her fangs, she turned to her bound hand.

Aiden realized with horror that she meant to chew her hand off to free herself. He yelled, “No!” and clamped his left hand on her bound one and the other on her wrist to stop her from cutting it off.

Siamura screamed again and launched herself upwards to the ceiling. Aiden lost his grip on her free hand and the bed rail hit his chest. He released her bound hand and slid off the bed. He landed on his feet and fell back into the chair. Looking up, he saw the bed was completely off the floor. Her scream frightened Aiden — it wasn’t human or animal, and entirely unearthly. It made the hairs on his neck and all the way down his spine stand on end.

The bed stopped ascending with a crash. Ceiling tiles rained down on Aiden. Throwing up his arms, he managed to deflect the worst of it. With a metallic clatter the bed landed on the floor beside him. Siamura was flat on the bed, covered with ceiling tiles, strips of metal and other building materials, her left hand still handcuffed. She shook off the building debris and launched herself upwards again. Her wings arched clear across the room, and they still weren’t fully spread.

Again, she hit the ceiling and fell back to the floor with a deafening crash. More of the ceiling came down. Ears flattened, her eyes were wide and glowing. Aiden called to her, but she ignored him and leapt to the ceiling again. The bed hit the floor a third time, dragging her down with it. Siamura sat on her haunches, panting, with her tongue hanging out like a tiger after a run.

Detective Tirzynski stood, and in the next instant, one of Siamura's wings shot out and sent her sprawling onto the floor. Siamura might be chained to the bed, but the wings could reach anywhere in the room. The detective stayed down.

Aiden yelled, "Siamura! Siamura!"

He stared as the half-beast pulled on her shackled hand, making the metal bar screech in protest as it deformed to the center of the bed. He knew she was strong, but this was unreal. It scared the crap out of him. She was like a caged animal in a panic.

Suddenly, Siamura's wing snapped out and slammed against the door. Then she roared. That almost made Aiden wet himself. He saw the detective cringe on the floor by the door, cradling her hand.

"Siamura, stop!" Aiden shouted. He grabbed her bound hand — he had to distract her before she killed someone.

The detective hit the light switch, flooding half the room with brightness. It relieved Aiden that Tirzynski was uninjured. Agent Kerns was on the floor between the two beds, trying to avoid Siamura's tail as it darted at him. Siamura bared her teeth to tear at Aiden's hands. Siamura still wasn't a cat or a human. She was humanoid in shape, but with sparse black fur over her green skin. Her mouth and nose protruded to form a feline snout, yet the rest of her head was human-shaped, her eyes glowing green.

"It's me, Aiden. You're safe." He didn't loosen his grip. There was no way he was going to give up on her. He could sense her underneath the rage and fear she was projecting.

Detective Tirzynski reached for her gun. Siamura paused a moment, then the door opened. The cops outside must have heard the commotion and were trying to enter. Siamura growled and her wing whipped over the detective's head, slamming the door shut. Her tail snared both of Agent Kerns' hands.

Tirzynski crouched at the corner of the empty bed and pointed her gun at Siamura. “Stop or I’ll shoot!”

Siamura’s one wing held the door closed against the officers outside. The other wing remained pinned against the remains of the ceiling and wall. She looked like a large bird of prey trapped in a too-small cage.

Siamura growled again, a low rumble that made Aiden’s stomach vibrate, saliva dripping from her teeth. Her ears were flattened against her head, and the claws of her free hand scraped against the metal of the bed rail, traveling closer to Tirzynski. It was an idle threat, as Siamura was already at the limit of her cuffed wrist, even with the bent bed rail. Her eyes narrowed, flashing at the detective.

Aiden leaned in front of Siamura. “Stop! Both of you!” He turned to the half beast. “Settle down.” As the officers outside pounded on the door, Aiden stroked Siamura’s arm, while keeping one hand on her cuffed wrist. He stared into Siamura’s eyes, ignoring the claws that could gut him.

Siamura blinked her cat eyes several times. Then the half beast melted into her green, humanoid form. “Unchain me.” Her accented voice was calm yet frayed at the edges.

Tirzynski kept eyeing the wing that was above her. “Let Agent Kerns go.” The men outside continued to beat on the door.

Siamura spat, “Tell them to back away from the door.”

“Let him go,” Tirzynski repeated.

Aiden spoke, “Detective, tell the people outside to stay out of the room. Then Siamura will let Agent Kerns go.”

“Mr. Moray, she’s dangerous. She must release Agent Kerns immediately.”

Siamura rumbled, “Thee has thyne gun pointed at me. Tell those outside to stop or shoot me.”

The detective glanced at the door, probably figuring that they weren’t getting in anyway. “Hey, Evans, don’t come in unless I call for you.”

A voice called back, presumably Evans, “Are you all right?”

“For the moment, yes. Just be ready.”

Evans said, “The doc wants to come in.”

“No one comes in until Agent Kerns or me says so.”

“Yes, Ma’am.”

“Dad?” It was Tyler’s voice. “Are you okay?”

Aiden tried infusing his voice with calmness as he shouted, “Yes, just stay out there for now.”

Detective Tirzynski glanced above her, where Siamura’s wing stretched across the ceiling like an executioner’s ax. The other wing was behind Aiden and blocked the window. Then, her tail retreated onto the bed, releasing Agent Kerns.

Aiden soothed, “Fold your wings. I’m sure the detective will put her gun away.”

Siamura slowly pulled her wings back and folded them, sounding like heavy canvas curtains retracting. She took Aiden’s hand in her free hand, which was now free of any claws. Blood smeared his hand, and she began to lick it off. She turned his hand over and licked between his fingers.

Detective Tirzynski slowly stood, lowering her weapon. She grimaced at Siamura’s grooming. Agent Kerns picked himself off the floor.

Aiden tried to pull his hand away. “I’m not worried about me. It’s your blood. Just promise me you won’t try to cut off your hand again.”

Siamura held onto his hand and examined the other one. She had a nasty gash across her bound wrist. “Mine claws can kill, but if it pleases thee, I will not cut off mine hand.”

Aiden had heard of wolves gnawing off their paws to escape a steel-jawed trap. If he hadn’t put his hand in the way… he didn’t want to think of it. She was desperate and scared and he needed to calm her down before something terrible happened.

Siamura rattled the cuff. She frowned and her ears flattened again. Aiden ducked beside the bed and withdrew the ice chest he had brought in earlier. “This is for you.” He set the chest on the bed and opened it, hoping to distract her.

Siamura stared at it. There was at least twenty pounds of raw meat there, maybe more.

Tirzynski offered, “We should cook that for you and refrigerate the rest.”

Agent Kerns reached for the chest. Siamura laid her hand on his arm. “That will not be necessary. I prefer it fresh. Can ye leave?” Her eyes narrowed and her tail swung over the side of the bed. Aiden worried she would assault the agent again.

Tirzynski adjusted the grip on her gun. "We're not leaving the room, so if you want to eat, go ahead."

Aiden said, "I've watched you eat. What's the problem?"

Siamura's nose and mouth twitched, becoming more cat-like. "Thee has seen me eat, not feed."

Agent Kerns pulled his arm from Siamura. "There's enough meat in there for several meals. There's no way…"

Siamura's head transitioned to panther in an instant, although the rest of her body remained human. She reminded Aiden of the old Egyptian gods with animal heads atop human bodies. She growled deeply in the law officers' direction. The agent backed away, slowly waving Tirzynski back. Aiden stood there, transfixed. Agent Kerns stage-whispered, "Mr. Moray, move away slowly."

Siamura, or rather the panther-headed beast, ignored Aiden and reached into the chest with her free hand. The hand had transformed too and now had the long talons that Aiden had seen earlier. Her other hand, bound by the cuff, clattered against the deformed bedrail. She sniffed at the meat and then glanced at the agent. She growled low, eyes narrowing at him. She was protecting her food, her kill.

Aiden had to calm her. "Siamura, eat." He didn't move. The beast paused.

Agent Kerns took a step around the bed towards Aiden. Siamura roared at the agent, head tilted, her eyes glowing green. A thread of saliva dripped from her mouth. He did the wise thing and froze. Her eyes flicked in Tirzynski's direction. The detective's lips were a thin line, hands gripped tightly on her gun pointed at the floor, but she didn't move either. Aiden worried that any motion could prompt an attack, and he would be powerless to stop it.

The door opened a crack, and before anyone could react, Siamura's wing shot over Tirzynski's head and slammed it shut. Evans' voice on the other side yelled, "Detective, are you all right?"

The detective glanced at the cat-headed woman on the bed. Siamura's eyes glowed, baring her teeth with another thread of saliva dripping onto the meat, but she didn't growl. Aiden was thankful for small favors.

Agent Kerns took a breath. "We're okay. Stand by."

Tirzynski added, "We're fine."

The half-beast chuffed and pulled out a large hunk of meat from the chest. Her eyes never left Agent Kerns or Detective Tirzynski. She began tearing at the raw flesh and swallowing huge chunks. It was like watching a nature program of lions or tigers at a kill, except scarier, because this wild animal was within arm's length. Blood quickly covered Siamura's muzzle and claws. Within minutes she'd consumed the entire contents of the ice chest.

When Siamura had finished, she cleaned her clawed hand with her large feline tongue. Slowly, her head reverted to her green human form. The cut on her handcuffed wrist had disappeared. Aiden closed the chest and slid it under the bed.

Siamura licked her fingers. "Thee can put thyne gun away, detective. If thee did not shoot me while I was feeding, thee will not ever shoot me."

The detective's brows shot up at Siamura's comment, but she remained motionless, her gun still out.

"Come, Detective Tirzynski. I have put away mine weapons. Thee can holster thyne. If thee is not going to kill me, why am I chained? I saved ye lives — in thyne case, detective, twice."

Agent Kerns glanced at Tirzynski. "Twice, detective?"

Siamura nodded. "After everyone left the upstairs area, the detective did not think I spoke the truth about Talot, the red spirit, so she and her assistant climbed the stairs."

"You were in danger. I was doing my duty," Tirzynski snapped as she jammed her gun in her shoulder holster.

"In the matter of magt, thee would be a casualty. It is mine responsibility to prevent thyne death. I apologize for knocking thee down the stairs, but a fall was more survivable than Talot gutting thee. Agent Kerns can see the damage at the top of the stairs where the corner of the wall used to be, if thee wants verification."

Agent Kerns asked, "Detective?"

"That's not the point. She's —"

"Why am I chained?" Siamura shook the cuff.

Detective Tirzynski shot back, "Because you are a suspect and you tore this room apart."

"Of what crime am I accused?"

Agent Kerns sat on the edge of the bed. Aiden knew he was trying to be friendly with her but hoped that Siamura wouldn't hurt him. The agent said, "I'll tell you what. If you'll answer a few questions, we'll help you with the legal proceedings."

Siamura laughed. It sounded so perfect, so close to music, that Aiden almost didn't catch the sarcastic note coursing through it. "Agent Kerns, I will answer thyne questions, but thee must believe me a child to think thyne magistrates are going to show any leniency to a being such as I. Aiden told me that Christianity is still practiced in this time. Once I appear before them, I will be condemned as a demon. The only mercy I have a possibility of getting is torture lasting mere days rather than stretching for years or decades. In the end, they will put me to death."

Agent Kerns pressed on, "You may not believe this, but it's against the law to use cruel and unusual punishment." She raised her brow in disbelief and Agent Kerns continued. "I'll start simply. We've heard you called by a couple of different names. What is your real name?"

"Siamura is the name I use now. Demosura is a name people called me over seven centuries ago. The boys found it in a book written at that time. That is why they call me by that name. I have had hundreds of different names in mine existence, most in languages no longer spoken. If Siamura is not satisfactory, then give me another."

Agent Kerns continued, "Siamura is fine for now, but what did your parents call you?"

"Parents? I am born of the forest and the creatures within. None name was spoken or needed."

"Do you have any identification or papers of any kind?"

"Why do I need identification? I know who I am, and others will give me a name if they find it necessary."

Agent Kerns paused, realizing he wasn't getting very far with that line of questioning and withdrew a plastic sheet from his jacket. It was a clear plastic sheet protector containing a few twenty-dollar bills. "Have you seen these before?"

Siamura held out her hand. "May I?"

Agent Kerns passed the sheet to her. Siamura examined the bills, her fingers stroking the sheet rather than looking closely at them. "I made these. Not the shiny plastic part, but the money." Aiden winced. He'd watched enough cop shows to know you never admit anything to the police.

"How can you be sure?" Agent Kerns asked. He seemed to be giving her a way out, even though he had her confession.

"I know mine own magt when I see it. The closest translation for magt is magic." Aiden wondered how the agent would handle that answer.

Agent Kerns frowned. "You're saying that you used magic to make these bills?"

"Yea, assuming the translation is correct."

"How do you expect us to believe that?"

"To be frank, I care not what thee believes. Humans are amazing creatures, able to rationalize things into and out of existence. I find it a never-ending source of fascination. What if I called magt a science?" She handed the sheet back to Agent Kerns.

"The bills are so perfect, yet why are the serial numbers the same?"

Siamura shrugged. "Eric told me to make the money exactly like the bill he gave me. Therefore, I did. I duplicated every fold and tear from the original bill. Why do the numbers need to be different?"

The agent glanced at the bills in his hand. "I'd wondered about that. It was weird that every bill was missing a small corner in exactly the same place." He marveled at the bills, and then shook himself. "Anyway, when the bills are printed, every one of them has a unique serial number. Most people know that."

Siamura's tail flipped and her ears shot up. "I would not know as I have not been of this world for the past few centuries. Furthermore, I did not want the money to be usable, and lastly, I made them with a time limit."

"Time limit?"

Siamura smiled and her ears perked up. "Hast thou heard the stories of the leprechauns and their gold? If a human catches them, they give the human the gold, but the fey-one fools the human. He gives the human what looks to be gold, but after a while, it turns back into leaves and bark. I used the same principle. By dawn, that entire pile of money I made, including those in your hand, will become carpet once again."

"Why did you do it in the first place?" Detective Tirzynski pointed at the sheet. "Seems like a waste of time."

"I am bound to follow the instruction of mine summoners. Their first request was for me to injure someone. I refused, of course. I reminded them that they would need to point out the victim to make sure that I injured the correct one and they weren't prepared for me to leave the circle. When one of them asked for money, I thought it would be less damaging than harming someone. When I made the money, I cursed it to be unusable for any exchange. Anyone receiving it for payment would find handling it uncomfortable. It would raise their suspicions and cause them to not accept the money. So, yea, I made the money, but made it impossible to be spent."

Agent Kerns said, "When Eric Tallman tried to spend it, the cashier noticed the serial numbers matched."

"They told me to make the bills match the one they gave me, but I did not know that the numbers had to be different. Everything worked out in the end."

Agent Kerns frowned, obviously thinking of another form of questioning. "Where do you come from?"

"I came from here, but in recent times from Irgale. This has been a very entertaining chat, but I must hunt, if I am going to have any chance of defeating Talot tomorrow."

Agent Kerns said, "That's the red demon, I assume. How do you know its name?"

"He told me. He shall be killing tonight to grow stronger, which is why I must stop him."

Tirzynski snapped, "How do you know that? Do you know where he'll be?"

"He must eat creatures of this world in order to gain strength. I must also feed, although not humans, if I am going to defeat him. Ye must let me go."

Agent Kerns shook his head. "You admitted counterfeiting the money. That's a very serious charge. You're staying right here and then will be going to a trial."

"Thee is willing to have thyne people be food for Talot because of that? I made the money useless in the first place." Siamura pulled the bedcovers over her lap and hand that was handcuffed to the rail. Aiden kept his hand on her wrist. He wanted to be sure that she wasn't going to cut it off.

Agent Kerns continued, "That's why a court will decide whether you're guilty, not us."

"Meanwhile people die. I must feed right away."

"How do we know you aren't the killer?" The detective narrowed her eyes.

"I saved thyne life twice and brought Eric back from near death. Both of ye, and the others too, would be dead now if I had not intervened. Why would I save ye if I was the killer?"

Tirzynski shrugged. "We'll handle Talot or whatever he is."

"By this time, it is probable he is immune to ye weapons. He is a destroyer spirit, one who feeds on humans. Thee must let me go!"

"What do you eat?" Tirzynski continued like she hadn't heard her plea.

"Ye saw me eat venison. I only eat wild game. I do not prey on people or their livestock."

Agent Kerns stated, "We can't release you. You've committed a crime and must remain in custody until your court date."

Aiden felt the handcuff fall from Siamura's wrist and in the same instant, her arm slipped from his grip. She sprang from the bed, her wings shot out and around Agent Kerns and the detective. She was so incredibly fast that Aiden could barely follow what was happening. The wings pulled the law officers against Siamura in a close embrace.

Aiden reached for her. "Siamura, wait."

Siamura's hands grabbed at the two people enveloped in her wings. Then her tail whipped up in front of her and disappeared downwards. Aiden saw two guns wrapped in the end of Siamura's tail. An instant later, she flung them at the window, smashing through the glass so they fell away into the night air.

Siamura pulled the law officers closer, her wings wrapped around them like a cocoon. "I need to eat. When I am gone, ye will not arrest, detain, or otherwise harm Aiden or his son, Tyler. Am I clear?"

The detective struggled, but she could barely move. She yelled, "Evans, get in here!"

Aiden shouted, "Siamura, don't do this!"

The door handle rattled, but it remained locked. Aiden's panicked mind wondered at it. The cops had been able to enter before.

Siamura growled, "Heed what I say, or else Talot will not be ye only worry." A wing smacked against the window, knocking out the remaining glass. In the next moment, she jumped onto the windowsill, and leapt out the window, spreading her wings to glide away.

Evans and the others kicked the door in. Guns drawn, they charged into the room. Aiden could only flatten himself against the wall.

Chapter 20

The Blue Amulet

Aiden stared out the window after Siamura. He pressed himself against the wall, out of the way and out of sight, hoping none of the cops would notice him. She had left him, abandoned him to a roomful of cops. On the other hand, she was right about the cops and the general justice system – she would never get fair treatment, never mind a fair trial. This was becoming more complicated.

Detective Tirzynski ran to the window. "Shit!" Agent Kerns and the three other cops looked out the window too. The detective barked orders to the officers to pursue Siamura. The officers hurried out of the room as Agent Kerns continued to peer out the window, craning his neck like he expected to spot her in the darkness.

Tirzynski whirled on Kerns. "It was your idea to play along with the kids' hoodoo crap, and…" She gritted her teeth, biting back what she was going to say.

Agent Kerns turned. "At least now we know the red demon has been murdering all those people."

"Do you hear yourself? How do you know that Siamura, or Demosura, or whatever the fuck her name is, isn't also killing people?"

"If she was, why save us? Why save Eric from certain death and allow herself to be captured? It doesn't make sense for her to be the murderer."

"Whatever. They're both… aliens… demons… God knows what. We need to catch them both now." Detective Tirzynski turned on Aiden.

"What the hell was that? I thought you were going to keep her calm and manageable."

Aiden gawked at her. She was obviously upset and he didn't want to argue with someone who could arrest him. Tyler peered around the shattered doorway.

Detective Tirzynski continued, "Do you know where she went?"

"Uh, not really."

"Fat lot of good you are. I've got a prime suspect in a murder case running around free and you told me you had the inside track, that you knew her. Instead, you feed her and then help her to escape."

Aiden's face heated. "I did not help her to escape."

"How else did she get out of the cuffs?"

"I don't have a key. How could I unlock it?"

"You've been helping Siamura since day one. Why would you change now? You had your hands over the handcuffs."

Aiden stared the detective down. "You're crazy! Siamura would have cut her own hand off if I didn't put my hands over hers. I prevented her from escaping sooner!"

"Yeah, right. I know it was all a ruse to give her time to recover."

"That's not true."

"She's out there killing someone right now! And it's your fault!"

Detective Tirzynski kept Aiden trapped between the bed and the wall. He tried to step forward, to no avail. "She isn't killing anybody. She saved Eric's life, not to mention everybody else's in the house, including yours."

"Why do you defend her?"

"Because she's innocent, she doesn't understand our world, and I'm the only one that can help her."

"I should arrest you."

Agent Kerns had been observing the exchange silently until now. "I don't think so, detective. Mr. Moray, you're free to go home, but no leaving town."

Detective Tirzynski grabbed Aiden's arm. "I know you're at least guilty of being Siamura's accomplice. This isn't done."

Aiden glanced at Agent Kerns, who nodded for him to leave. Aiden said, "Siamura's not the killer. She wouldn't heal Eric's bullet wounds if she was." Aiden pulled his arm away and left as quickly as he could with Tyler.

***

The sun brightened Aiden's room. It seemed like he had just collapsed into bed. Glancing at the clock next to his bed, he realized that it was almost true. He'd gone home, but the police had followed, setting up in his living room. When he questioned them, they said they were waiting for Siamura to come back.

There was a strange rustling coming from inside the room and the scent of pine tickled his nose. It wasn't the harsh smell of cleaning fluid, but the pleasant soft odor of a conifer forest after a rain. He snuggled down in his covers, happy and safe, until he remembered he wasn't in a forest. Despite falling asleep a few hours ago dead tired, he sat up with a start. On the carpet beside the bed was Siamura.

Agent Kerns and Detective Tirzynski would be right downstairs, waiting for her to come back to him.

"What are you doing here?" he whispered.

He heard a muffled groan as a wing twitched.

She sat up with a start, scrabbling a few feet away from him. Her ears were down, tail and arms wrapped securely around her legs and her wings tightly folded. She looked up at him, her head down and brow raised.

Aiden continued, "Listen! Half the police force is downstairs or looking for you."

She said, "I know. I slipped past them earlier to get here."

"You did?" For the life of him he felt he was talking with an irresponsible teenager.

Her ears stood up. "Of course. How else was I going to be with thee?" Then her ears lay back down. "Is… Is thee angry with me?"

"Angry? It's too dangerous for you here," he hissed. "They will capture you and slap you in irons, chains, and who knows what else." Aiden pointed at the closed door of his bedroom.

"But does thee think me a monster? After seeing part of mine cat form with the detective and others."

"Never mind what I think. You're not safe here! You have to leave!"

"It will be okay, as thee says. Both Talot and I wounded each other last night. Therefore, both of us have to hunt to restore ourselves." She smirked. "I hunt deer. He hunts humans. Humans take umbrage at the latter, so the police people will soon leave to investigate the latest atrocity. We just have to wait."

"Siamura! That's horrible. You did nothing to prevent those people's deaths?"

She shrugged. "I had to hunt to heal and rest or I am not going to be able to stop him."

"But people died!"

She blinked at him, tilting her head. "That is true, but I would not have been able to prevent him anyway for I did not know where he was. Better for me to prepare for the next battle."

Aiden shivered at her cold reasoning. He didn't want to admit it, but she was right. She was fey, a spirit, and thought differently than normal humans.

The sound of car doors slamming outside drew Aiden out of bed and to the window. Discreetly pulling a corner of the drapes aside, he saw that the police were leaving his house. The sun peered over the hills to the east, casting long shadows as its pink light glinted off the dew on the cars. He dropped the drapes. "So how did you know that?"

"Logic — no magt involved. As I said before, the result of the Talot feeding will upset the police, therefore they will investigate. Do not be distressed when thee enters the bathroom. I had no other place to put the head."

"Head?" Visions of a severed human head with a river of gore flowing from it filled his imagination. She'd always said she never killed humans, but maybe he'd been wrong. Maybe she'd been lying this whole time.

"The head of a deer. We shall need it for the ritual tonight."

Relief and horror flickered through him. "Why don't you tell me these things? You bring home a deer's head, turn into a panther, fight with the police, and then you leave me there with them?" He could feel his anger rising.

Siamura scooted away a few feet and resumed her knees to chin pose.

He stepped around the bed. "Well? You almost took off your hand at the hospital, and you would have if I hadn't put my hands over your wrist.

Then somehow you escape, leaping out the window abandoning Tyler and me to the cops."

She blinked at him, ears down, hugging her knees. "Sorry, but I was still weak. I could not fly while carrying thee, much less Tyler. I wanted not to leave thee or Tyler, but I had to feed again to recover mine strength. If I do not feed, then I cannot stop Talot and even more people will die."

"Do you realize how close I came to getting arrested? Siamura, I have never had problems with the cops and now I do."

"I want not thee in trouble either. I told the detective not to harass thee or Tyler before I left. That was the best I could do."

"If Agent Kerns wasn't there, Detective Tirzynski would have arrested me. She's convinced that I helped you kill those people."

Her ears flicked up. "I do not kill people."

He stared at the mearoch hugging her knees in the middle of his bedroom. He sighed. "Okay, but you scared me to death. You were saying something about your cat form earlier. I saw your claws with the reverend, but last night… What else am I missing?"

"That was not mine full form."

"How many forms do you have? Can I see this full form of yours?"

"I have two. Mine cat and the one thou sees now. Thee likes not mine claws."

"I'm not used to people sprouting claws."

"Thee shall hate me."

Aiden knelt just in front of the bed facing her. He didn't want to frighten her. "Look. If I hated you, I wouldn't be talking to you. Your full cat form, is this what Tyler saw at the summoning at Eric's house?"

She nodded.

"I thought it was just your head like I saw last night. I'd like to know what everyone is talking about. After all, Tyler and the boys have seen it too."

"It is not the head only, or the claws."

"Don't you trust me? If I'm going to be arrested for being your accomplice, I'd like to know who my partner in crime is."

"Please, Aiden, do not make me do this."

"I need to know."

After a moment of thought, she nodded. Almost at once her entire body shifted into a black panther, the size of a tiger, large paws, pointed cat-like ears on top of her head, a black furred tail. The bat wings remained. At the hospital, it had been just her head that assumed a panther shape. Aiden held his breath. In an instant, an enormous panther with green wings occupied the space where Siamura sat. Her chin was on the carpet and her eyes closed as if afraid to see his reaction, but somehow, he knew she could sense him without her eyes.

He tried to force his heart out of his throat and back down in his chest where it belonged. His mind knew that this was Siamura, that she was in front of him, but something primitive inside him screamed against the vision of a large carnivore in his bedroom. Long teeth peeked out from under dark lips, teeth too long for any normal panther. However, the large green wings were another giveaway this was Siamura. She wouldn't hurt him.

He closed his mouth and managed to swallow a portion of his fear. Siamura hadn't moved. Her tail was uncharacteristically still and lay straight on the floor, though black fur covered it rather than the usual green skin color. Her eyes remained closed. He knelt and willed his hand to touch her head. Slowly he reached out until he felt her fur tickle his fingertips. It wasn't as soft as a housecat's fur but was sleek and smooth to the touch. His hand brushed against her ear, and he instinctively rubbed behind it as he would a cat or dog. She leaned into his hand, except that her head was huge and easily overpowered him, unlike any domestic pet. He rubbed more vigorously to compensate and she opened one large eye, with a vertical pupil as her humanoid form.

Aiden gazed into her eye. This was his Siamura. "It's okay." He brought his other hand around to stroke her other ear.

She turned her head to push into his hands to get him to rub harder. Her black tail started to flick side to side. Aiden began to relax and crawled closer until his knees contacted her paw.

"I should tell thee," she said, but the panther's mouth didn't move.

"Siamura?" Aiden stopped petting her. "How are you speaking?"

"It is I. I cannot vocalize in this form so I need to use an alternate method." Her eyes blinked as she raised her head to look at him. *"It is not mind reading. I can only read what thee wants me to know."*

"So, I don't have to talk?"

"Talking puts thyne thoughts in order so that I can understand thee. Otherwise, I get a jumble of confusing ideas. I used this technique with Tyler last night, though he might not have realized it in the midst of the excitement."

"You said something last night about your claws being dangerous. There was something more to that wasn't there?"

"Yea. Mine claws secrete a poison of magt. That is why I was checking thee for any scratches. May I change back?"

"Yeah, sure." As if talking to a telepathic panther wasn't unnerving enough.

A ripple flowed through her body and the familiar, green-skinned woman appeared. She sat up, stretching. The dark green bands undulated down her body, revealing her nude form. She yawned, baring her upper and lower fangs. Her injuries from the previous night were gone. Siamura shook her head, her hair flying about her face. She brushed it back with a hand and crawled forward to put her head in his lap. Her wings trailed behind her as her green-skinned tail continued to twitch. "Good. I like not frightening thee."

"How did you do that?"

"I move the magt within me. I can shift mine body into mine other shape or somewhere in between."

"Is this your true form or is it the cat?" He smoothed her hair.

"I understand not the question. Both forms are true and real. I am at ease in either one." She hesitated. "I misspoke. I am more at ease in this appearance with thee. Mine cat form is best for hunting."

"Why didn't you tell me before about this? Why did you hide it from me?"

She raised her head and sat back studying him. "What would have been thyne reaction to a panther carrying a deer leg that first night after mine hunt? Thee was upset at this appearance, never mind a panther. I mean not to hide things, Aiden, but I was afraid. I was afraid of what thee would think of me, that thee would turn me out, that thee would hate me. I was afraid of thee. I am still afraid of thee. But Aiden, I need thee. Thee and Tyler are the only people I can hope to trust. This land is foreign and the people within are so antagonistic that I fear for thyne safety. I am surprised that I found thee in thyne own bed last night. I expected to parley with the detective for thyne release." Her wings splayed out behind her.

"How can you be afraid? You're the one who can turn into a panther and destroy a house in a matter of seconds."

She ducked her head. "Yea, I can, but I cannot fight the entire town and survive. There are too many people and only one of me. If they threaten thee or Tyler, then what can I do? Thyne is the first human kindness that I have received in centuries. If it were only weeks or months, that would be bad enough, but seven centuries have changed me. I know that now." She looked up.

"How did you get by the cops downstairs?"

Siamura shrugged. "I climbed in the window. To the police outside, I appeared as none-thing more than a shadow flickering across the building."

Aiden frowned. "How is that possible?"

"The same way I used mine disguise on Wendy and her priest friend. I influence people to see what they expect to see." She ruffled and refolded her wings.

He threw his hands up. "So, what am I supposed to do now? The police told me that I'm supposed to call them when I see you."

"They were expecting me then." Her tail arced upwards.

"What?"

"Thee said when, not if. They were convinced that I was returning here. That is true. I should give Agent Kerns and the detective more credit."

"I'm still in trouble. The detective told me to call her when I see you. If I don't, they'll arrest me. If I do, they'll arrest you."

She shrugged. "Tell them that I threatened thee with thyne death, should thee call them."

"But then they'll blame you…"

Her ears flicked down. "They already blame me for the money and they suspect me for the murders, so one more charge will not matter. I cannot have thee in jeopardy."

"I'm not going to say that."

"But thee must or thee will be in trouble with the law officers. I am an outsider and I always will be, so the onus will not be as hard on me." Her tail curled about her knees. “But thee should not worry about the police. We need to plan for this evening.”

“What’s happening tonight?” This conversation was confusing, and he was having trouble keeping up.

“I must meet Talot tonight and either I end him, or he ends me. I cannot have him killing any more people. I am loath to, but I must ask for thee and Tyler to help to summon Talot. That is what the head of the deer is for.”

“You want to summon Talot after he almost killed you?”

“I do not want to. I have to. If I fail to stop him, he will kill everyone in this town.”

“Can’t the police do anything about him?”

“Talot is a destroyer spirit, sent to destroy this town and everyone within it. The only thing the police will do is to become the first casualties.”

“If Tyler and I help you, how do we not end up dead too? I don’t own a gun.”

“I imagine by this time he is immune to any guns. I will protect thee in such a way that he will have to slay me before he can touch any of ye.” She stood. “We should prepare, if thee agrees to help me.”

Aiden opened a drawer and pulled out a T-shirt and shorts. “You’ll need to wear something.” He handed them to her.

Siamura changed the material into a black halter top and shorts like the ones she’d lost at the hospital and pulled them on. “Thee is not going to make me wear these things when I am in mine panther form, is thee?”

“No, people realize that animals don’t wear clothing.”

“By animals I assume thee means non-human-like animals.” She grinned flashing her fangs.

Aiden laughed. His laughter quieted as Siamura went into the bathroom and picked up the deer’s head. He grimaced at the dead thing. Though it was a beautiful creature with three points on each antler, the eyes were lifeless, the tongue lolling out.

“How did you get out of the handcuffs last night? You practically destroyed the bed, pulling on it. Then a few minutes later, it’s off your hand.”

Siamura's tail snapped. "I was weak and disorientated when I first awoke. After I recovered and thee fed me, I had enough magt to unlock the handcuffs."

"That's why you wanted me to bring the meat. How do you do it? Unlock things, I mean."

"I used the ability on the first night after I hunted to unlock the back door and get in, remember? I used it again last night to open the window to get in. I become part of the lock to learn how it wants to move and then I nudge it. It is similar to what we did to put the house right the other day." She glanced at the door. "We need to hurry to leave before the police come back in force."

Aiden frowned. He didn't understand why they would return so quickly.

She continued, "There is a car sitting on the street outside, but only two are downstairs at the moment, so we should go."

He quickly shaved and changed into jeans and a shirt. Siamura grabbed his hand and led him past Tyler's door and down the stairs. She changed into her human disguise with green top and blue jeans.

A tall cop stood beside the stairs. "Excuse me Ma'am. Who are you?"

Siamura stepped up and placed her hand on the man's head. A green flash, his eyes went wide then they closed. She caught him in her arms and carried him to a chair.

Another cop standing by the kitchen table pointed a gun at Siamura. "Stop! Hands up."

Another flash of green as the cop yelped and the gun flew across the room to land beside Aiden's feet. Siamura set the first officer in the chair and stepped to the second.

The man's eyes grew wide. Waving a hand at her, he said, "You're her! Stay back!" With his other hand he grabbed his radio hanging from his shoulder.

Aiden rushed to the kitchen. If the cop made that call, then they'd have the Feds and the entire police department on their heads. Siamura dropped her disguise and continued to amble towards the panicked officer. She wasn't in any hurry. Aiden wondered if she realized what the radio was.

The cop spoke into the mike. "Suspect is at the Moray house! I repeat. Suspect is at the Moray house!"

Siamura shook her head and extended her hand. "It works not. I shall not hurt thee."

The man glared at the mike and released it. His hand slapped at his utility belt and came up with a canister.

Aiden said, "Watch it!" He threw up his arm to ward off the coming spray.

The cop yelped again as the can flew upward and bounced off the ceiling.

Siamura's tail swung in fast arcs behind her. "Please stop." Her tail was a sign that she was becoming irate.

The man snatched her arm and tried to throw her. He stopped, tugging on her arm was like he was trying to move the house itself. Absolutely nothing happened. She touched his lower back with her other hand and his legs dropped from underneath him.

Siamura caught him easily. "Have a care. Let me help thee."

The cop screamed, "What happened to my legs?! You bitch! What —"

"Silence!" she growled, her fangs lengthening, "Or I will take thyne arms too." She raised her hand and her claws emerged as the cruel black daggers they were.

The man stared goggle-eyed at the claws in front of his face.

Aiden shouted, "That's enough! You've proved your point."

Siamura whirled, eyes glowing, mouth distended by fangs that no longer fit. Her change halted as she noticed Aiden's horrified reaction. She blinked once or twice and her fangs and claws retracted. Her eyes ceased to glow. She turned back to the cop. "I am sorry. Thee will have thyne legs when thou awakens." She touched his head and he fell unconscious. She carried him to the living room and set him in another chair.

Tyler ran down the stairs. "What's going on? Siamura! You're back!"

"Wait!" Aiden held out his arm to block Tyler. "What the hell was that? Why did you do that?"

Siamura's ears flattened. "I forgot mine-self. But he attacked me!"

"Yes, he did, but you didn't have to scare the living shit out of him. What did you do to his legs? Holy crap Siamura! That's… hideous. You practically laughed at that poor man as you pulled his strings like some sick puppet master."

Her ears stood up and she took a breath as if to shout. Then her wings sagged on either side of her. She murmured, “Thee is right. I am hideous. But they keep attacking me… and I forgot.” She stared at him. “I forgot that I am a terrifying, horrible monster that deserves to be put down like a rabid dog.”

Aiden motioned for Tyler to go upstairs and dress. Aiden sat beside her. “Siamura, you scared me. You were playing with that man like a cat would play with a half dead mouse.”

Her eyes hardened. “The man attacked me. I could not help mine-self. It happened. In the world out there, it is kill or be killed and teach the survivors to fear thee. If thee does not like it then I do not know what we can do.”

Aiden blinked. “That’s why I’m here. To help you navigate this new world. I’ll be with you to help you through this. Okay?”

She shook her head.

He pulled her into a hug. “You’re with me and I still need your help to get rid of Talot.”

She softened into his embrace and hugged him back. They stayed like that for a couple of minutes.

Tyler came back downstairs, now dressed. “Are you guys, okay?”

Siamura said, “Yea, we are good. I need to get something from upstairs.” She left them below.

Aiden turned. “We need to have breakfast. Something fast. No idea when we’ll eat again.”

Tyler pointed to the sleeping cops. “What happened to those guys?”

“Siamura put them to sleep, temporarily.” He waved for Tyler to follow him into the kitchen.

Siamura came downstairs and set the deer’s head on the counter farthest from the stove. It still bothered Aiden to have some dead thing in the kitchen. He poured two bowls of cereal while Siamura began searching through the cabinets. “Does thee have any red wine?”

Aiden put the bowls down and turned to her. “In the bottom of the pantry. Why?”

“We require it for the ceremony. I should have a large bowl to hold it.”

Tyler got up from the table and pulled out a large metal bowl from a cabinet. “We’re doing a ceremony? What’s it for?”

Siamura set the bowl on the counter and poured the red wine into it, while Tyler and Aiden finished their hasty breakfast and Aiden began to clear the table. "We need to summon Talot so that I can defeat him. Let me concentrate a moment."

Each of her fingers grew an impossibly long black claw, sprouting from her fingertips, or rather her fingertips became claws as long as her fingers, curved like scythes. Aiden stopped clearing the table and stared. No matter how many times he had seen them, they always gave him a chill.

Using a claw from her opposite hand, she slit her left palm. Blood flowed down her fingers, over her claws, and dropped into the wine. Her eyes glowed faintly as she muttered something under her breath. The blood turned green as it ran down her claws, spattering along the surface like skipping stones on a pond before finally sinking into the wine. Siamura stirred the wine with her bloodied talons. Her claws retracted into her fingers and she carefully poured the wine back into the bottle, spilling a little in the sink.

Replacing the cork she said, "Do not drink this. It is poisonous. We shall need it for the ceremony later." She thoroughly cleaned the bowl and sink. "Tyler, can thee get some paper to write on?"

He returned with a pad of paper. Siamura took several sheets and waved her hand, merging them together, using her magt. She made several of these larger sheets. Then she smeared her blood on the sheets, and the paper drank it up without leaving a red smudge behind. She rolled the sheets up and handed them to Aiden. "We will need these later. Tyler, please call Kevin and Matt. Tell them to meet us by the old house beyond the park."

"Wait a minute," Aiden said, "You know that they have our phones tapped. The cops will know what we're up to."

Siamura stopped. "I assume by tapped, thee means they can listen to our conversation. What does thee suggest then?"

Tyler said, "I could go to Kevin's house. He hasn't left for school yet. Which reminds me, what about school?"

Siamura put her hand on his shoulder. "For the safety of thyne town, thee should come with me today to the park. I am going to need thyne assistance."

"Woo-hoo! No school!"

"Tyler, thee should not celebrate because I am asking both of ye to risk thyne lives to allow me to fight and defeat Talot. And knowledge is important. If I fail, he will kill both of ye first before destroying the rest of the town. I like not having to ask thee to this, but I do not want to spend days hunting him while he gets stronger and more comfortable in this world. The sooner I face him, the better."

"Can't we just run away and hide?" Tyler asked.

She glanced at Aiden then back to Tyler. "Thee is asking me to leave the entire town to perish. I cannot tolerate that. Though I am only responsible for thee, Tyler, and thyne three friends, I cannot permit all the inhabitants of thyne town to die without trying to prevent it."

When she put it that way, how could anyone refuse her? Aiden said, "It's okay. We'll go with you and help you any way we can."

She smiled. "Many thanks, Aiden. It means a great deal to me. There is one more thing to be done. Tyler, does thee have the blue amulet?"

Tyler said, "Yeah, it's in the car."

"Can thee get it?"

He ran to the garage and retrieved it. Siamura cringed and shrank away from him when he returned.

Tyler's eyes widened in concern. "What's the matter? I did what you told me to."

She hung on a kitchen chair for support. Her voice was quiet. "I know, but…" She shook her head. "This is… Does thee trust me?"

Tyler nodded. "Yeah. What's wrong?"

"Aiden, does… Does thee trust me?"

"Of course, I do. I'm agreeing to risk both our lives for you. What are you getting at?"

"I am going to ask thee to destroy that blue amulet. That act is going to change me, although I cannot predict the exact events. By destroying it, thee will break mine curse and therefore mine charge to protect the four that summoned me. That is why I am asking if thee trusts me. The amulet ties me to the four. Without it, I am free. I believe the energy released will make me stronger and better able to face Talot. But there is a chance that I will be cast back to Irgale and unable to return to help thee. But I do not think that will happen. I cannot have thee destroy the amulet without knowing the possible consequences."

Aiden stared. It was strange to have her lay bare her vulnerabilities. "What happens if we do nothing with the amulet?"

She said, "Everything remains as it is. Which means whomever gains possession of the amulet controls me, and the magt locked up in the amulet stays within it, preventing me from using it to defeat Talot. It is thyne decision. That is why I asked ye if thee trusts me."

Tyler took the amulet and handed it to Siamura. "Here, you take it."

She cowered. "I cannot."

"Hold out your hand."

With some hesitation, Siamura did so. Tyler put it into her hand. It rolled off his palm and fell through her hand as if it wasn't there to stop it. She cried out as the amulet clattered on the floor, glowing balefully.

Aiden picked it up. The amulet was cool to the touch, but it disturbed him, setting off a sharp pain in his shoulder. As he held it, it became progressively colder, traveling up his arm until his hand was almost numb with the cold. He gave it back to Tyler before it caused permanent harm. "Destroy it. Whatever it is, it's an awful thing." He washed his hands in the sink to clean the cold sickness from his flesh.

Siamura stared at him. "Why does it affect thee so?"

Aiden dried his hands on a towel. "I don't know. Maybe it knows that I'm sympathetic to your plight."

She shook her head. "Tyler is sympathetic too, yet he can hold it. Perhaps it is the fact that he was one of the four summoners."

Tyler grimaced. "It still gives me the creeps. I don't like it either. How do we get rid of it?"

Siamura said, "Set it on the hearth and smash it with a stone."

Tyler ran into the den to the fireplace. Setting the amulet on the bricks, he searched for a rock. The gold symbols spun madly around the amulet as if it knew of its impending doom. Siamura stayed back, ears folded down, drawing her wings and tail tightly around her.

Tyler found a rock and brought it down on the amulet. Nothing happened. The amulet didn't break. Tyler raised the rock again and with all his might, he smashed it down. A flash of blue light burst out as it shattered, but otherwise it was strangely silent.

Siamura screamed and dread filled Aiden. She fell and tucked into herself, upsetting a couple of chairs on her way down. Her tail writhed behind her on the floor, then twisted about her leg twitching.

Aiden rushed to her and tried to help her up. She stumbled and leaned on him. She was bleeding profusely from her left hand. Her right clasped it and blood oozed between her fingers to drip onto the floor. Visions of her transformation on her first night here ran through Aiden's mind.

Tyler rushed to her. "Oh my God! I'm so sorry."

Aiden guided her to a chair. Siamura panted, "Tyler, please take… the rock off the amulet."

Tyler froze.

Aiden implored, "Tyler, hurry!"

Tyler went back to the fireplace and lifted the rock. He yelped, "Oh my God! What do I do with it?"

Aiden couldn't see what he was reacting to. "What is it?"

Siamura got to her feet unsteadily. "It is mine finger that Father Elringson cut off. We need to take it and the remains of the amulet with us to the old house where I was first summoned. We should leave now. Tyler, can thee call Kevin and Matt to meet us there? Tell Matt to bring the book, the Spiritorium, and the stone of Talot."

Aiden said, "But our phones are tapped!"

Siamura nodded. "I thought of an old spell. Trust me."

Aiden still held her. "Shouldn't you rest? Smashing that amulet seemed like it hurt you pretty badly."

"We have not the time. Get a bag and gather the remains from the hearth. I will take the head. Do not forget the wine and paper." She leaned against the table.

Tyler went to the phone while Aiden found a small plastic bag. At the hearth, Aiden saw Siamura's finger, but it wasn't a dry, mummified thing. It looked like it had been cut off a few minutes ago, lying in small pool of blood. He grimaced and gently placed it in the bag along with the broken pieces of the amulet. "Can't you reattach it?"

Siamura said, "Nay, we have to take it to the old house." She picked up the deer's head in her good hand. Her eyes glowed briefly and all the spilled blood vanished.

Tyler returned with his phone. “It’s Matt. He won’t come unless he talks to you.”

“I will not use that device. They are recording everything.”

Tyler spoke into the phone. “She’s here, I’m handing the phone to her.” He put the phone to her ear.

Siamura shied away. Then her expression softened and she mouthed words silently. She stepped away from Tyler.

Tyler put the phone to his ear. “Matt? Matt? Are you there?” He lowered the phone. “He hung up. What did he say?”

Siamura said, “He said he would meet us there. Before the police arrive, we need to be away.” She didn’t look well. The destruction of the amulet seemed to drain her instead of augmenting her strength.

Tyler picked up his book bag and placed the wine in it. Aiden carried the baggie with Siamura’s finger and the rolls of paper. Aiden locked the back door behind him out of habit leaving the unconscious cops inside. “What did you say to Matt? I didn’t hear anything.”

Siamura was halfway across the back yard. “Good, then they will not steal mine voice. I told him to bring the book and the stone and to meet us at the old house behind the park.”

They climbed through the fence behind the house. Aiden said, “But how was he able to hear you?” He had to help the mearoch through the fence.

“It is similar to the method I used to talk to thee in mine other shape. I merely directed it to the device that connected Matt and mine-self. Any human being listening on that connection will hear me. The two of thee did not hear anything because thee was not listening through that device. Any machines attached to the connection will only hear what thee did - silence. I took the chance that the devices connecting us would conduct the information. It seems that they did because Matt agreed to meet us.”

Aiden nodded, impressed how quickly Siamura adapted to the technology. They walked behind the houses to the park. He’d expected her to fly, but she walked with them though she occasionally stumbled. Perhaps she didn’t have the strength or was scared she’d be seen in the daytime. He winced at the sight of her bare feet on the rocks and dirt, but they didn’t seem to bother her at all. She still cradled her hand, but it wasn’t bleeding anymore. There was a stump where her left index finger used to be. Aiden asked, “Why did you lose your finger when the amulet was smashed?”

“Father Elringson cut off mine finger seven centuries ago. He encased it in that amulet so that it would control me. Mine finger cannot be in two places at once. I should have remembered that. Once freed from the magt of the amulet the duplicate finger had to disappear.” She held up her left hand, now with only five fingers. She wriggled the stub of her missing digit. “We are going to give mine original finger a home soon enough.” She stumbled and Aiden caught her.

“Where?”

“In mine new grove of course.” She smiled, and then collapsed in his arms.

“Siamura?” Aiden held onto her.

Tyler rushed over.

“I should be stronger, yet mine strength ebbs from me. We must get to the forest.”

Chapter 21

Sacrifice

Aiden said, "Tyler, here take this stuff. I'll have to carry her." He was always amazed at how light she was.

Tyler picked up the paper and the baggie with her finger and put them in his bag. Finally, he picked up the deer's head with a grimace and followed.

Siamura's eyes drifted open as Aiden started to walk. "Mine hero. And fearsome callous faterras fluttered on his head to fill it with the depths of mallous… Deux et…" She continued to mutter or sing in a language that was both captivating and frightening, like a Hieronymus Bosch painting of Hell set to verse. He tried not to listen, but it was difficult when the bushes nearby would undulate with her voice.

Tyler stayed close to Aiden. "What is she singing?"

Aiden shook his head, concentrating on avoiding as many plants as possible. Eventually, she fell into silence.

After a few minutes, Aiden saw the woods where a few days ago only a handful of trees stood. Now the forest surrounded the old house on three sides, making the structure look shrunken and frail in the company of the massive trees. And the trees weren't neat rows of straight-trunked lumber. Instead, they were enormous, the woods looking like it was a millennium old.

Some of the trees were tall with wide, majestic trunks, others were sprawling things with twisty trunks and branches, ready to grab wayward travelers. There were all kinds of trees — pine, oak, cedar, maple, and others that Aiden couldn't begin to name. The smell was familiar — Siamura's dark, earthy, scent redolent with arboreal scents. Yet beneath it all a quiet power crackled. Thick moss covered the trunks and all manner of crawling things darted about at their approach. Though it was late October, all the trees had their leaves in full green as if impervious to the cool weather.

Aiden could sense human beings were not welcome in or near the trees. It wasn't a friendly place. Aiden had the feeling each individual tree sensed he and Tyler on some primal level. He and Tyler stopped, staring up at the trees, entranced.

Siamura murmured, "Come along." She rolled out of Aiden's arms and stood on shaky legs. She retrieved the deer's head from Tyler and stumbled.

Aiden rushed to support her. They took a few steps closer to the nearest tree, a particularly gnarled specimen. The branches shook — or was that the breeze?

The pressure in Aiden's shoulder went into overdrive. This was old and powerful magic, unlike anything he had experienced before. For the first time in his life, the urge to run away nearly overwhelmed him. He entertained the thought of grabbing Tyler, running back to the house, and calling the police to arrest him so that these trees couldn't touch him.

A corner of his mind recalled the news stories a couple of days ago about plants growing suddenly behind the park and Jen's recounting of the bushes growing quickly in this area. At the time, he'd put it down to exaggeration and the usual media sensationalism. If it weren't for the string of murders occurring at the same time, this forest would have been the main talk on all of the programs.

Siamura said, "Aiden, is thee all right?"

Aiden asked, his voice a whisper, "How'd it get so big?"

She tilted her head. "Only in the last few hours has it grown to this size."

The bark on the tree in front of them seemed to shift almost forming a face, the face of an old man twisted as if bent on murder in the most foul and painful way he could manage. When Aiden blinked it was gone. Its branches reached out far beyond its trunk and a branch stabbed Aiden's cheek. "Ow!"

Siamura dropped the deer's head and caught the branch. She held it a moment then slumped against him. She barely whispered, "Pick up the head. Take me to the trunk."

Aiden did so. He shuddered as some of the tree's limbs twitched and touched them briefly as they reached the trunk. At least he wasn't stabbed again.

"Put the head next to the trunk."

Aiden placed the deer's head at the base of the trunk. Siamura fell to her knees by the head. Aiden knelt down to help her but stopped. She caressed the trunk like an old friend. No, not like a friend, more like a lover or favorite child. A pang of jealousy shot through Aiden, surprising him, until he reminded himself that she was a mearoch, a forest spirit. This was her home, her relationship with the trees.

"Carry me. I cannot walk. We must go to the center."

Aiden picked her up, carefully folding her splayed wings in the process. "I don't know. The rest of the trees seem like they want to kill us."

Tyler joined them, the leaves on the dark trees around them shivering with resentment.

"Thee must take me and mine finger to the center of the clearing. Bury it there. Please I know not how much time."

A motion drew Aiden's attention away from the trees. It was Kevin running down the hill from the direction of the park. He carried a pack and wore a black T-shirt with his khaki pants. Aiden had never seen him in black except for last night.

Kevin, out of breath, pulled up just out of reach of the tree. He eyed it, then Siamura in Aiden's arms. "The cops know about what we're doing! There's a police car in the parking lot!" He pointed behind him towards the gate and Franklin Park.

Tyler said, "Did you see Matt?"

Kevin shook his head.

Siamura whispered to Aiden. Aiden said, "Kevin, Siamura says to wait here for him. We need to go into the forest. She says this tree will protect you, but you have to stay close to it. We have to hurry."

Kevin trembled, clutching his bag tighter.

Tyler said, "It looks mean, but he's… I mean, the tree is all right." He pointed to the correct one.

Kevin nodded and shuffled to the old gnarly tree.

They dove into the forest leaving Kevin behind. Limbs whipped past them. Aiden clung to Siamura in his arms and dodged around branches and trunks. The oppressive feeling persisted, like a weight increasing on his shoulders. He stumbled over a root, shook his head at a limb that slapped his face.

Then he was falling. Aiden curled his body around Siamura trying to protect her on the way down. His back hit a tree trunk and she tumbled from his arms. She opened her eyes as Tyler ran up and gripped the root near her. Aiden caught his breath. Tyler put his arm around her.

The branches around them lifted and the roots sunk lower. Aiden didn't ask why. He picked himself up and gathered Siamura in his arms. He and Tyler continued their journey, ducking branches and jumping roots.

Then they were in the open in a small clearing about five large car lengths across covered in young grass, where the branches of the surrounding trees almost closed off the sky above. They ran to the center of the ankle-deep grass. Aiden set the mearoch down as gently as he could. With his hands he dug into the soft soil, remembering Siamura's instructions.

"Ok, give me the baggie."

Tyler knelt beside the hole. "Shouldn't it be deeper?" He doffed his pack. Unzipping it, he fished for the items.

With a shrug, Aiden dug further until Tyler opened the baggie and poured the contents into the hole. The finger grew a long black claw and undulated in the dirt like an earthworm trying to bury itself. Aiden stared first at it, and then at the unconscious form of Siamura. Tyler kept glancing between Siamura and the finger, as if he expected something to happen.

Aiden said, "I'm hoping that's a good sign." He backfilled the hole, patting it down, afraid the finger with its claw might escape.

A great gust of wind came from the ground. The grass lay down radially away from them. Then the gust hit the surrounding trees scattering small animals and birds. The breeze passed and the grass stood up again.

Siamura coughed and struggled to her knees. Her wings flapped around them like a large tent. Aiden didn't dare move. Tyler likewise watched her. She remained on her hands and knees, wings outstretched and still as she trembled. Out of the corner of his eye Aiden saw small wisps of green light zip across the ground towards the mearoch. He felt a tingling as his hands and body interrupted the little wisps. His fatigue vanished.

After a few moments Siamura inhaled deeply and sat up facing them. She shook her head and folded her wings behind her. Brushing her hair behind her erect ears she said, “That is much better. Many thanks to ye.”

Tyler said, “What did we just do?”

“I gave something to establish mine presence here — an offering of goodwill.”

Tyler said, “You mean like a sacrifice.”

Siamura hesitated. “Yea, everything has a price.”

Aiden said, “What did you just buy?”

She spread her arms. “All what ye sees. I am complete. I owe ye both so much for helping me, again. We should return to Kevin quickly.”

As Siamura walked to the trees, the ankle-deep grass bowed out of her path. As She approached a tree and caressed the trunk, the branches parted enough to let them through. Now the attitude of the trees had changed from ominous to welcoming and Aiden no longer felt the weight of the trees’ anger in his shoulder. She waved them forward. He nodded to Tyler and tentatively stepped forward.

Siamura said, “The trees were not yet used to ye. I let them know that ye are mine friends and without both of ye, they would not be standing here today. The word will pass through the forest and they shall not cause ye any distress.”

Tyler spoke up, “Why were they so mean before?”

“They knew not ye. As ye become more acquainted with them, I am sure ye shall feel a sense of welcome. Like me, they are very old. Most of these trees are mine original grove from centuries ago. Have patience with them because they are relearning what it is like to be in this world again. They are very much like I was when I first came to ye almost a week ago.”

When Aiden touched the tree, he expected it to do something, to grab him or crush him, but only a tickle of warmth on his fingertips gave him the sensation of gratefulness. The trees seemed to be welcoming him, making him feel like this was his home too. Tyler also touched the trunk, and after a moment he relaxed, a smile forming.

Aiden and Tyler followed Siamura into the forest and he noticed the trees and their branches lifting and parting in front of Siamura, as they would have done if she had put her arm up to move them. Luckily, the limbs remained parted to allow him and Tyler through too. It sure would have been easier if they had this help on the way in.

Tyler tapped him. "Dad, don't the trees seem healthier than before?"

"They do, although I wouldn't be able to say specifically why."

"Maybe they're greener."

Aiden noticed that the shadows they were walking through had a tinge of green. No direct sun reached the ground, not like other forests where a slash or speck of bright sun marked their path. The smell was a fragrance of trees and moist earth even stronger than before, and he could feel a palpable moisture in the air. Everything seemed to be amplified. Siamura's index finger was still missing, but he noticed that she was moving with more energy with each step she took.

They reached the familiar gnarled tree at the edge of the forest, the tree appearing healthier and greener than before. The old house stood to the right of the tree. Kevin stood beside the tree within the shelter of its branches, but at a distance from the trunk. His attention was directed at several officers coming down the hill from the park on foot.

Another cop opened the gate at the top of the ridge. A police SUV eased through and down the small hill and came to a stop just outside the reach of the trees. Aiden heard the trees' agitation and felt a rippling underneath the ground as if the tree roots extended towards the vehicle. Siamura's eyes narrowed and her tail snapped, signs that her mood darkened considerably.

Chapter 22

Parley

Aiden had to walk faster to keep up with Siamura as they approached Kevin. He didn't want to leave Siamura alone with anyone, especially in her worsening mood. The branches stretched towards the cops like questing fingers. Grass shot up from the ground in a wave of verdant green stopping a few feet beyond the grasping limbs.

Detective Tirzynski climbed out of the SUV her trench coat flapping in the breeze, eyeing the encroaching vegetation with raised eyebrows. She shouted, "Kevin, come over here. It's too dangerous under that tree." Two officers stayed with the vehicle, while the other two climbed out and flanked her and Agent Kerns.

Agent Kerns said something to the cops around them.

Detective Tirzynski shrugged and called again, "Kevin, come…" She stopped after seeing the three of them emerge from the forest.

Siamura called in her accented English, "Good afternoon, Detective Tirzynski, Agent Kerns, and officers. Please keep ye distance for ye safety."

"Are you threatening us?" the detective called, her voice carried to them on the wind.

Agent Kerns said, "I'd rather not shout. Come closer and we'll talk." His tone was the opposite of the detective's — conversational and relaxed. He too, stayed several steps from the suddenly appearing grass.

Siamura said, "We shall meet ye in front of the house — only the two of ye, not the rest of the officers."

Aiden was about to object, but Agent Kerns said, "Okay, good enough." This prompted the detective to turn to him, her hands on her hips.

Aiden turned to Tyler. "Wait over next to the tree by Kevin. He doesn't look very comfortable."

Tyler opened his mouth to protest, but Aiden cut him off. "Tyler, please. Siamura is not in a good mood and Kevin looks like he's going to bolt at any moment. We need him to perform the ceremony with us and I can't be in two places at once."

Tyler nodded grudgingly and jogged over to Kevin. Aiden sighed with relief.

Siamura and Aiden met Agent Kerns and Detective Tirzynski in front of the house, which looked even more forlorn than it had. Maybe the forest around it made it seem smaller. Lush grass covered the ground here, and the air was moist and smelled of earth and trees, in contrast to the park, which was drier and less alive.

The detective started, "What happened to your wounds from last night? The doctor told us it would be days before you recovered."

Siamura's ears stood up. "I healed mine-self, similar to what I did for Eric."

The detective raised an eyebrow. "Where did you go last night?"

"I hunted." Siamura nodded in the direction of Kevin and Tyler standing beside the tree. "The head of the deer is there."

"You didn't take any detours?"

"Detective, why should I tarry when I was weak and hungry? Nay, I hunted as quick as I could, then I healed mine-self."

"You don't remember going into a house where the hunting might be easier?"

"I do not kill people, detective." Siamura shook out her wings, her eyes beginning to glow. "Last night I could have stood aside and let Talot eat the both of ye and all the people with ye. I could have said that I was powerless against him. Ask thyne-self, detective, why did I put mine-self between the destroyer, Talot, and thee? He would have eliminated thee and mine trouble with thee, leaving me blameless. Nay, I stopped him from harming anyone at the house last night. A nervous officer shot Eric. Again, I could have stood by and done none-thing. Thee would not have suspected that I could save him, yet I did." Her tail twitched like a cat's would, a sign the detective was irritating her.

Tirzynski said, "You assaulted us last night at the hospital. You obstructed the investigation."

Siamura's tail snapped. "Thee chained me! Is that mine reward for saving the life of Eric? I prevented thee and the others from becoming victims of Talot."

Aiden took Siamura's hand. "Stop this." Her hand had warmed more so than normal.

Tirzynski set her hands on her hips. "We've spent the better part of the morning trying to pick through the remains of four people. Hell, at first, we couldn't be sure exactly how many victims there were. There was so little left of them. That makes eight people dead at this point. How do I know you're not working with Talot?"

Siamura stepped closer, arching her wings over them. "Thee dares!"

Aiden pulled on Siamura's arm. "Stop! Both of you." He was amazed that Siamura hesitated.

The detective reached for her gun, but Agent Kerns put his hand over hers. He said, "Everyone stay calm."

There was silence for several seconds as Detective Tirzynski and Siamura stared each other down. Thankfully, the detective looked away first and the glow dissipated from Siamura's eyes. Agent Kerns glanced west, and everyone followed his attention.

A figure ran towards them dressed in a black duster, carrying a backpack, Matt. Tirzynski called out, "Matt, come over here."

The teenager ignored her and continued running.

Detective Tirzynski shouted, "Evans, Perkins, I want that boy in protective custody."

Aiden didn't think that was a very good idea as Siamura's eyes began to glow again. The two men left the SUV and ran across the grass towards Matt. But as they got closer to the trees, vines leapt out of the ground and pinned both men. They screamed as the vines thickened, wrapping securely around their limbs.

The other two cops ducked under the branches and headed for Tyler and Kevin. Siamura's eyes glowed and the branches plucked the men up into the foliage. They shouted as the limbs wrapped about them preventing their escape.

Detective Tirzynski said, “Let them go! I swear…” She pulled her gun and yelped as her fingers splayed open. The gun fell into the grass where vines burst out of the dirt and entwined themselves around it. The detective bent down to get it and the vines entangled her hand. They shot up her legs and pulled her to the ground.

Agent Kerns shouted, “Detective!”

She shrieked, “Shoot her!”

Aiden stepped in front of Siamura, in part to distract the mearoch, but more importantly to prevent Agent Kerns from attacking her.

The agent stepped away with his hands up in front of him. “Everyone needs to calm down. We’re just talking.”

Matt stopped near them, surveying the scene, and laughed. “Wicked!”

This was quickly getting out of hand. Aiden pointed. “Matt, go stand by that tree with Kevin and Tyler.”

Matt hesitated, grinning at the men screaming on the ground. He really seemed to enjoy other people’s pain and fear. If they didn’t need him for the ritual, Aiden would have gladly handed the bastard over to the cops without a second thought.

Aiden shouted, “Move it!” The boy jumped as if touched by a cattle prod.

Aiden murmured to Siamura, “Let the men go. They aren’t your enemy. It’ll be all right, I promise.” He had to repeat himself, stroking her arm but eventually the limbs around the men in the tree slackened and the two men scrambled to get up. Their eyes were wild, and Aiden wasn’t sure if they would attack or run. He thought he should help them decide and yelled, “You two get out of here.” They didn’t pause, and high-tailed it back to the park. The vines loosened on the pair in the grass, and they followed the other men.

Aiden turned to the detective. “Okay, she will release you, but please leave.” The vines uncoiled from the detective’s body. Tirzynski stood and brushed herself off.

Detective Tirzynski snapped, “I want my gun.”

Agent Kerns shouted at her. “Will you shut up! I don’t know what the fuck is going on here, but don’t make the woman mad. Wait for me in the SUV.”

Tirzynski twitched her lip and stalked to the vehicle.

The agent turned. “Aiden, what is going on?”

Aiden said, “We’re going to call Talot so that Siamura can defeat him. Every day that he’s out there, he’s growing stronger and will keep killing.”

“I can help.”

Siamura rumbled, “Thyne weapons are going to be useless against him. Leave here. I cannot be responsible for people dying if they get in the way.” Her patience was sorely tried already, and Aiden hoped he would take the hint and leave soon. He wasn’t sure how long he could rein in Siamura’s temper.

Agent Kerns pointed at the tree. “Aiden, what about your son and the other boys? Do they need to be here?”

Siamura’s ears stood up. “Yea, they are three of the four original summoners. They are necessary to bring Talot here now. I am taking measures for their safety and for Aiden too.”

Agent Kerns said, “I can’t believe there isn’t some way that we can help you.”

Siamura said, “Keep people away from here. If I fail, evacuate the town. Take the gun. I dislike the thing.”

Aiden said, “Agent Kerns, I’m sorry this didn’t work out better.”

Agent Kerns picked up Tirzynski’s gun and pocketed it. “Hey, I’m sorry too. Good luck.”

The agent turned and walked back to the SUV. As Detective Tirzynski drove back up the hill to the park, she and Agent Kerns seemed to be exchanging heated words inside the vehicle.

Chapter 23

Battle

Aiden watched as Detective Tirzynski drove the SUV carrying her and Agent Kerns back over the ridge. Even if they were successful, they would still have to deal with the detective, along with everyone else. She wouldn't let up on Siamura, even if she did succeed in defeating Talot. However, he would worry about that later, if they lived. It was just before noon, as a cool breeze swept about him and Siamura. The weather was crisp and pleasant, which seemed odd with what they had planned for later.

Siamura walked with him to the run-down house where the boys waited for them. "They watch from the hill."

"Of course, they are." It didn't surprise him, but it still peeved him on some level.

"I have damaged thyne standing with the community. Detective Tirzynski is going to exact some kind of retribution against thee for helping me."

"Don't worry about it."

"I will not have her arresting or harassing thee or Tyler."

"Let's get through this first." If he thought about tomorrow, he would lose his mind.

She blinked with a flicker in her golden cat-like eyes as if she was going to argue, but only nodded. "Of course."

As they approached the boys, Kevin stepped back, glancing nervously at the ground. Matt maintained his cool, arms folded, nodding like he was in charge. Tyler came forward. "What happened?"

Matt snorted, "My demon kicked some cop butt! That's what happened."

Siamura stared at Matt, tail up, and Aiden thought she might hit him. Instead, she said, "Matt, did thee bring the stone and the book?"

"Yeah, I did. They're in my bag."

When he wasn't forthcoming, she held out her hand. "May I see them?"

He gripped the strap of the bag slung over his shoulder tighter. "No, it wouldn't be right. Demons shouldn't see the Spiritorium."

"Would thee rather be the next meal of Talot? Without that information I cannot build a protection strong enough to keep him at bay."

Aiden stepped forward. "Can I see them?"

Matt hesitated.

Aiden continued, "We're wasting time."

Matt grunted. "All right, all right." He handed the bag to Aiden.

The excessive weight of the bag surprised Aiden as he eased it to the ground. He unzipped the pack and felt an annoying buzz in his shoulder as he saw the leather-bound tome within. Steeling himself against the distraction, he opened it on top of the bag and found the pages were slick with an oily texture, not like normal paper, and the lettering on the pages small and cramped.

Siamura looked over his shoulder. "Writing bound tight and confined, reflects on the mind of Father Elringson."

Matt stepped towards Aiden and the book. "Hey, don't let her see that."

Siamura snapped, "First, I am not a demon, I am a mearoch, and second, where is the section on Talot and mine-self so that we can create a spell to summon him?"

Matt knelt down and turned the pages. "There, that's you." Then Matt flipped several pages over as if he knew this book backwards and forwards. "And that's Talot." It was no wonder that Matt was as twisted and arrogant as he was. Aiden could feel the slimy taint of the book on him.

Siamura sat beside Aiden as Matt moved away. Despite his bluster, Matt wasn't comfortable being near the mearoch. Siamura read the crabbed Latin about herself and laughed bitterly, "He describes me as an arch-demon, second only to the Princes of Hell in power. I know not any of these creatures. All of this is to make him appear a hero for defeating me."

Matt said, "But you had an evil forest full of vile, crawling things, right?"

"Is this forest evil?" She pointed to the trees. "I know not what the definition of *his* evil is."

"But you killed people before," Matt continued.

Siamura was silent, and her smile vanished. She ignored him and flipped to the section on Talot. She became more agitated, her finger darting on the page, poking aggressively at the various words.

Siamura grumbled, "I do not kill people."

Matt said, "But you did."

Aiden raised his hand to ward off Matt. "Stop it. Siamura, you need the boys to summon Talot. What am I doing during all this?"

Siamura raised her head. "Take the stone from the pack."

Aiden dug in Matt's pack and found the black obsidian. As soon as he touched it, cold numbed his fingers and he pulled it from the bag. "Here, take it." It wasn't just the cold. It was also distasteful to handle, like he wanted to wash his hands. It reminded him of Talot, the same distasteful taint he'd felt at the house where Talot and Siamura had fought.

"I cannot. The same way I could not touch mine own device, the amulet."

Aiden placed the obsidian back in the backpack, staring at her.

She continued, "The boys are going to summon Talot with mine help, and because of that, they will need to stay within the circle. That leaves thee to carry the stone."

There it was — so simple and matter of fact. Aiden needed to carry the beast's obsidian.

Aiden asked, "So I carry the stone. What does that mean? What do I do with it?"

Siamura cocked her head. "I know not. But if it is inside the circle then we cannot use it without exposing the boys to Talot."

Aiden said, "Why did you assume that I would carry this? That's what I find upsetting. You had everything planned and you didn't tell me. You knew about the stone. Why didn't you tell me about it?"

Siamura's ears flicked down and her eyes smoldered. "Oh, perhaps being isolated for the past seven centuries, I have forgotten to consult with others in any plans. I did not mean to exclude thee, Aiden. I am not in the habit of having to talk or deal with people."

"When you're asking us to risk our lives along with yours, we have a right to know what's going on."

"All right. Does thee agree to assist me now that thee knows what is required of thee?"

"Are you sure about this? I know it's not safe, but are you sure that this is the best we can do?" Aiden asked.

"If we wait or I spend time hunting him, Talot will get stronger. The more bodies he consumes, the more powerful he becomes."

He looked into her eyes, at once eerie and pleading. He could not hope to understand her motivation any more than to understand what it was like to live a thousand years. He did know she was attempting to save people. She wasn't being malicious, but she didn't know how to live with people or reason with them. In her own way, she was trying to make up for her past mistakes. "I'll help you because I know that red spirit is on a mission to kill everyone, including me and my son, but please make an effort to tell me what's going on in your head beforehand. I hate being blindsided."

She blinked, absorbing what he had said, and threw her arms around him. "Sorry, and many thanks."

He hugged her. "Don't thank me yet. We still have Talot to deal with."

"True. We should take this book behind the house where we can have some privacy in our preparations."

The back of the house looked even more forlorn from this angle. As they went, Aiden saw several cops standing at the gate looking in their direction. He'd always been careful to keep his abilities hidden. Helping Siamura heal Eric last night and his broader relationship with Siamura would prove to people that he was different in a profound way. They may not understand his ability to communicate with spirits, but they couldn't ignore a mearoch and her forest. If he survived this, his and Tyler's life would be different. They wouldn't be returning to their former life.

Siamura set the Spiritorium on the grass and opened the section on Talot. She handled the pages as if they left a greasy residue on her fingers, wiping her fingers on the grass after pointing to a passage or turning the page.

Matt faced Siamura, with his hands on his hips, his duster waving behind him. "Where is my blue amulet? That little thief, Tyler, has it, doesn't he?"

Aiden whirled on Matt, but Siamura was closer.

She rose from the book. "Do not dare disparage Tyler." Her voice was like ice as her wings unfurled above him. Though she was a full head shorter than Matt, the boy backed up. "He and Aiden have done more for me than anyone for millennia. Do not test mine temper."

Matt dropped his arms as his back bumped into the exterior wall of the house, his eyes wide. The tree limbs reached down scratching the wall behind him. The scent of oak and acorns pervaded the area. Aiden could have sworn a cloud shaded the sun, but it must have been the tree branches.

Siamura snapped her wings shut and turned from Matt. The branches lifted and sunlight returned.

Matt took a breath and brushed his black shirt off, though there wasn't anything on it. "Um, so where did the amulet go?" His voice had lost its bravado from before.

Aiden didn't trust Siamura to respond, so he said, "We destroyed it, and good riddance."

Siamura showed off her missing finger with a smirk. "Not without a price. Worry not. Ye summoned me to protect ye. I intend to honor that contract."

Matt gawked at her. "That means you're free to do anything, including killing us."

"I am free, but I am not dishonorable. I will not kill ye and I will do everything in mine power to make sure Talot does not either. To do that I need to contain Talot before he kills more people and I need thyne help to do so. Are ye willing to help me stop Talot?"

Tyler nodded. "Yeah, I'll help."

Kevin stood by Tyler. "Me too."

Everyone turned to Matt. "I'm here, aren't I?"

Siamura scowled. "I need a better commitment than that."

Matt glanced at the leaves at his feet. "You told me the voices might leave me alone if I helped. Is that true?"

She said, “There is a chance that they could lessen. We can try and hope for the best.”

“All right, then I’m in.”

“Good. Did thou command Tyler get the stone of Talot and mine amulet?”

He opened his mouth. “Uh…”

Her ears flicked forward. “’Tis a simple question.”

Matt shook himself. “Eric and me tried to summon Karses.” Matt sat in front of the book and turned the pages to another entry. “That’s Karses.” He pointed at an entry in the open book. “When we did the ritual a book fell, but nothing else. We couldn’t see him. So Karses went to Tyler and it was Tyler who told us what Karses said. Where to find the stones.”

She knelt beside Matt, who quickly scrambled away from her. She read the section, her tail flipping in wide arcs back and forth by the time she had finished. Whatever Karses was, he was in trouble. She simmered in silence and then said, “I shall deal with him later.”

Aiden said, “Who is Karses?”

Siamura spat, “He is a glavhen, one who trades in spirits and objects binding them.” Her tone indicated that she didn’t want to discuss him further.

Matt reached into his bag. “I guess you should have this then.” He handed the black stone to her.

She recoiled. “I cannot take that. None spirit may handle an object that controls another spirit.”

“Oh yeah.”

Matt gave it to Aiden and Aiden again felt a soft coolness begin to spread across his palm. “It almost feels like the amulet.”

She turned to Aiden. “How is thyne hand? Has it worsened?”

Aiden moved his fingers around the stone. “It feels the same. I’ll be fine, but it gives me the creeps.”

“Good, hold onto it. Tyler, bring the paper and the blood wine.” She picked up a nearby stick, and forming a claw, split the end of it. She sliced a lock of her hair and stuck it into the slit she created on the stick. Placing it near the ground, a small vine grew out and wrapped around the end of the stick to secure the hair. She examined it. “That will make a fine brush.” Waving her hand over the ground, a plant sprouted forth, forming a single hand-sized leaf, shaped like a bowl. She spread out one of the large sheets of paper, and vines grew to pin the corners down.

Uncorking the bottle, she poured wine into the leaf bowl and dipped her brush into the liquid. The blood wine was thicker now, the consistency of motor oil rather than wine, with an unsettling kinship with blood. She glanced at the Spiritorium one last time as she began painting on the paper. It was an angry image with similarities to Talot's symbol, but with lines breaking out of its confining circle. It could also have been lines of energy penetrating the circle, smashing the barrier.

As Siamura finished the illustration, she placed her injured hand over it and the paint flared like burning lighter fluid. It died quickly, leaving everything she painted a dull red. The boys were suitably impressed and Kevin was more than happy to hold it while she prepared another sheet of paper.

Once again, vines crept out of the ground and held the paper down as Siamura, like some impassioned painter, began another symbol. Repeatedly dipping the brush in the leaf bowl, she created a design with marked differences from her own in which a tree occupied the middle, the branches protecting a skull and a litany of other insignia. As she made the final stroke, she put her hand over it and it flared. When Aiden looked back, the design was all in green with a vine border along the edges. She gave this one to Tyler.

Then she began another design, very organic, with barely a straight line anywhere in it. After it flared, it was a deep brown, and she handed it to Matt.

Siamura lay down three smaller sheets of paper and refilled the leaf bowl with blood wine. Furiously dipping and painting, she stared at Matt, while seemingly ignoring the page. Moving to the second, she looked at Kevin. Finishing that, she went to the third, and regarded Tyler as she painted in a frenzy.

She stopped. "Who has something sharp?"

Matt pulled out a wavy-bladed dagger with a dragon's head on the hilt from his bag. "How about this?"

"Very good." She took it, slipped it out of the sheath, and said, "Kneel down and hold thyne hand over the first paper."

Matt did so and in one motion, she grabbed his hand, pricked his finger, and touched his bloodied digit to the paper, as it too flared like the others.

Matt yelped, and then grinned abashedly as she handed him the page. "Keep this with thee. We will need it later."

She turned to Kevin. "Is thee ready?"

Kevin nodded and knelt, sticking out his hand. Again, Siamura pricked his finger, touched it to the paper and watched the paper flare. She did the same with Tyler. As she handed his sheet to him, she said, "These are protection glyphs. Fold them and keep them in ye pockets. If I fail with Talot, these may shield ye from him. I know not how well they will work against him, but it is better than having none-thing. If I do fail, ye are to run from here as fast as ye can to the policemen up there at the gate. Does ye understand?"

Tyler said, "What about you? We can't leave you."

Siamura smiled. "Ye must, because the circle that we will set up will no longer work to keep ye safe."

Matt asked, "We're going to cast a circle? But there are only three of us."

She sheathed the dagger and handed it back to Matt hilt first. "I shall be acting as ye fourth with the help of the head of the deer." She closed the book. "I believe this belongs to thee."

Matt took the dagger and the book. "Don't we need these for the circle?"

"The book, nay. If thee would like to use the dagger, thee may." She snorted. "I trust thee will not stab me with it."

Aiden watched as the leaf bowl drank up the remains of the wine and more green leaves sprouted with blue-red veins in the same bowl shape. Siamura stuck the brush into the dirt, bristles up, and it too propagated with purplish-green, bristle-like tops for blooms. Aiden would have stood in awe of Siamura's power longer except that she straightened, picked up the bottle, and walked out from behind the house. Aiden wasn't the only one who had to shake himself to follow her.

Now more than a dozen men were arrayed on the hills and the gate between them. A few with binoculars began talking on their radios, which made Aiden uncomfortable, as he didn't know if they were merely watching, or plotting something more sinister.

Siamura led them eastward from the house to the sprawling tree with an attitude, in full view of the cops on the hill. She picked up the deer's head from the base of the trunk and stepped in the direction of the hill just outside the edge of the branches. With the toes of her foot, she marked a large circle in the leaves and debris.

"Matt, step inside the circle and give me the large paper thee carries." Taking it, she unrolled it and put it inside the circle, more vines emerging to hold the paper flat against the ground. She placed the deer's head beside it.

He stepped inside the circle and turned to face her. She remained outside the circle and held him by the shoulders. Putting her thumb to her fang, she pricked it. Touching him twice above each eye she intoned, "Thee is mine charge and mine is bound to thyne."

Matt raised his hand to his head, but Siamura stopped him. "Do not wipe it off. It shall protect thee. Thee wanted to perform blood magic. We are using mine blood for this spell. Mine blood is in the wine and the paper and now it is upon thee." She did the same to Kevin, who was white as a sheet and stumbled, close to fainting. Siamura caught him, kissing him on the forehead, and whispering in his ear. Kevin stood up straighter with a look of renewed determination on his face.

Aiden stood next to Tyler as his son stepped into the circle. Siamura performed the same rite on Tyler as the other two. Tyler set his paper on the ground and turned to Matt. "Give me the knife."

Matt frowned a moment but handed him the wavy-bladed dagger.

Siamura put her hand on Tyler's and the knife. "What is thee doing?"

Tyler said, "What you did for us." With that, he pricked his finger and dabbed his blood above each of her eyes. "As we are protected, so are you."

She blinked with obvious surprise. "Many thanks."

He handed the blade back to Matt. The boys and the deer's head took positions at the four compass points of the circle.

Siamura said, "Tyler, Kevin, unroll the papers I gave ye and place them side by side in the middle of the circle." As the boys complied, placing rocks to secure them, she poured the blood wine around the perimeter of the circle. Thick purple-red vines sprang from where the wine hit the ground, leaving a ring around the boys. "Do not leave the circle until either

Talot or I are defeated. Tyler, thee will know when that time comes. Now let us begin."

Siamura intoned a litany, a poem of sorts, in a language foreign to Aiden, yet the power contained in the words raised an electrical energy in the air. Wisps of cloud appeared in the clear sky above them. His hair started to stand on end and he smelled moisture in the air as if a storm were coming.

She dropped into a song for a short while and pointed to Matt to begin the invocation of air, followed by Tyler with earth, and Kevin with water. Siamura invoked fire and then she launched into her poem again. When she finished, she walked to Aiden and pricked her thumb again. She dabbed blood above his eyes. He felt a jolt, starting from his head to his feet. He was aware, yet not jumpy, senses primed. She kissed him and leapt into the air, flying large circles above them.

They waited. Aiden walked towards the old house, holding the obsidian close, his hand growing number and number. The cops on the hills had their guns drawn and continued to watch. Once or twice, Aiden lost sight of Siamura, but she maintained high above them, flying her circles. It was taking too long. He thought maybe it wasn't working, yet the air continued to have a charge to it. The tension hung like a weight on him.

Tyler yelled, pointing east.

Aiden heard a faint tread. From around the trees a man ran towards them. Aiden blinked. It was no man. He covered the distance impossibly fast as the footsteps became louder. He was large, no, huge, bigger than anyone Aiden had seen before and his skin, without any clothes covering it, was a deep red that shown in the sunlight. Occasionally his skin would gleam with a brighter red, reminding him of the glow under a crack in a lava flow.

It had to be Talot.

The red creature had two large tusks that protruded from his lower jaw to his cheekbones and was powerfully muscled like a giant, nude bodybuilder on so many steroids that it should have pained him to move. Anger permanently twisted his face into an ugly mask. The acrid odor of melted iron, the same smell he'd sensed at Eric's house reached Aiden's nose, making him grimace. Talot's dark yellow claws worried him. Aiden was sure a poison much worse than Siamura's covered them.

Talot approached the circle and with a grunt took a swipe at Kevin, the nearest boy to him. His hand bounced off an invisible, dome-like shield. A smattering of sparks took flight, trailing his claws. The boys cowered at the far side of the circle, eying the ivy barrier but not stepping over it. Talot roared at them, revealing his black tongue.

Siamura in her panther form dove out of the sky, smacking Talot in his chest. He screamed as the impact of their collision shook Aiden and the boys. She pushed Talot away from the boys but failed to knock him from his feet. He staggered and attacked her with his claws, throwing her off and high into the sky.

As she travelled away from Talot she spread her wings to slow herself, much like a parachute. Talot turned again to the boys, his claws sparking just above them against the invisible barrier, pounding and scraping against it. The boys relaxed a bit, realizing the circle would shield them from Talot's onslaught.

Siamura growled low. Instead of flying directly for Talot, she climbed and swung east. Then she abruptly turned west and headed for Talot, tucking her wings close to her black-furred body, building speed. He was still trying to pound the circle down. She hit him, driving him away from the boys. Aiden felt the impact again and headed for the relative safety of the woods. This time Siamura held onto her opponent with her forepaws. She tried to bite Talot's neck, but he dodged her while attempting to do the same to her. Her wings flapped to keep her on top of him. Talot twisted while striking with his claws. Siamura raked him with her rear talons and leapt into the air then tore at his abdomen. Talot howled. She took off again, hovering aloft, blood dripping from her talons.

Where the blood hit the dirt, narrow black vines shot from the ground, growing several feet in a fraction of a second. The ebony creepers waved in the air as if searching for prey finding Talot and cinching tight around his legs. The vines expanded to the thickness of Aiden's arm preventing Talot from moving his feet. The dark dagger-shaped leaves impaled themselves into the red beast's flesh.

The demon roared.

A motion to the west drew Aiden's eye from the action. A police SUV pulled up on the opposite side of the old house from the boys. A quick turn brought the right side of the vehicle facing the fight. The cloud of dust it kicked up blew towards Talot, who now had vines covering him from his feet to his waist.

Siamura wheeled in the air and dove on Talot. She tore at him about to become the victor when Talot snapped forward and grabbed her hind feet. Smoke rose and flames burst from him. Siamura screamed as Talot immolated. Even from Aiden's distance he sensed the flames were hotter than any normal fire and seemed to burn not only his skin but his spirit too. The ashes of the vines blew away as the panther beat her wings, trying to escape. Leaves and dust blew about them.

The front doors of the SUV flew open and two people in blue windbreakers stepped out. Aiden recognized Agent Kerns but didn't know the other man. But that stopped mattering as both pulled out pistols, pointing them at the combatants. The one agent ran around to the rear of the car and crouched while Agent Kerns used the vehicle's engine as cover.

Aiden waved them away, shouting, "Get out of here!"

They ignored him, lining up their shots. Aiden hoped they were waiting for Siamura to get out of the way, his heart in his throat.

Talot threw Siamura aside, her fur still smoldering. She hit the ground and rolled, righting herself. Talot turned and charged the agents. They opened fire. The slugs impacted the red creature, but he didn't even flinch. Talot kept coming, never slowing. The agents dashed away from the SUV in opposite directions. Talot changed his trajectory to go after Agent Kerns.

Siamura leapt into the air after Talot. Aiden thought Agent Kerns was already the monster's lunch, but Siamura put on a burst of speed and hit Talot from behind. All that seemed to do was to drive him closer toward his intended prey, but Siamura deflected him away from the agent. Using their combined momentum, Siamura pushed Talot into the side of the SUV.

The creature crashed into the SUV with such intensity that the vehicle practically folded in half. Glass and debris exploded from it. After a moment the SUV tipped over onto its side.

Siamura just missed hitting the SUV and skimmed over it, her claws leaving furrows along the metal. She flipped over in midair and took on her humanoid form. Beating her wings, she flew and grabbed Agent Kerns with one arm. Flying to the other agent she dove and snatched him up with her other arm. They yelled as she hauled them towards the hill. She could almost lift the both of them, but only on the down strokes of her wings. The effect was like she was taking long hops across the ground holding the two men. She dumped them at the base of the hill like two sacks of dirty laundry.

The one agent jumped up. “Hey, watch it!”

Siamura flowed into her panther form and roared furiously, baring hand-length fangs. The men wilted with fear. A patrol car descended the hill, stopping in front of the agents. The doors flew open and two cops jumped out to help the agents.

The winged panther bounded upwards, circling back towards Talot. Talot, meanwhile, had set the SUV on fire and tossed it a hundred feet in Siamura’s direction. She easily swerved out of the way and it smashed on the ground, burning bits of metal flying everywhere. She increased her speed and headed for Talot, veering off at the last second, flinging her talons out to slash at him.

Talot hunkered down, but as she contacted, he sprang up, hooking his claws into her. They hit the ground and rolled. Talot landed on top of her, tearing at the panther, tufts of fur sailing through the air.

Aiden couldn’t stand there and do nothing while Siamura got filleted by Talot’s claws. But after seeing him toss an SUV through the air he wasn’t going to get any closer. So, he picked up a rock and threw it at the red creature. “Hey, ugly! Lay off her!”

It didn’t appear the rock did anything to Talot, but Siamura brought up her rear claws to rake his gut. Wrapping her tail around his neck, she pried him off. The two creatures separated and then crashed into each other, growling and snapping, wrestling, and slashing with deadly vigor. They were big, yet incredibly fast. Aiden retreated from them. He couldn’t tell who had the advantage and he feared for Siamura.

Then they stopped and Siamura flew towards the house.

No, Talot had flung her away. Her wings trailed behind her as she sailed through the air, crashing through the wooden wall as if it was cardboard. The house shifted and sagged lower.

An angry red bolt cracked through the ground from Talot on a path to the house, almost like lava under the surface. The house exploded into flames. Bits of fiery wood soared into the air. Aiden felt sick. Siamura wasn't going to survive that.

Another bolt ripped through the ground at Aiden. He didn't have any time to dive out of the way, so he gripped the black obsidian tightly in both hands, hoping it would do something. The ground around him detonated. His ears rang, but as the smoke cleared, he realized he was unhurt. The obsidian felt incredibly warm instead of being cold, as if it had sucked up the energy from Talot's blast.

When the smoke cleared, Talot faced the patrol car. Those idiots were still there. The federal agents were nowhere to be seen, but the two cops beside the car opened fire. The bigger officer knelt behind the hood of the car using a pump action shotgun while his taller partner stood behind the open driver's side door firing an assault rifle of some kind. Their shots hit home, Aiden could see Talot flinch as each slug or blast struck him in the chest. He couldn't tell how much damage the bullets did, as Siamura's talons had slashed Talot to the bone in many places, but they didn't seem like they were doing much.

Talot sprinted to the car, so fast no one had time to react and grabbed the taller man behind the door by the arm. The red demon jerked the man's arm holding the rifle from his body, pulling it off completely. A stream of blood followed the severed limb and rifle as it arced away from him. The poor guy stared at his missing arm as Talot's other hand caught him under the chin, the claws driving upward through his skull. Talot lifted the carcass and flung it behind him like a forgotten rag doll. The red creature didn't laugh or growl but was steady and dispassionate as he killed the officer.

The bigger cop jumped away from the car just as Talot brought his fist down on the hood. The car buckled like soft clay and burst into flames. It didn't make sense, since the fire shouldn't have spread so quickly, yet the blaze engulfed it in an instant. The cop struggled up the hill, but the ground cracked under him, and he too flared up like the car. His screams sickened Aiden. Some of the cops at the top of the hill began firing at Talot.

A crash made Aiden turn to the burning house. Siamura burst out of the roof, fire trailing behind her. Glowing bright green, she rocketed towards Talot, the flames on her body snuffed out by her speed. She plowed into Talot, hurling him into the burning car, which crumpled like an aluminum can. A green shock wave of light propagated outward from the impact, traveling up the hill to shake the patrolmen at the top. They stumbled and stopped shooting. The earth buckled underneath Aiden, knocking him down. The shock extinguished the burning car and the remains of the unfortunate cop beside it.

The smoking wreckage of the car slid aside, revealing the winged panther hauling Talot away from the hill by his foot. Her jaws clamped down on his foot, fangs sinking into the flesh. He seemed dazed by the blow, groping blindly for Siamura. Her left wing dragged behind her, broken. The skin on her paws and forelegs was black and cracked, showing the muscles straining beneath. Flaps of burnt skin hung from her forelegs.

As she reached the front of the burning house, Talot snatched her rear leg. She twisted away, but he curled around and sank his teeth into her lower hind leg. A snapping sound resonated and Siamura howled in pain. She released his foot, falling to the grass. She slapped the ground not with a paw, but with her human-like hand, now burnt and blackened, emerging from her panther foreleg. Talot turned, releasing Siamura's leg from his mouth and pulled her under him. Her tail caught his leg, and using his momentum, rolled him over so she was on top straddling his hips. Her tail whipped around his legs to hold him down.

A sapling shot up where she had struck the ground with her palm. She reached for the young tree and missed. Siamura's right wing smacked the ground, shifting the pair slightly closer to the sapling. She snatched the young tree and it leapt from the ground. Instead of holding onto the dirt, the roots squirmed free of it, waving in the air like tentacles. Siamura took the sapling and thrust it at Talot's torso.

Talot seized her right arm and Siamura transferred the young tree to her left hand. Desperately, Talot brought his other hand to stop her, but it was too late. She rammed the roots into his abdomen. Her jaws latched onto his free arm, immobilizing it. Talot shrieked as the sapling took root in his guts. It drilled through him and rooted his lower abdomen into the ground.

She scooted off his hips, her tail releasing his legs. Maneuvering her left hand from around the rapidly expanding tree, she dug the claws of that hand into his chest. Ribs broke and snapped. "*Aiden! Come!*"

Aiden dashed closer, gripping the black stone tightly. Blood covered both creatures and the smell of burnt flesh, blasted iron, and trees saturated the air. The sapling's trunk swelled further, its coloring a dull red and its width as big around as Aiden's leg. He could hear bones breaking in Siamura's mouth.

Siamura yanked on two of Talot's ribs, creating a gap in his chest. "*Push the stone in the hole as far as thee can!*"

Aiden knelt on one side of the beast, obsidian in hand. Talot's eyes flicked to him. As the red beast's far arm slipped free of Siamura's grip, her jaws crunched down harder on his near arm and the bones shattered. Aiden saw Talot's freed hand, claws extended, reach for him from underneath Siamura. It moved too fast for him to dodge or jump away. Siamura couldn't stop Talot's hand, but she snapped her paw up to deflect his blow.

The panther shuddered as Talot jammed his claws deep into her ribcage. Her paw held him there so he couldn't strike again, but it had to have hurt. She nodded at Aiden, indicating he should continue. He forced the stone between Talot's bones, scraping his knuckles as he shoved it in as hard as he could. Suddenly, he pushed through, and his forearm sank beneath Talot's ribs.

The ground shook under him and Aiden wrenched his arm free, leaving the stone behind. The earth quaked again and Aiden rolled clear. Then all was silent, save for the crackling of the burning house.

Chapter 24

The Woods

Aiden raised his head. Siamura lay face down a few feet from him, curled slightly about herself. The broad red leaves of the flesh-eating tree behind her were unfurling and misting in the sunlight. There was no sign of Talot. Aiden expected blood and gore to cover his arm. Instead, it was coated with gray dust similar to iron filings. He patted himself and seemed to be okay.

Aiden crawled over to Siamura. She wasn't in her panther form but had reverted to her green humanoid appearance. Blood coated much of her skin, and other places were black with burns. Dirt buried her left arm and leg, and she wasn't moving. One of her wings stretched away from him and the other wing lay broken beneath her. The scent of barbequed meat assaulted his nose.

Aiden brushed her hair aside. "Siamura?" He was sure she was dead; there was so much blood.

She groaned, a wet rasping sound emanating from her lips and chest. "Aiden?" He could barely understand her.

"You're alive!" A thrill shot through him. He pulled at her left arm. He was afraid it was gone at the elbow; she was so badly hurt. He gently eased it back and forth to free it from the earth. The ground here wasn't pale brown like normal dirt, but gray, like the filings that had covered his arm.

The ground released her arm swathed in dirt. Glints of muscle appeared in spots as some of the soil fell away. The smell of cooked meat intensified. Tears came to Aiden's eyes. She was dying. Her breath whistled and rattled in her chest. He couldn't stop though. He went to her buried leg and tugged on it.

She yelped, "Stop!"

"I can't leave you like this."

"Dig… dig it out." She sagged back down onto the ground.

Tears streaming, he began to scoop the earth from her leg. Another pair of hands joined his, then another. He looked up and saw Tyler and Kevin helping him. They nodded and continued. Aiden was relieved that Tyler was unharmed. With the three of them digging, they freed her leg and saw that her shin was broken in two places. Talot must have snapped it when he bit down as Siamura was dragging him by his foot.

Aiden gingerly rolled her face up. Tyler positioned her shattered leg straight as Kevin rearranged her broken wing, taking care to align the bones. She didn't make a sound, though it had to have hurt. Aiden sat with his back to the carnivorous tree, the bark of which warmed him through his jacket. Ignoring the oddness, he cradled Siamura's head on his outstretched legs. A large hole marred the right side of her ribcage where Talot had jammed his claws into her. White bones poked out of the wound amongst the blood and dust. Aiden attempted to put his hand over it to keep her insides from spilling out.

Siamura caught his hand in hers. "It is all right." Her grip was firm, despite the lack of skin and in some areas lack of muscle on her hands.

Aiden looked around. Where was everyone? Matt was talking to the cops just beyond the branches of the tree Aiden sat beneath. Not only was Matt keeping them busy, but other people investigated the wreckage of the car and the bodies. The SUV and the house still burned, though not as vigorously as before.

Agent Kerns and Detective Tirzynski approached, although hesitantly, keeping their eyes on Siamura. Two men followed them. The tree branches above them blocked their path, forming a barrier. They stopped.

Agent Kerns spread his hands. "Can we talk?"

A soft growl came from Siamura, surprising Aiden. Her ruined fingers lengthened into claws.

Aiden stroked her hair. "Let them in, Siamura. I'll stop them if they try anything." Tyler and Kevin stood beside her, and Siamura's claws receded from view.

Agent Kerns lifted his gun by the barrel with two fingers and set it on the ground. He said, “We’re unarmed. Can we come closer?” The detective also put her gun down. She seemed contrite, or at least not as openly antagonistic as she was earlier.

Two men were behind the agent and the detective. Aiden guessed they must be federal officers of some kind, because they held themselves like Agent Kerns, and didn’t wear police uniforms. Aiden said, “Those two behind you have to stay back. Only Agent Kerns and Detective Tirzynski can come forward.” He hoped that the detective wouldn’t rile Siamura.

Agent Kerns turned and spoke to the men. Matt folded his arms beside them like a guard. For once, Aiden appreciated Matt’s bluster, but doubted it impressed the agents. Yet, the men stayed behind as the branches parted to allow Agent Kerns and the detective through. When Agent Kerns drew closer, he exclaimed, “Oh, my God. I didn’t realize. I’ll call for an ambulance.” He knelt beside Siamura and pulled out his cell phone. Detective Tirzynski stared at the mearoch, while Tyler and Kevin drew protectively around Siamura.

Siamura tapped the Agent’s knee with a skeletal finger. “I am not going back there.” Her voice was weak and raspy, but still audible.

Agent Kerns shook the phone. “It’s dead. Detective, try yours.”

Siamura raised her hand to get his attention. Aiden could see the individual muscles working under the blackened skin and dust. One finger was just bones, lacking any flesh, still moving as if muscles still operated on it. She said, “It will not function.”

“Why?”

“The forest likes it not. Too much noise.” She put her other hand on the broken ribs at her side.

Agent Kerns pocketed his phone. “You need medical attention. You saved my ass out there. I’m not going to let you die.”

“I am in pain, but I will not die. Am I still a suspect for the murders? Detective, what say thee?”

The detective gazed at Siamura. Aiden couldn’t tell if she had lost her mind or if she was going to fly into a rage. She took a breath and said, “It does appear that you stopped the perpetrator, but I’ll reserve judgment until I review the case. Where is the red giant?

“Under thyne feet.”

Tirzynski snapped, "Why can't you give me a straight answer?"

Talons shot from the ends of Siamura's fingers. Her head shifted into her panther form as she raised herself from Aiden's lap. A low growl rumbled in her throat. Agent Kerns scrambled backwards crab-like and the detective retreated, eyes wide. Aiden's heart quickened. He understood their fear. Siamura's injuries made her quick to anger, more so than normal.

Aiden put his hand on Siamura's furred shoulder. "Hey, hey. She's not attacking you. Just explain what happened."

For an extended moment, the panther stared the law officers down. Then slowly, Siamura melted back into her human form. "Talot is under us. He is still here, but in a different shape. The forest will surround this place to keep him safely bound to this spot." She tapped the ground twice with her hand and the fires burning the SUV and the house went out. The agents at the tree line glanced between the mearoch and the previously burning structures.

Her eyes narrowed. "Are Aiden and the boys afoul with thyne law?"

The two law officers took a deep breath but retained their distance. Detective Tirzynski cleared her throat. "I don't believe so. Agent Kerns?"

The agent shook his head. "No, not on my end."

Siamura continued, "Do not harass or arrest Aiden or the boys. Leave this forest unmolested. I have seen what people can do to trees."

"What's the connection between you and the woods?" Agent Kerns dusted himself off. He never took his eyes from Siamura though.

"It is mine grove, mine trees. I told thee last night that I am a mearoch, a forest spirit. This is me that ye are standing in."

Detective Tirzynski said, "You can't do that. What about the owners of this land?"

Siamura's ears snapped up. "It is already done. For the safety of everyone, the resting place of Talot must be protected. Are these owners going to prevent the trees from growing? Are they going to keep the rodents and insects out, the wolves and birds out?"

The detective continued, "But the owners will want to be paid if they no longer have access."

Siamura held up her damaged hands. "I have paid with mine flesh, blood, and spirit for the safety of the owners and for the town. Thee can make the necessary arrangements with these so-called owners. The trees tend to have their own opinion regarding trespassers. People should tread carefully between these trunks." She waved Aiden to bend down and she whispered in his ear. "Carry me to the large tree, the one thee first met."

Aiden said, "You need to rest."

"Aiden, please, I need to heal."

"Why can't you stay with us?" He picked her up. Her tail wrapped around her shattered leg to immobilize it. With her hand, she tried to hold onto her broken wing. Aiden walked a few steps but stopped when she gasped. He set her down and Tyler came over to position her wing so that as Aiden picked her up, it tucked underneath her like the other wing. He walked a few more steps, trying not to jar her.

Agent Kerns approached at a distance. "Siamura, come to the hospital. We can help you."

She growled in Aiden's arms, turning to face the agent. Aiden felt a shock of pain through her body, yet she growled louder. The pain made her more aggressive. She couldn't run, so she was going to fight. Her face and upper torso shifted to her panther form and she quickly became heavier.

Aiden shouted, "Stop!" He put her down before he dropped her. He'd made it within five feet of the sprawling tree's trunk. He turned to the agent and waved to him to stay back. Being an astute man, Agent Kerns stopped, knotting his brows.

Aiden turned to the mearoch. "He wants to help you."

The panther still faced Agent Kerns but wasn't growling anymore. The claws were out and her forearms were still black. Her tail swung in large arcs.

Aiden stepped in front of her, blocking her view of the agent. "He doesn't want to fight you. I'll tell him to go away, but you must rest."

She blinked, her alien cat eyes regarding him. Her tail hovered in midair. He didn't know if she was going to pounce on him, or just crouch there. The claws quivered and retracted as her body melted back into her humanoid shape. "Do not allow him take me from here." She laid face down on the ground, flattening herself as if the more skin contact with the earth made her feel better.

Aiden stroked her hair. “Just rest.” Her eyes closed, but he knew that didn’t mean she couldn’t sense him in her other ways. He walked to the agent. The tree branches above him opened to let him pass. Agent Kerns stepped back, glancing at the animating limbs.

Aiden forced a smile. “I’m sorry about that. She doesn’t want to go with you to the hospital. I can’t really blame her after last night’s experience.”

The agent eyed the tree above them. “Yeah, I understand that, but she’s seriously injured. She’ll die if she doesn’t get to the hospital.”

Aiden remembered Siamura’s story of reconstituting herself from a bone fragment and a drop of blood. He smiled at the thought. “She’ll be fine. Tell you what, if she gets worse after twenty-four hours, I’ll bring her into the hospital myself.”

“You’re nuts. She’ll be dead in that time.” Agent Kerns stepped around Aiden, but a wall of branches blocked his path to Siamura.

They watched as the mearoch got up, dragging her broken limbs behind her. She propped herself against the trunk. A black opening appeared on the trunk and she hauled herself into the darkness. Aiden charged through the branches, but before he could reach the trunk, she had disappeared. The black opening vanished, leaving behind a normal trunk. He stood beside it, disheartened. He couldn’t follow her. The tree relaxed its branches, lifting them out of the way.

He touched the bark. His fingers felt a normal tree, but it tickled his senses, and he heard her voice far away, but still audible. “Walk into the thick of the woods and call mine name three times. I shall be with thee.” Aiden glanced around. Tyler was nearby, coming closer, but he didn’t appear to have heard anything.

He stepped to his son. “Don’t worry. We’ll see her again soon.”

Tyler looked up with surprise and then smiled slightly. They walked back to Agent Kerns. Aiden spread his arms. “I don’t know what happened, but she’s not here anymore.”

Agent Kerns shook his head. “How about you two? Are you okay?”

The question struck Aiden as odd. He was so concerned about Siamura or Tyler that he looked himself over. “I’m fine. What about you, Tyler?”

Tyler shrugged. “I sat in the circle the whole time. Talot never touched me.”

"I'm going to have you guys checked out at the hospital anyway, just to be safe." The agent paused. "At least with you two, I know what I'm dealing with, so I expect you to comply."

Aiden smirked to himself, *if Agent Kerns only knew why Siamura stayed with them, he might think differently*. At their feet, small seedlings burst from the ground. Already the forest was laying claim to the area where Talot fell.

***

Agent Kerns and Detective Tirzynski picked up their weapons before the forest could claim the guns and holstered them. The boys retrieved their backpacks and the group headed up the incline to the gate. A flatbed tow truck drove down to retrieve the charred SUV. The destroyed police car with the two bodies already had police tape surrounding that area and a team of people marking debris.

When they reached the park above, it was thick with activity. The late afternoon sun glinted off the ambulances and squad cars crowded in the parking lot casting a soothing glow, in contrast to the harshness of their flashing lights. Cops and other officials hurried about. The entire park was also marked off with police tape, several officers keeping onlookers and news crews from entering the area.

People turned to watch them pass as Agent Kerns led Aiden and Tyler to an ambulance while Detective Tirzynski took Matt and Kevin to another. Aiden saw that each of the boys' parents waited there. When the boys approached, there was much hugging and kissing. Despite their evident happiness of their sons' return, Aiden knew the parents wouldn't be inviting him or Tyler over for dinner anytime soon, if ever.

Aiden waved off the paramedic, telling Tyler to go ahead. He turned to Agent Kerns. "Can we talk in private?"

Agent Kerns glanced around and walked to a temporary break table, grabbing two cups of coffee and leading Aiden to a squad car. Handing one to Aiden, he motioned for him to get in on the passenger side. The agent closed the driver's side door and took a sip of the beverage, wincing at the bitterness. "What did you want to talk about? You know we're going to be seeing a lot of each other in the next few weeks."

Aiden took a sip. Agent Kerns' statement caught him off guard. "What do you mean by that?"

"You're going to be de-briefed by me and a host of other people who want to know what went on here. One of the first questions will be is how a bunch of old trees grew up overnight."

Aiden felt exposed. He had spent his whole life trying to blend in and now he stood out in the most obvious way. At the time, he felt brave for defending Siamura, and helping to defeat Talot. Now, he was back in the real world. But he couldn't forget about Siamura. He wouldn't.

"So why are we sitting here?" Agent Kerns asked.

Aiden gathered his thoughts together. "What about the forest? What's going to happen to it?"

"Tough to say. Since she disappeared into that tree, I don't want to do anything, but the owners are going to be upset."

"She's not gone and that is her forest. You saw the trees sprouting to protect Talot's resting place as we walked out of there."

"I can make recommendations, but the story is so unbelievable. Hell, the Secret Service should dismiss me if I write up what happened here."

"The one thing they can't dispute is a forest springing up in a week. All they have to do is look at satellite photos to see that. They need to protect the forest or Siamura will cause a lot of trouble."

"If she survives her injuries." The agent took another sip of his coffee.

"She will, and she will remain in the forest, but what I worry about is people getting too curious and walking in there. She's extremely protective."

"I saw that. Okay, I can't promise anything, but we'll keep in touch. You can count on it. Now do me a favor and have the medic check you out."

Aiden exited the car and joined Tyler at the ambulance. While the medic went through his procedures, various people — mostly cops and emergency personnel — stopped by and glanced in. Some asked if he and Tyler were all right. It dawned on Aiden that he couldn't hide his connection to Siamura. The cops had watched the whole fight from the ridge line and had probably passed the word he was a friend of the mearoch, not to mention last night when she healed Eric with Aiden's help.

He and Tyler wouldn't be able to deny or play down their participation. Funny, the thing that he once feared most, being singled out as different, didn't really bother him anymore. He was concerned about Tyler, though, because being different in high school could be a traumatic experience. He would have to support his son — not only support but go out of his way to make sure that nobody took advantage or demeaned his relationship with Siamura or his unique abilities.

Aiden realized that his life promised to become even more unusual in the future. He sighed. He could think about that later, all he wanted now was a hot meal and a bath. It might not be a lot, but it would resemble some sense of normalcy for a short time.

Epilogue

The next day, Friday, Aiden and Tyler were brought in to file statements with the Secret Service in the counterfeiting case and with the FBI and local police about the serial murders. The difficult thing for the Secret Service was that they had bags full of carpet pieces for evidence that no one would ever mistake for US currency. The case was quietly dropped so as to avoid any undue embarrassment. Though to the Feds credit, they made Eric serve two weeks of community service.

The biggest problem arose with the eight murders committed by Talot and the two officers killed in front of the forest during the battle with several law enforcement people as witnesses. The advantage with the last two was there was no doubt that Siamura had actively tried to prevent people from getting hurt and that witnesses saw Talot kill the last two, however fantastical his methods were. The FBI was particularly upset about not being able to procure Talot's body to perform a proper forensic study of the wounds on the previous eight people.

This highlighted the root of the problem. A large, very old, forest had appeared within a week where previously an arid scrubland existed before. Within two days large trees grew where Talot and Siamura fought, preventing the forensic teams from studying that area. When the teams did enter the forest, they discovered all electronic devices, including flashlights, wouldn't work. That meant all cell phones, GPS positioning devices, digital cameras, even battery powered watches ceased to function. Magnetic compasses would spin, never resting on one position, so finding one's way through the dense forest was impossible. The forest frustrated their attempts to even to map its interior with reports of the trees seeming to move when they weren't looking.

The FBI and the police absolved Aiden and the boys of any blame in the murders, although they wanted more information about Siamura and her forest. From Agent Kerns, Aiden learned that Homeland Security deemed her a security risk because they couldn't contact her, didn't understand her motives, and couldn't determine what a mearoch even was.

Rumors of demons and of an enchanted forest drew people from all over. The story of Siamura's battle with Talot eventually leaked out, though increasingly garbled, despite attempts by the authorities to classify all information about it. The one thing that people could see was the forest and its effect on electronics and compasses. Within days Oak Springs became the next 'Area 51' except for fairies and bizarre forest happenings instead of space aliens. People flocked to the forest bringing placards saying that the forest was a sign of the coming apocalypse, others expressed their support of fairies and the trees.

Three weeks after the battle the situation in front of the forest became more and more chaotic. By nightfall, people were yelling and chanting, fighting, setting fires. The local police had their hands full just trying to maintain any order. The state's National Guard was called out and was due to arrive any minute when a fire started at the forest's edge. The fire department couldn't reach the forest very quickly due to the masses of people fleeing the conflagration.

But the fire never burned the forest itself, only the edges. And the fire department kept it from spreading up the hill and threatening the houses of the neighborhood.

People filtered back to the park after a few more weeks. The Feds erected a chain-link fence around the forest at the top of the hill to help with crowd control. The cops kept the crowds from getting too close and most people were satisfied observing the trees from the top of the hill. Without wild things happening people gradually drifted away and the news crews left to follow the latest disaster or celebrity gossip.

Aiden and Tyler returned to the forest after the hubbub died. When they touched one of the oaks a black portal opened like the one Siamura used to escape Agent Kerns. Then they heard Siamura's voice inviting them to her world.

With a look at each other, they stepped inside.

Unfortunately, nothing ever stays hidden forever.

The story continues in Consort to a Dark Fey.

Made in the USA
Las Vegas, NV
21 September 2024

95360366R00173